JOHN MULLIGAN

shopping
cart
soldiers

Scribner Paperback Fiction
Published by Simon & Schuster

SCRIBNER PAPERBACK FICTION
Simon & Schuster Inc.
Rockefeller Center
1230 Avenue of the Americas
New York, NY 10020

First Scribner Paperback Fiction edition 1998
Published by arrangement with Curbstone Press

SCRIBNER PAPERBACK FICTION and design are trademarks of
Simon & Schuster Inc.

Manufactured in the United States of America

1   3   5   7   9   10   8   6   4   2

Library of Congress Cataloging-in-Publication Data
Mulligan, John, 1950–
Shopping cart soldiers / by John Mulligan.
—1st Scribner Paperback Fiction ed.
p.   cm.
1. Vietnamese Conflict, 1961–1975—Veterans—Fiction.
2. Scottish Americans—California—San Francisco—Fiction.
3. Homeless veterans—California—San Francisco—Fiction.
4. Alcoholics—California—San Francisco—Fiction. I. Title.
[PS3563.U3976S56   1999]
813'.54—dc21   98-36814
CIP

ISBN 0-684-85605-0

ACKNOWLEDGMENTS

I would like to acknowledge the following persons for helping me survive to tell this story. My former wife, Francoise Mulligan, for not giving up on me. To Dr. Spence Meighan likewise for not giving up and for always being a good pal. To Maxine Hong Kingston who saved Finn MacDonald's fictional life, and taught me how to hope again. To my dear friend, Tillie Olsen, who taught me how to fight back and who reminded me of why I wrote *Shopping Cart Soldiers*. To James Kelman, man of honor. To George Long, a great neighbor and a great painter. To Bill Cody, who listened to me rant and rave while writing the book and, of course, for all his wonderful poetry. To my pal, Dennis Doherty, for his wonderful smile and for his courage. To Alan Black, my countryman and friend, without whose prompting and faith I might never have finished this book. My heartfelt thanks to all of you. God bless!

DEDICATION

I would like to dedicate this book to my daughter, Marielle Mulligan, to her twin brothers, Finn and Quinn Mulligan, to my mother and to my father, and to all of my brothers and sisters. I love you all dearly!

I would like to dedicate *Shopping Cart Soldiers* in a very special way, to all of my brother and sister veterans, and their families, who still suffer because of the effects of the Vietnam war and its aftermath. In particular, to those veterans who have gone before us. From the bottom of my heart, God bless!

SHOPPING CART SOLDIERS

──── PROLOGUE ────

ON SOME LEVEL he knows me. He wonders who I am it's true, yet it's all so simple. I am a woman. A simple enough statement to be sure, but laden with complications at the same time. At least as far as Finn and I are concerned, now that he's begun to know me, now that he's begun to feel me. He thinks my name is Madman. That's what he calls me anyway. Madman! But what does he know?

In spite of acknowledging me to some degree, he won't take me back, won't let me back in. And therein lies the problem. For twenty-five years or so I've been trying to get him to open up, but he doesn't even see me; nor does he listen to me. He can feel me though. I know he can feel me, the blackhaired, blueeyed, paleskinned, selfnegating bastard, yet he won't let me in. I don't often talk about him that way, I don't enjoy talking about him like that, not really. But he does anger me. Perhaps he won't take me back because I'm a woman. That's a hard pill for him to swallow. He feels me though, senses my femaleness and locks me out. Perhaps he won't take me back because my beauty intimidates him.

I am a beautiful woman. My hair is short and black, as black and shiny as newcut coal, trimmed in the style of a bonnie wee schoolboy. That's another thing! I talk in a strange dialect just as he does. But he's an Albanach remember, so I talk just like him.

I must excuse myself; sometimes I forget. Alba is the ancient name for an ancient country filled with an ancient race of Keltic people. It's been Finn's delving and diving into his distant past that has compelled him to employ such an archaic term. But he likes it; it makes him feel closer to his ancestors, and I like that! Knowing from whom he descends might save him. Alba, you know, predates even Roman civilization and probably the Greek too. Some say the Kelts came from a place Northwest of the Alps and that they were like both the Scythians and the Persians who lived and flourished in the millennium before the time of Christ.

Finn first saw the word *Alba* as a child growing up in Scotland. He saw it in an ancient manuscript handed down through the years by father after father of the Donald Clan, his ancestors. Finn's father knew it as *The Red Book of Seeing and Believing*. His father told him that Alba is the ancient Gaelic name for Scotland, the land of his birth. But he forgot all about the book and its lessons until one night in the jungle many years later.

He is sitting in a bunker with Romeo Robinson, waiting out another tense night of guard duty. The monsoon season has finally decided to assert itself, and the night is black, heavy and still.

"Hey, man, where you from?" asks Romeo, sitting back, leaning against the sandbags of the bunker. Romeo's holding a roach between his thumb and index finger and, after taking a long toke, passes it to Finn. Finn takes the joint, thinks for a minute, then laughs.

"Nowhere," he says. "I come from nowhere!"

"I can dig that, man, but ya gotta be from somewhere."

For a long time Finn is quiet, lost in his thoughts of Alba and of his family.

The whole MacDonald clan is gathered around the kitchen table listening to the da espousing the wonders and benefits of living in America. The da of course sits there sternfaced and grave; the ma has a worried expression on her face, as if the subject is one she'd rather not even think about let alone consider with any objectivity or seriousness. The da notices her confusion, her consternation. He rises to his feet and paces around the table.

"We haftae leave," says the da. "There's no point in livin' here without work when I've been offered a job in America." He is adamant; he has made up his mind. "Christ, Kate," he continues, "ah've been outa work for nearly a year now. Me! One-a the best machinists in the westa Scotland. An' why? Because ah'm a Catholic, an' a staunch trade unionist! Aye, that's right, a bitter combination in this tinyminded, dour wee country." The da is revving up now. "Ah'm sick of it, Kate. Ah'm sicka the bigots, an' ah'm sicka the bluidy weather. Clouds in the sky every day, rain, rain, rain! Ah've had it." The da sits down again in his chair. "Ah want these weans of ours to have a better life than we did, give them a fightin' chance at least!"

Finn, the oldest of the children, is beaming, obviously happy at the prospect.

"Where would we be going," he asks the da. "What part of America?"

"Detroit," says the da, rather grimly.

"Magic!" says Finn. "Motown! I can go an' see the Four Tops any time I feel like it. The Temptations, Joe Tex, the Supremes! It'll be great, da!"

The da just rolls his eyes heavenward; the ma looks worried. The younger children shout and laugh, oblivious to the huge and impending changes under discussion at the table around which they play. It's a tense time at the MacDonald's dinner table.

"What about the war, Joe, what about Vietnam for God's sake?" the ma asks of her husband in a whisper she would usually save for church or the library. "He'll be eighteen soon," she reminds him, pointing to Finn who isn't smiling any more.

"Aye, that's right, da," says Finn. "Ah forgot all about that. Ah'll get drafted!"

"No yae won't, son. It's a government contract. We'll be makin' helicopter gears, helpin' wi' the war effort. There's as much chance they'll draft me as they will you." The lame joke backfires.

"They wouldnae do that would they?" asks the ma, now absolutely terrified.

"Don't be daft, Kate, don't be so bluidy daft!" says the da, who is fast becoming exasperated.

3

"Are yae sure ah'll get a job, da?" asks Finn.

"Aye ah'm sure. Ah made them put it in my contract. As soon as yae turn eighteen they'll hire yae on as a machinist. Ah told them yae had three years experience already. They'll be glad to have yae they said!"

"Let me see it," says the ma. "Let me see the contract!"

But Finn hated the job making helicopter gears. They stuck him on nightshift six nights a week. In no time at all he was fired for sleeping on the job. In even less time he was classified 1A and was drafted shortly afterward. Now he is sitting in a sandbagged bunker smoking a big fat doobie with his pal, Romeo.

"It's funny, Romeo, but I don't feel like I come from anywhere. I was born in Scotland, but after all this war bullshit I wonder if I have a home any more. I can't go back, an' I sure as hell don't know where I'll be tomorrow."

"I know what you mean," said Romeo, lost in his own thoughts. "But how d'ya get here in the first place?"

"Same as you. I got drafted!"

Romeo burst out laughing.

"Drafted?" he says. "What d'ya mean drafted? You're a god-damn foreigner, a Scotsman. How can they draft a Scotsman?"

"You live in America, you register with the draft; that's the law. The price you pay. You don't get nothin' for nothin', Romeo! An' don't call me a Scotsman again. Scotland doesn't exist any more! In the olden days it was called Alba, so I come from Alba now."

"I hear that, Alba man, I hear that! Ain't no Chicago neither."

"Anyhow, when I got drafted the whole family went back to Alba. I think the actual shock of me being drafted was too much for them."

I thank God regularly for keeping Finn alive and somewhat hopeful during these past years of difficulty, all twenty-five or so of them. But he's shown signs of late that he might have found an exit to the twisting maze he's been wandering around in for so long. I'm relieved about his new clarity, because I came out of him; I need him well and healthy. All that stops him from accepting me is his pitifully closed mind. But it's begun to open up somewhat these past two or three years. Not much, mind you, but I am hopeful.

My eyes are green like the North Sea is green, and even though it's common to say so, they are shaped like almonds. How that particular oddity came about has always been a source of mystery, if not consternation and complete confusion to me, ever since The Leaving at least. After all, if I come from Finn, a Kelt, how can I possibly have almond eyes? It's easy! I figured it all out. It is so easy I laugh, because the part of Finn that I am is Asian. That's all there is to it!

Perhaps we're from a land farther east than has been imagined. One of the Asia Minor tribes perhaps. A long time passes before I can comprehend that myself, so I can easily understand why he's having such a difficult time with it. That I'm a woman goes quite against his grain to be sure; that I'm an Asian woman really does confuse him. It isn't as bad as it used to be, because for the last two or three years he has begun, finally, to learn more about his heritage. He's discovered that Keltic people and Asian people aren't so far apart, not in a mythological sense certainly and probably not, as I mentioned, in an anthropological sense either—a few thousand years perhaps, not much more.

My almond eyes became easier to understand after I began to know, through Finn's delving and diving, our Keltic heritage. Thanks, again, to Romeo Robinson and his quiet questions that dark night in the still jungle. They began a process that might, in retrospect, have saved Finn's life.

I am tiny, petite if you will, and my skin is pale like goat's milk. By contrast, I wear a flowing, bloodred robe fastened at the waist with a long, silver umbilical cord. After quarter of a century it continues to drip dark, thick blood. I alone can see the cord, though sometimes even I can't see it, but I know it's there. Somehow it's just there! And whether truly there or not isn't important; I need to think it's there, because that's all that keeps Finn and me together in some small way.

Finn and I separated when the Great White water buffalo, the bull, is murdered during The Leaving. Until then we are happy together, as one.

July, nineteen-seventy, is a bad month. All five of us are flying in a helicopter gunship, armed to the teeth, somewhere above Vietnam. We're out during the monsoon rains searching for the downed cargo plane; it has smacked into a mountainside. The plane carries twenty-six passengers, all soldiers, homeward bound after a long, hard year of jungle-rot, growing pains, and broken, bloody bodies. Ivy League, our friend, is one of the twenty-six, one of the dead twenty-six, a waste no matter how one looks at it. It is the waste more than anything else I can't come to terms with. All that violent waste, the pitiful pouring away of precious life into the already red Asian soil. Finn, at the time, doesn't understand why part of him thinks, no, feels the way it does. More like a woman, that is. I think he feels there is something wrong with being sensitive to the madness going on all around him every day. It isn't manly to be sensitive. Who knows! But we split apart that night and he chases me away. A hundred years ago it seems, perhaps longer.

I've been following him around ever since, plodding relentlessly after him, like the Hound of Heaven, watching the years tumble along one after the other, wondering always who is the shadow, wondering always who casts the shadow. In all fairness you'd have to say we had an equal right to dwell inside that physical shell everyone knew as Finn MacDonald. But he cast me out, doesn't want to share himself with me, doesn't want to believe that I come along with the package, that I am part of the package, though it's not as simple as you might think, this twoness.

Finn wants to be a man, a soldier, a hero! There are times I can't help but laugh when I think of it; it's all so insane. There are times too when I can forgive him; there are times when I can't.

He's a grunt, an infantryman, just like the rest of his pals. He's up in the control tower visiting a friend when they finally give Captain Peterson permission to take off. The weather has cleared. Too soon into the rain perhaps. God only knows, too soon. The plane crashes into the mountain when the weather unexpectedly closes in again.

Finn and four of our friends go to look for the plane. I know; I am there with them! We jump into the gunship laden with bullets, and go to look for our pals. A mission, a mission of mercy to save our comrades. I remember Finn telling Frankie Chen he's scared shitless; he's never been on such a dangerous adventure. Frankie tells Finn he's scared shitless too.

The weather's clear again. But we've been smoking dope ever since we first heard of the crash. It might as well be raining still we're all so stoned. It's that sort of place, the war zone. Crazy! Topsyturvy! For the first hour or so we can't find the lost plane, though we're hungry for some sort of action. When we don't find any we invent our own, such being our need, such being the depth of our rage. We have to, we need to, for we are filled with anger. We have to hit back, and we have to hit back hard! The enemy's elusive! They like to set their boobytraps or ambush us, then scarper down the holes of their tunnels leaving us frustrated with nothing to shoot back at, filled with teethclenching, bloodred rage.

The moon is big behind a break in the clouds and we can see quite clearly. We happen to pass over a fenced-in pasture and see a huge water buffalo, a bull. I can't believe how big he is, how huge. At least ten feet long and six feet high. Romeo Robinson can't believe it either. Romeo, when he isn't pulling guard duty, is our door gunner; he is itching for relief, itching to do the job he's been so well trained to do. I don't think he cares much any more. He's been out on so many missions, flying above the jungle so often, he lives on borrowed time anyway. What amazes me more than anything else as I sit there in the chopper, cradling my rifle in my arms, is how young we all are.

Ivy League was the oldest in our group. He was twenty-three and an old man already. We looked up to him. He knew a lot about things we'd barely heard of. When he played his saxophone underneath the sultry Asian sky my skin would tingle. Ivy League came from the east coast and had gone to a posh university. He volunteered for combat, same as Finn. I think that's why they liked each other so much. Ivy League was aboard the lost plane. We had to go look for him. He was what we all wanted to be when we grew up. Tough soldiers all, we would never have admitted how much we loved him, how much we looked up to him, as we might an older brother.

The bull charges around the pasture. Romeo screams with delight as he maneuvers the gunship's big doorgun into a better firing position. He lets go a burst of bullets and catches the bull right on the arse. It bellows and rages. Oh, how it bellows and rages against the night. Careening around the field, the White One searches for his tormentor, his pain-spitting persecutor.

I feel as if I've taken acid, because I sense things much more intensely. I'm hot and flushed and my skin tingles and prickles as if I'm wearing a hair shirt or hearing again Ivy League's saxophone. In the distance, lightning bolts jolt and shatter the sky, but I'm enjoying myself listening to the rotor blades throbbing, making mincemeat of the surrounding air. They sound out a hard-driving dancebeat, and we are dancing all right! Dancing high above the bloodwet earth we hate so much, freed for a time, disengaged, disentangled, divorced, away from it! Every so often Romeo fires a burst and we watch the tracers make their way down to earth. Our pilot, Tommy-up-front we call him, makes a sharp hundred eighty degree turn and flies back over the pasture. The White One careens around the field lost in his madness. I wonder if he's enraged that something so evil, so malevolent, could invade his domain so completely, so definitely. We fly just a few feet above him, following him like a shadow. Tommy-up-front is good. He sticks to the bull as if he were a part of him, as if he were a hawk in pursuit of a sparrow. Romeo puts a bullet into the White One's balls and everybody laughs. I begin to know then that something isn't quite right between Finn and me.

When the bull is shot, as we turn and cross behind his charging form, his balls explode, and I watch that two thousand pound creator jump ten feet off the ground. Does he know Death is close at hand, that Death stalks him? How does he feel when his peaceful night is disturbed by the huge and noisy monster following so fast, so close, behind him? The bull's red fury becomes almost perceptible, almost as red as the tracers blasting into him. He charges toward the barbed-wire fence surrounding the pasture, intent only on escaping the unseen thing that has rent his world asunder, split apart his quiet, fucking life. He jumps but, alas, catches his forelegs on the topmost wire and, caught in the barbs, he rages at the injustice of it all, his big brown eyes like deep water, mirroring the puzzled fear in his soul. We turn and come back around the pasture. I look over at Romeo. He smiles gleefully, almost greedily, and I know the bull is big in his gunsights. The whole world becomes quiet then. I hear not a sound, but my eyes are full, full of the color of blood as each of a long line of bullets blast their way through the neck of the bull.

We circle the pasture, we fly back and forth across the path of the bull, we watch him in his death throes. We see the beautiful horned head fall forward over the other side of the fence, attached only by a thin piece of skin and ligament, followed at once by a gush, a fountain, of thick red buffalo blood. Red, red, red! A river of blood as red as my robe. And as the white bull lies twitching on the wires, I watch his soul escaping, drifting out through the gaping hole in his neck. The whole world turns red as we fly through our sea of blood. Tommy's circles above the pasture become tighter and tighter as we rise higher and higher into the dark night sky. I feel myself leaving Finn then, coming out of his body, though I can't leave him completely. Like the head of the bull I, too, seem to be attached by a sliver of skin and ligament. Part of me remains attached to him, and all the world is bloody. The soul of the White One hovers above the quiet pasture and Finn, as if coming to, screams and kicks like a man gone mad.

I feel in that instant a terrific force pushing me out of his body, out of the whirling, vibrating aircraft, out into the cold, rushing air. I hear Finn scream as I, covered in blood, topple toward the bewildered soul of the dead white bull.

During my descent I feel a chill of such bonepenetrating coldness it defies definition, though it goes through me like a spear of ice, then swims around me, filling me with dread and foreboding. Then it is gone!

The bull and I swirl around and around, caught in the turbulence generated by the gunship's rotor blades, clinging to each other, wondering what has happened, wondering what could have put us outside of our bodies. The body of the bull is dead; I can see it still, hanging across the barbed wire fence. The bull can see it too, his big eyes wide, filled with fear. But my body lives. Finn lives. His arse is numb from sitting on top of his steel helmet. What's ironic is that we sit on top of our steel helmets to protect our own balls from those nasty bullets coming through the floor of the aircraft.

As I dance about the sky, riding the bull, I wonder what has compelled us to kill him so senselessly. What have we become after all? I take great pity on the bull after we shoot his balls off, after Finn casts me out of his body. And as the soul of the bull and I drift above the jungle, I cling to him tightly as we follow the gunship until, at last, we find the downed aircraft. I've been riding the bull ever since, riding the confused white bull, in one form or another, through the maze of our bloody madness for quarter of a century.

The gunship drops us off in a clearing nearby. The rain has stopped, but the trees are dripping as if it is still raining. Drip, drip, drip they go, monotonous and annoying. We walk, all five of us, single file, along the jungle floor, doing our best to dodge tripwire boobytraps, snakes and tiger shit. The bull is drifting above the treetops. Finn walks in the middle of the file; he is less experienced than the other grunts at jungle games. I walk ten feet behind him, but I've tied the umbilical cord around his waist; I don't want to lose him. Without that cord, or the idea of it, I would surely have lost him long ago and, just as I am new at this particular way of living, Finn isn't yet aware that he's lost his soul, that he's kicked me out of his body. What becomes immediately apparent to me is that at the very moment before my expulsion from his body I have only the same abilities as he. I am humanly limited; yet, when he kicks me out, I go immediately back to what I truly am: a pure spirit, an Invisibility, as some folk call me. I have all the accompanying attributes of a spirit: I can see things and hear things no mortal could ever hope to see or hear. No ordinary mortal, that is. A visionary, perhaps, might see many of the things

I do. Finn doesn't yet know that unless he embraces me once more, takes me back into himself, he will never be complete. He will always be an Empty.

We smell the downed aircraft before we see it. Among all the other odors associated with a burned-out aircraft, we smell the horrifying and unforgettable stench of roasted human flesh. The plane has burned almost completely, though it still smolders in spite of the heaviness of the recent rains. Many of the bodies remain strapped into their seats; others are scattered and strewn about the jungle floor all around us. We stand motionless, staring with horror at our barbecued pals. Some of the bodies are still intact and of those, most have been stripped of any valuables, including wallets, rings, watches and the like and, naturally, their weapons. We find Ivy League tied to a tree, his face beaten to a pulp and what seems to be a bullet hole in his forehead.

"Jeezus god," Finn blurts out before dropping to his knees and throwing up all over the ground before him. When he recovers he gets up and, with an angry jerk, pulls the dogtag from Ivy League's mutilated body. He wonders why the other whole bodies haven't been mutilated and why they haven't all been robbed of their personal belongings. Then, a moment later, he knows.

The explosions rip apart the drip, drip, dripping night and Frankie Chen falls dead to the ground.

I think Frankie died of a heart attack; he was such a frail wee sparrow of a man. Finn goes down too, but fear buckles his legs rather than bullets or shrapnel. He pisses himself, and his long black rifle falls by his side. Before he can pick it up a tiny young girl, no more than sixteen, dressed in black, silk pajamas, whose eyes are shaped like mine, comes charging out of the undergrowth and stands, smiling, over my sprawled-out Finn, her long black rifle pointed menacingly at his head.

Before she can pull the trigger, Romeo Robinson's machete comes swinging out of the darkness we have landed in and sweeps cleanly through the young girl's neck. The machete is Romeo's favorite weapon. He likes the closeness of it, the personal touch. Finn does too. Romeo told Finn he liked feeling death creep up along the blade and through the hilt into his arm. He said he liked the power it gave him.

The pretty head falls beside Finn. He looks straight into the eyes of the dead soldiergirl and he swears on his very soul he sees life there before the head lolls to one side, now finally dead. Had circumstances been different, he might have enjoyed sleeping with this girl with the almondshaped eyes. When Finn looks at the decapitated head, its eyes still open, lying there as still as stone, he snaps.

"Ya fuckin' bitch," he screams. "Why'd yae have to go an' do that? I don't even know yae."

Romeo Robinson laughs and, in a voice filled with disdain says, "Welcome to the war, Alba man!"

"For chrissake," Finn said many years later, "that coulda been my Mary lyin' there!"

The ambush ended almost as abruptly as it began. We are well-versed in counter-ambush tactics, because we've trained well, and we've lived through ambushes before. In spite of Finn's panic-induced pissings, we rip the enemy to shreds. There's nothing like fear to make the adrenaline flow, or to make a man a heroic warrior. After it's all over, the smoky smell of cordite hangs thick and heavy beneath the canopy of leaves and the jungle goes back to its drip, drip, dripping monotony.

We hear then a soft whimper nearby and when we look around we see Johnny Quinn's broken body lying a few feet away. Finn lets out a loud, piercing scream; Johnny, after all, is his best friend, Mary's brother. And Johnny is a poet. On many a warm southeast Asian night he would read to us from a big fat book of poems he kept by his bed.

The dead white water buffalo, bellowing madly, comes crashing through the leafy canopy, his legs flailing wildly. He doesn't understand why he'll never get back into his body, broken as it might be or why, with the same suddenness, he can now fly like the birds who once perched, picking and pecking, upon his haunches.

"Help me, Finn, help me," begs smiling Johnny as if his mouth is filled with toffee and marbles.

Johnny has blond, curly hair which he's always trying to straighten. I never could understand why he didn't like his curls; they matched just so his perfect smile they were so beautiful. Johnny's legs are severed just above the knees and half of his face is shot away.

"Goddamit, Finn," the young Johnny pleads. "For the love of the good God in heaven, kill me!"

Johnny tries to push himself up onto his elbow, but the strain overwhelms him. He falls back onto the grass and looks up at Finn, his eyes imploring, beseeching, begging.

"I can't, Johnny," says Finn. "Don't ask me to do that, please don't ask me to do that!"

Johnny sticks out his hand and grabs Finn's ankle tightly. "YOU PROMISED!" he screams, as best he can, blood and bits of broken teeth flying everywhere. "Don't send me back to my ma like this." He knows he's a goner. Both he and Finn have talked about the possibility many times over.

Finn stands, picks up his rifle and looks down at his fallen brother. He kneels beside Johnny and kisses him full on the bloody red lips. "Sssh, Johnny," he says." Then he stands over Johnny once more. When the shot rings out, echoing though the trees, the smile leaves Finn's face forever.

He drops to his knees, crying like a baby, as Johnny Quinn's spirit comes out of his body. Confused, it hovers above us.

I crouch beside Finn. He is still alive and, though I can no longer rest inside him, inside our body, I can no more leave him than the day can leave the night. Having no place else to go, moving on instinct alone, Johnny straddles the back of the great white bull, and I remember hoping then they might comfort one another as they ride away together to the Place of Truly Dead Souls.

Finn the Albanach, newly turned twenty, kneels down upon the wet leaves of grass, at the very moment of Johnny's death, and cries.

I realize that when he killed Johnny, Finn also killed something inside himself.

He rushes over to Romeo Robinson and grabs the machete from the startled gunner's hand. "Gimme that fuckin' thing," he snarls, then begins hacking wildly at the bodies of the dead Asian soldiers, aiming for their genitals. And seeing themselves so mutilated, their spirits scream and dance wildly among the treetops.

Finn becomes a cold, insensitive killer that night; life means nothing henceforth, and the realization that death really is his business becomes clearer than any textbook, story, or drill instructor might ever hope to tell.

Though Finn has no way of knowing it, the chopping in two of the White One and the hack, hack, hacky beheading of the smiling Asian soldiergirl have forever put their numbing mark on him, and the bullet now resting inside the brain of Johnny Quinn will forever have Finn's name etched upon it. Nonchalance and apathy become an integral part of him that night, more so perhaps than even the blood running through his veins. They are now as much a part of him as are his eyes or his hands or the color of his hair.

His emptiness is now complete; he did become an Empty that night, doomed to traipse around the earth without me, without his Madman, without his spirit. I remember falling to my knees as I watch him, then beg him, for the first time, to take me back.

"Please, Finn," I beg. "Take me back. I am your spirit, I am your passion, I am all the love, all the creativity you could ever hope to muster. Anything you want to love," I tell him, "I am that which will enable you to do so."

He doesn't hear a word of it, and the deep, red blood of the rainfilled night strikes my Finn, my blackhaired warrior, deaf, dumb and blind.

Tommy-up-front is as nervous as hell, though he's the most fearless gunship pilot I've ever seen. He doesn't fly his aircraft. He rides it like a wild bronco. I think he could have stood and flown it, still managing somehow to operate both the foot-pedals and the hand-controls simultaneously. But he's jittery; we've left the gunship, his baby, unprotected and, in spite of the monsoon rains, the area seems to be infested with Viet Cong. What's worse, though, is that we're illegal. We don't have any orders to go on this mission. We've simply taken it upon ourselves to go look for our friends. The implications, since we're returning with dead comrades, could be terrible.

"Let's get the hell outa here," says Tommy, as he grabs the body of Frankie Chen and throws it over his shoulder. "Now!" he demands.

"Bullshit, man," says Romeo. "The gunship's just up the way! Go get it an' pick up these bodies."

"You're crazy, man! I don't give a rat's ass if Jesus H. Christ's just up the way; we're gettin' the fuck outa here. Let's go, move it!"

"I ain't goin' nowhere, asshole. Ivy League's tied to a fuckin' tree back there," says Romeo, clenching his bloody machete more tightly than ever.

Tommy-up-front spins quickly around, pulling out and cocking his sidearm as he spins and, grabbing Romeo by the shirtfront, sticks his pistol into Romeo's temple.

"You disobeying a direct order, lover boy?"

They each stand their ground, staring one another down for a very long and tense moment.

"Shit," said Romeo, and spins away. "Watch your fuckin' back, asshole," he mutters through clenched teeth.

"Huh? Watch my back? I'll mess you up real bad if I hear that kinda shit again," says Tommy-up-front. Then he chuckles. "Don't you have no respect for your elders, Romeo?" he says. The tension evaporates. Even Romeo smiles.

"Awright, you guys. Grab Johnny an' the rest of 'em an' let's get the hell outa here. We'll take the bodies to Triage; the nurses can bag 'em up!"

The flight back to base camp is uneventful and quiet. All except for the dull, boneshaking throb of the mincemeat-making rotorblades. All of us are lost in our own thoughts as we watch the pools of blood gathering under the bodies of our dead pals.

◆ ◆ ◆

"I want that bullet," says Finn.

The nurse, who is in her early twenties, looks at him and chuckles sardonically. She leans over the body of Johnny Quinn, then stares straight into Finn's eyes.

"And which bullet might that be?" she asks. "There's half a dozen in him."

"I want the one stuck in his head. That's the one that done him in."

"How do you know that?"

"I know it because I fuckin' well know it! Is that no' enough?"

The nurse looks at him and shrugs her shoulders. She is haggard and tired, exhausted. A dark brown curl hangs over her forehead.

"I don't have time for that kinda crap," says she. "I'm too busy patching up the living."

"Nurse, I want that goddamned bullet."

She runs her tired eyes over the grim figure of Finn.

"Then get it yourself, soldier," she says, and hands him a long-nosed tweezer-like instrument.

He stands there for a moment gawking at the nurse, not quite sure if he heard her properly. Romeo bursts out laughing. Tommy's purple with rage.

"You're one cold-hearted motherfucker," he says.

There's a smile on the nurse's face.

"Man, you ain't really gonna do that, are ya?" asks Romeo.

Finn steps up to the gurney. He probes the bullet hole in Johnny's forehead. He hits soft stuff at first. He feels sick. Then solid stuff. Maybe he got lucky right away. Is it the bullet? Forget it, man! It's just bone. Skull. He's nauseous. There's a hole in the solid stuff. The path of the bullet? Get through the hole, through the forehead. Oh, christ, it's soft, soft and mushy! The brain, he's reached the brain. Wait a minute! Is there a hole in the back? He reaches under Johnny's head. Feels. Should be a hole as big as a baseball. There ain't no fuckin' hole in the back. Where's the bullet then? Must still be inside. Was it bouncin' off bone, ricocheting from bone to bone? Where did it rest? Could be anywhere. Don't talk to me now, Johnny, please don't talk to me now. His hands are covered in blood. My hands are covered in your blood, Johnny. He gropes, twists, scratches the skull. Sounds like a hundred fingernails screeching down a blackboard. Bloodcurdling. He heaves. He purses his lips, expands his cheeks. Heave. He holds it back. Reactionary forces are at work now, they've taken over and conquered his will. Heave. He's lightheaded, ready to swoon. He wishes he could. Heave. Can't back off now. Save face. He's a dangerous warrior now. A hero. Why am I doing this, he wonders. What the fuck am I doing here inside my buddy's brain? Evidence? Take the evidence and hide it in a deep, deep hole somewhere so that it will never, ever, ever be found? The vomit rises. Heave, Finn, heave! With all his will he swallows hard, forcing it back. Romeo pukes for him, sickened. The tweezers strike something solid in the middle of Johnny's mush. He grabs at it and pulls, pulls out the killer part of an M16 bullet. He stares at the nurse, his eyes blazing with fear and hatred. Why'd she have to make me do that? He sticks the bullet into the top left pocket of his jungle fatigues as if it were a pack of cigarettes, then heaves once more.

He rushes off towards the door of the Triage tent, holding his bloodied hand to his mouth. The nurse stares after him, a look of abject disgust creasing her face.

"Body bag!" she shouts to a medic, tears of exasperation and pity welling up in her eyes. "Bring me another goddamnfuckin' body bag!"

Before Finn reaches the door he hears the whistle, the sickening whistle of an incoming rocket, followed by the dull thud of the impact before the explosion. He hits the deck, smiling, and holds his rifle tightly.

"Missed, motherfuckers," he says.

Then the second whistling noise disturbs the night, wiping the smile from his face. It smashes through the flimsiness of the Triage tent, thuds into the floor underneath the table where Johnny's being bagged and blows Johnny's remains and the body of the brown-haired nurse to smithereens. Finn, shocked into inertia, is splattered with bodybits and blood. His numbness is immediate and so complete he can't speak, and from that moment on he is unable to smile. For the second time that night he throws up, and throws up, and throws up.

In whispers, the doctors mumble, "Battle fatigue!" A numbness has taken him over, and he has a vacant stare in his eyes, as if he isn't really there at all. A month or so later, his commander, with as little fanfare as possible, relieves him of his immediate duties and shoves him into a quiet occupation for the remainder of his time in-country. He shuffles papers from morning until night. He cries a lot. Quietly and softly. He goes back to his hootch after his duty day is done, plays hard rock music loudly through his headphones, and loses himself in the dreamscapes, the fantasy world, of his heroin-prompted wanderings, his only comfort.

◆　◆　◆

I stick with him every moment of every day until at last his war is over, all three-hundred-sixty-five days of it. I send him messages, I niggle him and pester him. I'm thankful he's still intact. In body at least. He's glad to be away from it all as he stands there next to the huge air terminal in Saigon. He'll be twenty-one soon. He's looking forward to his first legal drink when he arrives in San Francisco. Finally an adult in the eyes of the world.

The air terminal buzzes with activity, with the movement of people. As he stands there, he thinks how strange it is to be in a war zone one minute and out of it the next, back at last in mufti. He's just returned from a walk around the teeming streets of Saigon city. It really is like San Francisco, he thinks: beautiful, sultry, sexy! But like the city by the bay, Saigon also entices like a whore, a shameless goddamn whore.

Saigon city in the Maygone month of June is a magical place too, spiritthick and colorful, teeming and pulsing with a mysteriousness that transcends even bombs and bloodhungry bullets. I can feel the mystery myself, can almost see it in the heat-rippled light of the hot summer day, standing there at the airport with Finn, wearing my long crimson robe, waiting to go home, filled with regret. It could have been so beautiful, he feels. If only.

If only this, if only that! His post-Vietnam list of if-onlys has tripled, perhaps even quadrupled, compared to the days before Vietnam. "If only! The words of a dreamer," he says. What a waste. If only I'd stayed at home, if only I'd stayed in Alba. Now there's a thought for you. Alba, what a strange word it is right enough. These days at least. So ripe with emotion, bursting so with such a profusion of moods and feelings. His head pounds with memories as he stands at the terminal gate in his new silk suit, Hong Kong cut for a few lousy bucks. He had it tailored to fit to perfection some months before; but the suit now hangs miserably over his heroin-mangled frame. Home, he's sure, is where the blood is. Aye, that's it all right. Where the blood is!

When the White One's soul leaves his body, on the night Finn kicks me out, I feel sure it'll be easy to get back inside him, but he's so confused himself he doesn't have the slightest idea how empty he is. He doesn't even know he's an Empty. I feel certain it'll be easy to somehow communicate with him; even as a child his openness to mystical considerations is mature beyond both his years and the strictures of the ordinary, workaday world; that's why I'm so surprised he doesn't yet know he's now an Empty himself.

He always loved Alban winters, particularly during those long nights when thick fog descends over the fields in which he plays. He could feel the mystery then too, and knows intuitively that spirits and other Invisibilities roam around on such subdued nights. The wispiness of spirits, after all, blends well with fog. Proofs and the like are of no consequence. He just knows! He feels the presence of Invisibilities much too strongly. He is open to the feel of them!

I have always been inside Finn, though quietly. It's only since I've been outside him that I have to niggle and annoy him. When inside him, I am simply a part of him. I remember one particularly foggy night when he awoke disturbed from a fitful sleep.

He is around twelve years of age at the time and has awakened to the sad and plaintive moaning of the bagpipes. They beckon him, invite him to seek the source of the sound. He jumps out of bed and dresses hurriedly, not daring to awaken his family. He slips out the door into the night like an Invisibility himself and walks off into the darkness. All is quiet but for the sound of the pipes coming to him wrapped in the droplets of water forming the earth-embracing clouds. So enshrouded in music and clouds, he feels the pull of his heritage, the inexplicable pull of some ancient mystery, as if he's become one with the trees and the grass and other things beyond the usual ken of man.

And so pulled, he passes the homes of all his friends and loved ones, into the fields, through faerie rings and thistles, until he feels as scratched as the suffering Christ himself. He stops, half dead, and drops before a high hill where the music began. On top of the hill stands the piper, dressed in an ancient kilted plaid. The sad and plaintive dirge plays on, crying to him. For the first time in his life, he feels a great heart-heavy pain. The prostrate Finn looks up and the piper turns, his eyes filled with tears. "Mo thruaige ort!" says the piper in the language of the ancients. "Woe to thee!"

Oh why, Saigon? Oh, why those scratches of Christ from the mists of Alba to the teeming, pulsing mystery of Saigon city? Alba, light years away, is real only at a gut level and in memories. Finn's last memory of Alba is of getting drunk, sitting around a fire with his friends in Fingal's Park, a few hours before being poured onto the plane for America, land of the free, home of the bygod brave.

And America, what of America? He lived there just a few short months before being drafted, but he's learned so much about being American as he plods through jungle and guts with his fellow warriors who are all as young and as innocent as he. He knows even then he will never be an American, that he never can be an American. Nor is he a Scotsman any more. The many thousands of miles of separation and the many rounds of spent ammunition and the blood and the guts and the heroin overdoses have seen to that, have made him a stranger, a loner.

He stands at the air terminal in Saigon city in the Maygone month of June feeling like the Steppenwolf. And he weeps.

He's sure it's the killing of Johnny that makes him a loner when, in fact, it is the killing of the bull that makes him so. I've often wondered what they were thinking, those young men, when they took the life of the bull, when they killed the bull so certainly, so irrevocably. Were they killing themselves? Did the bull represent manhood, virility, propagation of the species? Or was it something more basic, more primordial even than that? Isn't Zeus, the father of all the gods, represented by the bull in classical mythology? Were they, killing God? Perhaps that's why, since then, Finn has felt that he belongs nowhere, but that he belongs everywhere too!

He feels the mystery of Saigon, though he doesn't know exactly what it is he feels; nor can he possibly know how to describe it, yet there we both stand at the airport feeling it. I've learned by now that Finn won't let me back into him without a tremendous struggle. Had I known then how long the struggle would be, I might have given up and let him do as he would, with or without me. But I know what we are, what our existence means, because I come from the Land of the Truly Alive which he knows so little of. I am the spirit; he, the body and the mind. He calls it toughness, will, one-and-one-equals-two pragmatism. I know better. I know it to be ignorance. No more, no less. Ignorance and pride!

But I won't let him go. No matter what, no matter whatever happens to him, I'll keep the blood-dripping umbilical cord wrapped safely around his waist, and I'll continue to plod along by his side until he takes me back or until he kills himself. Perhaps I'll hang him with the cord myself; it might be better than suicide.

He's been trying to kill himself ever since he put the bullet into Johnny Quinn's brain. Not so much by suicide, but through careless bravado at first and, now, through the extravagant use of heroin, pure China White.

He is loaded to the gills now as he stands here waiting for the plane to take us to San Francisco, where he plans to live after a short visit to Alba, as he will always call it. He has a vial of heroin in his pocket. He's going to stick it up his arse and smuggle it into

America. It will last him a long, long time and will enable him, he's sure, to withdraw completely from the awful stuff. But he's afraid. When his flight is announced, he runs into the bathroom and snorts enough of it up his nose to choke a horse. Though he's become emaciated through guilt and the consequent heavy use of dope and is thirty pounds underweight, his tolerance is high. As a junkie, he is at his peak. He feels somewhat normal as he stuffs some more of the heroin into the end of a cigarette. If nobody bothers him, he'll smoke it on the other side of the Pacific; if it doesn't go so well, he'll simply drop it on the ground and hope for the best, withdrawals be damned!

And so it all is, over and done with—history. A year, every minute of it spent counting down the days, accompanied by the agents of madness as they do their best to mold him and make him what he will become for the rest of his mortal life.

I hope that a visit to Alba after the war and a life in San Francisco will bring him around. But it doesn't! We grow farther and farther apart as the years fly by, as the years tumble headlong, one into the other.

— 1 —

WHILE IN HIS
WANDERING WALKABOUT

IT IS DARK and a light drizzle falls on Paranoid Park, a small park stuck in the middle of North Beach. The name lingers on long after San Francisco's hippies took their last bad acid trip. Nowadays the park is living room and bedroom to many of the city's homeless. At the edge of the grass, next to the bench where he sleeps, a Shopping Cart Soldier dances wildly as if his feet were on fire. His name is Finn MacDonald. He is an Albanach, a sick Albanach, withdrawing from alcohol against his will. He grabs and pulls at his clothing, and beats himself violently about the face and head until blood trickles from his nose. He crouches behind his shopping cart hiding from demons he can see but cannot touch. He's familiar with the demons, knows them by name. They've visited him often over the last twenty-five years or so, ever since he left the war behind.

"Get away from me!" he screams. "Fuck off, ya bastards."

The fear in his voice makes me want to scream myself. I try to console him, but I just make him worse. After all, he still can't see me. I wonder if he ever will. All I can do is watch him suffer. When

I'm about to despair, Arkansas, an old pal of his, now dead, comes running towards him. Arkansas's been sheltering in the nearby bushes, but when he hears Finn's cries he leaves his blanket beside his own shopping cart and runs to help his friend. Arkansas knows what's happening; he's seen it so many times before. He pins Finn's arms behind his back; he doesn't want his friend to hurt himself again.

"Is it the voices, Finn?" he asks. "Are the voices at it again?"

"Aye," says Finn. "It's that bastard Madman. I don't know what he wants wi' me. Do this, do that—he's drivin' me outa my goddamn mind!"

Arkansas knows all about me too. Madman, that is!

"Here, have a swig at this," says Arkansas, offering Finn a half-empty bottle of vodka.

"Arkansas!" says Finn, "You're a darlin'! I didn't know yae were in there," he says, referring to the bushes.

Arkansas chuckles. "I'm always in there, you know that!"

Finn takes a long pull at the vodka bottle then sits down on the bench.

"I was nearly sleepin' myself," he says. "Then it started! That nigglin' voice tellin' me I'm killin' myself, tellin' me to get it together. Screw it, Arkansas, gimme another drink. I'll drown that bastard yet!"

That's about as much credit as he ever gives me. All he seems to think about is how to drown me with his stinking booze. It breaks my heart, because I do everything I can to keep him alive. He should've been dead a million times, but I always manage to keep him holding on another day, just one more day. Because I do love him so.

Arkansas isn't the only one to hear Finn's cries of withdrawal. The police hear him too. They show up a few minutes later, flashlights flashing, nightsticks in hand, wondering what the hell's going on. Arkansas scarpers into the bushes again. They catch Finn, vodka bottle raised to his lips, chugging for all he's worth in a last desperate effort to get enough booze inside him to still the shakes. They handcuff him and, as they escort him to the patrol car, he shouts over his shoulder: "Take care of my shopping cart, Arkansas. Put it in the usual place." Finn is lucky; Arkansas's loyalty is beyond question; he stashes Finn's shopping cart safely in the usual place. But Arkansas's own luck ran out a few days later. A park attendant found him dead among the same bushes he slept under most nights, as rigid and stiff as a railroad tie. His killer had caved his head in, caved it in as if he hated Arkansas, and the contents of his shopping cart were scattered around on the ground beside him. The same miserable bastard stole his boots too. They were good boots, black boots with thick, leather soles. Arkansas was fond of his new boots.

On his way to jail Finn is in a panic. He doesn't have enough booze in his system. It'll be a long night in jail. The withdrawals will get to him. He'll have an alcoholic seizure! DT's!

"Fuck this bullshit," he mutters, straining against the too-tight handcuffs, sick and tired that it's happened again.

Some men aren't meant for war; their souls are far too old. They've seen it all before. The Albanach is just such a man. I knew it and he knew it the very first moment we stepped onto the red soil of Vietnam. I can say this with some certainty, with some impunity, for I am his soul, his spirit. I do know that much at least, though I don't know everything! But Vietnam's a million miles away now, and Finn's busy looking for his shopping cart.

He finds it, safe and intact, where Arkansas left it behind an abandoned building, a safe place they used whenever they needed to.

Finn lives in a small, compact world about ten city blocks or so in diameter. His world is centered at the intersection of Columbus Avenue and Stockton Street. He stops to paint and panhandle there every day; it is his favorite spot, his moneymaker. Only rarely will he make a foray into the world beyond; it doesn't make much sense for him to wander anywhere else, because everything he needs exists within the perimeter of his circular world, a world so like the one he lived in while fighting the war. He doesn't have to guard the perimeter of his present world, but he doesn't venture beyond its boundaries either.

He likes to paint, but because he doesn't have a home, let alone a studio, he paints out of doors whenever he gets the chance. He simply ties a canvas or a piece of wood, or whatever other flat surface he might find, to the top of his shopping-cart, takes his brushes and paints in hand, and goes to work as if there were no tomorrow. Today he's working on a canvas given to him by a sympathetic student from the Art Institute. He rarely experiences such kind gestures in the harshness of his shopping cart world.

"Why, thank you, kind sir," he says, with such a condescending tone the student raises his eyebrows questioningly.

"Do you want it or not?" asks the student, his feelings hurt, his hand still gripping the stretcher bar.

"Oh, I do, I do indeed!"

"Then why are you being such a prick? I don't have much either, you know!"

Finn looks hard at the student, then smiles grimly, already regretting his condescension.

"Sorry, buddy," he says. "Maybe I just ain't used to such kindness. But at least yae acknowledged me, saw me; most of the time I'm invisible. People don't see me, y'know, an' they sure as hell don't see my shoppin' cart. I'm what you might call an Invisibility," he says with a throaty chuckle.

The student smiles too, and I burst out laughing myself when I hear Finn talking about being an Invisibility; it's an unusual term certainly, but an accurate term, though not usually applied to the still-alive.

Long ago Finn grew accustomed to the stares and the snide remarks of the commuters, and there are many snide remarks these days; his shopping cart home and his appearance, though threatening enough in themselves, are nothing compared to the intimidating images he paints. Everything he paints is bizarre and disturbingly unreal. He feels sure that most of the commuters are threatened by his presence on the corner, and when they tell him to "Fuck off!" or "Go back to where you come from!" he puts their bellicose barbs down to fear, fear that they themselves may be just a paycheck or two away from the same fate, then he'll shrug nonchalantly and go on about his painting.

He enjoys painting the people in his head, the Visitors *he calls them. He's now busy painting a rather frightening image of me with chalk-white skin and a separation at the waist which looks both brutal and painful as if I'd been pulled apart, ripped in two by some awful force. Why the separation I don't know, but he seems to think it's important. He's got my body right though, for I am small, even my breasts, though they're plump and full. Blossoming, if you will, for I am young. He doesn't know who I am of course, since he hasn't seen me anywhere but in his mind; all he knows for certain is that I enter his mind, that my image keeps recurring in his dreams, and that he feels compelled to paint me.*

He's putting the finishing touches to this latest painting when, out of the unusually overcast sky, another alcoholic seizure slams him to the ground without mercy, without even a nod or a tip of its hat in warning, his canvas and brushes flying wildly, his arms and legs askew, his head jackhammering against the cold concrete.

The commuters try to ignore Finn and walk around him as he lies on the hard pavement shuffling and shimmying around in his fit. A small pool of blood gathers under his head. When the convulsions subside he reaches out, shaking to his bones and, grabbing onto the end of his shopping cart, tries to pull himself up off the sidewalk. But he falls back exhausted, shattered. He feels as if he's just been stung with a cattle prod, for his body tingles head to toe, and a dull thumping pain pulses in the back of his head. He's pissed all over himself, and for a few long minutes he feels disoriented and confused, not knowing whether he's in San Francisco or lying on a sandy beach on the other side of the world.

"Are you okay, son?" an old woman asks. She stands before him wrapped in an old rag of a coat as worn as Finn's.

"No, missus," he says. "But I'll be fine."

"Should I call an ambulance; you look like you need an ambulance."

"No thanks, missus; I'll be fine, I really will! It's a seizure! Just another damn seizure!"

He feels like weeping. He's been on the streets, homeless and miserable for more then twelve years now, ever since Mary Quinn, his wife, left him, her own heart nearly broken at her inability to help him. When Mary leaves she takes their son with her too. Many a time, in his dreams throughout the years, Finn sees Mary leaving their home with their son, Finn Johnny Quinn. She always carries the same heavy suitcase in her hand, her head bent low, tears streaming down her face as she trudges along the street, away from their home, away from him, the child hanging onto her sleeve, wondering what the hell's become of his quiet, safe life. The look on his son's face when he turns to see his father in the window of their home is etched upon Finn's heart forever. Not even in his wildest dreams could Finn imagine Mary leaving him. He is ultimately filled with wonder when she does, because his most far-out dreams of her have been so fantastic, so poignantly intimate they tell him only that they're meant for each other and that nothing in the world could ever come between them. Then the alcohol does, and so too does Finn's consequent withdrawal into himself.

"You're swallowing yourself whole," Mary tells him as she stands before him, hands on hips, her dark eyes ablaze with anger.

"Bit by bit, feet first, past your gut, and now you're up to your neck. One more swallow and you'll be gone. I don't want to see that, Finn," she told him. "I don't want to see you disappear inside yourself."

Then she left.

She was right too, because I saw the swallow coming myself. In truth, I do the best I can to help him allay the inevitable, to make the inevitable less destructive; it's a hard thing to watch a man swallow himself whole, feet first, all the way up past his stomach to his neck and the last fatal swallowing, gone forever into the hole of his retreat into himself.

He's lost all of his old friends too, and he hasn't been back to Alba since that first time after the war. He hasn't seen any of his family in over twenty years and none of his American friends can take his self-abuse any more either. Their love for him is so much they can't bear to see him continue to kill himself with booze. Not even for one more day. It's too painful by far, because they know that, ultimately, he's a decent fellow with a strong urge to live peacefully. It is too great a burden for his loved ones to witness his destruction. Nor can Mary and the child continue to watch him die so slowly, day after day. He finally leaves all of them behind. His struggle will have to be gone through alone. All that keeps him from swallowing himself whole is his need to paint those wild and bizarre images he loves so much. The painting seems to keep him rooted in something resembling life. He took up painting just after the war and it seems he must paint his life story on those flat surfaces. He knows intuitively that there's something beyond himself which compels him to paint, that there's a reason for his existence after all. He paints for his life, from the inside out, needing somehow to communicate. It's all that's left and he holds onto it with a quiet desperation.

Finn is tall and thick as an oak, yet, at the same time, he's nimble on his feet. He has coal-black hair gone grey, and blue Keltic eyes. At best, he looks ten years older than his forty-five years, though he feels older even than that.

As he picks up his brushes and paints, he wraps his tattered coat more tightly about him. He still has some pride left, and his incontinence embarrasses him. He stinks. Stinks of piss! Piss is a death smell. Dead bodies smell of piss. "I smell of death," he mumbles through a resolute grimace. He's been trying to stay away from the bottle, trying to quit drinking, but without medication a seizure is inevitable. Nowadays at least. He knows that to be true because it's happened so many times before, but he wants so much to quit drinking that he feels the risk worthwhile. Maybe now, he thinks, I'll be okay; I've had my seizure. Then he thinks back to the jail cell.

He remembers having one, probably two, seizures in jail. And he remembers the hallucinations and DT's setting in during withdrawals. Another seizure is certainly possible too, though he's never experienced a doubleheader before, let alone three in a row. He wonders whether his brain will remain intact if he has another seizure. Maybe this time he'll have a heart attack or a stroke, maybe his mind might snap.

But, no, it's just the drunk-tank again, arrested once more, dead-drunk in public, arms and legs shackled to the wall of the cell, his head hanging low, wondering why he can neither live nor die, wondering why he can't stop drinking, why he has to be arrested again and again, marriage broken, life a shambles, drunkdrunkdrunk! Overwhelmed with fear!

I'm there in the cell beside him, filled with grief at my inability to help him. Everything he experiences, I experience, though I see only the pictures, hear only the sounds; I never feel the pain he feels, though my breasts ache knowing what he's going through. I become angry with him at times. "Take me back, damn you, take me back!" And though there's a stirring of loss somewhere inside him, a feeling of something not quite right, he refuses to open up his thick, fat heart.

As I watch him, a cockroach moves across the floor, turning first this way then that, searching, searching as Finn is searching.

He looks up and, seeing a Grotesque walk into the cell, screams with all his might. He can't believe his eyes. She is tall and thin, a hag, as ugly as sin, whose single breast droops to her navel and drips an ugly, green putrescent liquid; her lipless mouth shows long, sharp teeth. Yet even though she's lipless, she can still smile in a chilling sort of way, which she now does as she walks over to Finn who has fallen silent, petrified beyond speech or even sound. The hag smiles her grotesque smile. It is a calm and determined sort of smile which makes it all the more chilling. Then he notices her eyes. They are red, malevolent red, and almondshaped.

She approaches him in a demonically sexual way, first sticking her dripping wet breast into his mouth trying to make him suckle and, failing that, kisses him passionately with her lipless mouth. Then she begins to rub his cock as if it were her own, slowly, softly, arousingly as Finn, screaming silently, stiff in his shackles, knows he is about to die or go to hell. The Grotesque loosens his shackles one by one and, terrorized, he finds his voice again and screams as loudly as his lungs will allow. As soon as she has untied the last shackle, the Grotesque picks the Albanach up in her long wiry arms and backs off toward the door of the cell.

Finn becomes even more rigid and screams harder than ever, but to no avail, for the Grotesque holds him ever more tightly, determined to take him from the cell; with each step backward she takes, he grows stiffer, struggling for his life. When the redeyed bitch Grotesque reaches the door of the cell, it flies open with a loud crash, but no matter how hard she tries to pull him through, he won't budge. He remains as stiff as a brick and the Grotesque pulls and pulls, battering him against the doorjamb. For long minutes she batters the brickstiff Finn against the doorjamb, growing angrier by the minute until, at last, in a complete rage, she throws the Albanach to the floor where he lies weeping and sore, thankful he's still in the Land of the Living, thankful that his will has somehow been stronger than that of the bitch Grotesque.

When Finn first notices the walls and floor of his cell moving he thinks it might be an earthquake; when he sees a number of Grotesques, both male and female, climbing out of the crevices created by the movements, he knows his mind is slipping or that it is indeed time to go to hell. He scuttles, crablike, into the middle of the cell floor, but these Grotesques are many, and they look just like the first Grotesque, red eyes and all; they grab every part of him they possibly can and, as he screams and kicks, they pull him down into the hole in the floor— the magical Saigon City in the Maygone month of June long-gone as down and down he goes into the hole.

All I can do is go with him.

Many of these Grotesques are naked too, and of those that are naked, their genitals have been horribly mutilated. The rest of them wear silky black pajamas. They are strong, and they carry Finn high above them as they travel through the dark, dank places of the jungle until they reach an encampment of sorts, surrounded by trees, lit with bonfires. In the middle of the encampment sits a bier, upon which they place him. When they've tied him down they dance around him, chanting all the while.

I am helpless, unable to interfere directly, though as I always do, I try to go inside him, try to fill him up.

As an Empty who became so through no fault of his own, Finn has an opening through which he can still receive messages from that of which he is empty. But, though he's open, he is more closed than open. He trusts nothing; he trusts no one. He manages to receive just enough of my signals to save him from complete and utter destruction.

The Grotesques continue their ritual of dancing and chanting around him. He has now calmed down somewhat, resigned perhaps to whatever fate might befall him. Wide-eyed, he watches a small group of his adversaries dance towards him, wide grins on their faces, their red almondshaped eyes bright and malevolent. He feels sure he knows those eyes the Grotesques all have in common. He's seen them before. Images of the dead soldiergirl in the jungle come back to him. He sees again her head being lopped off by Romeo Robinson's cleansweeping machete, and he sees again the bewildered look on her face as the life leaves her. But he knows those eyes from another place too, from somewhere in his far and distant past. Another life perhaps. He knows intuitively that those red, malevolent eyes belong to He Who Walks Only At Night, and that these Grotesques now surrounding him are the disciples of that very same Redeyes. Finn has seen Redeyes before. He knows him! And when he notices the mutilated genitals of the naked Grotesques he knows he's seen them before too.

Tied down as he is to the bier, he is a prisoner. They've caught up with him at last. Payback time has come for sure! Ivy league, Johnny Quinn, Frankie Chen, Tommy-up-front, Romeo Robinson and all the rest of the youngdead soldierboys he knew in Vietnam will forgive him at last; he is about to join them. Perhaps now he can rest, find some sort of peace.

He stares up through the treetops at the vast, unfamiliar sky with its countless unfamiliar stars, and he's afraid. The treetops frighten him. That's where snipers live. Maybe they're still up there in those treetops, he thinks. Maybe they've been up there all this time, waiting for me. "Help me. Oh, God, help me," he whispers through half-closed lips. He hopes the Grotesques won't hear him, won't see him looking so terrified, won't hear him beseeching his God. But they don't seem to be too concerned with what he feels or that he is afraid. They just do things to him. They take off all of his clothing and smear him with a foulsmelling oil. The oil smells like piss, like the smell of a newlydead corpse. And they touch him. They run their hands all over his body. All of them touch him. Over every inch of his piss-smelling body, all the while chanting their strange incantations. Perhaps they rub him with their oil because he too will soon be dead. Perhaps that's why they touch him.

They touch the soles of his feet and the palms of his hands; they run their tongues over his belly and his balls and down the inside of his thighs. A female Grotesque takes his cock into her mouth and Finn becomes aroused as his enemies make love to him underneath the countless unfamiliar stars. I'm making love to the enemy, he thinks. "They're fucking me," he murmurs. "They're raping me, for chrissake!" Then the youngdead soldiergirl with the lopped off head walks over to the bier and holds her head just above Finn's face. She lowers the head, and her cold lips, smiling faintly, find his and kisses them, her now-red almond eyes burning with a fierce passion. She kisses him, kisses him passionately, lovingly, then slides her tongue deep down into Finn's throat. Tears fall from the Albanach's eyes and the huge heaviness of impending doom wraps itself around his insides. He closes his eyes and waits. Nothing happens. On and on goes the droning sound of the unintelligible chants, hypnotic and spellbinding. On and on go the mesmerizing dances. Finn can smell the fires now, can smell them now more than ever. What's that? he wonders, then realizes it's diesel fuel. I can smell diesel fuel. They're gonnae burn me. They're gonnae burn me like a lamb. Then he shouts as loudly as he can: "I AM INNOCENT!"

The youngdead soldiergirl, now busy licking Finn's balls, looks up, momentarily startled, then her disembodied head smiles. A number of the Grotesques gather around Finn and untie the ropes around his limbs. Soldiergirl barks a few loud commands to the Grotesques who then grab Finn more tightly, more violently than before. At Soldiergirl's command they drag him over to a huge boulder lying near the funeral pyre. His fear is all-consuming, suffocating and terrible, like childhood fear, but he daren't make a sound lest he anger his captors, lest he goad them to worse violence. The Grotesques each take a separate limb and pull Finn's naked body across the rock, belly down. That done, they tie his arms to stakes hammered into the ground, then do the same with his legs.

The Grotesques begin a hypnotic dance around the rock. They begin again their strange chants, but this time the chants have more of a musical quality to them. Some of the Grotesques hold candles; some hold hollow pieces of wood with which they beat out a dance beat. Finn watches them, too terrified to move. Then suddenly the dancing and chanting stop. He is certain his end has come. Quietly, the Grotesques sit in a circle around him. They sit there for a long time whispering to one another, pointing from time to time to the wide-eyed Finn. A hush falls over the clearing so suddenly he can hear even the insects in the grass nearby. Then a loud, throaty, gurgling scream rips the night apart, followed at once by a choir of nightmare voices mumbling unintelligible sounds. The Grotesques directly in front of him break the circle and part to either side of a small path leading out of the thick trees.

The ropes around Finn's wrists and ankles are so tight he thinks he might rip apart at the waist. Struggling is out of the question. It occurs to him that the image he often paints of the splitapart woman is similar to the way he now feels about splitting apart himself. He wishes the Grotesques would just let him go, let him go back to his jail cell. Anything would be better than lying here trussed up like an unholy offering. He feels helpless and, naked as he is with his bare arse sticking up in the air, more vulnerable than he's ever felt in his entire life. Why are they doin' this to me? he wonders.

In a moment, more hair-raising screams. It's an animal, he thinks. It sounds like an animal screaming. Then out of the jungle steps the female Grotesque who came to him in the cell. She is naked still and her single breast continues to drip its horrible putrescent liquid. But this time her whole body is adorned with golden chainwork, and in her hand she holds a golden cord. Three feet behind her, attached to the other end of the golden cord, walks the biggest Billy goat Finn has ever seen. His coat is shiny and jet black and he stands fully three feet high. The horns upon his head are nearly a foot long. The Billy goat has been brushed so that his coat has a beautiful sheen to it, and his horns and cloven hoofs have been manicured until they shine like polished ivory. The billy goat's eyes are red.

The Grotesque walks over to Finn and lets the Billy goat stand there looking at him. Then the Billy goat licks his face, almost making him collapse with fear. The billygoat's foul breath reminds him again of piss and some kind of hellish decay. The stench is so bad it conjures up images of pus, open sores and feasting maggots, as if he's stumbled upon a week-old battle scene in Vietnam. He heaves, but nothing comes up, except more horrible memories, each heave bearing with it another grisly picture.

The female Grotesque kneels beside the Billy goat and rubs its cock arousingly. The Billy goat snorts and grunts with pleasure and the Grotesque drools dementedly. Some of the other Grotesques become agitated and excited while moving toward Finn. They massage him with more of their pissoil until he is covered with it and dripping once more. Then they spread the cheeks of his arse wide and apply the oil there too, all the while chanting and moaning to the hypnotic beat of the drums and the sounds from the other Grotesques. Finn stiffens when he feels objects enter him. He begs his lord God in heaven to please help him and don't let this happen. He continues to heave up memories, and as the remainder of the Grotesques dance in front of him, holding onto their mutilated genitals, Finn's mind roams some-where up in the trees of a Vietnamese jungle twenty-odd years before. It is all so familiar.

At last, the female Grotesque leads the Billy goat away. Finn feels a sense of relief wash over him, and he is thankful. He is so afraid, so exhausted, he can't scream any more. Then he hears the snortings and gruntings of the Billy goat louder than ever. He can hear the drooling of the bitch grotesque too, and he becomes terrified all over again. What are they doing back there? he wonders. What the fuck are they doin' back there? The grunts and snorts of the Billy goat grow louder still. Finn hears and feels the Billy goat clamber up onto the boulder, its forelegs resting on the rock on either side of him. He knows then what they're up to back there. He struggles, but to no avail. His greatest fear is realized when he feels the Billy goat force itself into him. Finn is sure his insides are burning, and he can feel the Billy goat all the way up in his stomach as it rips and tears into him, filling him with its vile, demonic expulsion. At long last he is able to let out a long, heart-ripping scream, and all the birds in the jungle for miles around rise into the air all at once and beat their way frantically away from the hellish clearing in the jungle. Finn, mercifully, gasps and collapses into unconsciousness.

After the Billy goat has had its way with him, and after the Grotesques are done with him, they untie the Albanach and throw him down onto the ground where they clean him and attend to his wounds. They are most gentle, and treat him with respect as if he were a prince or a god, or even one of them. The Billy goat is nowhere to be seen, although his smell permeates the clearing.

When the cleaning is completed the Grotesques help Finn dress, then they hoist him once more above their heads as if he were indeed being carried along, alert and alive, on top of a funeral pyre, his own funeral pyre. They walk back through the dark places of the jungle. They continue to chant their mad sounds as they enter the pitchblack places again, and when they reemerge once more back in Finn's cell they throw him into a corner, done with him. Waving cheerfully, the Grotesques disappear back down into the crevice just as quickly and as suddenly as they came. When the last Grotesque jumps into the crevice, the floor closes up and becomes as solid and flat as before. Finn sits in the corner shaking and crying, and knows he has lost his mind, that it has slipped down that very same crack in the flatagain floor.

He remembers every detail of the experience, from the

Grotesques and their chantings and ravings to the clawing and sucking of his genitals, to the Billy goat buggering him. All of it. Even the smell of the diesel fuel and, worst of all, the smell of piss— a sure sign that a newlydead corpse is close at hand. He is wet too. He reaches down and feels the wetness at his crotch. I've pissed myself, he thinks. Goddamit, I've pissed myself. Maybe it's blood. Nah, I've had a seizure. He feels numb, exhausted, his mind fuzzy. He wonders how long he's been lying there in the drunk tank. There are no windows; he can't be sure. Must be hours, though, if I've had a seizure. He hears the sound of wood being pulled across the bars of the cells, accompanied by a loud, brash, official voice, dripping with sarcasm.

"Rise and shine, gentlemen. Time to go home to your nice cozy beds!"

Finn smiles, thinking of his home. He wonders whether his shopping cart is safe. He remembers telling Arkansas to hide it in the usual place, just a few hours before, when they were taking him to jail.

Dragging himself up off the floor, he stands by the cell door, shaking and trembling for want of a drink. He waits until the jailer lets him go, lets him go out into another day of shopping cart madness, in search of his ever-elusive bottle of peace and tranquility.

Still trembling for want of that same drink, he holds his shopping cart tightly lest he fall and crack his skull again. He trudges along Columbus Avenue toward Paranoid Park. As far as he's concerned, it's the safest park in San Francisco. "For a no-hoper like me," he once said, his voice thick with irony, and a strangely rebellious smile, childlike, creasing his face. He repeats his dictum as he walks, pushing his shopping cart, all the while noticing the distasteful and sometimes menacing expressions on the faces of the people who pass him on their way to work.

"The hell with them," he mumbles. "They don't know a god-damned thing about life anyway."

And so he truly believes, for Vietnam taught him, in a twisted sort of way, everything he'll ever need to know about life, about living. It's funny, he thinks, how death and killing can teach us about living, even about how the hell we ought to live. It has made him more honest with others, less able to hurt another human being. But at the same time, the war did something to his very being, something inexplicable and mean.

He came back from Vietnam feeling empty, unable to smile, unable to mix with people for very long. Crowds of people in particular. Mary stuck by his side for as long as she could. Far longer, perhaps, than any other woman might have done, but she burned out too; she couldn't take it anymore either. Not even Mary who was always staunch and strong. It didn't matter that he'd known her more intimately than he'd ever known anyone. Or that he'd known her for such a long time too. She left him because she had to.

Shortly after leaving her in Hawaii, Finn saw Mary in a dream and, as soon as he wakened, wrote her a letter describing the dream. When he was sure Mary had read the letter, Finn called her in Boston where she lived with her family and asked her to marry him. She accepted immediately, as if she'd been expecting his call and his consequent proposal.

Ever since their first meeting, Finn had felt as if there had been some sort of inevitability to their relationship, and his dream had confirmed this. They were meant to be together in a strange and inexplicable sort of way. But the dream had been beautiful after all, and the resulting letter equally so.

Pushing the rattling old shopping cart in front of him, he thought back to the day he sent Mary her letter, a wry smile creasing his face as he remembered the dream. He stayed up most of the night trying to make some sense of the craziness he experienced in the dream. And it *was* craziness, but a craziness of such beauty and wonderment it shook him to the core. How could he have known they once loved each other in such a far away place, and in such a distant time? Later in life he would laugh at how ridiculous his dream had been, and how hopelessly romantic they were to believe it, to fall for it.

"I saw you in my sleep," he wrote. "You were beautiful then

too. We stood inside an old, old cottage with a thatched roof. Perhaps it was in ancient Ireland, or in the Highlands of Alba long ago. I'm not sure. We stood at a long table covered almost completely with herbs and potions of various sorts. We mixed and measured them as if we were apothecaries. The people of our village came to us and gave us things we needed in exchange for the potions they needed. We were healers or we were wizards; I'm not sure which. Every time I looked up at you as we worked, you would smile knowingly at me and I would burst out laughing. I remember in my dream wondering what it was you knew, what wonderful knowledge you had, that made me laugh so much. We were happy, Mary. I do remember that much at least."

But that was the crazy part of the dream. He actually felt he knew her in some other life. He keeps a beautiful picture of Mary in his head, and an overwhelming feeling of love for her in the pit of his gut. Still, to this very day. After meeting her in the world of his dreams, he came to feel for her a love reserved only for impossible stories and poems too good to be true. He now knows differently, knows that loving Mary is possible because, in the dream, he experienced Mary's passion, her passion for living, and for him. He felt her love for him, so strong back then when they were young.

That's all he thinks about now as he trudges along Columbus Avenue pushing his damned shopping cart ahead of him. And that's how it's been for the dozen years they've been separated. Hell, he thinks, I don't even know if we're divorced. His hands, unclean from days without a decent wash, tremble and shake as he grips the plastic handle of his cart, and tears roll down his bewhiskered face. "Fuck off," he mumbles to the world about. "I'll cry when I need to. I'm cryin' because I'm thankful, thankful that I'm still alive in some sort of way at least."

"I even love you!" he screams, scaring the daylights out of a Bureaucrat hurrying along on his way to work.

"Oh, Mary," he says. "Where are you, because I miss you oh, so much!"

He stops and leans against the wall of a shop. From his

shopping cart he pulls out a small package, neatly tied with a thin red ribbon, wrapped in a covering of soft purple velvet. The picture, the picture of his darling Mary within. He kisses it and looks briefly at the letter inside, all worn and stained from much reading. But he knows it, word for word, by heart. And he remembers mailing it to her, after making love to her in Hawaii, knowing that his love for her is his to keep forever. His first love letter to Mary, naive and true as all first love letters must be, full of such high sentiments. Do you remember, Mary? he wonders.

But there's no need to ask; Mary remembers the letter too, though more vaguely than he. More comes back to her the longer she lives with Finn, the Albanach; more comes back to her as the years pass by. She loves him for being such a dreamer. But he lives less and less the more he drinks his awful potion, his awful anesthesia. Mary gives the letter back to him when she leaves.

In spite of everything, Finn won't die. He refuses to die. Some kind of hope, some kind of faith, holds onto him and refuses to let him go. He knows this, he knows there is some reason for his continuing to walk the face of the earth, even if he is homeless and mostly drunk. But he truly believes he can kick the alcohol and return to life. There is something about his past, something about his Keltic ancestry, that nags at him constantly, unfailingly, and keeps him from completely destroying himself.

The grass is dewdamp in the park, for it is still early morning. Various groups of Chinese people are up and about as usual, practicing their taichi exercises. Groggily, Finn looks around the park and, finding a quiet corner, pulls his sleeping bag out of his shopping cart. His old, filthy sleeping bag. Kinda like a bodybag, he muses. Just jump into it and zip it up. Simple! He calls it his *hotel room*. But with a suddenness that astounds him, he feels another electric shock hit him as if he's been whacked across the back with a thick piece of wood. "Oh, God," he moans as he drops like a stone to the mercifully soft grass.

I'm as helpless as usual in that moment. All I can do is kneel beside him, send him messages of comfort, and hope that someone will come to his aid. He shakes and rattles around on the ground as he did on the avenue, but his head, mercifully, jackhammers against the soft grass rather than the terrible concrete of the sidewalk. My heart splits in two at my helplessness, but as I watch him suffer I notice that more than just a few of the Chinese grannies and grampas doing their taichi exercises have begun to notice Finn's shaking. They walk toward him until a circle of half a dozen or so have gathered around him.

"The poor man," says one of the grannies. "Help him; his spirit is dying."

Little does she know!

One of the grampas kneels before Finn and tries to comfort him by moving his hands over Finn's shaking body.

"There's blood," he says. "From his head and from his ears. His heart is in trouble."

Amidst the ensuing gasps and groans from the taichis, we hear the slow creaking sound of wagon wheels turning. The grannies and grampas part the circle and I see coming torward us, slowly and deliberately, a water buffalo, a bull, who is huge and whose head is bent as if in prayer. I can't help but notice the bloody bullet holes encircling the water buffalo's neck.

He pulls behind him an old wooden-wheeled cart inside of which is a bed of fresh straw. The water buffalo is driven by an old man whose hair is long and silver. He wears a saffron robe tied at the waist by a simple cord. The robe is short enough to show off his spindly, hairless legs. He holds a whisk in his hand with which he gently coaxes the water buffalo. Finn is quite still though he bleeds now from his mouth as if he's bitten his tongue.

When the cart pulls alongside the prone figure of Finn, the old man with the silver hair steps down from the cart, and he too kneels in front of the Albanach. Gently, the old fellow takes Finn's hands in his and strokes them lovingly.

As I watch them, I see tears rolling from the old man's eyes.

He picks Finn up off the ground as carefully as he would a newborn lamb and, walking through the quiet and still crowd of old taichis, places him gently onto the bed of straw. When he has once more mounted his old wooden-wheeled cart he turns to those gathered around him.

"He is one of us," he says. "I will take him to the Land of the Truly Alive."

Then he looks at me and smiles. He knows me and I realize I know him too. He points to Finn and beckons me. I step up into the cart and sit beside Finn. I can no more leave him than the fish can leave the sea. I sit there beside him in the cart, cradling his painfilled head in my lap, as the water buffalo, the bull, pulls us across the soft green grass of Paranoid Park in search of the Land of the Truly Alive.

◆　◆　◆

The miles have tumbled headlong one into the other. We've climbed hills, descended down into dales, and traveled through wooded areas. We've forded rivers, too, until the park and the old taichis are many hours, many miles, behind us.

Traveling on the old wooden-wheeled cart feels like journeying through a dream. A sense of lightness and unconnectedness fills me. The trees and the roads and the rivers appearing before us somehow don't seem quite real, though they are there nevertheless. At times we hear the noise of life all around us; at other times, quiet prevails. After a while we cross a long bridge over turbulent water. We wander through a thick forest of fragrant eucalyptus trees for many long hours, taking a great many turns, mistakenly it seems; the old silverhaired driver doesn't mind, isn't in any sort of a hurry at all. From time to time he looks back at me and smiles. Eventually, with the steady plodding steps of the water buffalo, we arrive at a house made of thick, strong stone such as might be used to build castles. The old man steps lightly from the cart, walks over to the water buffalo and speaks a few soft words into his ear. The bull bellows and shakes his head. Silverhair turns to me and smiles a big, toothless smile.

"Hello...eh...what is it he calls you? Ah! Madman is it not? It's grand to see you again. Aye it is, grand indeed!"

"I'm sure I know you, too," says I, "but I don't know what you're doing here."

He chuckles. "No matter," he says. "All will become clear in time. But this is where he must begin the real work. This is the beginning of the road to the Land of the Truly Alive. I'll leave him by the door. Yae must continue to guard him and guide him as yae have done all these years."

He picks Finn up again, so effortlessly for such a skinny old man, and lays him down on the topmost step. He looks comical standing there with his spindly legs sticking out below his saffron robe.

"Watch him well, Madman," he says, as he boards the old wooden-wheeled cart. "He'll recover sooner than yae think!"

I sit beside the Albanach and hold him, though he can't feel me. I look down at him for a long, long time.

Our relationship is strange at best. I don't feel things the way he does. I know he's exhausted after all those years plodding through the mudsludgy streets of his Shopping Cart Soldier's life. I tag along beside him, trying to direct him, to guide him as best I can. I keep telling him I love him. I must; I have to keep him going. He is, after all, my body, my shell. Wherever he goes I must go too, though my footsteps grow heavier, my heart more sore as the years fly by. He still can't see me.

He does recover quickly. He sits there, bewildered, on the top step of the entryway. He knows he's had a seizure, because his body still feels as if it's been jolted by a cattle prod. His surroundings look vaguely familiar, and his bewilderment stems mainly from his inability to understand why he isn't still in Paranoid Park. But, trembling and shaking, he pulls himself up onto his feet and enters the grand house. He doesn't care whose house it is; nor does he care who might be inside. He needs a drink and that's all that matters, that's all he cares about. When he enters the huge kitchen, he sees a bottle of whiskey sitting in the middle of the kitchen table as if it's been placed there by someone expecting his arrival.

It sits there like a chalice, splendid upon an altar. With careful deliberation he puts the bottle to his lips and swallows the liquor in great gurgling gulps. The relief from the shakes and tremors comes almost immediately, the possibility of another seizure no longer a consideration. He takes a few more healthy gulps from the whiskey bottle just to make sure, then wanders about the huge house. Exhausted from the seizures, he collapses onto an empty bed and falls deeply into a drunken stupor.

He wakens disconcerted from a sleep inhabited by more of his Grotesques. They always come after a hard night on the booze; though they frighten him, they are still unable to send him completely over the edge. Yet, in spite of his strength, a familiar fear hangs cold over him, as if he were wrapped for the crypt. There are times when a fear such as this makes him laugh. Laugh and laugh and laugh, as if he doesn't give a damn, as if he doesn't care. At other times, the same fear grips him with icy talons. He wipes the sleep from his eyes and looks up at the ceiling.

Catching sight of the grey stone high overhead, Finn feels as if he's in his old home, the same home he left when he began his Shopping Cart Soldier's life. At the same time the grand house feels unfamiliar. Perhaps even dangerous. Something isn't quite right, isn't quite as it ought to be and that, as well as the creatures of his dreams, throws him wildly off kilter.

He lived in the house for a long time back then, before his breakup with Mary Quinn. It's a huge house, a grand house. The floors are made of dark, grey slate and are always dusty. Mary sweeps them often. Nowadays, many people live in the house. It isn't his house any more. Not any more. It doesn't even look the same. It's been gutted on the inside and instead of rooms there are now a great many plateaus on three different levels. It is on the plateaus that the inhabitants keep their bedding. Many people live in the house now, and Finn doesn't know any of them, can't possibly know any of them. There's usually a lot of business going on in the house, a great many comings and goings, but tonight it's quiet and he's alone. Alone, out of sorts and frightened.

It is late evening and the house is dimly lit. He gets up and wanders from one plateau to the next, stopping from time to time to stare through the windows at the darkness without. Windblown rain beats wildly against the windows. He shudders and wonders again why he feels so fearful. He finds some discarded clothing scattered about the house. Though it's cold, he wears only a pair of jeans and a red velvet robe hangs loosely about his body. Dark leather slippers fit snugly on his feet. He wraps his arms around his body in an attempt to ward off the chill and whatever else makes him feel so ill-at-ease. With downcast eyes, he continues to trudge through the uncomfortable house. Up and down the stairs from one level to the next he wanders, dark thoughts pestering him.

Bed, he thinks, I'll go back to bed. I'll sleep an' I'll dream again. Whether good or bad he always enjoys his dreams; they tell him things he might never otherwise know. He feels them as if they're as real as living.

When he reaches the plateau he claims as his own, he throws his robe down onto the stone floor beside his bedding and slips under the woolen blanket, still wearing his jeans. In a moment or two he's as warm as he could wish to be, and for the first time that day he smiles, anticipating the adventure of his dreams, looking forward to meeting those who people them. Outside, the rain continues to beat against the house and the wind howls, happy at the havoc it causes. Drifting, he wonders at his fear. What causes it, what makes his heart feel so leaden and heavy, what makes his chest heave with anguish and his eyes fill with tears? Soon he sleeps, and dreams.

He sits on top of a grassy knoll, leaning against an oak tree, a very old oak tree. He can feel the age-old wisdom of the tree coming through the bark, from the skin of the oak through his own skin. The sensation from the tree feels comfortable. Night has fallen, such a beautiful night too. The sky is filled with uncountable twinkling stars. The moon sits among the stars smiling and bright, as huge as happiness. Finn can see for miles and miles. He's astonished at the beauty surrounding him. The sky blazes with silver light and all around him are flowers whose bright and vibrant colors would set any painter's heart on fire. There are poppies and anemones, and violets are so abundant their perfume hangs heavy in the air. He sits there ogling, taking in all that natural beauty, all that natural loveliness. Then he sees a movement in the trees beyond the knoll. He sees a shape move toward him, the shape of a man, a very old man, stooped with age, whose hair is long and thick and as silvery as the moon. The years show in the old man's wrinkled and weathered skin. The stories in his eyes speak not only of peace, but also of pain and tribulation. He wears a long, flowing saffron robe. It is the old man of the wagon. From the moment Finn sets eyes on the old man, he knows he looks upon a seer, a visionary. A strangely-colored stone hangs around the old fellow's neck, attached to a leather string.

I look once more at the driver of the wooden-wheeled cart, and I know instinctively that his name is Silverbright.

Finn and Silverbright smile a warm greeting to each other. The old fellow sits beside Finn, leaning as he is, against the comfortable old oak tree. It seems they talk for days. They talk of Alba, and they talk of leaving it, for Silverbright is an Albanach too. They talk of the flowers around them; they talk of abstractions such as love. They laugh a lot, happy at the beauty surrounding them. Finn can't help but laugh, for when Silverbright opens his mouth all he can see are the old man's gums. He doesn't have a tooth in his head, but that doesn't seem to bother Silverbright, and his carefree manner makes Finn laugh all the more. Laughing makes him uncomfortable. He isn't used to it, hasn't laughed like that for a long time.

Suddenly, without warning, the toothless old fellow turns to Finn, a vicious smirk stretching across his face. He slaps Finn resoundingly on the mouth. The old fellow stands and, shaking his fist at the astonished Albanach, he speaks.

"Come to my cave," he says, in a tone belying any thought of refusal. "Yae must go back to Alba," he continues. "Yae must go back. That's where you'll find your salvation, your peace of mind. I'll show yae the way." Then he turns and walks off back along the way he came.

Finn awakes rigid and stiff with his now-familiar fear. He rubs the side of his face unconsciously and looks around the room, half-expecting to see the old man, but he's disappeared. What he sees instead is the prone figure of Mary Quinn lying in bed beside him. Why is Mary in my bed? he wonders. She left such a long, long time ago.

He watches her pack. He sits on the edge of their bed, devastated, literally filled with dread. Young Finn is standing in the bedroom doorway, leaning against the jamb. He too is devastated. He doesn't understand why his parents have to go and fuck things up. Finn's leaning on his knees, his head in his hands. He just woke up, woke up to find Mary packing a huge suitcase. He's hungover, blearyeyed and sick from the drink.

"For chrissake, Mary, don't go!" he says. "Don't, goddamit, just leave!"

Mary throws a last piece of clothing into the overloaded suitcase. She angrily closes the flaptop then snaps the locks into place. She looks at him with determined, steadfast eyes.

"By this time tomorrow," says she, "Me an' Finn'll be back in Boston. If you get a grip you can call me at my ma's. But don't call me unless you're sober."

There's an imploring tone to Mary's voice as she continues.

"For God's sake, Finn, get some help. Go into treatment or somethin'. You're gonna die if you don't."

"Ah never asked for this, Mary, you know that. Ah don't know what the hell's wrong wi' me." He is naked but for his underpants. He walks over to where young Finn is standing and grabs his robe from a hook behind the door. When he's tied the cord around his waist he walks over to Mary and takes her into his arms. "Don't leave me, Mary," he says, quietly, holding her tightly. "Ah'll go absolutely mad if yae do. You're all ah've got, you an' the young fella!"

"Oh, Finn, Finn," says Mary, pushing away from him. She holds him at arms' length. "I have to go. Don't you see? It's the only chance you have! You have to do it on your own. For the love of God go back to the VA!"

Finn pushes Mary away, angry now.

"Screw those fools! They don't do nothin'. Same old shit every time yae go near them. Forms up the yin-yang, some young-arsed, trainee psychiatrist takin' notes for his latest research paper. Don't know sweet fuck-all about the war, what it was like. Screw the VA, Mary. Buncha goddamn lazy-arsed Bureaucrats makin' sure they don't lose their comfy wee jobs workin' for the government. We're nothin' but guinea pigs out there us vets."

When he hears the sobs he turns to his son. He kneels before the boy and takes him into his arms.

"Ach, don't cry, young Finn," he says. "Ah'll be okay, ah really will. Ah'll fight like hell, ah'll get some help somehow!" He turns to Mary. "Tell him, Mary, tell him ah'll be okay."

"Don't drink any more, daddy," says young Finn.

"Christ," says Finn. "Ah'm so scared, Mary. Ah don't know what's happenin' to me. Ah'm scared to death!"

"I'm scared too, Finn. We're all scared." She kneels beside Finn and puts her arms around him, the boy sandwiched between them. "We're all scared, Finn," says Mary, as a single tear begins its crooked, fitful path down her cheek. "Scared to death."

Mary opens her eyes and looks at Finn, surprised to see him lying on her mattress on the highest plateau. Her eyes pop open wider when she recognizes him. She springs from the bed, naked, and flees from the plateau. Mary looks young, as young as on the day she left him. To Mary, the Albanach is an old man. But why does she flee, her eyes so full of terror? Does Finn, in his sleep, touch her thinking she is still his wife, someone he might have touched that way? Does he touch her thinking they are still together? He thinks again of the old man who slapped him, and the word Alba tapdances behind his eyes, bothering him like a troublesome dream.

He feels fearful again, but this time he recognizes the source. He sits up as rigid as a doorpost.

"What the hell?" he mumbles. "I've lost somethin'. What is it I've lost?"

In a panic, he springs from the bed and pulls his robe about him. What have I lost? he wonders again. He searches his pockets, one after the other, and chuckles when he realizes that what he has lost can never be found in any pocket. Frantic, he flees from his plateau, but stops abruptly when the house fills with people, happy smiling people, champagne glasses in their hands. It's a celebration. Everyone is singing and dancing, roaring with laughter. Finn is terrified, his eyes as wide as Mary's. He looks across the crowded room and there she is. She's wearing one of those print frocks he always liked to see her in. She stares at him with those terror-filled eyes of hers. Frantically she sweeps the floor. He can't for the life of him understand why his wife is so afraid of him. As the house fills with people he becomes much more afraid himself. Amidst this sea of happy people, Mary and Finn are terrified. Then a tiny young man with an east coast accent walks over to Finn. He wears dirty, worn jungle fatigues soaking wet at the crotch. The young man's left hand is clasped around his balls, his right hand held over his heart. Bright crimson blood spills through the spreadout fingers of both of his hands.

"I'm leakin' like a sieve, but I'm goin' home!" says Frankie Chen, a joyous smile spreading across his face.

The Albanach stares at him.

"Where?" he asks.

"Home!" Frankie repeats, then slaps the Albanach on the back in a comradely fashion.

"Aye, in a bodybag, Frankie. Yae never made it, buddy!"

Then the Albanach walks away from Frankie, repeating over and over again the word *home*. "Home, home, home!" Where is home? he wonders. Is there such a place as home? "There is no home," he says, quietly, as he stands trembling by the window wondering again why he feels so goddamned numb.

Frankie stands motionless for a while looking after Finn, deep in thought, his brow creased deeply. He shakes his head. "Fuck you," he says, pivoting. He walks away from his old pal, his hands still clutching at his heart and balls.

Finn stares through the window at the darkness beyond. An armless black man whose face is covered in blood, walks over to

Finn. He pushes a battered shopping cart ahead of him. There's a large bundle inside the cart, covered by a crimson cloth. The bloody-faced man has splints tied to the stubs of his arms and these, in turn, he slips into holsters fastened to the sides of the shopping cart. Looks like he's dead, or should be dead, thinks Finn.

"Fuck you!" Romeo Robinson screams into the Albanach's face, splattering him with spittle and blood. "I *am* dead!" Then the crimson cloth is pushed to the side and a soldier with bluewhite skin looks up at Finn and grins knowingly. A huge syringe, filled with blood, sticks out of the soldier's arm. The blood runs down his forearm and forms a pool in the cup of his hand.

"Hello, Finn," says Ivy League. He throws the cup of blood over the Albanach before covering himself once more with the crimson cloth. Romeo resumes his journey, pushing the shopping cart ahead of him.

Finn, dripping with blood, screams. Like Mary, he flees. He recognizes the dead soldiers. He can't remember Ivy League's real name, but he remembers shooting up with him in his hootch over there in the jungle. A little bit at first, then huge amounts. He watches Ivy League become consumed with the heroin. He also remembers asking Ivy League to change the music one night when they were both high. Ivy League's too stoned to hear. He doesn't answer. Finn gets up and taps him on the shoulder. Ivy League drops to the ground. He turns blue. Finn runs from the hootch, not wanting to become involved in an overdose death. All that's left after that is the memory of his old soldier pal turning blue. Another grunt from a different hootch finds Ivy League and Ivy League lives to catch the unlucky flight on the night of *The Leaving*. He is one of the dead twenty-six.

For a long time Finn wanders about the house among the happy, laughing people. He's confused. He wonders how much madness one man can bear. Then he recognizes Johnny Quinn sitting among a group of people on a lower level of the house of stone. He feels safe; Johnny is his old pal and the Albanach loves the curly-haired man like a brother.

Poet Johnny's words often saved the Albanach from a scrape

he couldn't cope with. The words often save him from death itself. Johnny also saves Finn in the jungle when Finn tries, without awareness, to kill himself chasing the need to be a hero. Whenever Johnny and the Albanach meet they hug one another, smile as if they have a big secret, and kiss each other on the cheek like Europeans. Sometimes, when they're stoned, they would kiss one another full on the lips and slap each other on the back happily. That's just the way of them. Many of the other grunts think the two are queer, but they simply love one another as only one man can love another. Like brothers. Like soldiers struggling together on the battlefield.

The Albanach shouts down to Johnny, his friend.

"Johnny...Johnny, I've lost somethin'!"

Johnny laughs with the people he sits beside. But Johnny always laughs, is always happy. Perhaps that's why the Albanach loves him so. Johnny looks up at him.

"Don't bother me, Finn; I'm reading them a poem!"

Finn turns to walk away. Johnny rolls his eyes resignedly.

"What is it you've lost?" he asks.

"I don't know," replies the Albanach, "but I've lost somethin'!"

"Well, when you've figured out what you've lost, maybe you should go look for it!"

Then Johnny bursts out laughing again and slaps his knee; the people among whom he sits laugh too. The bloody, armless man who looks as if he should be dead comes back toward the Albanach.

"Fuck you!" he screams again into Finn's face, again splattering him with spittle. Again, the needle-armed corpse flings aside his crimson covering and smiles knowingly at his old pal.

"Hey, Finn, how ya doin', buddy?" he says.

Screaming like a stuck pig, Finn flees from the house, grabbing his old coat as he runs. Mary watches him with her terror-filled eyes. Outside, in the darkness, the wind howls like a banshee and the rain, which once beat wildly against the window, now pounds Finn as if it means to punish him. In his haste, he's forgotten his shoes. Barefooted, he runs along the street toward the sea, his instincts alone prompting him. The wind grows stronger, pushing violently at his back. The sea beckons, "Come closer, come to me!" He loses control as it pushes him faster than his legs can move. He feels trapped, caught up in a wild, frenzied concert played by the strings of the wind and the brass of the sea, and he can't for the life of him figure out who the mad composer might be, who it might be that wants him so badly to become a part of the wind and the sea. "Don't let me drown," he cries, but the wind picks him up as if he were as light as lint and hurls him toward its cohort, the beckoning sea. With luck, or perhaps with the help of the old man of his dream, he manages to grab onto the branch of a tree and hold fast. Presently, the wind dies down a little and the Albanach clings to the trunk of the tree crying with happiness and gratitude.

Little does he know that it was me, me and my umbilical cord that has saved him.

"No' this time," he says. "Ah'm no' gonnae drown just yet."

He pulls his worn, old overcoat about him and walks, headbent, into the wind. He has no idea where he might go, but he has to find whatever it is he's lost. He trudges on. The rain continues to beat down on him. The wind continues to howl to the tune of the raging, crashing sea below. The Albanach hears a woman screaming in agony. He looks toward the sound. On the hill above sits an enormous, prison-like building surrounded by a wall. The agonized woman lies on her back on top of the wall; it seems her back is broken. The wind has blown her there. She looks young. She wears a nurse's white uniform. A huge red cross hangs around her neck.

"Help me. Oh, God, help me!" she screams. "Help me, I'm dying!"

Tommy-up-front stands over the nurse, looking down at her, an expression of disdain contorting his face.

"Shuttup, ya damn fool," he says. "If ya don't shuttup the gooks'll hear ya!"

Then Tommy picks the nurse up and throws her into a rickety old shopping cart; the pushed and the pusher disappear into the darkness amidst the screams of the broken woman. The astonished man from Alba shouts out to the retreating figures. He doesn't recognize them in the darkness.

"Hey, you, hold it there! Who are you, what are yae doin' with that broken woman, where are yae goin' with her?"

Out of the black night he hears a loud and piercing laugh. A voice speaks out to the Albanach in a strange, singsongy voice, sending a chill up his spine.

"I'm a hero, so is she. She's finished and broken. I'm taking her to the garbage dump; nobody needs her any more; nobody gives a rat's ass these days!" Then all is quiet.

The Albanach continues his journey feeling fearful, overflowing with his terrible sense of numbness. He knows he must find whatever's gone astray, but knowing what he fears makes him less fearful. He crosses a railroad track and looks up to see a strange-looking engine emerge from the train station a few yards along the tracks. The engine is unlike any he has ever seen before. It reminds him of a pod, a giant, transparent pod. Inside the engine, a single word dances a mad dance as if in time with a tune crazier even than that played a short time before by the wind and the sea. As the engine pulls out of the station, the Albanach notices a train of smaller, podlike carriages, each with a word inside, being pulled by the mother pod. The words are dressed gaily as if on their way to a party. The words smile happily, but Finn is unable to read them.

"Yae shouldn't be goin' out on a night like this," says Finn to the word inside the mother pod. "The wind might blow yae into the sea! The wind and the sea are hungry tonight."

"Mind your own damn business," says the word inside the podlike engine, then she laughs and chug-chugs along the railroad tracks into the night. The man from Alba thinks he hears one of the pod-entrapped words telling the mother pod to stop, but he can't be sure; the wind and the sea are roaring so.

He continues his walk, dripping wet, and soon realizes that he doesn't know where he's going. He chuckles. "It's a goddamn guide I need," he mumbles. He has no idea of his whereabouts or of his destination. He wanders aimlessly through the dark, wet night.

After a while, the rain finally ceases its punishment and the wind dies to a mere whisper of its former self. On and on he walks until he comes to a well-lit street where he meets a kilted Albanach warrior. The warrior's hair is long and sandy-colored and his thick mustache sweeps across his cheeks back towards his ears. He looks fierce this warrior. But at the same time, he seems peaceful and has a look of wisdom about him that's unmistakable. Instead of the targs and claymores or other weaponry of ancient Alba, the warrior carries a set of bagpipes slung across his shoulders. Finn is shocked, not only at the unusual sight of the Albanach himself, but also because he wears the colors of Finn's own clan, the Sons of Donald. In his formal and colorful attire, the Albanach looks as if he's just returned from some festivity or another, for the bag of his musical instrument steams hotly in the cold night air. When he sees Finn approach, the Albanach stops and looks at him curiously. As Finn passes, the warrior stops him.

"Hello laddie," he says, "what's wrong with yae, have yae somehow lost your way?"

"Aye, but more than that," Finn replies, breaking into the speech of Alba. "I've lost something else too, but when I came abroad to look for it I became lost myself."

"When I came abroad to look for it...." The words are music to my ears. At least I know now that he's looking for something. He doesn't really know what it is he's looking for, but at least he's looking. When he discovers he's been looking for his soul all this time he might throw a fit, he might become more angry than he has been, more determined to keep fighting me. But I'll just have to take that chance. I'll just have to keep hoping that he'll learn enough on the way to help him realize that without me he's doomed. I'll do everything I can to keep him going towards the light! It's all I can do.

The warrior studies Finn for a moment then casts sideways glances up along the road in both directions as if he expects someone to walk along the path towards them.

"I can tell by your speech that yae're an Albanach like me. But tell me, where are yae goin' on such a foul night?"

"I'm no' sure," Finn replies. "I'm just no' sure!"

"Then where d'yae live?" asks the man.

"I live in a big house made of stone, strong stone the likes of which is used to build castles. Our house has grey, stone floors and they're always dusty. Mary Quinn sweeps them frantically, but still they are dusty. A great many people live in our house." Finn looks down at the ground. "But it's no' my home any more."

The Albanach looks at Finn more closely, more curiously.

"I know of such a place," says the man. "I'll take yae there, though I don't for the life of me know why yae would want tae go there. It's a strange place, a strange place indeed."

"Why would yae do such a thing for me?" asks the man from Alba. "Why would you help me? Yae don't even know me."

"Och, I know yae well enough," comes the reply. "I understand such a one as yersel' for I'm searchin' too. An' like me, yae're a warrior. Warriors help one another. Come on, I'll take yae to this place yae call home." Finn smiles, hearing himself described so, as a warrior.

The warrior looks off into the distance as he speaks these last words and he chuckles at the mention of the word home. Finn seems disconcerted all the more by the strange humor, but when the Albanach marches off through the well-lit street Finn follows right behind him happy, at the very least, to be moving again. When they move off, the Albanach warrior strikes up a happy marching song and Finn, feeling considerably cheered, smiles as his spirits rise. Perhaps, he thinks, when I find my home I can begin again my search for whatever it is I've lost. They march for a very long time before Finn finally sees his house perched high up on a cliff by the seashore. It is the same house where the old man and the water buffalo dropped him off earlier.

"That's my home," he says. "I had a feelin' it might be!"

The Albanach looks at him with curiosity once more.

"I was happy to help yae," he says. "But if yae want to find what yae've lost, laddie, yae must first know *what* yae lost." He has a voice like a whispering wind.

Finn thinks of Johnny Quinn just then. He thinks too of a warning he heard as a child and, when he looks again at the Albanach, he remembers where he saw him before. The Albanach turns just then and walks back the way he came, gaily playing his pipes. Before he's gone more than a few yards the warrior turns once more to face the man from Alba.

"Look for Silverbright, the auld man of your dream," he shouts. "He lives in a cave by the sea. Go to him!" Then he turns again and begins once more to blow on his pipes. This time, though, he plays a dirge, a mournful tune of loss. Finn recognizes the music. It is the same mournful lament he heard as a child when he went out running through that long, misty night such a long time ago during his childhood when he first saw the Albanach warrior.

Finn appears stunned by the words of the warrior and wonders how a stranger could know of his dream. When he looks up at his house he feels comforted at the sight of the thick, strong stone. Enjoying the moment, he looks through the picture window at the front of the house. There stands Mary, naked once more, her eyes closed rapturously. Romeo Robinson, who looks as if he ought to be dead, has his splinted stubs wrapped around Mary's waist. He's naked from the waist down himself and Finn notices that he has artificial legs. The armless, legless man nibbles Mary passionately around the earlobes and humps and bumps his body into hers. The blue-white soldier pulls the syringe out of his arm and a geyser of dark, black blood rains over the happily coupling couple. As Finn watches, the drug-addict corpse drops his fatigue pants to the floor and, holding his huge erection proudly, hobbles over to Mary. He stands behind her and, timing himself to the rhythm of the lovers, takes Finn's wife from behind, all the while pouring blood all over them. The Albanach's heart races and his old fears return. What is this place? he wonders, and the odd chuckling of the Albanach warrior becomes clear to him.

"This isn't my home!" he screams into the turbulent sky.

Behind the passionately kissing lovers stands Johnny, hands on hips, head flung back, laughing heartily. But Johnny always laughs. Poet Johnny, the Albanach's brother, finds humor in the strangest places and is always happy. Turning, the Albanach walks off toward the sea, his old wet overcoat clinging to him like seaweed on a rock. He walks the walk of the dejected, he walks the walk of one who has had the wind, the gumption, kicked out of him; as he walks, he looks up to the high promontory between his old home and the sea.

There stands the girl who tried to kill him in the jungle such a long time ago. She stands looking out to sea, her head held high in her hands. A look of abject hatred creases her once lovely face as she tries to find Finn. She blames him for her beheading. Finn's despondency at what he's just seen at his old home is so great he barely cares what happens to him. A small light penetrates the dark veil around his heart and spurs him forward.

Little does he know that it is me, his Madman as he calls me, who has spurned him onward. He knows that if anything happens to him nothing will be resolved, that none of his questions will be answered. For some reason, he thinks, I've been given a chance to see things through to some sort of conclusion, and that's what I must do. To feel him think like that makes me smile. Though his heart is filled with dread, he trudges on toward the shore. I plod along with him, holding on tightly to the umbilical cord.

When he reaches the sandy shore, he sits down by the now calm sea until the sun comes fully up into the sky. On the horizon, far out to sea, a line of transparent pods bobs gaily in the dark water. The warmth of the sun dries Finn's robe and he feels better, more hopeful, though he wonders, with a terrible sense of loss, of betrayal, why Johnny laughed at him. He thinks of what the Albanach warrior said. What is it I've lost? Shouldn't I first know what I've lost before I can find it? For hours he thinks, as the waves lap upon the shore. He thinks and thinks and thinks until it comes to him as naturally, it seems, as breathing. In knowing, he realizes his deepest fears. He finally knows what made him flee from the house made of strong, castle-like stone, from the house filled with happy, laughing people, out into a night made in hell.

He looks out to sea once more, but it is quiet and calm and the waves lap lazily against the shore. The horizon looks as straight as Truth, clear of gaily-bobbing pods, and he feels just then like a transparent pod himself, though without the words to fill him up inside. Had Mary seen his emptiness when she looked into his eyes? Had she seen through his transparency? Is that, perhaps, what terrified her so and made her flee from her plateau? And the sea, what of the sea? Had the sea not beckoned him in the night, had not the wind pushed him toward the roaring, crashing sea? Why does the sea want me so badly? he wonders. He chuckles. Back to the beginning? Maybe it wants to start all over again with me. Maybe it realizes it fucked things up the first time when it sent me up onto the sandy beach. He chuckles again.

He gathers his overcoat tightly about him and walks toward the waves below. Gulls shriek and swoop all around him, shouting, screaming, mocking. The sun shines brightly, warming him. And the sea, the ever cold sea, splashing lazily against the shore, with all the time in the world, whispers in his ear and calls to him once more:

"Come to me, come closer."

The Albanach walks, smiling, toward the beckoning waves, holding in his mind the knowledge of what it is he's lost. Putting one foot in front of the other, he begins his search for Silverbright, the old seer who intruded upon his dreams, he with whom he laughed and talked in his vision.

And the sea says yet again, "Come to me, come closer."

As he walks along the shoreline, Finn thinks about Alba. He knows he has to go back, that something calls to him, but he knows neither how to get there nor what it is that has called to him. Nothing makes sense. He just knows that getting to a place called Alba means more to him than he can imagine. He hears the prolonged scream of a train as if it's passing in the night on the outskirts of town.

"Johnny, Johnny, Johnny," it screams. "Frankie, Frankie, Frankie!"

The sound is awful. He doesn't understand the words. They remind him of something, but he isn't sure of what. On and on scream the words. They don't stop! He looks high up over the coastline to a distant hilltop and sees again the same podlike train he saw before drawing closer, filled with words and letters, emerging over the crest of the hill. It moves slowly, chugging along contentedly, forming new railroad tracks as it goes wherever it has a mind to. It draws abreast of him. Then the pods concertina, piling one on top of the other, until all the podlike carriages break loose and the words escape from the pods and lie scattered on the wet earth alongside the gleaming railroad tracks. The Albanach notices how many of the letters from the broken words have fallen in such a peculiar way that they form new words. The newly-formed words jump up angrily into his face. "Romeo!" "Tommy!" "Frankie!" they say. Terrified, he clamps his hands over his ears and screams his own familiar, silent scream.

For a long time the names attack him and he screams so long and so quietly that every animal in the woods nearby hears him and becomes frightened, as if they feel an earthquake beginning its preliminary belchings and rumblings. Then, as suddenly as the names came, they pull themselves together, jump back into their pods and chug off back along the railroad tracks, their task completed. The mysterious and vindictive names disappear over the crest of the bare, black hilltop. Just like that they are gone—like magic! Finn has a good laugh to himself as he continues his walk, as he continues his long journey: *magic*, that's it! He hears again every word spoken in Silverbright's vision, that and other strangely significant words. It all comes back to him. There's a cave, he feels sure, near the spot where he now stands, the very same cave the Albanach musician spoke of, the same cave Silverbright mentioned when Finn saw him in his vision. And he knows the old man still guards the entrance to this cave looking over the ocean. He just knows, can feel it. He feels too that the cave is inaccessible. But there sits old Silverbright, cross-legged, holding onto a piece of driftwood with the words *For Madmen Only, For Magicians* inscribed upon it.

"Sonofabitch," mutters the Albanach, "that's it—magic!"

He's pleased with himself, pleased to connect at least one of the driftwood's words with its source. "Maybe I'm not so crazy after all," he says.

But he wonders what's happening to him, and he needs a drink. For the umpteenth time that day, he wishes he had another bottle of whiskey to chug on. He hasn't had a drink for such a long time and his body has begun to complain vigorously. He hopes old Silverbright's a drinking man; he has to calm his trembling body.

Lost in his musings, the Albanach hasn't noticed a machine cruising slowly along the hilltop as if patrolling the area, as if in search of something or other. The cab of the machine sits perched on top of its frame in the shape of a bullet and the tires are as tall as a big man. The whole contraption has been painted like jungle camouflage. There's a huge cockroach painted on the door panels in black. As the machine approaches him, the Albanach finally hears the drone of its powerful engine. He looks up, surprised and fearful, when he sees Soldiergirl sitting in the driver's seat. The machine stops; Soldiergirl and half a dozen or so Bureaucrats in pinstriped suits step down from the cab, rifles slung nonchalantly over their shoulders. But before the Bureaucrats can use their rifles, the Albanach darts off toward the safety of the sea. One thing Finn's sure of is that Bureaucrats won't go within a hundred yards of the sea; nature and the elements frighten them. The Bureaucrats don't see him at first and when Finn looks closer he sees that they have small American flags stuck into their lapels. It angers him, for it is these same bastards, he believes, who are the real oppressors of the world. It is they who start wars and prolong them; it is they who control the purse strings of the government, and it is they who could do so much good in the world but choose not to. They anger Finn to no end, piss him off till his blood boils. That these same cocksuckers have the audacity to wear the flag he fought for on their lapels makes him fighting mad. His zigzagging run across the sandy beach makes him much more visible. Then they do see him. On and on runs the Albanach, bullets biting into the sand all around him, until he's certain that Soldiergirl and her riflemen won't follow.

I run with him, to be sure, though as an Invisibility I can't be hurt. But I can't separate myself from him either. I have to keep the umbilical cord intact.

He slows his pace to catch his breath before trudging on in the direction he feels he might find Silverbright's cave. He looks up at the sky and marvels at how closely the color of the clouds matches that of the rocks strewn haphazardly about the surrounding hilltops. The rocks look as if they've been thrown there by some frenzied giant or another. Finn takes in a deep breath, filling his lungs with the tangy-sweet scent of the ocean, then he stands quite still and listens to the roar of the waves as they crash against the shore. The sound of the ocean comforts him this time. At least the water's constant, he thinks, and makes his way closer toward it, accompanied by the screams of the gulls who glide playfully among the seaborne winds. He watches the birds, wishing he too could fly, at least for a moment. Just long enough to scan the shoreline for the cave. He presses on for many more miles, looking here, looking there among the crags and crannies, but there's no sign of the cave anywhere. Perhaps it was all just a silly dream! He sits crouched behind a large rock, exhausted. The climb down along the cliffside and the ensuing flight from the rifletoting Bureaucrats have almost beaten him, have almost made him turn back to the house made of thick strong stone. But he didn't see himself turning back in his vision. There is no going back! For whatever reason, he must continue his journey. He feels dejected and lonely sitting there by the rock. Then he hears a strange sound coming out of the wilderness around him. Laughter? Is that laughter I hear? he wonders. He stands and looks out over the water. Sure enough, there's old Silverbright sitting in front of his cave just as he should be. He grips his piece of driftwood with both hands. He still wears his saffron robe, but it's tattered and torn and flaps noisily in the wind. He wears nothing else.

"Must be freezin'," mutters the Albanach. "He's such a skinny wee thing."

Finn the Albanach watches Silverbright intently for a few moments.

"He's laughin', the auld bugger *is* laughin'. What the hell's wrong wi' him? Nah, can't be! Maybe he's cryin'!"

Silverbright's shoulders bob up and down convulsively, racked with either heartrending sobs or uncontrollable laughter.

The Albanach ducks behind his rock again and tries to make some sense of the situation. Silverbright looks different, as if he's been wrung through a wringer, and he acts as if he's lost his marbles. This isn't good, thinks the Albanach, peeking once more across the water. There has to be a way over there, but the ocean in front of him reaches to the cliff wall between the rock and the cave. Another rock sits in front of his rock, but nothing else. Maybe Silverbright will tell him how to get to the other side. The sea is too wild to swim, too deep to wade. The Albanach stands and walks out in front of his rock. The guardian of the cave can't see Finn; he's too busy convulsing. Finn can now see tears streaming down Silverbright's face, but he still can't tell whether he's laughing or whether he's crying. "Nuts!" says the Albanach. "The auld bugger's nuts!" Then he shouts out to him.

Surprisingly, Silverbright hears the Albanach above the sound of the crashing waves and looks up suddenly, casting wild, staring eyes at the Albanach, who falls immediately to his knees as if he's just been punched in the stomach. Silverbright convulses again and the Albanach looks up at him, a pained expression clouding his face. "Christ, what was that?" he asks, not in the least amused. Silverbright jumps up quickly, waving his piece of driftwood high in the air.

"For madmen only, for magicians," he screams over the noise of the wind and the sea. The Albanach stands, rubs his stomach, and stares at the old man. "Mad as they come," he mumbles, "away wi' the goddamned faeries!" But he can't keep from smiling as he watches the near-naked Silverbright prance around outside the cave, menacingly waving his piece of driftwood in the air.

"How do I get over there?" shouts Finn.

"Are yae mad, are yae a magician?"

"Aye, that's it, mad as a midnight in March."

"Are yae daft as well as mad?"

"No, not in the least."

"Then use the bridge there!"

"Bridge, what bridge?"

"The bridge right in front of your nose, in front of that big rock there," says Silverbright. "Stand up on that stone there—you'll see it."

The Albanach waits until the waves recede, then he wades the few feet out to the second rock in the water. It's slippery with seaweed and sea creatures, but he manages to clamber up onto it before the waves come crashing into the shore again. When he reaches the top he looks out over the water. Sure enough, there sits the bridge, hiding behind the big rock where he can't see it from the shore. It's nothing but a stone causeway, a thin stone causeway, sticking out from the base of the rock he now clings to. It reaches in a slight arch to the far shore. Silverbright stands, laughing and gesturing crazily. "Better hurry up," he shouts.

"It's too thin," says the Albanach. "It'll break, it'll collapse!"

"It's the only way out here," says Silverbright. "You don't have much time. It'll disappear, an' it won't come back—it's a magic bridge!" Then he bursts out laughing again, but that merely angers the man from Alba and makes him all the more determined. He scrambles down the far side of the rock and runs across the bridge over the ocean, across the causeway leading to the road to Alba. It is slippery, and he hasn't gone halfway when he skids and falls forward onto his stomach. He lies there for a moment, the wind driven out of him, then he wraps his arms around the thin bridge and holds on tightly. Silverbright is in hysterics at the fun of it all. The Albanach screams and jumps when he sees a multitude of wraithlike faces beneath the waves staring at him and smiling, their almond eyes big and dead, but open and searching at the same time. They too are screaming, but Finn can't hear them in their watery grave beneath the surface. He's thankful at least that he can't hear them. He's quite certain he doesn't want to know whatever it is they scream. As he attempts to regain his feet, a hand reaches up out of the water and tries to pull him beneath the waves. He feels cold, slimy fingers slither over his ankle.

"They want your Alban arse," laughs old Silverbright. "They want to make yae one-a them."

With a shriek, the Albanach jumps up and runs again, though a bit more cautiously, toward the shore. Silverbright brandishes his cross and screams gaily.

"Better hurry up, Madman, only half a minute left!"

I feel a thrill run through me when I hear Silverbright call him Madman. *His saying so makes me feel as if he were acknowledging me too.*

The Albanach runs on, filled with horror, filled with the fear of being pulled down into the wraith-filled ocean before he has a chance to begin his journey. He jumps the last few feet to the shore and lies on the rocks bleeding from his fall, gasping for air. When he turns to look back at the bridge, it rises into the air and, with a loud snapping noise, breaks into a million pieces and disappears under the waves as Silverbright predicted it would. The Albanach sits up abruptly, his big, wide eyes staring into a misty grey blanket, a misty grey nothing. America has disappeared too. He turns to Silverbright.

"Yae cannot go back now, laddie," he says. "No way to get there, nothin' to go back to."

"Away yae go, ya creepy auld bastard," says Finn, scrambling to his feet.

Silverbright chuckles. "Yae're late," he says, as he moves beside the Albanach.

"Late, what d'yae mean late?" says Finn, rubbing his bruised knees.

"Twelve years late. It took yae twelve years to get here. Yae were too busy drinkin' that bluidy awful booze-a yours. It's a wonder yae still have half a mind."

"I was going to ask yae if yae had any booze by the way. Anyway, what the hell are yae talkin' about? I saw yae just yesterday—yae came into my dream, remember?"

"Maybe yae don't have half a mind after all. Nah, nah, laddie, that was twelve years ago. It took yae twelve years to get here from that weird house-a yours. That's the truth of the matter. Look! Look at these rags I'm wearin'! That's from sittin' here for the past twelve years. No bluidy wonder I'm angry!"

Flummoxed, the Albanach sits down hard on the ground next to Silverbright. "Christ," he moans, "I'm confused!"

"You've always been confused, Albanach. You get messages all the time. Signals, signs, portents, omens—call them what you will, but all yae do is ignore them. You never listen to the voices, yae never listen to your Madman, as you call her."

"Madman, who the hell's Madman? Anyway, I listened to you, didn't I? You knew I was comin' here!"

"I finally had to go right into your dreams—like a sneak. We don't like doin' that."

"We?"

"Aye, we!" says Silverbright angrily.

"You were a lot nicer in my dream! Well, sort of."

"If I hadn't sneaked into your dream you still wouldn't be here. Too busy hidin' inside your whiskey bottle."

"It gets lonely sometimes."

"Ach, lonely my arse—you're spineless."

"Here, you, watchit!" says the Albanach, standing once more. "I don't need to listen to your crap. Who the hell are you anyway?"

"Silverbright's fine right enough," he says. "That's what I'm called nowadays."

The Albanach studies him for a moment, then he laughs.

"The Albanach warrior called you Silverbright," he says. "Because of your hair."

"Aye, an' he's called me much worse, believe me," says Silverbright with a throaty chuckle.

He studies Finn for a moment, then walks around him, deep in thought. He looks quite amusing, padding around in his rags, the piece of driftwood slung across his shoulder like the Bureaucrat's rifles.

"Who are yae, an' what do yae want with me?" asks the Albanach finally.

Silverbright now stands directly in front of the entrance to the cave. The Albanach looks up past the old fellow and, though the cave looks dark inside, he's sure he sees a movement within. He blinks to clear his vision and, when he looks up again, he would swear he sees a pair of red, almondshaped eyes look out from the confines of the cave. The eyes he sees are strangely familiar and fill him with dread.

"I told yae who I am, an' I want nothin' from yae," says Silverbright.

"You told me what your name was, but yae didn't tell me who yae were—nor did you tell me what yae wanted."

"I've known yae a long, long time, an' you're here because yae need me to tell yae how to get to Alba. That's where you need to be!"

"How come I'm meetin' so many Albanachs these days? In all my years in America I've never met so many."

"That's how it's supposed to be. The last person yae see is a countryman an', if yae survive, reach the other side, the first thing you'll see is a countryman—an Albanach, just like us."

"Survive? What d'yae mean if I survive?"

"Here," says Silverbright, taking the strangely-colored stone from around his neck and handing it to Finn.

"I don't want that," says the Albanach. "Why the hell would I want that?"

"It's yours, just touch it."

The Albanach takes the stone from Silverbright, and sure enough, it pulses along with the beat of his heart, as if it really is a part of him.

Silverbright bursts out laughing at the muddled expression on Finn's face. "We know each other, you an' me," he says, "but more about that later; you don't have much time to waste! You've got a lot of work to do in Alba. But first, yae have to go back to that house. Your guide will take you there."

At that moment Silverbright looks up at me and winks.

"Who the hell's this guide anyway?" Finn asks. "Never mind; I'm not sure I want to go now. Will I be able to come back?"

"You must do what you must do. There's no goin' back. Look!" says Silverbright, pointing into the mist. "There really isn't anythin' to go back to. When yae came here yae set laws in motion that won't be trifled with. Yae must go on. There's nothin' behind yae any more, Finn, except experiences. Yae have to learn from them an' move on. Yae have to put your experiences of the war and of life on the streets in their proper wee slots and go forward. Go on, go!"

Finn hesitates. "I've a really bad feelin' somethin's followin' me. I don't want to sound like I'm a coward, but I've been seein' these horrible eyes starin' at me. Red, almondshaped eyes."

"He's been followin' yae around for many a long day, an' there's more than just him followin' yae. There's always somethin' followin' us, Finn. That's just the way of the world. Somethin's always behind us, prodding us onward for one reason or another, making us run!"

Finn looks up at old Silverbright, surprised that the old fellow would use his proper name. He hasn't heard it in such a long time; it feels strange, though comforting too.

"Who is it that's followin' me?" asks Finn, not quite sure if he really wants to know.

"He's everythin' you're not, Finn. You're a good man in spite of yourself; he's the exact opposite of you. He's also a good part of the reason yae drink that awful booze an' try to hide from everythin' goin' on all around yae. A pained expression clouds Silverbright's face just then. It's him that wants your Alban arse. Him an' no other."

"Now what the hell are yae talkin' about?" asks Finn angrily.

"D'yae no' recognize me, boy?" asked Silverbright, chuckling. "Too much whiskey?"

"Let's have it then. Who are yae?"

Silverbright stares at the Albanach for a moment. "I knew you in another place an' time," he says.

"Oh, really," says Finn, looking at the old man as if he were daft. Old Silverbright was voicing the same thoughts Finn first had of Mary, that he knew her in another place and time.

"It's true, Mary," says Finn. "I dreamt that I knew you in another life, an' the more I think about it, the more convinced I am that it was in ancient Alba."

They are sitting in Paranoid Park, then still known as Washington Square Park, for the hippies hadn't all had their bad acid trips yet. They've been married two years, and young Finn is a year old. Finn holds his son, cradled in his arms, and Mary sits on the soft grass next to them. She giggles.

"I don't know if I believe all that kinda stuff," she says, "but it is very romantic."

"Aye, ah know. It sounds crazy, but it was too real to not be true. It was as if I could actually touch you. I felt as if I could actually hear your laughter, as if I was right in the dream itself."

"Did we have any babies then, Finn, did we have any children?" she asks, stroking young Finn's soft, dark hair.

Young Finn starts bawling just then and kicks out vehemently with his arms and legs as if to assert himself and demand that he should be a part of that life too.

"Ah'm no' sure, Mary, but ah've a feelin we were just gettin' started. We used to make love under a tree behind the cottage. There was a stream nearby, an' we used to make love to the sound of the gurgling stream. It was lovely, Mary, an' we made love all through the day an' night."

Mary giggles again, contentedly, and takes her son into her own arms. Goosebumps crawl and prickle all over her arms and behind her neck as she toys with the idea of having known her husband in another life.

"Another place and time," says Finn, astonished all the more.

"Aye," says Silverbright. "You an' I roamed the hills of Alba more than two hundred years ago. That's the truth of it! There was a redeyed devil then too. There's always a redeyed devil! It seems he's taken possession of the woman with the almondshaped eyes, the same young woman who had her head chopped off in the jungle. You've discovered each other again, an' now Redeyes an' Soldiergirl, as she is known, are both tryin' to find yae. They want you, laddie."

Finn sits down on a nearby rock, too stunned to move. How could Silverbright know about Soldiergirl? Finn has tried to forget about what happened to her for twenty-five years. Then again, he has to believe Silverbright; he speaks so sincerely. Finn can't see any reason why the old fellow would lie to him. When he began his journey he knew he would have to face many strange things, many strange ideas and concepts, but meeting someone he'd known in another life, someone who also knew about events in his present life was wilder than anything he could have imagined.

"That's a bit much, Silverbright!"

"Aye, maybe so, but yae better hurry up now. As I said, you're late. Go on, get in there!"

"Don't rush me!" replies Finn, trying to steal time.

"Yae better hurry. You've wasted enough time, an' there's a lot to do. Get in there an' follow the passages. When yae get to the sea pool, jump into it; that's the way to Madman—and Alba!"

"Jump into a pool!" says Finn, incredulously. "I don't even like to swim! An' who the hell's Madman I asked yae?"

"You'll find out soon enough. You just better get started. Your road might be a tough one, but it's the only road for you, laddie, the only road. Might as well get on with it!"

"What about all my things—my home, friends, Mary, my son?"

"Now he's got DT's," Silverbright whispers to the wind. "That stuff's all fiddledeedee, an' a long time ago too. You're tryin' to find your soul, boy. Better get on wi' it!"

"Just leave everythin'?"

"You knew that anyway. Leave them all like they never existed. You're fightin' for your very soul. But it might not be as bad as yae think. You'll meet people in there that yae know. Some will see yae in their sleep—they've already seen yae in their sleep. They'll think they dreamed about yae—just like you dreamed about me. That's how they'll try to explain it anyway. And others will be there."

"Christ, I need a drink," says Finn.

Silverbright laughs. "Good luck, Albanach," he says. "See yae in Alba!"

Silverbright slaps Finn on the back, then turns away from him. He sits down cross-legged as before. "Go on," he says. "Get on wi' it!"

"By the way," says Finn. "Who were those Bureaucrats up there on the cliff? They had AK47s. They tried to blow me away!"

"Oh, them! They're nearly as bad as Redeyes. They'll steal your soul, your energy, as quick as look at you. They're your mortal enemy!"

"They always have been. Bureaucrats that is."

"More so now than ever. They're lookin' for yae."

"What's wrong wi' them?"

"They're attenuated!

"What?"

"Thinned out. Most likely newer souls. All they've ever done in their lives is to take, get in the way of, put up obstacles against... everything! When you live like that you can't help but become thin, attenuated. Like a beam of light going out, it finally becomes so wide there's nothing left. It's become attenuated. That's what they've done with their energy, their spirit. By the by, were any of the suits empty?" asks Silverbright with a chuckle.

"Come to think of it," says Finn, "two or three of them did look sorta strange. Like there wasn't much to them."

"The Empty Suits. Watch them! They're the worst, the most dangerous, the most desperate. They're ready to disappear completely. There's not much they won't do to get what they need. Watch your back!"

"Don't you worry, mister, I always watch my back."

"Just as well."

Finn the Albanach then turns and walks toward the cave. As he approaches the entrance, he peers inside, half expecting to see the girl with the red, almondshaped eyes. The cave is dark. "Dark as the devil," he mutters, then shudders. It grows darker outside too, then a voice, as if from the heavens, shouts out to him: "Keep the faith, Albanach!"

Finn turns, but Silverbright's gone. He looks up at the sky and sees that the clouds are lower, thicker and darker, a dark, dark green. A lightning bolt strikes the causeway rock, splitting it in two. The broken halves fall backward into the ocean. Hundreds of gnarled, twisted hands pull the pieces underneath the waves. Rain batters down on the Albanach amidst the crash of thunder and, out of the core of the rock, a voice bellows out to him, "Go!"

As the Albanach dives over the threshold of the cave, a landslide of lightning-loosened rocks seals up the entrance, separating him from the world without. He's never before seen such absolute darkness, such a tangible darkness. He can almost feel it. The thick, musty blackness of the interior swarms over him. He becomes frightened all the more, his gaze searching futilely in the darkness for almondeyes. He's completely aware that within the confines of this cave for magicians or those as mad as he, nothing will be as he could ever have imagined. He knows instinctively that no laws of man govern this place and that all he ever held dear will be of no consequence in a place such as this. This cave, he feels, is a womb, a womb in which he'll find his beginnings. Or perhaps he won't.

Finn has never felt so completely naked in all his life, yet he's convinced that alone in the cave for Madmen only is where he should be. Slowly he turns toward the exit, but he can see only blackness. All sound and light have been locked out with the world as he once knew it. He can only go forward. He turns once more, taking comfort in being able to feel. He smiles, thinking: I'll feel my way through this darkness. I will too—until I face the madness so hell-bent on destroying me. I must stay here. If I don't face the madness I'll be doomed forever, without hope. If he somehow manages to escape the confines of the cave, without fulfilling his obligations, he knows he'll be doomed to ignorance, that the remainder of his days will be spent in the fear and the pain and the torment born of that same soul-destroying ignorance. No, I must go on, he thinks. If I don't face my demons I'll never know what's beyond all this fear and ignorance. I must go on! He puts one foot in front of the other, as if walking for the first time, and begins his long journey in search of Alba.

— 2 —

ON DALI'S
TILTING DANCE FLOOR

I HAVE NEVER seen such complete darkness either, not even as an Invisibility, so I have to admit to a certain edginess myself. I stick close to Finn. He's on edge, sweating profusely in the cold, damp darkness of the cave, sweating from a pure and primal fear. He sees nothing at all in this blackness. But he can hear, and he can feel. He'll have to feel his way along the cold, slimy wall of the cave. Most important perhaps, since it might save him, is that he can sense things. He senses something now. I try to encourage him, tell him it's me he senses, then I feel something else myself, another presence. Silverbright could have helped us here, I think, warned us at least. Then I remember that just as the gods won't interfere in day-to-day human concerns, Silverbright won't directly interfere either. Life and the world must move along the way they are, at that particular moment, moving along. To interfere would be to upset the balance.

The thing about Silverbright is that he's still in the realm of the spirits, and can most likely see, or at least sense, other spirits much better than I. It's a pity, I know, but as an Invisibility, I'm not able to communicate with anyone in a realm different from my own. Not with anyone in the physical world, nor with anyone in the spirit world. Another Invisibility, yes, but I doubt that that's ever happened. Certainly not to me at least. With Finn, though, it's different. He, after all, is my body, and I need to get back inside him. As for Silverbright, I can communicate with him only because he too is Finn's spirit guide, and he's here to help us get back together—if it's ever going to happen at all! I suppose I exist in a limbo of sorts that's neither here nor there but, if anywhere, then everywhere, and I'm beginning to think that Finn lives in such a limbo too, sort of in his own world, but out of it at the same time.

I'm beginning to wish I was out of this cave for Madmen only; there's something else in here beside us. I'm sure of it! The feeling of it permeates the cave, and it reeks of evil. I look about me, but can see nothing, not even the white of Finn's eyes though I know they're wide and staring as he decides what his next move will be. I try to encourage him, and give him strength enough to move forward. He finally turns himself around, away from the entrance, and walks off in the direction of the pool Silverbright spoke of, all the while feeling his way along the wet, slimy wall of the cave. That he has turned himself around and is now walking towards the pool, the gateway to the Land of the Truly Alive, gives me strength and courage. It's as if he's turned his back on all that has held him down, kept him from living all these years. It's as if he's turned his back on his emptiness and all that has made him an Empty. "I want to live," he seems to be saying. "I want to be full again!" I can't help but smile and walk along beside him.

There's a smell inside the cave too, of offal and piss, and who knows what else. I hear sounds, small, tinny, gibbering sounds the likes of which I imagine might come from a band of malevolent imps. And there's laughter too, cold, mocking laughter. Though Finn's sight is immaterial in the blackness of the cave without light, his other senses are almost completely overwhelmed; I feel then that if he doesn't reach the pool soon he might never reach it. He can feel the terrible slime on the wall, smell whatever revolts even me, and he can hear those demented gibberings grow louder and louder the farther along the passage he moves. Above all, he can sense the presence of his tormentor, he who has been hounding him all these years and who, it seems, is growing more bold in his pursuit of my body, my shell, my Finn. He seems to be growing hungrier for Finn's blood. Finn stops, he trembles, and stands with his back against the slimy wall. He wants to turn back, I know, but he can't; he knows that much at least. He knows too that he'll rot where he stands if he doesn't move. He can only go forward. He steps away from the wall and puts one foot in front of the other amidst the loudening voices and the putrid smells that grov stronger as he approaches the pool, the entrance to the Land of the Truly Alive. But, as suddenly as a seizure, the floor gives way and Finn falls forward into a great, black hole.

The umbilical cord tightens and, with the sharpness of a snapping whip, I am pulled over the edge with him; we tumble together in darkness for a long time before hitting the pool with a loud splash. The water feels good after the initial shock of the impact. It is lukewarm and soft. Finn is surprised to find that he can still breathe. He can't see me, of course, but I can see him quite clearly. The pool is deep, and in it there is light, a soft, green light. Finn smiles as we float downward in the warm amniotic fluid of his mother's womb. No wonder he smiles; those days in the womb were good days for him. Yet thoughts of loss suddenly come to him once more. Thoughts of loss and of the sea. What of the roaring, crashing sea? What is it with all this water, water? And all these beginnings of amniotic fluid and Alba! Christ, it's all coming together. Beginnings!

"I must go back to the beginning, to the beginning in Alba," he whispers, quietly, lest anyone hear him. "To the beginning inside my mother's womb when we lived in Alba. That's how I'll find what it is I've lost!" A revelation to be sure, he thinks. If I trace my footsteps back then forward, from the beginning until now, I'll discover what it is I've been missing all these years.

That's it! I float beside him, almost delirious with joy myself, knowing that he now knows where to begin his search for that of which he is empty. I feel so encouraged, and I have an inkling now that all will be well. But, as abruptly as the passageway of the cave ended, so too the water of the womb ends and we land with a loud crash on a solid, flat surface with the abruptness of a newborn calf falling from its mother's womb.

We enter into a kind of twilight, not quite dark, not quite light, and the light we do have, I notice, reminds me of African violets, though a little more subdued. The violet light colors the mist surrounding us, makes the mist look warm while it whirls and eddies about us, as if blown by a light, summer breeze. Finn lies on his back, out of breath, but he opens his eyes and looks about his surroundings. We have landed on a floor of sorts, but a strange floor.

Whenever Finn moves, the floor moves too, like an old-fashioned ballroom floor, the kind that tilts as the dancers dance. It tilts now, too much, and Finn grows afraid, afraid he'll fall over the edge of the floor, though he can't see the edge, doesn't know if there is an edge. He scrambles into what he thinks might be the center of the room until the floor rights itself. He stands and bumps his head on a lamp hanging from the somehow suspended ceiling, and a beautiful lamp it is too. It hangs low like those hanging over green felt tables in a clandestine cardroom but, unlike those, it emits the soft, purple rays now coloring the surrounding mist. Slowly, the mist swirls faster and faster, then evaporates. Finn looks up again at the lamp. Made of stained glass, it has three panels, each with an elongated violet at their center, done in the same art deco style popular during the early part of the century.

The mist clears only from the middle of the floor and it's still impossible to tell whether the room is big or whether it is small; it could have stretched to infinity for all we knew. A tall, wrought-iron table sits directly underneath the lamp. It has a glass top done in the same style as the lamp, and on top of the table sit two steamyhot cups of tea. At each end of the table there are two highbacked chairs matching the table. Finn likes the look of the chairs; they seem comfortable, and the colors of the stained glass, the enamel paints and the cushions are warm and inviting. He sits down in one of the chairs and waits, waits for whoever it might be who will drink the other cup of tea.

I, meantime, have been walking about the room as far as the umbilical cord will allow, but there's nothing more to be seen.

While he waits, Finn watches the mist as it continues to swirl about the room. From time to time it looks as if it might disappear altogether and, during those brief moments, Finn realizes that the room has no walls, just a ceiling and a floor, a floor that tilts whenever he moves across it. The floor reminds Finn of Salvador Dali. The whole setting reminds him of a Dali painting. In those brief moments when he looks outward through the violet mist he sees only sky, a blueblack night sky, filled with stars the likes of which he's never seen before, like those he saw in his vision with Silverbright when the old fellow slapped him back into awareness.

He sits there for a long time thinking about all that has happened to him of late, he thinks about his inability to stop drinking, about his life on the streets, and about Mary and everything else that ever meant anything to him. His disgust and his terrible despair begin to creep back into his thoughts. He's thought often about ending his life, about just getting it over with, when he's feeling such despair.

I become panicked then when I feel him thinking so. I've been sitting in the chair opposite him, beside the other cup of tea, and I jump straight out of the chair. I think the intensity of my panic nearly renders me visible for there is a welcome look of astonishment on Finn's face. I know he's just seen something, a shadow perhaps, because his eyes are big like a frog's. He sits back in his chair, his shoulders slumped, as if resigned to his fate, resigned to wait for whatever might come next. I learn a valuable lesson then. It seems that any sudden movement from me, if it's strong or sudden enough, might get through to him, catch him off guard, rendering me seeable. I promise myself to test my theory as soon as possible.

But Finn doesn't have to wait much longer for whatever might come next. As he sits in the comfy chair, surrounded by the mysterious violet-colored mist, he hears a rasping, hacking cough coming, somewhat muffled, through the mist behind him, then in front of him, then all around him. Hack, hack, cough; hack, hack, cough. Then slow shuffling footsteps followed by the dull clunking thud of a walking cane on wood. His senses are heightened to the point where he thinks he might go into another seizure. Shuffle, shuffle, clunk, go the sounds of the footsteps and the walking stick, permeating through the mist so that Finn still can't discern from whence might come the owner of the rasping, hacking cough. He sits straightbacked and tense, rooted to his chair like an unfortunate forest animal on a lonely country road suddenly gripped in the lights of a passing car.

He looks about the room but sees nothing. He hears only sound! Hack, hack, cough! Shuffle, shuffle, clunk, growing closer with each passing moment. The mist, intensely violet in the light, swirls faster, faster, faster as he waits. Then a face looms out of the mist directly in front of him. The face looks both sad and angry at the same time and the eyes, drooped toward Dali's tilting dance-floor, seem to be filled with a great and hungry yearning.

Shuffle, shuffle, clunk. The face moves out of the mist, exposing the frail and sickly body of a man clothed in the garments of a bygone era. His shirt and trousers are baggy, made of linen, and are light of color such as might be worn in a warm, humid climate. Around his neck, the man wears a purple cravat made of finely-woven silk. He wears calf-high leather boots on his thin, long feet. But what mesmerizes the Albanach more than anything else is the stranger's walking cane. It has been carved from dark wood like hickory, and it has been stained a deep, red color like that of the thick hot blood in a newly-opened vein. The crook has the shape of a serpent's head. Scrolls and sworls are carved in an intricate pattern all the way down to the tail of the snake. The strange apparition stands in front of the Albanach for a long time, staring down at him with those drooping, yearning eyes, his free hand all the while clutching at his breast as if to keep his heart from jumping out of his body. He lets go another rasping, hacking cough.

"Would yae like to dance," he says. But he says it with such venom, so angrily, that Finn jumps up out of his seat, startled.

"That's what I like," says the stranger, "enthusiasm!"

He grabs Finn, who is ready to faint, and waltzes him around the dancefloor so fast the Albanach thinks they must certainly go tumbling over the edge of the ever-tilting floor.

The apparition whirls the Albanach around and around the room till he feels dizzy and ill. In and out of the mist they dance as the apparition keeps time, singing spirited songs in the old Alban tradition of a ceilidhes. Round and round the room they go in ever-increasing circles until Finn feels a slight bump as over the edge of the floor they dance into the crisp-long darkness. Certain of plunging into hell or beyond, Finn's heart leaps into his mouth, making him speechless as if his tongue is cowtongue, thick and bloated. He struggles with all his might against the steelclawed grip of the strange apparition whose laughter rings out to the heavens above. Outward and outward, farther and farther away from the tilting dancefloor dance the two, and Finn sees clearly that it is indeed just a floor and a ceiling floating in midair with all the stars above and nothing below.

"Above, the stars," the apparition says, pointing. "Below, perdition!" Then he lets out a loud, guffawing laugh before being consumed by his rasping, hacking cough.

He dances Finn back to the dancefloor, coughing all the way, and sits down in one of the chairs, Finn opposite him. Both men sit there for some time, breathing heavily. When Finn looks up once more his dance partner stares at him, a knowing, Mona Lisa-like expression etched onto his face. The apparition reaches out across the table and Finn shakes a cold, clammy hand, long and thin and pale like a lady's. Finn thinks he knows the stranger; the man's cough, dialect and appearance all stir a memory in the Albanach who now looks more closely than ever at the man who likes to dance out into the firmament of unknown worlds. His hair, mousebrown and streaked with strands of silver, hangs just below his ears. His face, gaunt and sallow, shows evidence of a long and dreary illness. He has a thin and wispy moustache and a sprouting of hair grows just below his bottom lip. The stranger begins again his rasp-hacky cough, his ladyhand clutching again his troubled breast. He's ill, thinks the Albanach. The poor bastard's tubercular; then a glimmer of recognition passes over Finn's face.

"I know you!" he says. "It took me a minute, but I know you. You're...."

"Aye, quite right, quite right," growls the apparition. "I *am* ill, I *am* tubercular, but that's not what will get me in the end." He grasps once more Finn's hand.

"Robert Louis Stevenson," he says. "I am your guide."

Finn bursts out laughing; he can't help it. This meeting is beyond his wildest hallucinations. Well, perhaps not, he thinks. Not after all that's happened lately.

"Aye, quite right, quite right, to be sure," says Finn, mimicking his visitor. "There's as much chance-a that as there is for peace in the world," he continues, laughing loudly. He becomes quiet then and wakeserious. He could have sworn the visitor's eyes had turned red and almondshaped, if but briefly. He rubs his own eyes and studies again the man in the chair at the other end of the table. I don't know what's going on here, thinks the Albanach, but he can't look any more like Stevenson than he does now. It must be Stevenson! But....

"I know you too," says Stevenson, a malicious smirk fleetingly twisting his face, as when Finn saw his red, almondeyes. "Have done for quite some time," Stevenson continues. "Don't you remember, Mac-Don-ald?" He sounds out Finn's name in a long, drawn-out manner as if savoring the sound of it. And Finn does remember.

He is doing well at the time. Sober as an oak tree, working hard at his painting. Painting is all he wants to do; it helps keep him sane and he feels compelled to pick up his brushes every day and paint, paint the images of his dreamscapes. I am often flitting around in his dreamscapes. When he paints me back then, the likeness is astonishing. I must have been getting through to him— at least on the level of dreams. He got my face right in that painting, almondeyes included, though my robe he paints blue-white rather than the crimson color I've worn ever since The Leaving. *God help us, but it is a lovely piece of work. He even manages to capture my sadness, and when I watch him putting the finishing touches to it my heart bursts with love for him. I know for certain then that we'll be as one again; he's on his way back into the realm of the Truly Alive.*

Sober as an oak tree indeed, out and about painting amidst the warm San Francisco streets, looking for a studio where he can live and do his work. I must confess here to a certain amount of interference on my part; I can't help but push him toward Bush Street, the six hundred block of Bush Street to be exact, for it is on that site that Robert Louis Stevenson lived when he visited San Francisco nearly a hundred years before Finn. I have to interfere because their lives are so intertwined, so similar.

They are both Albanachs, though Stevenson comes from Edinburgh, the eastern city, whereas Finn comes from Glasgow, the city in the west. Both of their fathers had been engineers, but the sons rebelled against such a structured way of life. Stevenson came to San Francisco in pursuit of a woman he loved; Finn came to the city by the Bay to get away from a woman he loved. Both are artists. Stevenson a writer; Finn a painter. When they felt the pangs of homesickness come upon them they would each sit up on Telegraph Hill and watch the seagoing ships sail back and forth in the San Francisco Bay feeling lonely and terribly sorry for themselves. Perhaps what's most important though, in a spiritual sense or in a universal sense, is that Stevenson was born in November of 1850, and Finn was born in November of 1950, exactly one hundred years later to the day. Some would say that such occurrences are coincidental which is okay if one is willing to ignore the obvious. But the truth is, there are no coincidences, no chance meetings, no meaningless feelings of déjà vu. Everything happens for a reason as Finn discovers in no uncertain terms.

He all but bumps into the plaque fastened to the wall in the entryway at the Bush Street address which proclaims to all the world that Robert Louis Stevenson did indeed live on this very same site. Finn rings the doorbell.

"But there's nothing available this month," says the apartment manager after much beseeching by Finn. "There won't be anything available until next month; come back then." He's a tall fellow and slender, whose near-white hair is pulled back in a ponytail. His penetrating blue eyes are red and watery as if he were ill or drank too much. He looks like an artist himself, thinks Finn. Maybe he's a kindred spirit.

"I don't need much," says Finn. "A place to sleep and paint. That's all I need."

The manager studies Finn for a moment and Finn can see the wheels turning behind the other man's eyes.

"There's a room at the top of the building," says the manager after some moments. "It's fulla junk an' dust, but it's big an' there's lotsa light, lotsa windows. You can open them when the smell of the paint gets to ya. D'ya wanna see it?"

Finn can't believe his good fortune. "Sure, I'd love to see it," he says.

The elevator is old and has an arrow, like the big hand on a grandfather clock, indicating the floor. Finn watches it climb.

"1910," says the manager.

"Huh?" replies Finn.

"They built this place in 1910, just after the o-six earthquake."

"Oh, I see," says Finn. "It's a nice building. Beautiful woodwork."

"You look just like him," the manager says, studying the Albanach.

"What, what did you say?"

"Stevenson, Robert Louis Stevenson. You look just like him, only bigger. There's a picture of him in the entryway. You look just like him. Grow a mustache and a goatee. You'd be his double."

"Don't know much about him," Finn says, not daring to tell the manager he's read almost everything Stevenson wrote, and that *Jekyll and Hyde* is one of his favorite and most contemplated books. He doesn't want the manager to think him nutty if he explains his affinity for the longdead author.

"He lived in a duplex on this very site,' says the manager. It crumbled and burned during the quake." He studies Finn again. "I've seen him up here you know, up here where you're goin'." Finn freezes.

"What do you mean, you've seen him?"

"Only for a second at a time. He sits up here an' reads. Well...here we are, top floor. We hafta climb another flight to get to the room."

Finn sucks in his breath and rolls his eyes, wondering what the blazes he's getting himself into. The room is huge, and does have a lot of light. It's filled with old furniture, crates and boxes and rolled up pieces of carpet. This could be fun, he thinks. Just looking through all this junk. God knows what's under all this dust.

"Take a week to clean it," says the manager. "But it'll be good for painting when you're done. Come and see me when you're settled. I'll bring you some sheets and a key later. I'm sure there's a mattress underneath all that shit." Then he leaves in a cloud of swirling dust as he bangs the door closed behind him.

Finn pulls a dustcover off an armchair and plops himself down into it. "Oh, God," he moans, "Down! The damn thing's fulla down, what a luxury!" He closes his eyes then and dozes, quite comfortable in his new, if dusty, surroundings. He dreams of the work ahead of him and of the happiness he'll find painting every day in his very own studio.

◆　◆　◆

Gleaming, the room shines like a new penny. It takes nearly a week to clean it and make it livable, just as the manager had predicted. Five weeks have passed since that first day and Finn's hopelessly drunk once more. It seems that whenever his life is on the verge of going well he has to screw it up by drinking away all the progress he's made, as if he doesn't deserve it, as if a decent life's something reserved for those who are better than he.

Dejected and miserable, I can only sit there quietly and watch him. The frustration's tremendous.

He stands on top of a huge and strong oak table. He has tied the end of a rope around one of the many pipes criss-crossing the ceiling. The noose fits snugly around his neck. He's made sure there's enough slack in it so that, when he jumps, he'll drop two feet or so, thus allowing for a severe enough jolt to snap his neck. He closes his eyes and contemplates the jump. Should I? he wonders. But before he can answer his own question he hears a loud crash. He loses his balance and teeters off the edge of the table anyway, his decision made for him. As he falls, he feels a pair of arms grab him around the legs and push him upward. He reaches up and grabs the rope then, pushed and pulling, his feet find the table again, his life for the time being, still intact. He pulls the rope off his spared neck and jumps off the table as if his tail were on fire.

"Who're you?" he asks the stranger who stands, fuming, before him.

"I should thrash you within an inch of your life," says the stranger, "trying a trick like that. Who do you think you are? What makes you think you can take your own life just like that, eh?"

"Eh?" says Finn, flummoxed, confused now more than ever in his entire life. He stares down at the stranger.

"You scared the daylights out of me," says Finn. "Thought I'd had it!"

"You're too mean to die. Too bloody miserable. Don't know your arse from your elbow and you expect that killing yourself is going to solve a' your problems. Hah! That's just the beginning, my friend!"

"Hey, piss off, buddy! Who do yae think yae are anyway?" Finn has uttered these last few words before realizing he spoke, after so many years, in the dialect of Alba.

"Robert Louis Stevenson, at your service," says the stranger. "And you're in my house, my sanctuary."

Finn sits down hard on a nearby couch. "Oh, God," he moans. "Why me?"

"You should have left all the dust right where it was. I like the dust. I used to move through this room trying to disturb the dust. Sometimes I did. Just a smidgen. That meant I was still in this world a bit. Just a smidgen, mind you. I can't leave here you know. Isn't that awful? I'm stuck!"

"Me too," says Finn, a heavy sadness coming suddenly over him. He looks up at Stevenson. "Why are yae stuck?"

"I used to paint too," says Stevenson. "Aix-en-Provence. I love France. Met Fanny there," he continues, dreamily. "My wife, that is!" He studies Finn's painting where it sits on the easel at the other end of the room. Finn turns and looks at it himself.

"Nearly done," he says. "All it needs now is a heart."

A three-by-four painting sits on the easel. The background is dark, blue-black dark. He's painted a beautiful young woman on top of the background. Her hair is black, her skin chalk-white, and her eyes are shaped like mine. She's split violently in two just below the navel and the separation seems to be on fire. A crueler separation I've never seen. It's the first picture Finn has ever done of me, the woman in his head.

"Who is she?" asks Stevenson with a strange, knowing smile on his face.

"Dunno," Finn replies. "She just comes to me from time to time. I was on my knees prayin' and she just came to me. I don't know who I was prayin' to—either God or the Devil, I suppose. But when I was done I got up and painted her."

"So either God or the Devil helped yae?"

"I suppose so, aye."

"Stevenson giggles. "Oh, that's a good one all right. That's a real beauty! Seems to me yae might be a bit more careful who yae pray to, what yae pray for! Yae might get it!"

"Worked for me."

"If yae say so, Albanach! But meantime I'd better be off. Been here long enough, too long as it is."

Stevenson gets up and stands before Finn, his hand stretched out. Finn stands and takes Stevenson's hand. They shake.

"If I catch you up to your tricks again, I'll put my stick across your back!"

Finn notices that the stick is simply crafted, though lovely, made of a light-colored wood like yew. The handle, shaped like a shepherd's crook, is worn from much use.

"Remember," says Stevenson. "Stay away from noose-wrought

rope; it'll be your downfall. But most important, heed your dreams; follow your heart!" And with that he turns, laughing all the while, and leaves the room.

Finn sits down on the couch once more, heavily. He lights a cigarette and as he watches the smoke slowly swirl and drift above him, his mind wanders around in the shapes of the swirls, as if his mind were the smoke itself.

◆ ◆ ◆

He's back in the violet-colored mist, sitting in the chair on Dali's tilting dancefloor. He chuckles. Back to reality! When he looks up again he notices that Stevenson still smirks, and that he has a strange glimmer about his eyes. The stick too is different from the one the storyteller had when Finn first met him on Bush street. There's something fishy about the strange stick but, as usual, I can't say a word, can't warn him. Finn sits in his chair, bewildered, not a little worried.

"Thanks for the tea," says Stevenson, picking up the cup of still-steaming tea.

"Don't you touch that; it's no' for you," a voice rings out behind the mist, followed at once by another rasping, hacking cough. Startled, Finn looks off in the direction of the cough just in time to see another Stevenson break out of the mist, at speed, the Bush Street walking stick held aloft, ready to strike.

"Imbecile...devil!" he screams. "Be gone, back to hell with you!" And with that he takes a swipe at the dancing Stevenson who jumps up quickly, knocking over his chair on the way. When speeding Stevenson's stick connects, the dancing Stevenson bursts into a million fragments of fading light. The fragments, as they rise higher and spread out above the mist, begin to swirl, each on their own, faster and faster and, in their speed, form two faces etched with pain and grief. Finn rises to his feet, staring in wonder at the faces spinning within the violet mist.

"It's the Suicide Veterans," says Stevenson, every bit as full of wonder as Finn. "I've never seen them before. Heard about them, but never seen them." He looks across at Finn. "But you should recognize them!"

"It's funny," says Finn, "but they do have a familiar look about them."

"It's been said," replies Stevenson, "that there's a hundred an' fifty thousand of them out there somewhere, floating around lost. They took their own lives after the war; they don't know where to go."

As the Albanach watches in amazement, the veterans shout out a plea to him.

"Help us, Finn," they shout. "Help us to get home!"

The veterans spin faster and faster then disappear off beyond the mist. Stevenson picks up the fallen chair and sits down in it, coughing his rasping, hacking cough, his clenched fist once more pressed against his weakened breast. Finn sits too and takes a gulp of tea.

"I'll be dead afore this year is done," says Stevenson with a laugh. "Nothing like a nice cuppa tea, now is there?" He giggles pleasantly as he sips his tea. "Can you imagine, that miserable soul-stealing, shape-shifting bastard tried to drink my tea. What a nerve!"

"Hey, mister," says Finn, "what the hell's goin' on here? Who was that in your skin?"

"He did a good job too; that's what worries me. He's your nemesis, Finn. But he's a part of you too—a big part of you. Half of you to be precise. Silverbright recognized him for what he is—pure evil! That's the Redeyes he was talking about."

"Too bad you died, Stevenson; you've got a great imagination! Lotsa stories in you still."

Stevenson laughs. "Aye, you're right, I do. But what I'm telling you now is truer than you can imagine. Whether you believe it or no' is entirely up to you. But I must tell you that the most impor-tant for you to do just now will be to keep an open mind. Anything's possible, Finn. Anything! And there are no indubitable truths. When I realized that, I felt such an overwhelming relief. That's what makes life so wonderful, so exciting. Nothing is true! Nobody can prove that anything's indubitably true. All anything boils down to after all is faith. I believe that such and such is simply such and such, and that's all there is to it. Nobody can tell me I'm wrong, or that what I believe in is wrong—because nobody really knows! Nobody can tell me, beyond a smidgen of doubt, that a certain thing is a truth."

He pulls his chair closer to the table, places his elbows on top of it, and leans over conspiratorially towards Finn.

"This will be difficult for you to understand, you being a pragmatist an' all, but Silverbright wasn't pulling your leg when he says he knew you before. He really did, back there in the mists of time, more than two hundred years ago."

Finn fidgets uncomfortably in his chair. He's grown somewhat accustomed to these strange experiences of late, has accepted them as something he simply has to go through, with the same inevitability as seizures during withdrawal from alcohol. But he's becoming increasingly more aware of losing completely his ability to discern the difference between the real world and whatever he's now going through. He looks at Stevenson as if begging for a better explanation. Stevenson catches the worried expression clouding the Albanach's face.

"Och, it's no' that bad, Finn. It just is! That's all."

"Look, Stevenson," says Finn, "I'm getting a wee bit worried. What the hell d'yae mean *it just is*?"

"Some people are blessed—or cursed as the case may be—with a gift such as you have."

"Gift, Stevenson? You call this a damned gift. Why can't I just be a truck driver or a cop for chrissake. Why does all this craziness, this madness, have to happen to me?"

"It is a gift. Aye, an' a blessing too, some might say. You have a powerful ability to see things few men are able to see. That's your gift! Some call it the Second Sight. All it means is that you're more in tune with the spirit world, as you call it, than most folk. You can see beyond the realm you live and walk around in. It's your heritage, man, just as it was Silverbright's heritage. You can no more deny it than you can deny your eyeballs, or your arms and legs. It just is! All you can do in the end is learn how to use your gift, or let it destroy you! A gift like yours, unharnessed, out of control, will surely drive you mad. And it will drive you mad if you misuse it."

"Then it's a curse!"

"Perhaps, aye. But I'm here to help you—if you want my help, that is."

"Well, I don't want to be stuck here; I have no idea what's going on."

"Good, that's good! Just keep your mind open a little bit. Your heart's been open all these years. That's why the booze and your life as a Shopping Cart Soldier haven't completely killed you. And your feelings are still intact—even if they are but a wisp of what they ought to be."

Stevenson takes a drink of his tea, a long drink, all the while staring at Finn over the rim of his teacup. He smiles then places the cup back in its saucer.

"Why do you think you call Scotland *Alba*, Finn?"

Finn shrugged his shoulders. "I dunno," he says.

"Because that's its real name. That's how you remember the place wherein you were born. In the Gaelic, the speech of your fathers, that's what it's called; that's what it's still called in the Gaelic. To this very day. And that's what it was called when the Brittanish merchants traded there six centuries before the time of Christ. To you, that's its real name. That and no other. It's in your bones, in your gut! That's what's keeps you alive, man!"

"An' all this time I thought it was because I was a hopeless romantic," says Finn, laughing. "I thought it was because I was a hopeless romantic that I missed something about the old Scotland that I somehow had a personal knowledge of."

"You do, Finn, you do. That's why you have to keep an open mind while, at the same time, remaining careful not to go mad. Good lord, man, if I'd known all these things I'm telling you, helping you see, I could've written some beautiful stories."

"You did, Stevenson!"

"Aye, you're right, I did!"

Stevenson sits back in his chair and looks straight into Finn's eyes.

"I don't like to be called Stevenson; it's very crude, very rude. You may call me Louis hereafter. All my friends do," he says with a chuckle.

"My friend, my guide, Louie Stevenson!" says Finn, bowing low. "Louis...Louis!"

"Louis."

"Thank you."

"Well then, Louis, who are they then, these Suicide Veterans?"

"They call themselves the People of Peace. Most folk call them ghosts. We call them Invisibilities. They've nowhere else to go except to roll around the firmament, stuck between one place and another. They just need a bit of help, that's all. Listen, Finn. There's different parts, levels, to life in the Land of the Truly Alive. They're just stuck between one and another. They're confused because of the way they left the level they were living in."

"Goddamn," says Finn. "That doesn't seem right. I thought I had it bad, gettin' through the war. I even live in another kinda war zone, homeless, pushing my shopping cart around all day long, always lookin' over my shoulder. Can't even quit fuckin' drinkin'. But I'd hate to be stuck where they're stuck. Nah, nah, wait a minute. I don't even believe in all that shit. What is it you call them...Invisibilities? Horseshit!"

"Call them what you like, but you believe in them!"

"I do?"

"You do! What else would you call them? *Visitors* is how you name those inexplicable sightings and visions. That's just a word you use to explain the inexplicable, to describe that which can't be described. Like *Invisibilities*, it's just another word. Invent one of your own if you like, but you do believe."

"Aye, well, that might take a bit of time, a bit of thought," says Finn, facetiously.

"But you already do believe in them, Albanach. You know you do. That's your lot in life. Your confusion is your cross."

"Oh, christ!"

"Precisely! But let me ask you something. Do you really want to be so vain that you don't believe in them? What a lonely, empty life that would be—has been for you!"

"Maybe I *am* too much the pragmatist these days."

"That there's nothing else to life? That no other life exists besides that which you can see and touch? That the People of Peace don't exist?"

"Prove it!"

"Prove they don't! Those veterans you're so eager to discount know you—and you know them!"

"The hell they do!"

"If you'd talked longer with Silverbright he'd have told you more. He'd have told you about Mary Quinn too if you'd asked. Ask him next time you see him."

"About Mary Quinn?" asks the astonished Finn.

"Aye, the very same. The very same soul, that is! Everything comes full circle in the end. And that's a fact."

"So I was right after all. I did know her; my dream was real! I wonder what she's doing now, Mary Quinn?"

"A vision, I'd say. That's what you had. But I don't think you should be thinking of Mary at present, laddie. You're getting ahead of yourself again. First things first, as they say. You have to figure out how to get to Alba, how to face your demons. You've been running around the world an' Empty yourself all these years, denying everything, hiding in your whiskey bottle."

Finn squirms in his seat again, not liking one bit the direction in which the conversation's dragging him.

"How do I know for sure you are who you say you are? Maybe you're just a goddamn shapeshifter like that thing we just saw."

Stevenson chuckles. "I think you saw his eyes, did you not? His eyes can never lie, Finn. Remember that! They are the only part of him that won't change. As I mentioned before, he's been following you all your life. He was in the jungle with you too. When that young Asian woman met her end, he was there. When her soul left her body, he was there. He took her body. He stole her mutilated body as her soul began to leave her; that's what gave him substance enough to wander about among the Truly Alive. He took her body as her soul began its journey to the Place of Truly Dead Souls. But tell me, Finn, why are you trying to kill yourself with alcohol?"

"I'm not!" shouts the Albanach, and the floor tilts.

"Better be careful," says Stevenson with a smile. "You seem to have upset someone."

"You know somethin'," says Finn. "You really piss me off, sitting there in your tight kneebreeches and your fancy cravat, acting like you're God Almighty, all knowing and omnipotent. Screw you!"

"You have such a charming way with words, my friend, but don't change the subject. You've been doing just that all your life. Answer my question, Finn, and remember this: if you lie to me, even if you lie by omission, this floor we sit upon will tilt; if you tell a big enough lie it will tilt so dramatically you'll go flying over the edge—to perdition. Aye, perdition. Old Redeyes was right about that at least. Above, the stars; below, perdition! It's time, Finn. Time to look inside yourself and be honest."

"What are you talking about, I *am* honest."

"With others, perhaps, but you lie to yourself all the time. You couldn't do anything more silly than that. What's that nasty word you seem so fond of? Ah, yes, bullshit! You're full of bullshit, my friend. You have to learn to be honest with yourself. A scary proposition, is it not?"

"I am honest with myself," says Finn, and the floor tilts and trembles. Stevenson chuckles again.

"Really? What about God, Finn? You've always been a God-fearing man, Finn, yet you even try to pull the wool over the eyes of God. That's truly funny, though quite ridiculous I might add. Another lesson in futility. Bordering on insanity. Do you think that in the end you can get away with deceiving God?"

"Enough, Stevenson, that's enough! I don't do anything of the kind!"

The floor tilts dramatically, and Finn's chair slides two or three feet away from the table. Stevenson gets up from his chair and shuffles and taps his way around the table, all the while holding his fist up to his chest as the strain of his illness continues to overwhelm his lungs. He grows angrier by the minute.

"You know what really makes me angry?" he says, his stick held aloft as if ready to strike. "You know what I find really despicable? Your disgusting sorrow for yourself. And that you're alive and I'm dead. God damn you, man, but I was just coming into my own as a writer when this coughing business began to wreak havoc with my life. When I was alive, as you see me now, I was only months, nay weeks, away from death's door. Yet you play with your own life as if it were of no value whatever, as if you could buy another at the local market."

Finn stands, growing angrier himself. "Get lost, ya auld bugger! Go back to where you came from," he screams, reminding himself of the Bureaucrats who would shout the same to him as he panhandled at his corner in North Beach. "I do the best I can with my life," he continues with little or no conviction. And, as if in agreement, the floor tilts and trembles ever more forcefully. Finn has to struggle to keep his balance. "I haven't done anything wrong; I don't hurt anyone!" he shouts, and the floor tilts twenty degrees or so more. With a thunderous clap, the floor moves forward, then flies quickly through the firmament as Finn struggles to keep his balance, his eyes filled with terror. Stevenson smiles and leans on his stick as if he's strolling along Princess Street in Edinburgh on a warm, Sunday afternoon. As the tilting floor speeds through the sky, the mist disperses and Finn, now on his hands and knees, looks up. The ceiling too has disappeared, and he sees a sky filled with more stars than he has ever seen in his life before. And they are all of different colors too. Vivid, bright and energetic colors such as he's never seen before either. In the middle of all the luxuriant stars sits the moon, a huge moon, shinywhite, illuminated, it seems, by millions of candles. The features of the moon smile scornfully down on the Albanach.

"Well," says Stevenson. "Go ahead. Take a good long look. What do you see? That's life, you fool! That's what you're negating each time you take a drink of your awful anesthesia. You negate all life as if it were a tradable commodity. Don't you know it's the only life you have?"

"I love my life!" Finn shouts. And the floor tilts another ten degrees. The Albanach slides a few feet closer to the edge of the floor. Stevenson doesn't seem to be perturbed in the least. Seems, in fact, to be quite at home. Finn scrambles now to keep his balance. He tries to anchor his fingernails into the floor, but he continues to slide nevertheless. Then, quite suddenly, the floor slows and comes to a complete stop among the stars. Many-colored lights sparkle and dance across the floor. Near to tears, Finn looks up and sees that Stevenson has begun to change, to meta-morphose. The Albanach lets out a loud yelping scream and sits back on his haunches. He covers his eyes with his hands; Stevenson has begun to melt.

When Finn looks up again Stevenson no longer exists. In his place stands the white-robed figure of the Nazarene. He stands there with his hands spread out before him, supplicating perhaps, welcoming certainly. Finn notices the marks of the stigmata on the Nazarene's hands and feet, and from the gaping hole in his side streams a soft and subdued violet-colored light much like the mist in the room in which they stand. The thorns of the Nazarene's crown are much longer and more brutal looking than the Albanach has ever imagined they might be. Small rivulets of blood streak and besmirch his paleholy face. Tingling with fear, the Albanach creeps backward closer to the edge of Dali's now-still dancefloor.

The Nazarene looks down upon Finn, his eyes filled with love and compassion. "Why hast thou forsaken me?" he asks, and Finn screams all the more, scared to death.

"Leave me alone. Oh, please leave me alone!" he shouts.

"But you keep asking for me," says the Nazarene. "Well, here J am; what do you want?"

"Leave me alone. I just want to live without all this madness. I just want to be okay, to live normally."

"You have a good life," says the Nazarene, "yet you destroy it."

"I love my life," says Finn, and the floor tilts all the more.

"You lie even to me. Oh, why, Finn, why hast thou forsaken me?"

"No, I haven't. I haven't forsaken you," says Finn, now pleading. But the Man from Nazareth is having none of it.

"You have everything," he says. "You have been given everything, you have been given life, yet you destroy it as if it means nothing to you."

"No, no! That isn't true! I told you, I love my life." And the floor tilts even more.

The Nazarene drops to his knees beside Finn and covers his face with his hands. When he takes them away, tears of blood stream from his eyes.

"Where's my cross, Albanach? Did you throw my cross away? I need my cross, Finn! How can I rest without it? Where else can I rest my broken body?"

The Nazarene strokes Finn's hair gently, lovingly.

"What happened to love?" asks the Nazarene. "Don't you love anything any more?"

He stands then and looks down at Finn, anger now bubbling in the back of his eyes. Blood pours from the wounds in his hands and feet and from the cruel hole in his side; thick, dark blood trickles down his face from his crown of thorns.

"Was this all for naught?' he asks.

The blood from the body of the Nazarene runs along the floor, and when it reaches the grasping hands of Finn, the Albanach screams and jumps to his feet. He tries to wipe the blood on his clothing, but it won't come off. He retches and finally vomits all over the hands and feet of the Nazarene.

"Have we lost you forever, Albanach?" asks the Nazarene, as he wipes Finn's vomit on his robe.

"Leave me alone," says Finn, and takes another step backward.

The Nazarene's face lights up with anger. "You make me ill," he says, rage burning brightly in his bloodteary eyes. "Did you know that, Albanach?" he says, all the while prodding the Albanach with a bloodcovered finger. Backward, closer to the edge steps Finn. "You make me ill!" the Nazarene says again.

"Hey, what the hell's wrong with you?" Finn screams. "You're supposed to be God, ain't you?"

"I've cajoled you, and I've begged you. I've even pleaded with you, yet..."

"Piss off!"

The Nazarene laughs.

"You're funny, Albanach," he says. "But don't you forget, I can be human too. Remember that! You bring out the man in me. You seem to think you have a monopoly on suffering. You seem to think you're the only one who suffers. Don't you ever forget, I INVENTED SUFFERING." The Nazarene laughs sardonically. "I was in Vietnam too, remember."

"What!" Finn shouts out. "*You* were in Vietnam? You? Oh, for fucksake, that's the biggest piece-a-shit joke I've ever heard! Now I know I'm in la-la land."

"You don't remember the little shove I gave you in the triage tent when all your friends were blown to smithereens? No, the likes of you wouldn't. You were too busy thinking about how to hide, get rid of, the bullet you'd just scraped out of Johnny Quinn's brain. You selfish bastard, no wonder you feel guilty. You were scared they'd do an autopsy and find the M16 bullet in your pal's head. What was it you were so fond of saying? Oh, yes, I remember. 'Cover my ass!' Wasn't that it, Alba man? You've been living that same selfish way ever since. I should have pushed someone else out of the way."

"FUCK YOU, NAZARENE!" screams Finn. He's in a purple rage, the veins in his neck throbbing, his fists clenched until his nails pierce the skin. "Why didn't you, why didn't you push *everyone* out of the way? Why did you have to let that tent blow up in the first place? Huh? Why'd you have to let that fuckin' war happen at all?"

The Nazarene's shoulders slump forward. "You have such a strange, such an unrealistic comprehension of me. Do you think I can change all the things the likes of you instigate, incite, begin? Hah, that's a laugh, but it's typical. Take the easy way out. Don't accept responsibility for what you do. Typical! Why do you think you have the ability to reason, the gift of choice? I *can't* interfere.

It's that simple. All I can do, when all is said and done, is send you strength, that's all. Believe me, I pushed as many grunts out of the way as I possibly could. But I'm human too, remember?"

Finn is completely at a loss. He just sits there looking bewildered, thinking over what the Nazarene has just told him. The Nazarene kneels beside Finn and continues.

"The problem with you, Finn, is that you wallow in your pain, embrace it as if it were yours alone! Hah! I've shown you nothing but compassion all your life, all kinds of love, but you discard it, ignore it, deny it! Maybe by being a man again I'll get through to you?"

Still reeling from the smell and feel of the Nazarene's blood and his anger, the Albanach steps back, over to the edge of the dancefloor. The Nazarene's eyes blaze. He steps closer to the Albanach, pulls his leg back, and kicks him square in the groin. Finn loses his balance completely and falls into the blackness underneath Dali's tilting dancefloor. The Nazarene stands looking over the edge, watching Finn twist and spin farther into the blackness. The Nazarene turns away from the edge of the dancefloor and sits down heavily in one of the chairs. He folds his arms across his breast as if to warm himself from some awful chill. As he closes his tired eyes, the Nazarene shouts out loudly for all the stars and the shinywhite moon to hear.

"Perdition!" he shouts. "Perdition awaits you, Albanach!"

Tumbling headlong into the emptiness Finn, ever defiant, sticks out his right hand, the index finger pointing straight up into the surrounding air.

"Perdition my arse!" he screams as he falls, head over heels, down, down, down.

◆ ◆ ◆

Finn sits on the cold, stone floor of Coit Tower, and the remembered words of the Nazarene bump and bang their way through his seizure-beaten brain. He still feels like throwing up, throwing up

*over everything within reach, himself included. Sick to death!
When he falls over the edge of Dali's tilting dancefloor the word
perdition falls with him too, and as he spins and tumbles through
the firmament the word tumbles likewise through his mind. He
drifts, falling like a leaf, all the way down to the ground. It occurs
to both of us at the same time that we've been falling downward
ever since we entered Silverbright's cave. First down through the
pool and then down through the firmament underneath a sky we've
never seen before, where stars sparkle the likes of which neither of
us have ever seen before either. The word Hell crosses his mind, as
it crosses my own. Down and down we tumble and Finn still can't
get the Nazarene's last words out of his mind.*

"Perdition awaits you, Albanach."

"Perdition my ass," says Finn, wondering again where he's
landed. "What the hell's perdition anyway except an old damn
word nobody uses any more. Maybe it doesn't even exist; maybe
there is no perdition! No hell after all!" He looks up at the sky and
laughs into the wind. "Eternal damnation my ass. What a miserable
concept!" he says. "What a miserable fuckin' concept!"

He laughs when he thinks of Stevenson. After all, isn't
Stevenson longdead? And then there's the redeyed devil who
haunts him and follows him everywhere. The Shapeshifter! What
else could he do but laugh in the midst of all this craziness?
Laughing is all he can do to keep himself from going over that
other edge, the edge of sanity, out into the outer reaches of the real
madness, out into the realm of the real naked craziness where he'll
end up walking through lonely, crowded streets talking and
chuckling to himself.

But I smile too as I watch him sitting there on the tower floor.

He knows he's been in the Land of the Truly Alive ever since he
fell into the pool in old Silverbright's cave. That much is certain,
though it isn't anything like he's imagined. It isn't nearly as different
from ordinary reality as he thought it might be. He'd been expecting
beauty, birds singing in trees bountiful with fruit and all manner
of loveliness, and streets crowded with fine, golden figures; but all
he's seen so far is a dead writer, Grotesques, an evil spirit in the

form of Redeyes, bad memories come alive, and a man from Nazareth. As he scrutinizes his surroundings, he notices that Coit Tower has become a shambles, a wreck, with broken glass and bricks and pieces of painted plaster strewn everywhere.

He walks over to the wall where I sit watching him. I'm perched on top of a flat part of the broken tower, my knees tucked up under my robe, my arms around my legs, waiting to see what he'll do next, wondering what the fates might next have in store for him.

The sun peeks her head up over the horizon to the east, above the smoking remains of what used to be the city of Oakland. With some amazement Finn leans over the edge of the wall and looks down, looks down upon the ruins of North Beach and San Francisco. All of Telegraph Hill and the surrounding area lies in ruins below the tower. He turns and casts a furtive glance over the waters of the San Francisco Bay "Jeezus!" he gasps, when he sees two broken ends of the Bay Bridge jutting out over the water like the jagged ends of broken teeth. Plumes of smoke trickle up into the dawning day all around him, and the smell of fogdampened cinders grabs his attention like a nightmare, reminding him of the bitter night they found the downed cargo plane in the jungle so many years before.

"What's happened?" he says, very quietly. What in God's name's happened? he wonders, as if he really doesn't want to know, as a sense of dread fills his tightening stomach. He knows he's back in North Beach again, but it isn't the North Beach he knew. Something's gone awry. Maybe the last great earthquake came and went, he thinks. Perhaps at last the Big One's already been here. But where's all the people? Surely there are at least some survivors. Then he remembers he is indeed in the Land of the Truly Alive where anything goes, the place where spirits of every description commingle in some manner of strange communion, vying for the souls of those in the ordinary, workaday world. He wonders if the ordinary workaday world even exists any more, or if it ever did exist.

But it's all beginning to make some kind of sense, he believes. Even Mary and Johnny and that armless bastard Romeo who pushes Ivy League, the dead junkie soldier, around in his shopping cart. It's not even a dream.

"This is some hardcore reality I have to get through," he mumbles.

I'm relieved to hear him acknowledge that much at least, though I feel now a great sadness sitting there on the broken wall watching him. His nose tingles and his chest swells up with sadness, with loneliness, his eyes tearful and fearful. Will he survive? I wonder. Will he make it to the other side, to the end of his journey? I can hear the Great White Bull screaming in the far-off jungle, and I can hear again Johnny Quinn's desperate, begging plea through his shattered face: "YOU PROMISED!" Can Finn hear these things too? I hope he can. I hope he realizes his journey isn't done, that it's just beginning. No, he isn't done, not by a long shot, not even close! I feel my own nose tingle tearfully as I remember how young and naive he was when he kicked me out of his body. He was so confused then he didn't know what else to do. How could he know, really? Confusion is a natural reaction, I suppose, to the shock he experienced after the massacre of the bull. He doesn't know that by kicking me out he kicked out everything that was good in him, and that I was his saving grace. That's why I'll never let him go, that's why I can't let him go. I'll hold onto him with dear sweet life. Even if it's but with an imaginary umbilical cord that continues to drip dark, thick blood.

But twenty-year-olds know nothing, that's the sadness of it all. They think they know everything! Yet from the moment of The Leaving, *as I will always call it, Finn has to go through life living with his emptiness, wondering always what was wrong with him.*

He knows he's an Empty, yet he still doesn't know what has made him so, a fate worse than death itself, to be sure. Finn MacDonald lives with fear and bewilderment. He looks full circle again around the tower, then walks around and around in a circle going faster and faster, his eyes wide and mad, tears streaming down his face. Then he runs around the tower floor, jumping over and dodging the rubble strewn all about, going ever faster and faster. He stops and throws himself to the ground in the middle of the smokedusty floor and beats the ground with both his fists, all the while screaming like a poor soul locked up in Bedlam.

"Who are you?" he screams. "Where are you, where the hell are you, you sneaky bastard coward?"

I jump from my wall perch, stunned at this admission of his, this admission that he isn't alone. And I have hope, though it's soon dashed when he picks up a piece of the broken tower and beats himself around the head, as if possessed, until the blood bursts from him and mingles with the tears streaming from his eyes.

"Fuck you!" he screams, then stands, his arms now quietly by his sides, like a stonequiet statue. Presently he rubs his hands over his face then looks for long minutes at the blood on his hands.

I stand motionless beside him. He must feel my presence, because he looks through red-rimmed eyes in my direction.

"I know you're there," he says. "I know something's there. Why do you keep fucking with me, trying to hurt me?"

He walks in circles once more.

"Tell me," he says, looking down again at his hands. "Will I always have blood on my hands?"

He walks faster and faster until he's broken into a run once more, all the while screaming the word blood. "Blood, blood, blood," he screams. Faster, faster, faster, he runs, dervish-like, madly then, with a final great effort, runs and jumps straight out over the broken edge of the tower wall, out into the emptiness of the world beyond.

I feel within myself the dull, deadweight thud with which he hits the concrete below. I feel it as surely as if it is me who has fallen. I look over the edge and see him lying on the ground in a twisted, ugly position.

Finn MacDonald, the Albanach, looks dead.

I run down the stairs of the tower to where he lies bleeding and broken. He has already been joined by the Albanach warrior who took him back to the big house. He still wears the tartan and kilted plaid of the Alba of much earlier days.

"I come from the People of Peace," says the warrior. He's looking straight into my eyes.

"I know, I know quite well who you are," says I.

The warrior smiles and turns Finn over onto his back and ministers to him in the soothing language of the Old Ones, and by moving his hands, in a wavelike motion, over Finn's body. He looks up at me, the smile now gone, and speaks as solemnly as I have ever heard anyone speak.

"Redeyes has found him," he says.

"I know; he's been following us for a long, long time."

The Albanach laughs.

"Aye, he has. A very long time indeed," he says.

"And he's taken over the body of Soldiergirl!"

"Och, I know that too," says the warrior. "He did that a long time ago. But, come! We'll take Finn to a place of safety; we can talk more later."

Then he picks Finn up. He simply grabs him under the knees and under his armpits and lifts him effortlessly, then trudges through the dusty ruins of North Beach. As he marches, the warrior hums an old song, an old fighting song by the sounds of it.

I'm not so adept at the Gaelic as I would like to be; I haven't used it myself in such a long time. But I feel the spirit of the song, and I smile at the gay figure of the Albanach as he marches, carrying Finn's heavy body as if it were a rag doll, his kilt swishing proudly from side to side with each step he takes. When the song's finished I feel emboldened myself, filled with the old fighting spirit, if you will. And he is friendly, this warrior; he seems only to have Finn's well-being in mind.

"Who are you really?" I ask.

The warrior looks up sharply. "Yae don't know? Yae really don't know?"

"Well I know you're from Alba and I know you're ancient, but other than that, I have no idea."

"There's time enough for that," is all he says.

We've only walked a few blocks through the North Beach ruins when we stop in front of an old, dilapidated storefront on what is left of Grant Avenue. The windows are broken out and the door is missing, but we enter anyway. We walk into the back of the store and the Albanach places Finn down on the rubblestrewn floor. The warrior lifts up a trapdoor revealing a huge, candlelit basement. It is only with great difficulty that he reaches the bottom of the stairs but, that done, he puts Finn down onto a straw mattress, covered with beautiful woolen shawls.

The warrior ministers to Finn and, as I watch intently, marveling at his skilled hands at work, I'm sure I detect a fluttering beneath Finn's eyelids. Then I hear a cruel rasping, hacking cough coming from the shadows behind me. I spin quickly around and behold again the dandy figure of Stevenson, his walking stick still held tightly in his feeble hand.

"You!" I shout, both with fear and joy, not knowing which Stevenson it might be. "I never thought I'd see you again."

I can't help but stare at his walking stick.

"No snakes here," he says, holding his walking stick out in front of him. He's referring to the shapeshifter, of course. "Your memory mistreats you," he continues. "Do you not remember the words of old Silverbright, young lady? Or is it young man?" he adds with a cheeky smile. "Remember," he says, "I am his guide!"

"And I am his spirit, Mr. Stevenson. You should know all about such a disconcerting proposition!"

He lets out a loud, mischievous laugh at that, though it is sadly cut short by his awful cough.

"Aye, to be sure, to be sure indeed," he says, his clenched fist once more placed over his heaving chest.

"Look! He's returning!" interjects the Albanach warrior. "The man from Alba's coming back!"

Stevenson ignores him and looks at me solemnly.

"What you say is more true than you can imagine, Madman. I have had many a long day to study such a proposition, and I can assure you that neither you nor Finn is alone in this task you have before you. There is another part to this equation that had escaped me entirely until just very recently."

"Oh!" says I, my senses all suddenly on high alert.

"Has Finn acknowledged you yet, seen you perhaps?"

"Before he fell he acknowledged my presence. He was certain he wasn't alone."

"But did he know it was you, did he give any indication that it was you in particular he addressed?"

"Well, no," says I, feeling a bit miffed. "Not in so many words."

"It's as I suspected," says Stevenson, who then sits down heavily, leaning again on his stick with both hands. "It was Redeyes," he continues. "That's why Finn seemed to jump over the tower wall. Redeyes tried to enter him, tried to force himself back inside him. But he's fighting back, our Finn. He felt the evil bastard try to enter him and he closed himself up much more than usual. The force of the collision threw him over the tower wall."

"He does the same with me. Closes himself, that is."

"Aye, to be sure," says Stevenson. "But he doesn't feel so threatened by you. He simply doesn't know what's happening. He really doesn't know he's an Empty, doesn't even understand the concept."

"So it was Redeyes he felt, not me," says I, feeling both sad and not a little disappointed.

"Listen to me, Madman, the mistake I made when I was writing *Jekyll and Hyde* is that I thought man had a dual nature, that he is made up of two parts, good and evil. Well, that may be true to a certain extent. The mistake I made was to concentrate only on the evil side of man; I had a character who was completely evil, but I didn't have a character who, like yourself, was completely good. I should have!"

I interrupt him: "I'm not so sure I'm getting your drift," I say.

"Listen," he says. "All I had was a character who was a little bit good and a little bit bad, my Doctor Jekyll; and another who was all bad, all evil, my Mr. Hyde of course. But man's true nature is, more accurately, made up of three distinct parts: good, evil, and the composite whole, the man himself. One, two, three parts! The triad of man for want of a more precise term. And so it clearly is with Finn, Madman. He has you, the good side of his spirit, and he has Redeyes, the evil side. My story should have been named not *Jekyll and Hyde*, but *Jekyll and Hyde and the Other One!*" He lets out with a loud chortling laugh then, slapping his knee in accompaniment.

"Wait a minute," says I. "Are you saying what I think you're saying?"

"Most likely!" he replies, calming down somewhat. "If you are asking me if Redeyes is a part of Finn, as much a part of him as you are, then the answer is most certainly yes!"

"Rubbish," says I, furiously. "How can that possibly be?"

"Only when both you and Redeyes are back inside him will he be full, complete—a whole person!"

"Are you saying then that I must live within the Albanach alongside that old bastard Redeyes?"

"Precisely! He will never be complete, he will never be full unless you do so. And, remember, you did until Finn and his comrades massacred the bull. He kicked you out, yes, but he also kicked Redeyes out. You both resided inside him vying for his everlasting soul which, of course, is both of you."

I think deeply for a moment. "Perhaps that's why Finn calls me Madman," says I. "Maybe he feels Redeyes, a man, just as much as he feels me!"

"Most likely," says Stevenson. "You must remember that Redeyes is an integral part of what makes Finn Finn—just as you are."

I'm stunned. Too shocked to even consider further the proposition Stevenson has just thrown in my face. Meantime the Albanach warrior is growing more excited. Finn is indeed coming to! Stevenson notices the agitation. He gets up from his seat and walks over to Finn.

"Yae did a fine job," he says to the warrior, who beams a big smile, then says:

"Och, I know, Mr. Stevenson, but that's what I do! It was no bother after all."

Stevenson smiles and looks down upon Finn who now blinks in bewilderment.

"What the hell," he says, trying to rise from his bed of straw and, failing, falls back again.

"I think you'd better rest awhile," says Stevenson. "You've just been through a rather harrowing experience."

Stevenson chuckles, but the chuckle ends abruptly. We hear the sound of footsteps crossing the floor above us. When our company of friends hears the sound we stiffen, Stevenson included—even if he does know so much. When the trapdoor opens we jump to our feet, even Finn who has barely recovered from his own fall. The Albanach warrior tries to run toward the stairs to bolt the trapdoor, but before he reaches halfway, he stops dead in his tracks, rooted as if he's been growing there for years. For the first time in all of my wanderings through Finn's Shopping Cart Soldier life I see Redeyes closeup, though he still inhabits the broken, dead body of Soldiergirl, her head still held tightly under her left arm, her neck and head still dripping blood. She looks half-dead, her skin chalky-white and wan, and my thoughts harken back to what Stevenson recently said about the three parts of man. I realize that Soldiergirl *is* half-dead because she has no good side. All she has inside her is Redeyes, the ultimate evil, like Mr. Hyde, and he's dragging her body through the years like an old rag doll, refusing even to let her spirit rest in peace. Soldiergirl isn't even an Empty. She is less than an Empty, because her body has been invaded by a spirit other than her own. When Soldiergirl speaks, it is with the voice of an older man, a much older man, and the noise it makes is like the sound of words after they tumble around in a vat of thick mud and stone. It's an utterly demoralizing sound.

"At last," says Soldiergirl, "it's my turn to talk!"

She descends the stairs slowly, deliberately, all the while smiling and nattering in a very strange and, seemingly, very old language the nuances of which even I can't understand. Soldiergirl then takes her head in both hands, lowers it to her navel and points it straight at Finn.

"Hello, Finn," says she. "Remember me?"

Finn screams, then scurries, like a cockroach, into the furthermost corner of the basement, well behind the rest of us.

I stare, confused, at Stevenson. He looks back at me and smiles sadly.

"He's got a body, Madman. He stole a corporeal body and that's why Finn can see him."

"But I have a body too," I complain.

Soldiergirl lets out a loud, ugly laugh in her mud and stone manvoice.

"But it's *his* body I want," says she, pointing off toward Finn.

"Your body is that of a spirit," says Stevenson. "That's why he can't see you. He can feel you though; has felt you, but he can't see you."

I'm about to say something to Stevenson about my own confusion, my inability to comprehend all that's taking place, when Soldiergirl's head suddenly swooshes, with the speed of light, to the back of the basement where Finn sits cowering in his corner, pushing, pushing, pushing as if trying to force himself through the bricks of the basement wall. The head hovers above Finn for a brief moment, then lowers itself until Soldiergirl's nose touches the tip of Finn's nose and, in a voice like all the demons from the annals of history screaming in unison, it cries out: "TAKE ME BACK!" But it's all too much for Finn and he collapses in a faint against the wall. Unconscious as he now is, unable to protect himself, he has become vulnerable. Every bit as quickly as the head of Soldiergirl I rush over to Finn's side and lie on top of him, my arms spread defensively before me. The head of Soldiergirl laughs and, in a flash, is joined by her body. The arms reach out, take hold of the head, and sit it back on top of her neck. The complete though mangled body kneels before me and, in a voice surprisingly bereft of malice, speaks to me with great deliberation.

"I too am a part of him," says Redeyes through the mouth of Soldiergirl. "He is me also! Even if you do get back inside him, he will never be complete without me!"

I feel Finn stir beneath me, then I move to his side where I stand, challenging and unafraid. Redeyes laughs.

"Hello, Finn," he says when Finn opens his eyes completely. Finn tries to push himself through the wall again, though less vehemently than before.

"It wasn't my fault," he says. "You tried to kill me. If Romeo

Robinson hadn't chopped your head off, you would've. I didn't even know you!"

Soldiergirl reaches under her silky black pajama blouse and pulls out a pint bottle of vodka.

"This is for you," she says, handing the bottle to Finn. "Go ahead, drink it and open up your heart to me. Let me in; it's where I belong!" Soldiergirl smiles evilly before going on. "Don't worry about the past, Finn; it's over, unrecoverable, unchangeable! But you must take me back!"

Finn looks long and hard at the bright, clear liquid and trembles at the sight of it. He takes the bottle in his hands, unscrews the top and raises the bottle to his lips. He drinks deeply, thankfully.

Soldiergirl's body then walks into the middle of the basement floor and stands looking at us with an expression of pure hatred twisting her face. She metamorphoses just as Stevenson did on Dali's tilting dancefloor. In a moment, the body of Soldiergirl changes into the body of Johnny Quinn as it was when we last saw him: broken and bloody beyond recognition. Blood runs thickly onto the stone floor of the basement. He stands shakily on the torn and bloody stubs of his legs. He is in great pain, because the jagged ends of his leg bones stick out below the knee joints, and it is these pieces of bone he is forced to walk upon. He falls back, at last, onto his haunches and rubs at his stubs. Tears of unadulterated pain seep through his screwed-up eyes. "Help me, Finn," he begs. "For the love-a God help me." He sounds like he's got a lisp as he tries to talk through his shattered face. The whole right side has been blown away and looks like a naked skull. His right eye hangs out over his cheek and stares straight at Finn, who is filled with terror. When Johnny speaks through his lisp, it is with the same mud and stone manvoice as Soldiergirl used. Everything has changed except the voice, as if Redeyes can change everything except that which lives deep inside him. Perhaps even Stevenson hadn't realized this when he told Finn that Redeyes could change everything but his eyes!

"What she said about *The Leaving*," continues Johnny, "is true!

That's how it happened all right. No doubt about it!" he says, looking and pointing straight at me, ignoring completely the horrible pain Johnny is suffering, intent only on getting his point across. "But what *that* bitch doesn't understand," he continues, "doesn't realize, is that I was that undefinable, bonepenetrating spear of icy coldness that swept over her all those long years ago. I am *cold*. I *am* cold. I'm also many other things. The good one there thinks she's it, thinks goodness is all there is to life. Hound of Heaven my dark, evil ass; Hound of Hell's more to the point. She's so good, so fucked-up good, she doesn't even know I *exist!* You might say, then, that if I'm cold, she must be hot! Right? Okay, I'll buy that. We are, after all, opposites. The problem is that she can't see past her nose. She's so good, she doesn't even understand bad! It just doesn't register, penetrate her self-induced inability to see! That's how fucked-up she is. I *am* bad. What could be more simple? That's my fuckin' job, for chrissake, to be bad! It's me an' my ilk who make you fuck your daughters, bugger your sons, make you kick and walk over the beggarman lyin' in the street with his hand out lookin' for a few lousy PENNIES! Goddamn you. I'm every bit as evil as she is good. So fuck you! That's the truth of it! There's no denying my evil. I enjoy all the bad things, all the things you aren't supposed to enjoy. Like booze, dope, sex, war, pain, pedophilia, betrayal, violence— abuses of every sort imaginable. All that sorta stuff. Murder and mayhem. My specialties! I *am* murder and mayhem. That's what I *am!*"

Johnny seems ready to collapse, actually looks as dead as he should have, but Redeyes is having none of it. He won't let the dead man rest. He jolts Johnny as if he's just prodded him from the inside out; Johnny dances on his stubby legs, leaving trails of dark vein-blood behind him. As he dances, a slow, waltzy dance, he keeps time, or Redeyes does, by singing a popular American ballad. He looks straight into Finn's eyes.

"All of me," he sings. *"Why not take all of me...can't you see that I'm no good without you...."*

Redeyes makes the body of Johnny dance faster and faster around the room, pirouetting and swirling gaily on his hands and the strength of his still-strong arms. He sprays blood all over us as he spins and spins and spins. Johnny, or the remnant of Johnny that might still be lingering around his body, is anguished beyond measure. Redeyes makes Johnny smile and laugh as he speaks, a horror show of anguish, pain and laughter. It seems as if Redeyes doesn't care, that he knows something the rest of us don't know. He has a supreme confidence of sorts, as if he can do no wrong, or that everything will be just as he planned or imagined it might be. He drags Johnny's broken body around the room, stopping briefly here and there in front of each of us as if to emphasize his self-proclaimed air of superiority. Johnny leaves a trail of blood along the floor like the trail of a big black slug after a night of rain. Redeyes becomes more angry as he walks, more hateful.

"Piss everybody off I say," he continues. "Mix it up, that's my motto. Husband against wife. Son against daughter. The sky against the earth. Dark against light. I like to massage the earth, caress it with my firm, cold hands until it moves, until it squeals with delight and belches forth rivers of lava or creaks and groans in great rippling chasms underneath the skin, deep in the bellies of cities. That's what we do, me and my ilk. We create terrors of every kind. We alone create Vietnams in the minds of men and it is they who put our desires into action. Horror is our game, assholes! Don't *ever* forget it!"

Finn looks as if he's somehow beyond fear. He puts his hand over his mouth to stop the puke from rising, but it does anyway, landing all over his legs and on the ground beside him. Redeyes laughs and walks over to Finn.

"This is yours," he says, pointing to the bullet hole in his forehead. Just then a stream of blood shoots out of the hole and splatters all over Finn's face. "Remember?" continues Redeyes. "I don't want you to forget nothin', goddamn you!"

Finn puts his hand over his face in an attempt to get away from his tormentor, but all he does instead is go deeper inside his own mind, as if there is no possible escape from the horror, from his memories. He knows what Redeyes is talking about. He knows the evil well. Everything Redeyes says is true. The jolts Finn receives from Redeyes' hellish speeches take him back to the jungle. The bull is dead. Johnny is dead. Frankie is dead. The Viet Cong soldiers are dead and mutilated. Ivy league is dead and mutilated. Soldiergirl is dead and... Finn is standing still, his machete swinging by his side. Smoke and the smell of cordite and death permeate the air. It is quiet except for the rain dripping from the treetops. The spirits of the dead hover in the treetops, confused but not surprised. Finn lets out a loud anguished wail and, seeing the headless body of Soldiergirl, runs over to her, all his anger and fear and hatred once more filling him. He takes Soldiergirl's head in one hand and, with two sharp and steady swipes of his machete, chops off her ears. "Bitch," he shouts. He gets up and walks away from the dead and mutilated body of Soldiergirl and stuffs her ears into the breast pocket of his fatigue shirt.

Redeyes howls with delight. "See! I told yae so! That's what we do, me an' my ilk." He looks at Finn. "You do remember, ya sonofabitch. An' don't you ever forget that you do remember! 'Cause if yae do, I'll always be there to remind you!"

At this stage of Redeyes' macabre and mad performance, the Albanach warrior wails as if he's in great pain. Redeyes laughs all the more. Stevenson, strangely enough, now has a wry smirk plastered onto his face.

"We use men as if they were putty in the hands of a child!" says Redeyes. "She and her kind try to fix what we fuck up, but they're losing ground rapidly. We are winning! We have made wonderful leaps forward these last few years. Nobody tries to be like me; everybody tries to be like her. Or so they claim at least. What nobody understands is that you can't have one without the other. That is the first law of the universe: there is no good without me, without evil! Get used to it! Nobody would ever admit it, but some folk do like me, they like the power I give them. Your mother wouldn't like me. But your sister might. You see what I mean? You get my drift? Take Finn for example. He wasn't always the way he is now. He really was innocent at one time. I hate to admit it, but she had more of a grip on him at one time than I did. In other words, he *was* innocent. Perhaps I introduced him to the real world too soon, that night over there in the jungle, on the night of the bull. That's why he kicked us out, me an' the bitch, that is. The shock of the killing was too much for him. But after the killing he was *all* mine. I had him!"

"You take too much for granted," says Finn. "You didn't have nobody. I was in a war, that's all."

"You've got to be kidding," says Redeyes. "The way you mutilated Soldiergirl, the way you used her ears to scare the rookies? That wasn't evil?"

"That was just war for chrissake. Fuck you!"

But Finn knew Redeyes was right. He knew he was right, because he remembered what he was like after that night. When they pulled him from combat claiming "Battle Fatigue", he'd already done it all, seen it all. More combat in the booby-trapped, tiger-shitted jungle he hated so much. The muck, the squishy-wet boots, the redness of blood mixed with the green of the jungle fatigues, and the whiteness of splintered bone sticking out through traumatized body-bits; intestines held in pale, pale, trembling hands, and kids younger even than he crying through long hard tears for their mammies. Oh, yes, those tears, those goddamned heavy tears that no one walking around in a city street, going about his ordinary, daily business, could ever, ever understand. I don't know how many times I heard him praying to his God. "Oh, God, please help me. Oh, God, please, I beg you, please forgive me."

The hootches they lived in were hellish. All those grunts crammed into those stinking, tiny spaces, sleeping on those tiny little camp beds. Those hootches bred contempt. Contempt for the army, for the government, for everybody back home in "The World" calling us babykillers—contempt even for that stupid goddamned actress up there in Hanoi spouting out all her crap about how bad we were and how wrong it was that we were there. And contempt for all authority. Oh, yes, authority sucked.

"I had to work my ass off," says Redeyes, "wreaking havoc as usual, creating the carnage. All the brothers, the black dudes, are pissed off, as are their white brothers. The military police have cracked down on the mamasans who brought the heroin onto the camp, and the consequent shortage of smuggled heroin is becoming dangerously intolerable. Grunts are beginning to jones, violence is in the air, tempers are frayed. Something bad is about to happen, and it does one beautiful July night."

"Yeah, it was beautiful all right," says Finn, "depending on your perspective. It was beautiful for you, you hateful, Redeyed cocksucker, because the carnage was worse than anything I'd ever experienced, worse than anything any of us had ever experienced. But we stuck together, all of us, because we were brothers. You knew that and you used it to your own ends. You knew we'd stick together, an' you used that against us, ya miserable old fuck."

"Hey, come on, Finn," says Redeyes, laughing. "It was the fourth of July. The sky was a deep, midnight blue and all the stars were twinkling as they ought in that beautiful night sky. What more could you ask for? All you needed to complete the day were a few fireworks."

"You took everything we had left of our humanity. Every last remnant, every last vestige of our humanity—you took it all, the lot! I'll never be forgiven for that night. Every year when the fourth of July rolls around I go out into the country as far as I can, and I try to turn myself into an animal, I try to become a beast of the woods. Most of the time I just wish I were a spider or some other kinda bug so that I can hide under a hard rock and keep the world away from me. More to the point, I try to keep myself away from the world, because I know what's inside me, I know what I'm capable of. It scares me and it horrifies me."

"Oh, don't be so hard on yourself," interjects Redeyes. "You were just being your bad self. You can't deny your bad self, Finn; it's inside you and always will be."

Finn falls silent and, with his hand over his eyes, begins to cry like a man who is truly, truly sorry for some past misdeed. He cries and silently begs for forgiveness, and no wonder he thinks, God help us all. The hellish incident comes rushing back to him as if he's just left it.

It happens so quickly there is hardly any time to think about it. Finn goes to Leroy Hamilton's hootch to score some heroin; he is jonesing so bad the sweat pours from him and his limbs ache as if someone is pressing his bones in a vice, and the pain in his gut is excruciating. But Leroy, whom they called "Spider" because of his ability to hide in the bush and just seem to blend with it so well, doesn't have any to sell. He's getting ready to fire up when Finn walks into his hootch; they are good buddies, Finn and Spider, so Spider offers to share his hit with Finn. Spider is sure that another shipment will be reaching him soon, but it won't be enough for him to sell in the usual way; it'll be just enough for himself and his closest buddies. Spider always seems able to get that much at least and his buddies are ever so grateful.

The war within the war in Vietnam was nearly as bad as the war itself. The juice freaks against the "heads" as they called themselves. The juice freaks liked whiskey and beer, and the heads liked smoking dope and shooting up China white or dropping acid. The juice freaks liked the war, reveled in it; the heads hated it and they all wished they were back in the World, preferably in Haight Ashbury. The two groups recognized each other and tried to stay out of each other's way. But with the shortage of heroin becoming so acute, the situation had become intolerable; a tension had built and was turning into pure and unadulterated hatred. The MP's were doing all they could to keep the smack from the junkies, and that's not a smart thing to do—especially in a war zone where everybody's walking around armed to the teeth. Anyway, a soldier has to have something, after all, to get him through the carnage without losing his mind completely.

"It's them motherfuckin MP's," Spider says, as he ties himself off to shoot up. "We hafta do somethin', man; nah, we're *gonna* do somethin'!"

"What the fuck do yae think yae can do against them bastards?" Finn asks.

Spider closes his eyes, enjoying the ride as the heroin courses through his system. He almost nods off completely, but shakes his head a few times, then hands what's left in the rig to Finn. Finn ties himself off, getting ready for his hit.

"Tonight, man," says Spider. "We're gonna frag 'em tonight. Fuck them cocksuckers!"

"How are yae gonnae do that, Spider? Yae might get one or two, but that ain't gonnae help nothin'."

Finn's American accent has improved immensely since he's been in Vietnam.

"Nah, bro. They're havin' a barbecue in their compound. We'll get the whole fuckin' lotta them."

Finn's eyes close too when the heroin hits his bloodstream. "I don't want nothin' to do wi' that, man. That's fuckin' nuts."

Spider lifts up his pillow and there, underneath it, sit four fragmentation grenades and a Colt 45, stolen, no doubt, from some rookie Lieutenant.

"Take your pick," says Spider.

Finn stares at the armaments for a long time before picking up one of the grenades. He doesn't want any part of the Colt; it's too traceable.

Johnny Quinn's still hobbling around along the basement floor taking it all in, watching Finn like a hawk. I know Redeyes is inside Johnny's head and that he in turn is inside Finn's head listening to every word Finn's thinking. Johnny's smiling, because Redeyes is enjoying every moment of Finn's replay of his first fourth of July under the banner of his adopted country. Everybody else is churchmouse quiet, waiting, just waiting, for something to be said or something to happen. Each of us knows that it isn't our place or time to talk; it is either Finn's or Redeyes' and we all know that, so we are quiet, muted, waiting. It's Redeyes who speaks first, as usual.

"What's up, Finn. You too chickenshit to tell 'em what happened? If I'd known yae were such a chickenshit I'd have picked some other poor fucker to live in."

"I wish yae had, asshole," says Finn. He looks up at Redeyes. "Why'd you have to use Johnny's body anyway? You too chickenshit to show your real self. Why don't you leave the poor bastard alone; he never done you any harm."

Redeyes ignores him. "They are smart, these junkie grunts," he says. "There's only four of them. Spider keeps the Colt 45 and a frag grenade. The other three each have a grenade. They each stand at one of the four sides of the square compound which is surrounded by a six-foot-high wooden fence. They have coordinated the time so that each of the grenades will land at precisely the same moment. They have also been smart enough to wait until the big, fat juicy T-bone steaks have been barbequed and eaten. Satiated with food, the MP's turn up the country music and begin the serious drinking. In the darkness, the four junkie grunts, lovely lads that they are, lob the frags into the crowd of twenty-five or thirty drunk MP's.

"The ensuing pandemonium is a delight to watch," continues Redeyes. "Bang, bang, bang, bang! It is *lovely*. It is absolutely smashing, more than I could ever have wished for. Three or four dead and on their way to hell. And each and every other one of them hit by the awful shrapnel. Legs and arms, and even a piece of someone's head lie all over the concrete which is quickly being dyed red with spilled blood. Our smart friend, Finn, and his buddies run like hell, but only for a moment. They quickly return to the scene of my lovely carnage and help clean up the mess. They actually have the balls, the audacity, to go back there right away, acting surprised and shocked, and help to pick up pieces of bodies and other debris while, up above, gunships send down their floodlights hoping to find the perpetrators of the madness that has just occurred.

"They were never found out, and within two days the flow of heroin onto the base made it seem as if the Golden Triangle were just up the road a bit. Finn and Spider and the other two junkies received commendations for their bravery in helping their fallen comrades. I was in my glory, my pure fuckin' glory, and I chalked up another success, another victory for evil. Ladies and gentlemen it gives me great pleasure to introduce to you Finn MacDonald, mass murderer. Fuck you, chickenshit!"

Redeyes bursts out laughing; he's thoroughly enjoying himself. Finn is sitting in a corner, beaten down, and shaken. He looks as if he's just been given a large doze of some strong tranquilizer, something a violent mental patient might be given to keep him quiet and subdued. He seems lifeless. The Albanach warrior sits in front of him as if to protect him. Stevenson sits leaning on his stick as he does, with both hands, his chin resting on his hands.

The craziness of this whole episode is that as I watch Johnny, and as I listen to Redeyes' vitriolic speech, I see him in a different light. I begin to understand him, and to feel his desire to be where he and I both need to be: inside Finn. Like a revelation, an epiphany, I see him not as Johnny or as his old ugly self, but as a young man in his early twenties, much the same age as me. He is young, darkhaired, good-looking. He doesn't look evil at all. I become frightened, wondering where these thoughts come from. They are confusing. Like myself, Redeyes wants only to be back inside Finn's body. As I struggle with these warm thoughts of him, Redeyes turns on me with a venomous outburst, his eyes still blazing red! I know then where these thoughts come from. They come from him. He's working me as he's been working Finn. He looks at me with his hateful eyes.

"He was a soldier, ya crazy bitch! He was a goddamned hero! That's why I like him so much. He killed lots an' lotsa people. It wasn't easy for him though. Most blood he'd ever seen up until his war days was when he cut his goddamned finger or when he punched his pal, bloodying his nose. But that was me too. I made him punch his pal. That's my job! You know, Madman, you were right about the whole bull episode. Finn was such an innocent he went into shock when the bull was murdered. He just didn't understand that the universe was working exactly as it must, exactly as it should. It shocked him so badly he emptied himself. He did become an Empty that night. When he kicked you an' me out of his body, our home, he became an Empty. And Empties don't have no conscience! That much is true. It was on that night that he became more like me, more evil that is. I had him. Didn't I, Finn?"

Redeyes looks furtively around the room, almost desperately, as if he isn't quite sure of himself. Perhaps he's gone too far with his bragging, his wild bravado.

"Get used to the concept of Emptiness," he says, looking now directly at each of the gathered company of friends. "There are so many Empties, those whose spirits are gone, it's mind boggling! The problem here is that both he and the bitch think there's only two parts to this equation. Herself and himself! But she's so squeaky clean she doesn't even know I exist; Finn on the other hand knows I exist. He must; he's seen my handiwork first hand. He's lived it; he's been it! But they're both in denial, heavy denial. There's three parts to this equation. And I am the third part. I am the knitting needles of this triad known as Finn MacDonald. I am what makes him complete. You didn't tell them the rest of the story, Madman. You didn't tell them what happened later, did you? I was working my ass off, fighting for my very existence. He was my body too, my shell too. I needed him just as you did. I had to fight like hell that night to get back inside him. I like him. He's the only person in the whole wide world I like. But I'm a selfish bastard. I like him only because I need him, I need his body. I'm homeless, you see. His body is my home. I just thank the devil daily that I don't need sleep. I flit around in the atmosphere as you do. I can't do my work unless I get back inside him. But neither can you. That's my only comfort. That you're homeless too, that you're powerless too."

Johnny metamorphoses once more. First he changes back into Soldiergirl, then he moves over to where wide-eyed Finn sits on the floor, terrified. Redeyes takes on the shapes of all of Finn's old friends and acquaintances. He becomes Ivy League, then Romeo, Frankie, Tommy and the whole company of dead Vietnam veterans. Finally, he rests in front of Finn as Soldiergirl once more.

"Hello, Finn," he says. "You'll remember this part of the story I'm sure." Redeyes looks around the room at the rest of us. "He kept those ears. Oh, yes, kept them in his shirtpocket until they had dried up like parchment. That's when the fun part of his war began, that's when I was able to get to work, albeit within my limited capacity, driving him outa his fuckin' mind. I did my best! Oh, yes, I did my best! I *am* evil. Get used to me!" He points over at Finn. "Why don't you tell them what you used to do with those ears. No, you don't have the guts, ya whimpering asshole. He liked to scare people with them. That's what he did with them. Dropped them into his mamasan's soup one day. The soup flew into the air, an' the mamasan flew the coup. Ran all the way to Hanoi for all we knew. Eh, Finn, that was a laugh. We laughed for days on end over that one. We never saw the mamasan again, did we? Well that was me too, folks!"

Suddenly Stevenson jumps in front of Redeyes, his stick held aloft ready to strike.

"All right, that's quite enough," he says. "We do indeed get your drift, but you can leave now!"

"I'll leave when I'm ready!" screams Redeyes.

"Has your memory failed you?" says Stevenson, pushing his walking stick out in front of him. "Remember what happened the last time I whacked you with it."

Redeyes smiles, turns, and walks, again deliberately and slowly, toward the stairs at the other end of the basement. He pauses there, deep in thought, then turns back.

"Fuck you, Stevenson. You wish I'd just walk away, but I'm here for the duration. I'm a fighter too, you know. But you know that, don't you? No, siree, I ain't goin' nowhere. Not just yet!"

I look over at Finn. He looks as if he's at the end of his rope. He's sitting in the same place with his arms around his knees. He's bug-eyed, staring down between his feet, rocking back and forth like some poor soul lost and forgotten in an insane asylum. His mind has gone back to that awful night and his head is filled with the sight of those bloody ears. When he looks at his hand he can feel the ears there as he slaps them down on top of the bar. He's in Saigon again. Stand Down time, a break in the war when they're pulled back from the jungle for a rest, a respite from the carnage and mayhem. He goes to the same bar all the time, looking for rookies. He's found one. A good-looking kid from the Deep South by the sound of him.

"You just get in-country?" Finn asks the rookie.

"Yeah," says the enthusiastic youngster, beaming with pleasure and pride that a crusty old vet like Finn would even give him the time of day. "Got in last night."

"Well, goddamn, soldier," says Finn, "buy yoursel' a beer!"

He slaps Soldiergirl's ears down hard on the counter, and when the rookie sees them he lets out a yelp and jumps back as if he's been hit by a train. The color leaves the kid's face, and if there weren't so many soldiers standing around him he'd swear he'd call out for his mammy. The barman and the bargirls and all the other weathered veterans laugh like hell and the poor young rookie, trying to keep it together, stumbles off to his hootch where he'll say his very first and earnest prayer for deliverance from this hell he's just found himself living in.

Finn takes his hands away from his face and looks up. I've been sending him messages of strength, and I think they might be getting through. He is sick to his stomach, but there's a strength building up inside him that I've seen before. It's the same strength that has kept him going all these years. The same strength that has made him determined to live, no matter what the past has to offer.

Perhaps Redeyes feels the strength rise in Finn too. He walks off slowly towards the stairs, smiling all the while. When he reaches the top of the stairs he turns and looks back at us.

"I'll see you all again soon," he says, "it's time now for me to get some rest. But I'll be back! Oh, yes, I'll be back!" With a wave, he disappears through the trapdoor of the basement ceiling.

Angered, Stevenson turns a disquieting shade of purple. He grabs the half-empty vodka bottle from Finn, spins around on his heels and smashes it against the opposite wall.

"Temper, temper, Louis," says Finn, reeking of false bravado. "Better watch that temper!"

Stevenson looks around the room, studying the troubled expressions on each of our faces. Then he smiles.

"Ach, don't look so worried," he says. "That was just Redeyes remember. Illusion is his game. We can take care of him all right. And don't you worry, Madman, our friend here will be quite all right. I'll take him to Alba. Let Gemini sort him out. Are yae ready?"

I nod affirmatively, though I'm not quite sure if I can be a part of Stevenson's confidence. I know he's trying to bolster our spirits, but I'm not so sure it's working.

"You," he says to Finn, "are you ready too?"

"Piss off," says Finn. "I'm going nowhere with you."

"But I'm your guide," says Stevenson, sardonically.

"I don't trust you! You could be that other Stevenson, your pal the shapeshifter. I don't know who the hell to trust."

"Don't be daft, man; I am who I say I am. Anyway, you don't have a choice. You'd better hurry though. Time, as I'm sure you've just realized, is running out, old chum. He wants you now more than he ever did. He senses an ending."

Finn feels desperate. A sense of futility sweeps over him, blanketing him in its heaviness. "Well, he's no' gettin' me," he says with the bravado of a child. He fidgets for a moment where he sits, then gets up unsteadily to his feet, all the while holding on to the wall for support. "Anyway, Stevenson," he continues. "I needed that drink; I don't want to have another fuckin' seizure—an' yae can think whatever the hell yae like!"

"Be that as it may," says Stevenson, "but we must go—quickly!"

With that, he begins tap, tap, tapping with his walking stick all the way to the other end of the basement. As he taps he talks.

"Don't worry, Albanach," he says, quietly. "We'll be back. We must go where we must go, but we'll be back."

"I'll join you too," says the warrior.

"No!" says Stevenson. "You must stay here. You may be needed here. If he comes back!"

The Albanach is disappointed at having to stay behind, and I can tell Finn needs another jolt of alcohol to keep him in something resembling a normal state. Stevenson, on the other hand, does his best to maintain an optimistic outlook as official guide to our motley crew while I do my best to brace Finn, in my own peculiar way, for whatever lies ahead. But I must admit here that my usual feeling of hopelessness regarding him seems to be changing to a feeling of frustration and even anger. I can't understand why, after all we've been through lately, he still won't recognize me or talk to me. I feel utterly dejected as we climb the dusty stairs leading to the ruined storefront up above us on Grant Avenue.

◆   ◆   ◆

The misty morning light from the dustdappled sun casts an ochre glow over the recently ruined buildings of San Francisco. We are walking along Grant Avenue, Finn, Stevenson and I, taking in the ruins all around us. The sun's warm already and feels good on our faces. I'm looking forward to climbing higher to get a different view of the city as it lies before us. I wonder if it really is all in ruins. Finn seems more inclined to accept things, without question, just as they are, as if he doesn't care any more or, more accurately perhaps, as if he is simply resigned to the way things are. Stevenson seems to be enjoying himself, happy to be out of the basement. He points his walking stick in the direction of the Tenderloin area, that part of the city where the poor folk live.

"Onward!" he says, like a true leader. "To the Tenderloin!"

"The Tenderloin?" asks Finn, incredulously. "Why the hell would yae want to go to the Tenderloin? It's spooky down there!"

"Don't worry, Finn. Nothing's the same as it ever was. Remember that! Anyway, it's there where you'll find your Alba. But first, the Peep show!"

"Peep show?" asks an utterly confused Finn.

"Aye, Albanach, Peep Show! Just a little detour. An educational foray into the wilderness to help you find your metaphoric way."

We trudge up Vallejo Street to the intersection at the Kearny Street steps. When we look down the steep incline of the steps we see that the manycolored neon lights of the Horny Ho, a popular strip club, still blink and beckon to the lovestarved among the nonexistent populace. All the other strip clubs stand in an ominous darkness.

I finally get my better view of the city. I can now see more of Nob Hill and Russian hill, and all of downtown lies spread out before us. Not one building as far as we can see stands as it did before. But before what? What's happened to San Francisco, I wonder, but the crisis of the present moment straddles my shoulders and brings me back to now, to the sight that lies before me. Finn laughs nervously. Stevenson catches his nervous laughter and points to the strip club.

"Good," he says. "It's open as I hoped it would be."

"We're not going in there, are we?" asks Finn.

"Aye, we are! Indeed we are," replies Stevenson, now laughing himself. "But this is a special strip club. It will add new meaning to the word nakedness!"

When they step into the dim interior of the Horny Ho they are met by a scrawny old man in a dark suit who has a toobig derby stuck on top of his head. The grey skin of his face and hands stretches over his thin bones like a drumskin, and his eyes are sunk far back in his skull. The old man steps forward and holds out a bony, withered hand.

"Five bucks each," he says, rubbing his hands together hungrily. "Best show in all the world," he continues, giggling greedily.

The old man's voice, though disguised in a phony New York accent, seems familiar to Finn, and when Finn sees the twinkle in the old fellow's eyes, and notices that he doesn't have any teeth, he realizes he's talking once more to Silverbright.

"Silverbright!" he shouts—facetiously, but happily. "What the hell are yae doin' here?"

Silverbright bursts out laughing himself, as does Stevenson, and with a sweep of his hand pulls off his derby and lets his long silver hair fall and cascade about his shoulders.

"Welcome," says Silverbright. "Welcome to another world. I am the barker to beat all barkers. I will introduce you to worlds beyond your wildest imaginings; I am the doorkeeper to your very soul. Suck in your gut, throw out your chest, and cross the threshold to discovery!"

Silverbright winks at Stevenson. "Make sure you've got lotsa quarters. Don't want yae runnin out halfway through the show."

Stevenson smiles. "Don't worry, Silverbright," he says. "We have plenty of quarters."

Silverbright sticks out his hand and grips Finn's in a vicelike grip. Then he shakes Stevenson's hand.

"Good, good," he says. "It's a wonderful show. It's all you needed but never expected."

"To be sure," says Stevenson. "To be sure!"

"Let's go then," says Finn. "No point in dallying."

"Well said, young fella, well said," says Silverbright.

Silverbright pulls aside the heavy black drape covering the doorway. All is darkness beyond.

"You like guarding these dark passageways, don't you, Silverbright?"

Silverbright chuckles. "It's my job, laddie, it's my job!"

"Come on, Finn," says Stevenson. "Let's go see the peep show; it's time for class!"

"All the very best of luck to yae, gentlemen," says Silverbright. "Give my regards to Broadway!" Then he lets go of the drape covering the door and leaves the two travelers standing all by themselves in the passageway.

"I don't like it in here," says Finn. "Reminds me of that other tunnel I was in. The one that began this whole journey."

"Aye, well that may be so, but this is where you need to be."

"Black as the Earl-a Hell's waistcoat, that's what it is."

"Tread lightly, Finn. Don't step on any snakes."

"Snakes? What snakes?"

Finn tries to read Stevenson's expression, but he can barely see the storyteller though he stands only a foot or so away. But Finn knows his guide is smiling. Though the passageway isn't quite as dark as Silverbright's cave, it is, by far, more comfortable. A carpet cushions their steps and the walls at least are dry. As they walk cautiously across the carpet the travelers hear music, soft at first, then louder as they approach the source. The music is fast and heavy on the bass side, such as might be heard in a discotheque. Presently they see a dim red light at the far end of the passageway.

"Nearly there!" says Stevenson.

"It stinks in here," says Finn. "Like somethin' dead's been lyin' around too long."

Stevenson chuckles. When they reach the end of the passageway they see three doors, each with a huge number, one through three, painted in white and covering the door from top to bottom. Before the first door stands a warning sign which reads, FOR MAGICIANS ONLY!

"Uh oh," says Finn. "This looks strangely familiar."

Stevenson reaches into his pocket and pulls out a handful of quarters. He inserts one into a slot in the door and turns a small handle next to the slot. Slowly the door swings open and they enter a deceptively large room lit only by a soft bare bulb hanging from the middle of the ceiling. The bulb glows red and pulses to the beat of the music. The wall at the far end of the room is made of glass and looks like a giant TV or movie screen. Though there is movement beyond the screen, Finn can't make out what's happening there: the glass is either too opaque or the lighting insufficient. But there is certainly movement. The deadthing smell has disappeared too, replaced by the almost overwhelming scent of jasmine.

"It's nicer, but it still smells like death in here!"

"Beg your pardon?" says Stevenson.

"I said it still smells like death in here."

"Och, no," says Stevenson. "That's jasmine you smell."

"That's death we're smellin'—believe me! Cold, hard death. Smelly death! Death smells like a Parisian pissoir, Mr. Stevenson; so does jasmine!"

"You have a vivid imagination too, laddie!"

"That's what sustains me."

Stevenson steps into the middle of the room and turns around in a complete circle. "Welcome to the peep show," he says.

"Why can't we see it?" asks Finn.

"Money," says Stevenson, laughing. "Everybody wants money."

The storyteller reaches into his pocket again and pulls out more quarters. There is another coin slot near the movie screen as well as some control knobs, and when Stevenson feeds the slot a light suddenly comes on, illuminating the area behind the glass. The lone figure and everything else behind the partition becomes visible.

"Okay, so who is it?" asks Finn.

Stevenson doesn't answer; he just stands there staring at the screen. Beyond the glass a huge stepladder reaches nearly fourteen feet or so into the air. A middleaged man, nattily dressed in a dark, double-breasted suit, stands at the halfway point on the ladder. He has dark hair slicked back across his scalp. Rivulets of sweat run down his face and, though he climbs quickly, he seems exceedingly tired. A red carnation clings to his left lapel. Finn looks questioningly at Stevenson.

"Okay, I give up," he says. "Who is it? What's he doing up there?"

Stevenson smiles and nods towards the climber. When Finn turns again, the slickhaired man has reached the top of the ladder where he stands, his left arm flung out expansively. Stevenson reaches over to the coin slot by the movie screen and turns up the volume. They hear then the monotonous voice of the slickhaired man as he belches forth a waterfall of words. He seems pained at speaking, sorry for having remembered the words he spoke.

"That is not it at all. That is not what I meant at all," says the slickhaired man.

Then, his head bent sheepishly, contritely, he descends the stairs. When he reaches the bottom he stops short, his eyes wide, almost bulging out of his head. He tries stubbornly, but unsuccessfully, to step off the ladder. Then an elegantly dressed woman steps out of the shadows at the back of the room. She stands for a moment in front of the slickhaired man and smiles, pleased with herself—like a cat after having just conquered a mouse. She reaches out and puts her hand on slickhair's forearm.

"I have seen the moment of your greatness flicker," she says.

She speaks with such venom Finn jumps, completely taken aback. The woman then turns and walks back towards the shadows.

"Time to turn back; ascend your stair," says she in her dignified voice before disappearing into the shadows again.

Slickhaired man shrugs his shoulders then begins once more to ascend his ladder. He stops again, momentarily, at the midway point.

"I have measured out my life with coffee spoons," he says.

Then he resumes his climb, his journey, to the top of the ladder. Once there he repeats his expansive gesture and blurts out again his mournful litany:

"That is not it at all. That is not what I meant at all."

The lights behind the glass partition go out then; all that remains is the blurred shape of Slickhair and his lofty ladder.

Finn turns to the Storyteller. "Put in some more quarters," he says.

"As you choose to live in your world, so you will live in another," says Stevenson, rather haughtily.

"Huh?"

"An oversimplification, some would say. But true nevertheless."

"Why the mystery, why the riddles?" Finn asks.

"There is no mystery, no riddles. It's all very simple. You get an itch—you scratch it! You stub your toe, it'll most likely hurt. Cause and effect—karma! Call it what you will."

"But I don't get it. What are they doing back there?"

"Remember what your ma used to tell you? You make your bed—you lie in it! That's what he's doing back there. Lying in his bed! Simple; no mystery there."

Stevenson can see the confusion on Finn's face, the consternation. He smiles at the Albanach's attempt to make some sense of what he's just witnessed.

"He was a poet, Finn. An American poet. He was also a social climber. He went to England and became a socialite, a whore to the power of *look at me*. A wonderful poet, some have said, but a climber nevertheless. His wife got in his way, so he had her committed to an insane asylum."

"You've got to be kiddin'!"

"Man, mind thyself," says Stevenson. "What goes up will come down. Spousal abuse of the tolerable kind, the socially acceptable kind."

"Plain as day!" says Finn.

"Well, should we put in some more quarters, see what happens next?"

"Might as well; you're gonnae anyway," says Finn.

When Stevenson feeds the hungry maw of the glass partition a soft red light comes on behind the glass. The red light illuminates the naked figure of an older man who sits crosslegged in the middle of the floor. He is plump and flabby, his skin the same light-starved color as the belly of a fish, his glasses bottle-bottom thick.

"Goddamn!" says Finn. "He looks like a fuckin' frog."

Stevenson bursts out laughing. "Funny you should say that," he says.

The froglike man on the floor sits perfectly still, though he looks terrified. The only part of him that moves are his eyeballs, shifty bulbous eyeballs. They move up and down; they move from left to right. He is too afraid even to move his head.

"What's his problem?" asks Finn.

"We've disturbed his eternity."

Finn looks at Stevenson, a big smile on his face. "What d'yae mean by that?" he asks.

"That's the first light he's seen since he died almost fifty years ago."

"Really?"

"Aye, really. He was a world renowned philosopher. Didn't believe in anything. No, wait! I'll take that back; he believed in Nothing. He believed that after death he, and all the rest of us mind you, would go into some great emptiness, into Nothingness. Zilch! The Void!"

"The cheeky prick! Who does he think he is?"

"Precisely, my dear Albanach, precisely!" says Stevenson.

As Finn and Stevenson watch Nothing, a tall, darkhaired woman suddenly appears before him. She shines with a wonderfully translucent light, like a firefly in the night. One minute she is; the next, she isn't. Like the woman in Slickhair's movie, Nothing's woman looks dignified, and she has a look of defiance and imperturbability about her. Suddenly she bends over Nothing and screams into his ear.

"Merde!" she screams. "Merde du chien!" Dogshit! Both Finn and Stevenson burst out laughing, but the woman's face is contorted in anger.

"All I wanted was a child," she continues. "You denied me a child, you selfish MERDE!"

Nothing looks around the room in bewilderment, and I can't help but wonder if he knows that something is going on around him. The woman of the light continues her circling walk.

"If you could feel, I'd kick you," she says. "All along forever! You'll wish there *was* Nothingness after I get going on you!"

She stands behind him now, her face a mask of wonder and perplexity.

"Ah, hell," she says. "I'll kick you anyway."

And she does. Right on the arse. But Nothing feels nothing, and the woman disappears, like a firefly, into the night. Finn looks over at Stevenson, but the Storyteller is doubled up in a fit of laughter.

I don't know what to think though I feel particularly uneasy watching this man who believes in nothingness.

Slickhair at least could talk, could move, even if his speech and movements were limited. Nothing just sits there staring at nothing, his senses completely deprived. No warm touches, no cuddles, nothing to see, nothing to hear or feel; completely still and numbed. Slickhair's senses receive some signals at least, no matter how weak; the philosopher tries to receive, but nothing at all comes into him. Stevenson watches him intently for a moment.

"He can't even see, Finn. His eyes are open, but he can't even see; he's trying, mind you, he's trying!"

"Let's get the hell outa here; it's too depressing!"

The red light goes out above Nothing, leaving the room in complete darkness once more. Back in the passageway, Finn leans against the wall and lets out a long, heavy sigh.

"That was awful," he says. "Kinda scary—really depressin'!"

Stevenson laughs. "As yae sow, Finn, as yae sow! And that's the truth of it!"

"Do you find everything amusing, Louis?"

"I do nowadays," he replies.

Finn looks at the Storyteller as if he doubts his sanity. He slides down the wall and rests on his haunches. The music meantime continues its monotonous beat to the pulsing rhythm of the passageway light. He screws up his eyes and flares out his nostrils as he sniffs in the stale air.

"Is that smoke I smell?"

Stevenson sniffs likewise. "Can't smell a thing!"

"It's fuel. I can smell burning diesel fuel!"

"Your nose is too close to your arse!"

"Bollocks, Louis! Something's burnin'; I can smell it!"

Stevenson taps Finn on the shoulder with his walking stick. "Let's go," he says. But Finn has long departed, scurrying across the carpet on all fours. He stops and turns back to Stevenson.

"Get down, goddamit, get down; they're all over the place."

Is he back in the war zone?" Maybe not. Not this time! I realize, instead, that he's tied down to his sacrificial bier in the clearing somewhere in a Vietnamese jungle, surrounded by a multitude of Grotesques.

"Help me, Stevenson," he shouts. "They're rapin' me again!"

I have a hard time not laughing, as does the Storyteller, who just rolls his eyes and walks over to Finn.

"Get a grip of yourself," he says.

Finn looks up at Stevenson, wide-eyed and frightened. He stares at the Storyteller for a long time then he slowly gets up. He shakes his head as if trying to clear away all his crazy new thoughts.

"Let us go then you and I," says Stevenson with a chuckle. "Let's go next door!"

"Yae mean there's another one?"

"It's endless, Finn, endless!"

There is also a hint of worry or concern about the questioning glance Finn next throws the Storyteller. I can't help but wonder if Finn fully understands the implications of what Stevenson has just shown him. I wouldn't be surprised if his confusion is now complete. He's been through the wringer lately and now seems to be taking each new experience in his stride. Self preservation perhaps. He may be confused and, though new experiences fail to surprise him, it does seem to me that his level of tolerance is peaking to the point of rebelliousness. He is agitated and nervous as if he's had quite enough, thank you very much. But Finn has always been a rebel. If I succeed in making him see the light as it were, and if he will open himself up, look at things more objectively, I'm sure he'll realize that his rebelliousness is the root cause of all his problems. He isn't stupid. He is perfectly capable of thinking so and seeing so. If only!

Finn casts a perfunctory glance at Stevenson as if to let the Storyteller know he is indeed at the end of his rope, and that he doesn't want to play any more. Stevenson ignores him and continues simply to tap-tap-tap his way to the door marked 'two.' When Stevenson deposits a quarter into the coin slot the door swings open slowly of its own volition. The two cast quick furtive glances at one another and step into a pitch black room devoid of smells and sounds and sight. The door bangs shut behind them.

"This is too creepy," says Finn.

"I think we've just walked into a black hole," Stevenson replies.

"Put some quarters in the damn thing."

"I would if I could see it!"

"It's right there by the window—like next door!"

"Aye, so it is," says Stevenson, fumbling around until he's able to drop a handful of quarters into the slot. Nothing happens at first. The screen is dark and quiet. Then: soft moonlight illuminates a grove of trees and bushes. There's a shopping cart in the middle of the grove. Arkansas's sleeping peacefully beside his shopping cart. They look tough, the two younger men standing over him, observing Arkansas as if they were hyenas gazing, from a safe distance, in their cowardly way, upon their prospective prey. They are travelers like Arkansas, but more homeless than he; they have no shopping cart, nothing on their backs. No backpacks, no bedrolls, no possessions of any kind. Nothing! Just themselves and a big bag of hatred and bile between them.

"Don't wake the fucker," says the taller of the two. "We wanna see what he's got in that shoppin' cart."

"He ain't gonna wake," says the other. "He's probably drunk on his ass anyway."

But Arkansas wasn't a drinking man, not really. He drank with his friends to be sure, and he drank when it was particularly cold outside, but he wasn't a constant drinker like so many of the other Shopping Cart Soldiers. He was simply a man without a home. He had come back from the war with the blankness, the emptiness, of war stamped upon his soul, and he could no longer function in the ordinary workaday world. So he traveled, following the sun.

Always on the alert, even in sleep, he hears the two punks talking about him. He prepares himself, stiffening, eyes open wide, staring, alarmed and alert, he rolls over under his blanket, away from them. The first boot catches him on the side of his face. He grimaces, but gets up onto his knees, throwing his blanket aside. Fuckers, he thinks, sneaky, miserable fuckers. But he was a combat soldier, and he'd been in many a skirmish both during and after the war. He knows how to fight for his life. He attacks the smaller of the two robbers who is closest to him. He hits him in the face with all of the considerable strength he has in him. As he's about to turn towards the tall one, the tall one viciously whacks Arkansas with a log he'd picked up off the ground, and Arkansas's knees buckle out from under him. Unfair, thinks Arkansas as he goes down. That's cheating, ya miserable piece-a shit. He tries to get up, but he's bludgeoned again, then again. As he goes down for good, a brief thought flashes through his mind that this is indeed an ignominious way to die after all, after all that.... The little one rises groggily to his feet and, in the rage of a coward, kicks Arkansas again and again, and yet again venting all the rage and anger of his vile and miserable life on Arkansas's now-dead body.

As the two murderers pillage Arkansas's meager belongings, Finn looks over at Stevenson. But Stevenson's face is a complete blank, his lips tightly pressed together, his head bent low. When Finn sees the murderers pull Arkansas's new boots off he flies into a rage, attacking the screen, beating at it with both fists until, exhausted, he slides down the wall sobbing as if his heart would break.

"Why'd they have to go an' do that?" asks Finn when he recovers.

"We have to keep moving, Finn," says Stevenson. "We can't stop now. We must keep moving."

"I don't want to see anything else," says Finn. "I've had enough!"

Stevenson gently takes Finn by the arm and leads him through the third and last door of the passageway. Finn's head still reels from this latest hallucinatory burst. His fears are real. Watching these strange screens is like being in them, as if he were actually a part of them. Not only is his mind playing games with him, but the hallucinations seem physical too, as if he can feel his mind step out of his body, as if he can actually feel it permeate throughout his muscles and slip or seep out through his skin. In those moments he feels as if he's standing, tiptoed, on top of a very high and thin tower, looking down into a rushing, swirling torrent of water. Had Stevenson not taken him gently by the arm, he might still be tied to his jungle bier in a continuation of some wild hallucination or watching still the demise of Arkansas who would never have harmed any living thing, not even the bugs and other creeping things he slept amongst. As it is, Finn now stands staring into another blurred image behind a glass partition. Stevenson puts his arm around Finn's shoulders as he pumps the slot next to the screen full of quarters.

This time a purple light comes on behind the movie screen, illuminating a shopping cart standing alone in the middle of a bare concrete floor. Inside the cart sits a bowed figure dressed in combat fatigues; all around the cart a mountain of vodka bottles, in various states of fullness, litter the chamber floor. Finn looks at Stevenson, his brow creased questioningly. As if suddenly startled, the head of the figure in the cart snaps back. The figure pulls himself up onto his knees, his hands gripping the sides of the cart, and looks furtively around the chamber. In the cart kneels the disheveled figure of Finn MacDonald, Albanach, at the height of a bender. The hair on him stands out in every which direction; he has a two- or three-day beard, and his face is bloated from the drink. His eyes are big and wide with wonder and, though there is a hint of blue in there somewhere, they now look as red as those of Redeyes, as if he's rubbed sand into them. Finn feels the excruciating pain of a hangover come over him as if it came right out of the blue sky. He looks at Stevenson in complete confusion. The Storyteller merely shrugs his shoulders and points at the screen.

The sound behind the screen climbs steadily until it fills the outer part of the room, bouncing off the walls, floor and ceiling, filling the air like a heavy cloud of fog. The figure in the screen moans as if in great pain and, while Finn watches, a great force suddenly flings the figure into the back of the shopping cart. He thrashes around in a seizure and the ensuing sounds become earpiercingly loud. The cart bangs and clanks against the bottles, the bottles against the concrete floor; the figure's head and limbs bang against the sides of the shopping cart. Great screaming sounds emanate from bloodied lips. Finn staggers back into the wall of the chamber, but he can't take his eyes away from himself. The figure becomes quiet and still. Slowly, Finn of the screen comes to and looks around the chamber in bewilderment and confusion. He reaches out and pulls a half-full bottle of vodka from the pile around him and drinks deeply. He smashes the empty bottle against the inside of the movie screen.

"Oops! I don't think he likes the movie!" Stevenson says.

"Fuck you!" replies Finn, turning suddenly to leave.

"But it isn't finished yet. Look!"

Finn turns in time to see three other figures emerge, head first, from the pile of bottles surrounding the shopping cart. It looks as if the figures are being born of the bottles surrounding them. Romeo Robinson plops out first, followed by Johnny Quinn; Ivy League comes out last, swinging his saxophone through the air. All of them are wet and appear as they had before that dark night in the jungle: young and healthy, full of the vigor of youthfulness, brandishing smiles. They climb, slipping and sliding over the vodka bottles until they're standing by the shopping cart and the exhausted figure of the moviescreen Finn. They look down at him, shaking their heads back and forth.

"It's not him," says Johnny.

"The hell it ain't," says Romeo. "He's been like this for years."

"It might look like him, Romeo, but I'm tellin' you, it ain't!" argues Johnny.

Ivy League shrugs his shoulders, confused. "Sure fuckin' looks like him," he says.

Johnny turns and looks out through the screen, straight into Finn's eyes. He walks over to the screen, puts his hand up over his eyes as if shielding them from the sun, and presses his face against the back of the screen. He continues to look straight into Finn's eyes. Finn looks over at Stevenson who simply shrugs his shoulders. Finn is astonished, astonished that Johnny has targeted him so directly. He steps back. Stevenson smiles, enjoying such an intimate exchange between the two.

"Hey, guys, he's out there," says Johnny. "I can't see him clearly, but he's out there all right; I can *feel* him!"

Romeo and Ivy League walk over to the screen and stick their faces up against it just as Johnny did.

"I can see a shape out there," says Ivy League." But it don't look like nothin', man."

"Nah, bro," says Romeo. "There's two shapes out there."

"Goddamn," says Johnny. "So there is! But this one here, that's Finn MacDonald. I just know it."

"I think you're right," says Ivy League. "I'm beginning to feel him myself."

"Finn! Hey, Finn! It's me, bro," says Romeo. "Remember me?"

"Wait a minute," says Ivy League. "How the hell do we get to him, how do we get past this glass shit, this barrier here?"

"Dunno," says Johnny. "Back to the drawin' board I guess. Maybe we just need to shout louder."

All three of the dead grunts wave and shout at Finn who is now completely backed up against the wall, his eyes wide and staring.

"Shit, this ain't gonna work," says Johnny. "Come on, Ivy League, rev up your sax. Play him a tune that'll make him remember us, make him feel homesick for his old buddies. Give him a bit of the old nostalgia; works every time. Hey Rome, what was that tune he liked, that Irish thing."

"That was *Danny Boy*, man. He always liked to hear Ivy League's jazzed-up *Danny Boy*. Brought fuckin' tears to his eyes."

Ivy League turns to Finn and starts blowing out Finn's favorite, teary tune. Romeo begins to dance as if he doesn't have a care in the world. Johnny steps forward, smiling, and recites, over the top of the saxophone, part of a poem he wrote just before he died.

> There's a wall inside wrapped around my heart
> it won't let you in and won't let me out.
> This wall is made with the bricks of shame
> and it's there where I keep all my sadness.

Then he winks cheekily at Finn, turns, and holds up his hands for quiet. Ivy League stops playing; Romeo stops dancing. The three of them stand with their backs to us. The voice of a tenor comes over the speakers. He's singing *Miserere*. As the music reaches its climax, a figure emerges from the pile of bottles. It is the same nurse Finn asked to dig the bullet out of Johnny Quinn's brain, the same nurse who was blown to smithereens during the rocket attack. She wears the same white uniform she wore in the triage tent, and the same red cross hangs around her neck. The nurse looks over at Finn, a look of defiance creasing her otherwise benign face. She spreads her arms out before her like a madonna.

"Why have you forsaken us?" she asks. "This isn't the Finn we knew," she says, pointing to the Finn in the shopping cart.

"Yeah, why?" ask the three young warriors turning towards him. "What's happened to you?" they ask.

"Why have you betrayed us, Finn?" asks the nurse.

"I don't think he even remembers us," says Romeo. "How sad."

Then the light dims. The bottles and the shopping cart disappear. Finn is young again. He's wearing his jungle fatigues and he's lying flat on his back, smoking, staring up at a beautiful full moon shining over Vietnam. It's warm and comfortable and, for the moment, Finn MacDonald doesn't have a care in the world. He's at peace, just lying there thinking of home, thinking of his ma and da, and all his brothers and sisters. But mostly he's thinking of

Mary Quinn. It's only been a few weeks since he saw her in Hawaii. He misses her terribly, his first love, but he knows he'll see her again. He just knows it. Fuck this damn war, he thinks. I'll make it! Then his reverie is disturbed by loud laughter. He hears it and smiles. It's the lads, he thinks. One by one, the faces of his pals appear above him. Johnny Quinn, Ivy League, Tommy-up-front, Romeo Robinson, Frankie Chen, all of them, his buddies. All of them, excluding Ivy League, had arrived in Vietnam together, and they'd been together ever since.

"Hey, man, what happened to you?" asks Frankie Chen. "You missed the best part!"

"It was makin' me too homesick, Frankie. Anyway, I just wanted to be quiet for a while." He sits up. "I was thinkin' about your Mary, Johnny. I think I'm in love."

Johnny laughs. "You better take good care of her, Finn me lad," he says, imitating Finn's accent. "'Cause I think she loves you too. I got a letter from her today. Man, what a loada crap! 'Oh, Johnny,' she says, 'he's this, he's that, he's so *cuuute*! And his accent, wow!' It nearly made me throw up!"

"She said that, she really said that?" asks Finn. "Let me read it, let me read the letter!"

"No way, man. That's private stuff between a brother and a sister. That would be a breach of confidence." Johnny was having fun teasing Finn.

"Ya must've gave her a good hosin', Finn," says Romeo.

"Hey, man, that's my sister you're talkin' about!"

"Yeah, Rome," says Finn. "Cool it! We fell in love. This is true love!"

Romeo bursts out laughing. "It's always true love the first time you get laid," he says.

"Shit," says Finn, "you just don't understand!"

"I don't give a flyin' fuck about any of your petty crap," says Ivy League. "I'M GOIN' HOME TOMORROW. One more fuckin' day an' I'll be out of this hell hole. I'll be back in the World, gettin' laid *every* night."

"I just wanna talk about those dancers we saw," says Tommy-up-front. "Christ, did ya see the one in the pink dress. Man, I've never seen tits like that! Never in my whole life. An' that dress was so short you could almost see what she had for breakfast!"

"Yeah, Alba man," says Romeo. "You missed the best part for sure."

They had all gone to a USO show together, but Finn left early. USO shows just pissed him off anyway, frustrated him because every few months the government would fly in a group of beautiful, round-eyed white women with a half-arsed musical show, and everybody would go ape-shit at the sight of them. The first show Finn saw made him think of Alba for weeks after it. Tonight's show made him think more of Mary. He didn't feel right leering lecherously up at the women on the stage when Mary was in his heart and in his head. So he left, came back to their compound, laid himself down on the grass and dreamed of her. He dreamed of her and dredged up memories of their first days together, though the dredging wasn't deep. The moment they laid eyes on each other, after the letters and the photographs swapped back and forth, they knew there was some kind of magic at work.

It was that simple, that natural. A resumption it seemed like, rather than a beginning. Easy!

She is slight, Mary. Petite, like me. Her hair is copper-colored, her skin pale and soft like a powder puff. She wore no make-up when she came to meet Finn, but she smelled of wild hyacinths. She wore a flower-patterned dress like a sarong and she had sandals on her feet. A love-child, thought Finn. A beautiful flower-child-love-child. They were clumsy at first, but her wild red lips were willing and eager; she opened them up to him like a flower to the summer sun. They made love for six days straight and, when they left the islands, neither of them could tell you the name of Waikiki's main street nor the name of any of its beaches. On the seventh day they rested before going their separate ways. Mary went East, her belly filled with new life; Finn went west, caught between life and death, his own belly filled with two more reasons for living.

"Here, Finn," says Romeo. "Have a toke at this motherfucker!"

While Finn was in his reverie, Ivy League had gone to his hootch to collect his saxophone, and Romeo had rolled a huge doobie. They were smoking Thaistick, the best weed in the world. Romeo had rolled it two papers long and two wide, like a rasta-man might have rolled it. The hugeness of it was almost obscene. After he rolled the joint, Romeo coated it with opium. A joint fit for royalty. One toke was enough. Any more than that would put anyone out there among the stars, and all these fellows were reaching for the stars. Get the hell out of Nowhere for even a little while. In-country R&R. Ivy League began wailing on his saxophone, and all the lads nodded and swayed and tapped in appreciation. Stoned out of their minds, they became part of the melody Ivy League created. Finn felt as if he'd become part of the sound itself, reaching out with his mind, following the sounds until they disappeared, ended, then he'd swim back again and pick up another wave of sound like a surfer, like a soundsurfer. He giggled in appreciation, then he burst out laughing. Ivy League stopped playing.

"You're really gettin' off, ain't ya, Finn?" he says.

"I'm out there, Ivy League, keep playin', man, keep goin'!"

And Ivy League began again, pumping out the wailing sounds harder than ever.

"Oh, this is fuckin' great," says Finn. "This is outa sight, man!"

He looked up, up at the stars, and way off in the distance he saw *The Shadow*, a C-123 cargo plane converted into a murderous killing machine. Painted black, it looked murderous. It was said that *The Shadow* could put a bullet into every square inch of a football field within a minute, cover the whole damn football field within a minute!

"Hey, man, check it out!" says Finn. "*The Shadow's* on night-duty again." Everybody looked over in the direction Finn pointed and saw the tracers make their passes back and forth, back and forth, back and forth across a Vietnamese football field suspected to be full of Viet Cong players. The grunts cheered it on, got up onto their feet, fists raised in the air, and cheered it on. They hoped *The Shadow* would get a whole buncha the gook bastards so that *they* wouldn't have to deal with them. "Git the motherfuckers, burn 'em up," they shouted, feeling fortunate that they had such powerful, destructive fire-power supporting them. Lautreamont woulda loved this, thought Finn, sittin' here stoned senseless, watchin' the nightmare fireworks. This kinda show took surrealism to the extreme, to its far-reaching outer-limits. The difference between that surrealism an this surrealism was that this surrealism was real, like a walk on the beach.

SPLAT!!! The blood and the gore hit the screen so quickly, so suddenly, Finn outside the screen falls back hard into the wall behind him. Stevenson jumps back; I jump back too, it is so sudden. A great gob of blood and gore seems to rise from among the happily stoned grunts and splatters the inside of the movie screen as if some giant had cleared his throat and spat and angry gob of mucus at his worst enemy.

That's as much as Finn can bear. He lets out a loud, yelping scream and flees from the room, his hands held tightly over his ears. Stevenson beams delightedly. The blood and gore slides down the screen revealing again the three young soldiers. They smile and give Stevenson the thumbs up. The lovely nurse smiles too and, with a sweeping motion of his walking stick, Stevenson bows before the dead veterans. He turns then and walks toward the door, whistling a merry tune as he goes. "Progress," he murmurs, then quietly closes the door on the now-dark movie screen.

I find Finn sitting on the warm pavement outside the strip joint. He's leaning against the wall, his arms behind his head and his legs stretched out before him. He looks perfectly content sitting there enjoying the hot, noonday sun. Then I notice that he's shaking and trembling. Stevenson comes and stands beside him, hands on hips, staring down at him. Amused, I walk in a circle around them. Who knows what might happen next? Finn looks up at Stevenson and I see fear cloud his face again. Perhaps it's anger I see. Stevenson on the other hand seems full of himself, as if satisfied that his plans are going just as he hoped they would. He turns and taps his way to the other side of the entryway and sits down in the shade. Finn follows the storyteller and sits beside him.

"Happy now, Louis?" he says, facetiousness getting the better of him.

"It was all I'd hoped for," says Stevenson. "But more to the point, how do you feel?"

"What *is* the point you're trying to make, Stevenson? I'm getting a bit fed up with your scenarios."

"It's simple, laddie. Just helping you see things a little more clearly. When something doesn't feel right, it most likely isn't. You should listen to that voice inside you."

"I've read about people who listen to voices. Axe-murderers, rapists, weirdos! An' quit callin' me laddie, for chrissake."

"What I'm trying to show you is that you already know what you need to know. Now you have to act on what you know. You have to take your life back! Get off your arse and get some work done!"

"Oh, really?"

"Do you believe in God, Finn?"

"Uh oh—here we go, the big one, the sixty-four thousand dollar question."

"Well?"

"I do now, after meetin' that sonofabitch up there on the dance-floor. He was quite persuasive, you know, that Nazarene of yours."

"That's his job, Finn."

"His job, Louis? He kicked me in the nuts!"

"You're rather stubborn," says Stevenson with a laugh.

Finn laughs too. "So was he. But look where it got him."

"Listen to what you're saying!"

"Aye, well..."

"Everything that's happened to you lately is in your head. Always has been. It's a dialogue you've been having with yourself for years."

"You mean none of this is real?"

"Not exactly, no. These experiences are as real as you need them to be. You need all those people from your past. They're your lifeline. They'll help you come back if only you'd let them!"

"It doesn't matter, does it?"

"What doesn't matter?" says Stevenson, sighing heavily.

"I don't care if God exists, an' I don't care if he doesn't. It's moot, Louis, that's all! If he does exist, then he's so unknowable, I couldn't comprehend him anyway. So what's the difference, who cares? If he didn't exist I'd probably con myself into believing he did. I'd conjure him up, invent a God or the idea of a God. When all is said and done, it just doesn't matter."

Both of them fall silent. Finn thinks of the day after the war. He remembers it more clearly than he does any of the preceding days in-country. He still can't figure out what the hell happened to him when his war was over, or why he doesn't give a damn any more. Neither can he figure out why he does give a damn. All he knows is that the war changed him in some inexplicable way. He never ceased to be amazed how a few short months could have changed his life so dramatically, so absolutely forever.

I'm glad I'm able to follow Finn's thoughts. That's one of the strengths of being an Invisibility. I can feel him think. And I'm pleased with what I'm feeling. So too can Stevenson; he looks up at me and smiles. Finn has tried with all his might to figure out what changed within him after the war. The best he can do is to realize that he's just somehow different. He remembers walking up to the old family home in Alba, on the day after the war, thirty pounds underweight, jonesing like hell from the heroin. Vietnam and the White Stuff are less than twenty-four hours behind him. He's a corpse in a toobig suit, and his ma knows it.

She nearly has a heart attack when she sees him. The desperate intake of breath and the clutching at her breast when she sees her son tells Finn she's shocked to her soul. Finn tries to smile, but he can't. The muscles in his face just won't work like they're supposed to. He can feel it. He sees himself as a Grotesque standing there in front of his mother trying to smile. He imagines the awful contortions his face must be going through as he tries to smile for his ma. He's never experienced such an aberration, anything so awful. He realizes then that he's left his smile over there in Vietnam.

Little does he know, so soon after his war, that it is me, his soul, he's left on the battlefield.

"Is that you, Finn, is that you, son?" the ma blurts out, confused, not knowing what else to say. Then she wishes she hadn't said anything.

"Joe...Joe," she shouts in a panic through the house to her husband. "It's our Finn. He's back, he's back! Our son's come back!"

She grabs Finn and holds him tightly, daring any living man to ever come near her son again—she'd rip them apart, tear them limb from limb! Then the da comes to the door and grabs the two of them, and he holds them tightly, with the same goddamned fierceness with which the ma finally holds her son.

The ma and the da let the floodgates open, and the hardest tears anyone ever saw fell from both their eyes and all the pain and anguish of the past three-hundred-sixty-five days come hurtling out of their bodies and their gasps for breath are like those of someone drowning. Then the da looks at the ma with big bewildered eyes that ask her, Is this really our boy, ma? And the ma looks at the da with her own big bewildered eyes that ask him, Is this really our boy, da? And the soft and loving way they lean their heads against Finn's speaks volumes. Yesyesyes! He might not be whole, but he's ours. They too are confused, not knowing what kind of hellish weapon it is that could waste her boy's body so, make him so thin and transparent. The ma cries for a week, and the da works overtime at the factory.

Finn stays in his room trying to smile. He remembers the hellish feeling of his failure to smile for his ma and it terrifies him, really terrifies him—even more than the hell he saw in the war itself. He looks into the mirror and tries to smile again, but he can't! The muscles of his face won't work no matter how hard he tries. He stands in front of the mirror and tries, but he feels as if he's cheating, stealing smiles. When he attempts to smile his face twitches, as if he has a nervous tic. When he forces a smile onto his face he looks pitiful, like a macabre Grotesque. Better not to try at all, he decides. From then on he wears a mask of stone, though inside, deep inside, he's dying to live, dying to smile! He just doesn't know how any more.

"It's easier than it used to be," says Stevenson.

"What? What is?"

"Smiling. It used to be a lot harder for you."

"Time, Louis. Heals everything."

"That may be so, but it's been taking you too long. You have to help it along now, Finn. That's all you're going to hear from me until you get to Alba."

"Alba! I've been tryin' to figure out what it means to me, this elusive, mythological place."

"Any light bulbs going off?"

"Yeah, I suppose."

"I'm all ears."

Finn looks up at Stevenson and laughs.

"I dunno. It just seems like I need to be in Alba. I have a sort of yearning to be back there, as if I'm going to find out some wonderful big truth about myself, or about the war and what changed in me after the war. I can't help but feel there are answers waiting for me in Alba. That's why I don't call it Scotland any more. Scotland doesn't mean diddly-shit to me, except that I've got family there. But I grew up in Vietnam. I learned how to be an American fighting a war in a Vietnamese jungle with a buncha yanks the same age as me. Chrissake, Louis, I killed an American kid before I'd been in America a year! I killed my wife's brother before I even married her! Oh, for chrissake, those were fucked-up days."

"You had a deal with Johnny. He would have done the same for you. That was your deal! He probably wouldn't have made it back to the base."

"An' that's the clincher. Probably! I've been tossin' that word around in my head ever since then. What if, what if, what if!"

"That too is moot, Finn. It's done! You can't change the past, but you can certainly change the future if you have a mind to, if you have the courage."

"You really believe that?"

"Believe me! That's just one of those simple but beautiful truths."

Finn laughs, laughs like hell, a good feeling overwhelming him. He then scrambles to his feet. He feels good. He feels happy! It's so unusual a feeling. The enormity and the simplicity of Stevenson's proposition that he can change his future begins to sink in.

"You mean I don't have to live like this any more? Is it really that simple?"

"Not if you don't want to, and yes it is. Take my word for it!"

Finn had never even considered the possibility that life could be so simple, that it didn't have to be so complicated. He thought about what Stevenson said for a moment, then let out a great, loud belly-laugh. He actually felt happy. A daft sort of happiness, as if there was something not quite right about it or, worse still, that he perhaps didn't deserve to experience happiness. But he didn't really care about all of that; it felt *good*! That was enough for now—or was it? For some strange reason he thought about hot summer nights sitting in Paranoid Park with Arkansas and all his other old veteran pals, drinking, talking, laughing, without a care in the world. Ah, yes, good nights, wonderful nights, so comfortable and warm and safe sitting among the like-minded who knew the score, who knew what was happening, as if they each had one mammoth secret in common: what they'd done, how they did it. They trusted only one another.

Quiet Michael was there, sitting in the shadows beyond the reach of the lamplight's glow, quietly taking it all in. From time to time he would chuckle. So quiet, and always a ready smile on his face. Such a contradiction from the Michael who completed three tours in Vietnam. A marine lieutenant, he was, well-liked by his comrades, and brave too. Three purple hearts, two bronze stars and a silver star. Not to mention the two Presidential citations for bravery. He now sits in the park with his pals, his family, chuckling from time to time, trying to ignore the pain from the Agent Orange-induced cancer now riddling his body. He was probably eating that shit when he went into the north, into the Inchin Valley, to free the POW's from that hellish camp.

"Y'know, Finn," he once said, "that was the worst part of the motherfuckin war, goin' in an' gettin' them POWs outa there. It broke my heart, man, they were so fucked-up. But we got 'em all out. We missed one-a the gooks though. He musta been hidin'.

Cocksucker! Shot me in the leg, the prick. But my shotgunner got him. Blew his fuckin' head clean off. Best shotgunner I ever saw." Quiet Michael pauses. "We freed the whole damn lotta them. Seventy-four POW's, Finn. Took 'em home. Saddest sight I ever did see, they were so fucked-up."

Michael gets a six hundred-dollar-a-month pension for his service-connected injuries. He keeps twenty of it and sends the rest to his daughter up there in Sacramento. "What the hell do I need it for," he'll tell you. "I'll just spend it!"

Arkansas just sits there, happy to be among his friends. He's got medals and citations coming out of his ears, but he never talks about them, this old ranger. He'll always tell you *five-by* though when you pass him on the street and ask him how he's doin', then he'll give you that special ranger handshake that ends with him rapping his knuckles against the back of your hand. "Five-by, brother, you know me!" Yeah, sure, Arkansas, and your face is smashed and your boots are gone and all your belongings are scattered.

But it's the Pilot who's holding court this fine evening. Finn likes Pilot, because he's a real American sort of fellow, the kind of fellow Finn would always picture in his mind when he thought about America. A straight-up kind of man with lots of integrity. Pilot was tall and rangy and reminded him of Francis Phelan, a character in a book called *Ironweed*. Pilot was like the ironweed: strong, rangy, lean, almost indestructible. He came from Pensacola, Florida, and talked with a wonderful, southern accent—real American! He's talking now, telling his friends all about how he ended up sitting beside them drinking potent liquor, swapping war stories. He's told this same story a hundred times at least, but nobody ever tires of hearing it, least of all Finn. It seems like Pilot's story just confirms their belief, their conviction, that no one is to be trusted.

"Comes to money," says Pilot, "don't trust nobody, least of all your damn wife!" He smiles broadly, almost childlike and innocent.

"Used to fly them F4's," Pilot would begin. "Up there at Boeing Field near Seattle. I was one-a the top test pilots, you bet! I was up at forty-five thousand feet in one-a the newer ones an' all this smoke starts to fill the cockpit. Somethin' went wrong, but I don't know what. I tried to eject, well I did eject but the cockpit didn't open; I went flyin right through it, seat an' all. The TNT under the seat went off, exploded just like it was supposed to, but the damn cockpit didn't open, an' I went right through it. I landed okay, but just about every bone in my body was broke. They found me with the homing device. Spent a year in the hospital. Got brain damage from the lack of oxygen up there in the stratosphere. Ten thousand feet I fell without oxygen.

"Boeing paid me half-a-million as a settlement, an' the Air Force gives me a nice pension. Spend it on my kids. Got two daughters at the University of Washington. Doin' good too. My wife divorced me when I was lyin' in the hospital. She took all the money, the bitch. Nothin' I could do about it. I was too sick. She had the divorce papers delivered when I was lyin' in the hospital, an' if that ain't cold, I don't know what is."

Both Finn and Arkansas gasp exclamatory gasps when Pilot tells them about his wife and her ways. Even though they've heard the story so many times before, it never ceases to amaze them. But it's this bandying back and forth with stories from their respective lives that so enamors Finn, the absolute trust they have in each other that makes their lifestyle so precious and attractive in spite of the hardships. He tries to explain it to Stevenson.

"Aye, well there's the rub, Louis!" he says. "I *want* to live the way I do! I Like living like this. All I have to worry about is getting another drink. I don't pay rent. I don't have to work. I don't have to belong to anything, or join anything ever again. It's a worry-free, unstructured lifestyle which suits my sensibilities just fine, thank you very much."

"You don't mean that! You've wondered yourself a million times why your life had to be so awful, why you didn't have a job, a place to live, a family! You've also wondered a million times why you can't laugh without drink."

"I had all that, a long time ago. Even the laughter."

"Aye, you did, but you gave up the ghost! You stopped fighting. You forgot how to get your back up!"

"He doesn't have a back, Louis," rang out a voice from somewhere above them. "He's spineless, an' he knows it!"

Finn and the storyteller look up. There sits Silverbright on the roof of the strip joint, just above the neon. His spindly legs dangle over the side of the building. He jumps up and clambers down a pipe attached to the side of the building. In a moment he stands before Finn, resplendent in a spotless-new saffron robe which reaches all the way down to his ankles. A golden cord is tied around his waist, and a golden baseball cap sits jauntily on top of his head.

"An' he's a liar too," says Silverbright. "He lies to himself all the time."

Silverbright turns to look at Stevenson, a big smile on his face.

"He's a cop-out. Bursting with self-pity, that's what he is. But we'll do our best, right, Louis?"

"Aye, we will indeed, Silverbright, we will indeed!"

"Come on then, Finn, me lad," says Silverbright. "Hi ho, hi ho, it's off to work we go! No laggin' this time. Alba here we come."

Finn rolls his eyes heavenward and complains. But before he can utter more than just a few words, Silverbright does the most astonishing though wonderful thing. He turns around to where I am standing on the perimeter and speaks to me directly.

"Come on, Madman," he says. "You're part of this too."

Stevenson laughs. "She's the biggest part of this," he says. "She's the reason, after all, for all this commotion."

"She?" says Finn, completely bewildered.

"Aye, she," says Silverbright. "From now on we're going to acknowledge her. She's right here beside us."

"Then why can't I see her?"

"Yae could if yae tried, dipshit, but yae choose not to," says Silverbright. "Right, Louis?"

"Bang on, Silverbright!" says Stevenson. "But maybe we should describe Madman to him." He winks then at Silverbright. "Might help him see her."

Silverbright stops and looks Finn up and down, then he looks me up and down, then he looks Finn up and down again, all the while stroking his chin.

"Not a bad idea, Louis. Not a bad idea at all."

It's funny, but I begin then to see Silverbright in a different light. No longer does he seem like Silverbright. That name seems to belong to a different period, a different time. Silverbright seems more like a mythological name such as might suit someone waiting, in a limbo of sorts, just as he's been waiting for Finn all those years. But now he seems real, now he seems actual. Perhaps he should use his real name again.

"Thanks, Silverbright," says I, and both he and Louis laugh. Finn looks at them as if they're nuts.

As we walk to Alba, Silverbright tells Finn what I look like. Every so often Finn casts a glance in the direction where he thinks I might be walking, his face twisted in confusion. But Silverbright, with the help of the odd interjection by Louis, does a wonderful job describing me. He tells him first about the long silver umbilical cord and how important it has been to Finn throughout the aftermath of his war. Finn, I must admit, seems quite grateful. The knowledge of the cord seems to answer a lot of questions for him. Then Silverbright tells him about my complexion, my eyes, the color of my hair, my height, the size of my breasts. He tells him all about my crimson robe and why I wear it, and how delicate are my hands. Finn has a small, curious smile on his lips by this time, and he's looking in my direction. Can he see right through me? I wonder. Stevenson's shoulders bob up and down as if he's chuckling at something truly comical.

"But her feet are best," says Silverbright. "They are very tiny, more delicate than her hands. Like the rest of her skin, they are pale like goat's milk. When she walks it's like watching a butterfly in the height of summer bobbing from one flower to the next. Silently, joyfully, as if she didn't have a care in the world. Such a joy to behold."

I wonder what Silverbright's up to. He's being his old mischievous self again, and I can't help but smile. Sweat forms on Finn's top lip.

"Where is she?" he says, and turns in a complete circle looking for me. I make myself as visible as possible, but he still can't see me.

"She ain't married, is she?" he says, then bursts out laughing, as does Louis.

Silverbright feigns shock.

"Listen to him, Louis," he says. "Would yae just listen to him! All he thinks about at a time like this is sex!" He winks at Louis.

"No bluidy wonder," says Finn. "I haven't been laid in years, then I have to listen to that without gettin' excited? You're crazy, Silverbright!"

Silverbright stops dead in his tracks and looks straight into Finn's eyes.

"You've been screwin' your soul for years, son. Why don't yae just try embracin' her for a while. It might make all the difference in the world."

Finn smiles brightly when he catches the old man's drift, and I feel better than I have done in many a long year. I feel so good, in fact, that I walk over to Finn and put my arm through his and hold on tightly. He doesn't feel a thing, but I'm on top of the world. We walk on like this until we're right in the middle of Downtown. Finn can't believe the ruins that had once been the beautiful city of San Francisco. I look up at him and there's a look of abject terror on his face. Sweat seeps from his forehead and he shakes and trembles. I look over at Silverbright, but he's chatting away gaily to Louis as if Finn didn't exist.

"What have I done?" Finn whispers. "What have I done to myself. My world's a ruin! Oh God, Mary Quinn, what have I done? What the hell's happening to me?"

I let his arm go and he runs away from us. I am about to run after him, but Silverbright holds me back.

"Let him go," he says. "He's not going far."

And sure enough, he doesn't. He heads straight for a broken-down liquor store across the street. When we get there, he's already sitting on the floor at the back of the shop chugging on a whiskey bottle, shaking like hell, sweating like a pig. He looks up at us.

"Medication," he said. "Don't want to have another seizure. I felt like one was coming on."

"Don't yae think yae've worn that one out?" says Silverbright. "It's old hat these days, yae know."

"Are you tryin' to drive me completely over the edge, Albanach?" The emphasis isn't lost on Silverbright, but he simply laughs.

"No, not at all," he says.

"Then you tell me what's happening. Why is the city in ruins?"

"I told you what happened," says Louis.

"Not good enough," says Finn. "What happened to the city?"

Silverbright adjusts his golden baseball cap and sits beside his Finn.

"It really is all very simple," he says. "There really was an explosion. Everything blew up. Everything was pushed to the absolute limit. The haves continued to amass great wealth until there was nothing left for the have-nots. No food, no schools, no medical attention. Nothing! Starvation, hatred and greed prevailed! They became the norm, fed by fear. The haves wanted all of the pie! The revered concepts at the time were merge and mega. Merge this, mega that!"

"So what happened?

"The melting-pot became a huge boiler, and no one could turn it off or even down. That's okay for a while. A boiler can run full-tilt for a long time, but if yae keep the pressure on without a break it'll explode. The seams of the boiler became so stressed, they blew apart. An' that's what happened."

"Nobody tried to stop it?"

"Of course they did, but it was too late, much too late."

"It was greed, Finn," says Stevenson. "Greed and selfishness. Gimme, gimme, gimme! You should know all about that, you being a Shopping Cart Soldier, expendable now as you were then. Hardly anyone cared about you or any other so-called warrior for that matter. You already gave everything you had. There was nothing left for you to give, so you were either ignored or swept under the carpet. A great many people disliked you because you made them feel guilty. They stuck their heads in the sand like ostriches so they couldn't see you. And if they don't see you, you don't exist! It was the same for all the other poor folk; it was the same for the infirm, and the elderly, and the very young. Towards the end people would laugh, while they starved to death, at the thought of the Statue of Liberty and what she stood for. Give me your poor, etcetera became a huge joke."

"Bastards," says Finn. "What a buncha bastards! But where's all the people?"

"Mostly dead," says Silverbright. "There are a few scattered groups of people here and there. Tribes you would have to call them. Mostly in the country. They're all exhausted."

Finn falls silent as he tries to take it all in. He can't believe the devastation. But he isn't surprised. Selfishness and greed and the hatred they spawn have finally overcome every single ideal and value he fought for in Vietnam.

"Those bastards!" he says.

Silverbright stares at him. "It's a bit late for your cursing," he says. "You shoulda been doin' your cursin' a long time ago. You and your fellow warriors gave up the ghost, remember. Too busy feelin' sorry for yourselves hidin' in your whiskey bottles. That's the reality, Finn. You gave up everything you ever loved. Threw away life because you couldn't take it any longer. Thought you had a monopoly on suffering."

"Hey, wait a minute, Silverbright. A lot of those same warriors felt they had no recourse but to take their own lives—like around a hundred an' fifty thousand of them. The pain of their memories, and their guilt, was too great, Silverbright. That too is the reality."

"Aye, that's all very well and true. Unfortunate and sad, but you choose to keep on living the way you do. Why is that? You fought like the devil during the war, but when it was over you gave up. Doesn't make any sense!"

When we turn off Sutter Street onto Larkin, the Tenderloin district lies spread out before us. The poorest of the poor once lived down there among the violence and the drugs, among the mayhem. The Tenderloin, like the rest of the city, is desolate and ruined, empty of people.

"I wonder if Redeyes had anything to do with this," says Finn. "What was it he said about mayhem?"

"I'm sure it was him and his ilk; it's got their mark on it," says Silverbright. "Looks like they had a field day!"

"I used to love this city," says Stevenson. "When I lived here that is. I used to sit up there on Telegraph Hill and watch the sailing ships go by, going and coming. And I'd think of Alba too, Finn, so far behind me."

"Well we're nearly there," says Silverbright. "Alba, that is! It's just down the way a bit." He points down the hill, and he has a wry smile on his face. "Just a couple of blocks."

"Christ," says Finn, a hint of anger in his voice. "Now what?"

Silverbright turns sharply and looks at Finn. "But you've been trying to get there for years. Don't you want to go now?" Stevenson laughs.

"I never thought I'd find Alba in the Tenderloin."

"You're in the Land of the Truly Alive, remember," Stevenson says.

"Aye, that's right," Silverbright agrees. "Don't ever forget it. Anything goes in the Land of the Truly Alive! You'll find whatever you're lookin' for no matter where you're lookin'—as long as you've the eyes to see, Finn. That's the answer, son, that's the answer!"

I can tell Finn isn't in the mood for any more of Silverbright's conundrums. He rolls his eyes Heavenward as they trudge on deeper into the Tenderloin. Finn feels a tightening in his stomach. Apprehension is beginning to get the better of him, and he's begun to sweat. He thinks back to his experience with the Grotesques and all his other strange experiences. Most particularly his experience with Redeyes. That bastard really puts the wind up me, he thinks. A' that rantin' an' ravin' about how evil he is. What a loada crap! He won't get inside me!

I hope he's right, but the thought puts the wind up me too. If he does, how will I ever get back inside him? I still haven't fully accepted Stevenson's idea that Finn needs both myself and Redeyes to fully become himself again, to fully reclaim his life.

While thinking so, I feel a warm sensation in my stomach, like a warm tickle, not at all unpleasant. Finn must have felt it too, because he puts his hand over his stomach and scrutinizes his surroundings. *I'm certain he can sense me even if he can't actually see me. He stops looking when his eyes rest on the spot where I stand. I'm equally certain he feels the umbilical cord. I sense that he's finally putting things together; he's wondering about intuition and the source of all knowledge. It's a fleeting thought as he walks towards Alba. But it's progress too. I chuckle. Didn't Stevenson think the same thing not an hour ago at the peep show? Perhaps Finn really is on the right track, because it occurs to me that through the cord he will find knowledge, that precious, innate knowledge. The cord isn't there, obviously, but it's real nevertheless, insofar as Finn receives messages strongest there. That's where the knowledge of the cord is strongest. That's his lifeline to the Land of the Truly Alive. It makes perfect sense. That's probably why he feels apprehension there, as well as every other feeling in the book too: all the bad feelings such as fear, danger, anger and the like. And all those good feelings of love, compassion, sympathy and their ilk. As good a concept as any, I believe. After all, we Invisibilities don't know everything either. It just wouldn't be as much fun that way. When I look up again at Finn he has a slight smile on his face. As Stevenson says, an unusual occurrence unless he's got a good drink in him.*

"Well here we are," says Silverbright. "Alba!"

Finn pulls up abruptly, then turns and stares at Silverbright, a look of confusion and fear on his face.

"You're kiddin'," he says.

"Nah, that's it," said Silverbright. "Welcome home, son. Welcome to Alba!"

Directly across the street stands the house made of castle-like stone, and directly in front of the house stands a young man, no more than twenty years of age, whose eyes burn with fire. Finn's heart pumps like a piston and I must admit to a certain apprehension myself. I'm a bit confused too. I can't figure it out. I thought it was Redeyes, but this fellow is too young. Or is he? He looks to be the same age as me, twenty that is. But it occurs to me that if Redeyes has indeed been kicked out of Finn's body as I was, then he too would be twenty. We are both twenty, because that's how old we were when The Leaving *took place. Finn is confused more than ever. He looks over at Silverbright.*

"Redeyes?" he asks.

The old fellow rubs his chin; slowly and deliberately he says, "I do believe it is."

The young man's red eyes flame with a burning passion, either of anger or of hatred. I say this because his face wears a bitter scowl. Yet, underneath the scowl, he's quite handsome. Attractive, if you will. I am a woman after all and I know about such things. His skin is pale like my own, like goat's milk, and he has black hair, thick and wavy. It hangs almost to his shoulders and sticks out every which way. He wears a purple wool suit with yellow buttons which fits him snugly. His shirt is a deep crimson color, his tie as black as his suit. His boots too are black and quite scuffed and worn as if he walked a lot. His hands are stuck in his trouser pockets as he leans against the door jamb of the house made of castle-like stone. He looks altogether cheeky and arrogant, like a teddy-boy. As we look on Redeyes stares relentlessly at Finn and every so often he sticks out his tongue and licks his lips seductively.

Finn stares back at him, transfixed, as if under a spell, as if hypnotized. Imagine the surprise I feel, the shock I feel, as Finn steps off the sidewalk and crosses the road toward the young Redeyes.

"No, Finn, don't!" I shout.

Silverbright turns quickly to me. "Let him go, Madman, let him go."

"But, wait..." I protest, but Silverbright simply holds up his hand to silence me.

Redeyes straightens up and, taking his hands from his pockets, walks towards Finn, wearing again the look of the conquering cat. When he reaches him, Redeyes simply stands there smiling. Finn doesn't seem to have any control whatsoever. He seems completely captivated. Redeyes, luxuriating in his power, reaches out and caresses Finn's face lovingly, tenderly. I'm beside myself with hatred for this Redeyes who would dare to touch my Finn just so. Another feeling comes over me too as I watch them. I hate Finn for being so weak, and I hate Redeyes for being so powerful, so alluring. Ultimately I hate myself for being so, what is it, so jealous? Can I be jealous? I can barely take my eyes off Redeyes either.

"Leave him alone, ya sonofabitch!" I scream.

Redeyes ruffles Finn's hair playfully, then without a word, turns and walks away, laughing boldly. Finn stands there in the middle of the road in a daze, as if he's dreaming. Redeyes is by now out of sight and only then does Finn come to.

"What are yae waitin' for?" he shouts back at us. "Let's get this show on the road!"

He hasn't remembered a single thing. I'm still upset, apprehensive, at seeing Redeyes again, especially as such a young man, such an attractive young man, and I can only surmise that Silverbright and Stevenson are just as surprised. Silverbright shrugs his shoulders, and walks towards the doorway to Alba with Stevenson and me bringing up the rear. It dawns on me that the implications of Finn's not remembering young Redeyes could be great. I cast a glance at him. He smiles, standing there by the Gateway to Alba, oblivious to this new danger, to the possibility that he could be seduced by evil, that he could find evil so attractive.

3

DEBUT AT
THE ALBANACH THEATRE

"WE'LL BE LEAVIN' yae here, Finn," says Silverbright. "You're on your own now."

"That's right," says Stevenson. "You'll have to figure the rest out all by yourself." Thoughtfully, he pokes the ground with his walking stick. "I don't know what Alba means to you either," he continues, "but this is where you'll find it."

"Spoken like a true guide," says Silverbright, laughing pleasantly.

Finn's confusion is obvious. He walks in a circle, hesitating, deep in thought. He looks over at Silverbright and Stevenson. Then he looks at me. His eyes burn into mine, though he still can't see me.

"I'll do what I have to do!" says Finn.

Looking at him I wonder if he really will, or if he's just afraid, acting bravely. It doesn't matter, I suppose, as long as he's willing to go into the house again, into Alba. His willingness to do so now is he key to any expiation, any peace, he might hope to find.

The thought of another step across this same threshold doesn't appeal to him. All these crossings have ever done for him so far is to re-introduce him to his old warrior pals, or to show him his life as it is, or as it could be, neither of which please him. It takes a certain amount of strength to confront such knowledge or insights head-on. I'm not so sure he's that strong yet. Who knows what might happen next. All I am sure of is that his third step over the threshold will be the culmination of all our contrivances to bring him here.

In Alba he'll find what he's looking for, or discover some thing or another which will propel him off along the road to a true reclamation of himself. Most likely it is now or never for Finn MacDonald. If he doesn't make it through this next part of his journey, he'll probably be found some bitter morning asleep forever under a stairwell or, like Arkansas, underneath the bushes in a lonely city park. His epitaph will read simply,

Here lies another Shopping Cart Soldier.

Standing by the gateway, Finn nervously adjusts his clothing. Silverbright sticks two fingers into his mouth and lets out a loud, shrill whistle. Presently, the water buffalo comes into view, patiently pulling the old wooden-wheeled wagon. When he reaches us, the bull stops and looks at Finn. He stares for a long time then snorts loudly and tosses his horned head in the air. As might be expected, Finn is disconcerted by the bull's behavior. After all, he's only been stared-down by an animal once before. And the bull is an especially huge and virile-looking animal. More so, even, than the Billy-goat. Finn quickly shakes hands with Silverbright and Stevenson before turning toward the door leading to Alba.

But before he can open it I grab onto him and hold him tightly. I'll go with him of course, but I want to give him as much support and strength as possible before he actually enters Alba.

Amidst the goodbye's and the good-lucks and the strangely loud bellowing of the bull, Finn opens the door to the house made of thick, castle-like stone and crosses the threshold.

Thresholds are all I think of as we enter this other dark place.

Each crossing is a new experience, each experience more grist for the mill. Unlike Silverbright's cave or the peep show entrance, this passageway is huge. I can't see anything and neither can Finn, but this place has the feel of bigness. He stands still trying to take in the feeling. He is excited and nervous; this, after all, is where he needs to be. He has finally arrived at the place he's been looking for all these years.

After a moment we hear a soft chuckling sound coming through the darkness around us. Then a soft, red light illuminates the place ever so slightly. At least it's enough to help us make out the insides of this house made of stone. Again the house has changed; again it is different from what it used to be. The chuckling grows to a laugh, the laugh grows louder, then with a suddenness that rocks us, it stops and is replaced by a loud roll of drums. The drum-roll ends with the beating of a huge gong. A large red neon light blinks high above us. It reads: THE ALBANACH THEATRE, and underneath that, in smaller letters: COME IN YOU'RE NEXT!

Finn bursts out laughing; he can't help it. The sign reminds him of his younger days. "Come in, you're next" is a common term used by young Alban men. It is heavy with sexual innuendo. Maybe I'm gonnae get laid, he thinks.

"Dream on, sergeant," says a voice out of the darkness way off to his right. It is the voice of a young woman. Finn jumps back and the smile leaves his face.

"Who's there?" he asks.

The lights are dim; he can barely see. One or two other lights increase in brightness as if someone were turning up a dimmer switch. Finn looks off into the corner and sees a huge throne-like chair made of deep red mahogany. In the throne sits the broken-backed nurse he saw being carted around in the shopping cart, the same nurse who gave him the tweezerlike instrument to dig the bullet out of Johnny Quinn's brain. She still wears her nurse's uniform and her big red cross still hangs around her neck. She smiles.

"Sometimes it grows heavy like stone," says she.

Finn stands there, speechless.

"What's up, Finn, cat get your tongue?" asks the nurse as she fondles her cross. "The cross, dummy, the cross. Sometimes it feels heavier than other times."

"What are you doin' here?" asks Finn, after plucking up a bit of courage.

The nurse sings. *"They try to tell us we're too young, too young to really be in love..."*

He walks toward her.

"Stop!" says she, indignant, holding her hand up, palm out. She grips the seat with her other hand. "You've no right to come any closer; I'm not the kind of girl you think I am! Not that I had much of a chance, mind you." She laughs, a deep, throaty laugh, as if she's having a wonderful time. "I'm still a nurse, you know," she continues. "But it's different. No more blood. I lost all of mine. Lived for two days, you know. In pieces. The doctors couldn't believe it; they didn't want me to die. How could they let a young woman die in war. Went against their grain. I think I reminded them of their sisters. 'I'm a nurse,' I told them. 'I can't die!' But I did. You should've seen me. Holes everywhere, limbs hanging off, turning paler and paler as more and more blood seeped out, covering my whiteness with various shades of redness. My blood became thin as it made its pulsing way out through the holes in my body."

The nurse stops talking and slowly begins to metamorphose into herself as she was when she lay dying. Finn is so horrified he backs up then drops to his knees and sobs amidst the nurse's dying sounds. He looks up at her, his eyes full of tears.

"Can I touch you, nurse? I just want to touch you; I've thought about you for more than twenty years. Please let me touch you!"

"I told you," says the nurse, anger in her voice, "I'm not that kind of girl! I want you to see me as I am. I want you to know what it's like."

Finn's angry now. He jumps to his feet. "Know what it's like?" he explodes. "I was fuckin' well there!" he says. "Remember?"

"You didn't stay long. All I saw was your back."

"Fuck you, nurse, an' fuck your horse too."

"They call me Gemini here, you know. They say it suits me because I have two sides to me. The healer side and the pissed-off side. But no one's perfect now, are we?"

She stands. She spreads her legs wide. She raises her arms into the air. She spreads them out. She looks like the cross of St. Andrew. In a booming voice, she shouts: "I AM THE MEDIATOR!" Then she sits down again, smiling. Finn looks at her as if she's nuts.

"A wee bit fulla yoursel' too," he says. Gemini giggles.

"What do you expect?" she asks. "This after all is theatre. Show time. Come in, you're next!"

Finn smiles. The lights grow brighter. He steps farther into the house of stone. Off to his left, in the corner, a body bag hangs from the ceiling. It is black. Down the front, huge golden letters read, RIP. Above the body bag hangs another neon light. The words MADMAN'S CORNER, large and red, pulse in...pulse out...pulse in.... On the floor sits a three-legged stool. The ceiling is black. The floor is black. The walls are crimson red. It is warm. Exotic incense burns, soothing jangled nerves. *Come in, you're next!* The words run through his mind. Next for what? he wonders. The deep-throated sound of cellos fills the air. Behind the strings a helicopter approaches. Voices jabber instructions, directives, orders. A bull bellows madly. The music stops. The lights dim. Darkness returns. Jungle sounds encroach on the darkness, filling the Albanach with dread. He stands in the middle of the room feeling light, as if he's floating through the firmament as he did on Dali's tilting dancefloor.

The helicopter grows louder; the bull bellows. A voice booms loudly: "Come in...you're next!" Finn is terrified. It is quiet. It is dark.

I want to go to my corner and sit on my stool. It's my turn to just watch. I am the audience.

A soft orange spotlight finds the pale figure of Frankie Chen. He still clutches his heart and balls. Blood continues to seep through his fingers. His head is slightly bent towards the floor. His shoulders shake. The cellos play softly once more. Sadly. Frankie weeps. He lifts his eyes and looks at Finn through his tears.

"You were right, Finn," he says. "It was a heart attack. My heart blew up. It was the searing pain in my nuts. They shot me in the fuckin' balls an' my heart popped. They shot me like we shot the bull. Right in the nuts, Finn. What makes a man a man? Do the gonads make a man a man? Payback, that's what it was. I paid the debt for all of us. Nut for nut!"

When Frankie walks into the back of the room he fades away like smoke. Finn seems amused by this wispiness of spirits. He looks up at Gemini with a smile on his face.

"That's a good trick," he says, facetiously. "Can you do that, Gemini?"

"No problem," says she.

And she does. Just like that she disappears into thin air. She reappears standing next to Finn. He jumps back, startled, but Gemini puts her arm around him.

"Wanna fuck?" she asks him. Finn laughs. "That's the problem with dyin' young," she goes on. "You don't get to taste enough of the delights of life, the goodies."

"It hasn't been easy for me either, Gemini. All you dead fuckers seem to think it's been a bed-a roses. It hasn't. I've had a different set of problems."

"Tell me then, Finn. How are ya? How are ya really? Have you still got Johnny's bullet?"

Finn shrugs. "Oh, hell, I dunno," he says. "Scared I suppose. I feel dead inside but I don't know why." He ignores the Johnny question.

"Well that's why you're here, isn't it?"

"Yeah, but I don't even know where to begin."

"It's easy enough. You need a new pair of glasses."

"Glasses? I don't wear glasses!"

"You should. You need to see differently. You don't see well enough."

"Riddles," says Finn. "All you spirits talk in riddles."

"They're not riddles, Finn. You just aren't seein' right. It's that simple. Everything true and special is simple. Once you comprehend that you'll be fine. And that's a fact!"

Gemini breaks away from Finn and paces around the room, deep in thought. She walks back over to her chair, lifts up an arm of the chair, and pulls out a pair of glasses from a compartment within.

"Here," says she, "try these!"

"I don't need 'em; I told yae that!"

"Just try them, goddamit!"

Gemini looks over at me.

"Hey, Madman, tell him to try these. He'll be able to see you if he does."

That gets to him, shakes him up. His eyes grow big. They dart furtively about the room looking for me.

"He doesn't want to see me," says I.

"Is that true, Finn?" asks Gemini. "Don't you want to see your soul?"

"Not particularly, no, I don't."

"You have to make him see, Madman," says Gemini. "You've been wandering around the perimeter too long yourself, you know. Seems like you're hiding from him."

"But that isn't true," says I, a bit miffed myself.

I learn an important lesson then, because Finn is surprised. He heard something, I'm sure of it. I remember the other time he almost saw me. Something dramatic happened then too. My outburst a minute ago enabled him to think he saw me, as if the signals between us grew stronger or more direct just then. Things are looking up.

"Hey, Finn," says Gemini, "remember what it used to be like guarding the perimeters over there? Well I think you learned how to do it too well. You've become too adept at guarding your own perimeter. You won't even let the good stuff in."

"What the hell good stuff are you talkin' about?" Finn asks. "There ain't no *good stuff!* An' anyway, what the hell would you know about guarding a perimeter?"

He remembers the night when he and Romeo spoke so disconsolately about having no home any more, no Scotland, no Chicago. All is quiet. There hasn't even been any perimeter action for weeks. They are relaxed, chatting away to one another, but it just seems a little too quiet. They both realize this at the same time, for they look at one another, their brows furrowed. They get down behind the jungle-green sandbags and scan the perimeter a hundred yards away. Beyond the wire for another hundred yards it is clear, then the jungle begins once more. Romeo gets on the radio to the other guard posts five hundred yards away, left and right.

"It's too quiet," he tells them. "Fuckin' spooky! You gettin' anythin'?"

"Nothin'," comes the reply. "Don't see a thing."

"Well, keep your eyes open, bro; it's too goddamn quiet."

The quiet is eerie, nerve-jarring eerie. The adrenaline level is beginning to mount. It reaches a high point and stays there. If someone as much as farts it'll go rocketing sky high. Sweaty trigger-fingers tremble as they curl around the triggers of their M16's. Sweat runs down foreheads and along the length of noses, itching like hell, annoying till you feel like screaming. But don't take your eyes off the tree-line. Put your head down and wipe the sweat from your nose and you might never sweat again. Nerve-jarring. It's four o'clock in the morning. Probably too late for the sappers now anyway. The sappers come in at night—always! They're good. They have balls as big as elephants'. They're afraid of nothing. They have a cause. They sneak through the perimeters like snakes in the grass, low, belly-down, and plant their explosives. They retreat, then attack. Ferociously. You can't help but admire them. Night-shift devils, that's what they are.

Behind Finn and Romeo, the base sleeps peacefully. The grunts, to a man, have a huge resentment that it is they who have to guard these Air Force bastards while they sleep in their comfortable barracks. Beyond the tree-line there may be a hundred, or even a thousand, Viet Cong readying themselves to attack, to overrun the light defenses of the base. No one ever mentions it, but the defense of Khe San during Tet '68 is on everyone's mind. The mythology of that particular battle has reached epic proportions. For three more hours Finn and Romeo stare into the trees, wide-eyed and alert, not daring to speak another word. Nothing happens. "I know enough," says Gemini, "to know that you bastards did sloppy work. After all, didn't the sappers get close enough to the triage tent to blow me and all your buddies to hell?"

Finn becomes quiet.

I walk over to my corner and sit down on the stool.

Gemini smiles. She is pleased. Finn has a look on his face that could curdle milk. He's beyond fear. He looks as if he's just experienced some moral cataclysm or another, or just caught his parents fornicating.

"Impossible!" he gasps, staring at me, finally seeing me.

"He did it! He finally did it!" says Gemini. "How wonderful!"

"Madman? Is that really you? You *are* a woman!" he says, walking towards me. He's in a state of shock by the looks of him. "An *Asian* woman!"

"Is that so bad?" I ask. "That I'm a woman, an *Asian* woman as you so deftly put it? Asian, Asian, Asian. Are you afraid of *Asian?*"

"No, not at all. That's not what I meant at all. It's just that I never expected it. For you to be a woman that is, and an Asian woman to boot. It's just that I never expected it, that's all." He pauses for a moment, tongue-tied. "Well, I knew you were, but...I don't think I ever really believed it. It never occurred to me that you could be Asian. Why is that, how can that be? It's just confusing, that's all!"

"Well I am both, though I don't know how that can be except to say that it might be an anthropological mistake. Most likely it's simply that you see me exactly as you need to see me! I am the way I am, because that's how you need me to be so that you can forgive yourself, so that you can heal yourself. Quite frankly, I don't know the answer to your question. Perhaps it's because you killed so many Asians you now feel a need to go through some weird kind of metamorphosis of your very own soul. Perhaps you have to anthropomorphize your soul in just such a way to find the expiation you so badly crave. Who knows!"

"Maybe I just didn't expect you to be so, uh...so attractive," he says, obviously unwilling to face the issue head-on. I play out the rope; there will be other opportunities to confront him. It's still early.

"Does that mean you'll take me back?" I ask, disdain creeping into my voice. "Does that mean you'll always see me?"

He laughs. "It'll make it easier to look at you; you *are* a beauty!"

"Wish I could say the same about you!" says I. And it's true. He looks awful as usual, wearing the same soiled overcoat fastened at the waist with that old piece of rope; his hair's sticking out every which way, and he still hasn't shaved. I'm beginning to wonder if Redeyes isn't inside him already, his eyes are so bleary and red.

There's a staircase in the corner opposite me, but it's so dark down there I can't see the top. While Finn and I are bandying words back and forth a quiet and refined voice speaks out above us:

"Well, well, well," says the voice. "How cozy they seem. I think I'll join them."

I don't know the voice, but the facetious tone is familiar.

We look up. Gemini laughs. Finn recognizes the tone as well. He's looking fearful again. We hear the voice once more, loudly this time. Finn walks over to my corner.

"Light!" shouts the voice. "Let there be light!"

And suddenly there is. An orange-red spotlight comes on, illuminating the youthful figure of Redeyes. He's standing on a balcony at the top of the stairs. It's a Florentine balcony, beautiful and ancient, surrounded with manycolored roses. Redeyes too is beautiful. He's obviously taken great care with his appearance. His hair is washed and brushed until it shines. He has pressed his purple suit. His boots are polished to perfection. I think: he's clever, this one.

"My, my, my," says Gemini, "what have we here?"

"Good day, ladies and gentleman," says Redeyes, slowly descending the stairs, followed by the spotlight. Such a grand entrance! He looks like he should be carrying a top hat and cane. Finn is rigid, wondering what's going on. Redeyes reaches the bottom of the stairs and comes towards us. He smiles. His eyes are on me.

"How are you, Madman?" he asks.

I can't understand why it is I can now see and hear him so clearly, or why I would even feel compelled to answer him. But I do. Is it because he looks so young and handsome? Perhaps my eyes have opened too.

"Where's Soldiergirl?" I ask, getting up onto my feet.

"Ah, yes, Soldiergirl," he says. "She's resting. I laid her to rest at last."

"After all these years?"

"She was simply an illusion, Madman. That's all. Like everything else. No more, no less."

He smiles again. I don't know if it's condescension that moves him or if he just feels so terribly superior to us all. Whatever it is I don't like it. He's too crafty, our Redeyes.

"Would you look at the two of them," he says. He's talking to Gemini.

Gemini smiles and shrugs her shoulders. She's not being much of a mediator if she won't even talk. Finn's shaking, though it's not so much for want of a drink as it is from pure fear. Everything he's ever been afraid of goes through his mind where it rests a while before becoming physical. He can feel his fears leaving his mind, no longer thought, then circulating throughout his body and resting, one after the other, in the pit of his gut. There, they tumble around, each vying for superiority, for the best seat in the house. He is ill. Dread is in his blood, circulating through him. His time has come. If he doesn't come to grips with himself now, he never will.

For the first time in twenty-five years we're together, the three of us, acknowledging one another. Finn, Madman and Redeyes. I jump to my feet.

"Let the music begin," says I, wondering if I can be as flamboyant as Redeyes. I find that I can. The music begins. Ravel's *Bolero* starts somewhere in the middle, building already towards the crescendo. I didn't know I was so powerful—or uninspired. Surely I could have picked a more exciting piece of music to serve my purpose but, still, not bad for a novice. Dramatically, Redeyes does a walking dance into the middle of the room.

"C'mere, wimp," he says to Finn. "C'mere with your eyes open."

Finn pulls his worn coat about him, as if to protect himself, and follows Redeyes. I follow Finn. Gemini follows her instincts. She goes to her throne and sits. She's like the queen bee sitting up there on her mahogany throne. She has a panoramic view of her domain. She is our witness.

I look at Finn, at the deep craggy lines mapping their way across his face, the crow's feet around his eyes, the eyes themselves, watery and yellow from the drink, the unshaven face, the contrite look about him as he traipses after Redeyes, the penitent in search of the gallows. I feel pity for him, and for all the other men like him who daily trudge through city streets pushing their rickety old shopping carts in front of them, filled with their lives. I remember how proud he was at nineteen, boarding the big jet liner, bound for the war, wearing his clean, crisp jungle fatigues, his face cleanly shaven, proud as Punch. I wonder if he can feel pity for himself; or if he feels he hasn't the time for such a comfort. Most likely he feels that self-pity is wrong, that to feel compassion for oneself is a bad thing. Sometimes I grow tired of the rules of men who were taught by fools such as themselves, so rigid and stiff, so diametrically opposed to being soft and human. Stiff upper lip, old boy! Spare the rod and spoil the child! What a load of bollocks! But I can see Finn believes all that old stuff as he stands there in front of Redeyes with his shoulders stooped. Redeyes puts his arm around him, conspiratorially.

"Need a drink?" he asks.

Finn nods his head, affirmatively. Redeyes produces a pint of whiskey from inside his jacket and passes it to Finn. Redeyes watches the amber liquid burn its way down Finn's throat. I feel nothing, neither anger nor frustration. Not even remorse. I'm thankful he won't have a seizure. I look up at Gemini. Her brow is creased. What is she thinking? I wonder. She looks at me, smiles, then waves. I return her smile. She is in the theatre, her very own theatre. She is the theatre all by herself. The queen bee. Witness for the prosecution. Before disappearing offstage, Redeyes raises the curtain for the final act. He speaks to Finn.

"I don't know why I feel so compelled to show you this," he

says, "but I do. This is a city. It could be any city. It could be anywhere. This is your city."

Finn's confused. Redeyes waves his arm expansively and the ceiling recedes, exposing a deep night sky. He leaves. I stand alone, in the background. A few stars twinkle high overhead; there is no moon. The walls of the Albanach Theatre grow upwards, hundreds of feet, like the walls of tenement buildings. The walls don't stop. They just keep going until only a thumbnail of sky is visible above the buildings. Different-colored lights shine from anonymous apartments. The streets are wet. The sides of the buildings are wet. The streets are cobblestoned. Some of the lights are red, some blue; most are yellow. In the blue tenement at the very top Ivy League is sitting at his kitchen table shooting up, chasing the dragon, hoping to replicate the wonderful, heavenly high that almost did him in. In the red one down there in the middle, off to the right, Romeo Robinson sits in the center of his living room floor crying his eyes out because he can't reach his cock. He tries and he tries, but he has to reach over so far with his stubby arms his back hurts. "No point in jackin'-off if my back hurts," he says. "Can't concentrate!" He sticks his stubs into his wooden clappers and tries again. But it just isn't the same. His cock won't respond to the wood. In the yellow tenement at the very top, Tommy-up-front, veins-a-poppin', pumps iron. A single, solitary phrase dances through his mind: "Fuck you, I ain't dead...fuck you, I ain't dead...fuck you, I ain't dead..." Thomas the doubter. Two floors below, Johnny Quinn writes poetry by the flame of a flickering candle. He gazes out the window at the world beyond. He's finishing the poem he began in the peep show earlier.

> Behind this wall wrapped around my tears
> a broken man has fallen
> his face is smashed and his boots are gone
> and all his belongings are scattered
> a tattoo on his arm stands out sudden and sharp
> and it screams of the Khe San offensive.

In the red tenement on the ground floor, Frankie Chen sits in the window like an Amsterdam whore. "You were right, Finn," he says. "It was a heart-attack. But I wasn't scared. Oh, no, not this grunt. They shot me in the nuts and my heart blew up." Frank throws his head back and laughs a loud, sardonic laugh. Gemini, the mediator, sits atop her throne, her legs open like a man. She has no shame. Her nurse's uniform is hitched up around her waist. Her pussy is bare. Frankie is the first to notice it. His eyes bulge; he's never seen a pussy before. He's not impressed, but he has sense enough to know he should be. He leans out the window and shouts up to the thumbnail of sky. "Hey fellas, she ain't wearin' no knickers!" Before he can say nooky all the other dead, lovestarved veterans are down on the ground beside Finn, jostling and shoving their way to the front of the line. Gemini is in her element.

"Hello, boys," says she, a huge and self-satisfied smile on her face. Seductively, she spreads her legs, displaying further her delights. "Can you handle it?" she asks.

"No problem," says Tommy-up-front. "I've been laid a million times."

"At last," sighs Romeo, "I'll feel a warm human hand wrapped around my mickey again."

"I've never been laid before," Frankie confesses as he unzips his fly.

"Lift me up, for chrissake, somebody lift me up!" cries legless Johnny Quinn.

"Figures," says Ivy League, "I'm so fuckin' wasted I can't even get it up!"

Finn wants to join his pals, but he knows he can't. "Yae can't fuck the dead," he says, turning his back on all of them. He walks away, along the wet, cobblestoned street. "Now, can yae?" he wonders.

At the far end of the street a gas lamp spreads its yellow hand across the cobblestones. A small, rectangular shape sits at the base of the lamp. Finn goes towards the light. The small, rectangular shape is a bassinet. It is white. It is adorned with blue daisies. The daisies have tiny yellow faces. He looks down into the bassinet. An infant child looks up at him.

"Why'd you go and leave me, daddy?" asks the child.

A sledgehammer of pain and regret whacks him mercilessly in the stomach and he's thrown against the lamp post, filled with grief.

"Don't you know me?" asks the child. "I'm your son, Finn Johnny Quinn. I was named after you and my uncle Johnny, your pal. Don't you remember?"

"Of course I remember."

"You thought I was the cat's pajamas when you first saw me. Then you deserted me, me and my mom. You wouldn't even give me your name, MacDonald."

"You're wrong; it wasn't like that! Your ma and I decided to keep your uncle's spirit alive, keep his name going like he was still alive. I don't know what happened to me. I really and truly don't. It's as if I didn't know how to live any more. When I went to sleep at night I never wanted to wake up again. I never wanted to see the light of day again. I don't know what went wrong, Finn. I really don't. Anyway, it's best that I left. I would've caused you and your mother nothing but a sea of endless trouble and heartache."

"Tell me, truly, why you left us? Why'd you leave Johnny again? You left him in the jungle, an' you left him in the junkyard of your memory."

"Leavin' was the best thing I coulda done. If I'd stayed you woulda been miserable."

"Have I touched a nerve, Daddy?"

"Of course you've touched a nerve. I've still got some feelin's left! You've no idea how much I've missed you, son, how much I've missed your ma. I could fill lakes with all the tears I've shed."

The child laughs.

"Would you like to pick me up?" asks the child. He chuckles, a gurgling, baby chuckle. "Pick me up an' hold me tight, daddy?"

"Aye," says Finn. "I would like to pick you up, hold you tight. I've missed you terribly, you an' your ma."

Finn kneels beside the bassinet. He reaches over to lift the child. The child lashes out with arms and legs, and screams like a stuck pig. Shocked, Finn jumps back, retreating.

"Fuck off," says his son, in a cruel, Fagin-like voice. "Get lost, ya hopeless, chickenshit bum. Go back to your stinkin' alky life. We don't need you. Do you hear? WE DON'T NEED YOU!"

Terrorized, Finn turns and runs back toward the Albanach Theatre. He trips and falls on the wet cobblestone. He feels like staying there. He wishes the wet cobblestone would swallow him up. He even wishes the Grotesques would come back and take him down into their hole again. Anything would be better than facing his angry son. Slowly he gets up onto his feet again. While he's slouching off towards the theatre, Johnny Quinn hobbles out from behind one of the tall tenement buildings. The yellow light of the lamp post recedes behind them.

"Well, ya can't really blame the kid," says Johnny. "It's been tough on everybody, you know. Watchin' you tryin' to kill yourself with the booze."

"Don't you start, Johnny; I'm no' in the mood!"

"Go get that shoppin' cart, will ya. My knees're killin' me."

Johnny points off to the side of the street. There's a shopping cart sitting all by itself on the sidewalk. Finn laughs.

"Aye, sure, Johnny," he says.

He sits Johnny into the shopping cart and Johnny leans back with a sigh, facing Finn. He smiles.

"It's good to see ya, buddy," he says.

"It's good to hear yae say that, Johnny. I think about yae every day of my life."

"Yeah, man, I know."

Johnny becomes pensive. He sits there holding on to the sides of the shopping cart, staring up at Finn. After a while he speaks again.

"Some of the other guys are pissed-off. Ya gotta be prepared for that, Finn. They're pissed-off 'cause you lived an' they didn't, an' you're wastin' your life, killin' yourself with the booze. Ya can't blame them either."

"Come on, Johnny. It's no' my fault! I don't know what the fuck happened to me, man. It's like I didn't have any goddamn life left in me. I used to wish I'd copped it along wi' the resta yae. I don't know how to explain it."

"Yes, you do," says I. "All you have to do is take me back again. You've known that all along. You just won't admit it."

"Hey, Madman, how ya doin'?" says Johnny. I smile at him. "I didn't see ya back there."

Emboldened by Johnny's friendliness I continue. "You kicked me out, Finn. All you have to do now is take me back. Simple!"

"I don't even know how to begin," he says. "How do you take your soul back, Johnny? Can you tell me, Soul? How do I take yae back, Soul?"

"Don't be facetious," says I. "It doesn't become you. You're no good at facetiousness."

"She's cute, ain't she, Johnny?'

"Yeah, she's cute all right."

"Yes, I am," says I, laughing happily.

"All this time I thought she was a man, Johnny," says Finn.

"Yes, you are cute," says Redeyes. He's just walking out of the theatre, his arms open wide in a welcoming gesture. "An' so am I, Madman. Do you like my nice yellow buttons?"

I do like his buttons. I like his purple jacket too. He's very attractive, our Redeyes. He walks over to us and puts his arm around me. I smile. It feels good, yet I know it shouldn't. Then I wonder why not.

"Come in, you're next!" shouts Gemini when she sees us. She's still sitting up there on her throne, queen-beeing it over her domain.

All the other lads are there too. Romeo's over in the far right corner sitting beside his shopping cart. Slowly, methodically, he claps out a mournful dirge on his clappers. Ivy League's still sitting inside the shopping cart, though his head's sticking out above the crimson blanket, as if he's gasping for air. Frankie's in his window again, leaning on his arms, watching the wonders without. He looks happy. He winks at me and gives me the thumbs-up. When he thinks nobody' looking he blows Gemini a big kiss. Tommy-up-front's sitting on my stool pumping his pecs, looking confrontational.

As I take in the scene before me, the door over by Romeo opens and Stevenson walks in. He looks great. He's all dickied-up like a man about town. He's wearing a midnight-blue, velvet jacket and a white, silk shirt. Around his neck he wears a handsome, lavender cravat such as he might have worn in his younger days. A thick, golden chain hangs around his neck too. At the end of the chain hangs an ordinary-looking stone. It is worn and shiny as if it's been rubbed a lot. I can't help but smile when I look at him; he's so impeccable. His dark, knee-length breeches are immaculate, his black, calf-length boots highly polished. Behind Stevenson walk another two men. The first is Arkansas. His face is smashed and his boots are gone and all his belongings are scattered. His filthy overcoat is tied tightly about him as if he's afraid it might be lost or stolen. He's got a half-gallon bottle of vodka held tightly in his arms. The second man I don't know. I can't see his face clearly, but he's wearing faded, jungle fatigues and there's a heavy rucksack strapped to his back. He looks up briefly. I still don't recognize him. His hair is dark and thick as is his beard. His head remains bowed. He looks sad. His arms are wrapped tightly about him as if he's freezing. He has no shoes, and there's a red hole in both of his feet. He goes off by himself and sits in a corner. Behind everyone else sits Soldiergirl. She's wearing a beautiful, knee-length silk dress the color of a midnight sky in her own country. Under her left arm she carries her head. It still drips blood. When he sees her, Romeo jumps to his feet, his arm reaching for his machete. When he finds he has nothing to grab it with, he sits back down, forlorn and lost. Finn's bitch Grotesque comes out from behind Gemini's throne and sits down beside it. Soldiergirl disappears, and in her stead the Billy-goat follows behind the Grotesque, still tied to its golden cord. Finn's in a panic now, and is about to take off running for the door when the Grotesque speaks. "Don't worry, Finn. He's had his way with you. He wants to get inside you in a different way now." Finn is scared to death. He looks around the room, looking for a friendly face, some kind of support. None, it seems, is forthcoming. Gemini stands, her arms and legs spread wide once more. She's in her aggressive, mediator stance.

"Is the cast assembled?" she asks.

Perhaps she's in a director mode. Nobody answers her. Arkansas takes a long, healthy pull at his vodka bottle and staggers into the middle of the stage.

"I thought this was gonna be a party, Finn?" he says. "What the fuck's goin' on, man? I thought we were gonna have a party?"

Finn has his frog eyes of wonder stuck back in his head. He can't believe them. Poor old Arkansas doesn't know he's dead. Perhaps it hasn't been long enough. Perhaps he's just having a prolonged transition. It makes Finn sad; Arkansas's a good lad. He had a bad transition from war to peace too.

"Hey, Johnny," says Finn, "help Arkansas, will yae?"

"Sure, Finn," he says. "No problem!"

Johnny crosses to Arkansas and sits beside him.

"Gimme a swig, buddy," he says, sticking his hand out.
Arkansas looks at him, unwilling to let go of his bottle. When he notices Johnny's wounds he relents.

"Jeezus, man, you really got fucked-up, didn't you!"

"Yup, sure did," says Johnny. He takes a swig at the bottle through the good side of his mouth. Finn walks angrily towards them.

"We've been gettin' screwed ever since," he shouts, without for a moment taking his eyes off the Billy-goat. "What the hell're you doin' here?" he asks the bitch Grotesque. "Get that fuckin' thing outa here," he says, pointing at the Billy-goat.

"The bitch Grotesque smiles her lipless smile. She slowly extends her right arm and sticks her index finger up into the air. Finn's sure he saw the Billy-goat smile.

"One more word out of you and I'll let go of this chain," says she.

"I thought it was a dream," he says, "but the Billy-goat was real. It's really here now, too."

"What is, what dream?" asks Arkansas.

"That goddamned Billy-goat buggered me when I was back in the jungle. The Grotesque an' her cronies tied me up an' that Billy-goat screwed me. I thought it was all a dream, but it wasn't! It's really here again!"

"Yeah, it's here all right," says Arkansas. "Maybe it wants to screw you again." Arkansas bursts out laughing.

"Wouldn't surprise me," says Finn. "We've been gettin' stroked ever since we came back from that goddamned war. Right from the giddy-up. An' that's the bare-assed reality. They used us like pawns in a cheap chess game. Same ol' expendable flotsam an' jetsam. The great military experiment!"

"Didn't work," interjects Gemini. "Didn't damn well work. Did it?"

"What do you mean?" asks Frankie. "What didn't work?"

"The innocent. Look at him will yae?" says Finn. "For the first time in history, Frankie, soldiers went to war for a specific period of time. Three hundred an' sixty-five days to be exact."

"So what?" asks Frankie.

"So what?" Finn repeats. "It failed miserably. Men usually went to war for the duration. Some stayed forever. But with Nam we went for only a year. The generals thought it would make us better soldiers knowin' we were goin' home so quickly. But it backfired. No esprit de corps, no camaraderie. Nobody gave a fuck. Everybody was gettin' stoned, fucked-up. Instead of watchin' each other's back, we were shootin' each other in the back. A fiasco, that's what it was. All them mammies an' daddies who think their poor sons died nobly should check the real documented facts. Chances are their good sons got an M16 bullet in the back. Jack Daniels an' dope ruled the roost, Frankie baby—you should know that!"

Finn's thoughts go swooshing back to Vietnam, to the night he and Spider and their two pals fragged the MP's compound. "Yeah, it happened all right, Frankie. And the mammies and the daddies and the unwitting wives got a nice letter and a visit from two polished young officers. Sorry, Mrs. so-and-so, sorry Mr. so-and-so, but he was killed in action. He died nobly though, defending the Constitution, the beliefs, of the United States of America. Just ask Robert McNamara, he'll tell ya the whole goddamn truth. He has to. Mortality is kicking him in the ass, and he's trying to find his own expiation. 'Oops, sorry, it was all a big mistake. The best way out of it for me is to negate all the deaths, the suicides, pretend that there isn't a single Shopping Cart Soldier walking through crowded American cityscapes.' They are the real Steppenwolves, Frankie."

"Fuck you, ya fuckin' foreign cocksucker!" shouts Tommy. He's mad as hell; he gets up onto his feet quickly, and my stool flies farther into the corner. His bulging biceps strain against his shirtsleeves. Veins pop out on his neck. He continues to rant as he walks towards Finn who is also up onto his feet.

"So fuckin' what," Tommy continues. "Are *you* tryin' to negate what happened to us? You've been makin' excuses ever since you came back from the war. You were even makin' excuses when you were in the goddamned war."

"Fuckin'-A!" Romeo shouts.

"Yeah, man," says Frankie. "You really did wimp out, didn't ya?"

"Ya left me to die, ya sonofabitch."

Finn spins around to get a better look at them.

Tommy continues. "You're a fuckin' wimp, buddy. Pissin' your pants every time you heard a bang!"

Tommy has everyone's attention. Finn looks hurt and scared. Everybody else is looking at Tommy and Finn. Even the Billy-goat. And, I'll be damned, but it still looks like it's smiling. It shifts its position to get a better look downstage. The Grotesque strokes the back of the Billy-goat, now lying at his feet. Redeyes walks over beside it. He strokes it too. I don't like him any more. He's a backstabber, even if he is good looking. The damned Billy-goat is in its element, watching the confrontation. It likes the commotion, the turbulence. Finn is rigid; Tommy's in his face. Stevenson's smiling too. The sad-looking man in the corner is taking it all in.

"You always were a dumb-fuck, Tommy," says Finn. "Lotsa balls, but nothin' between your ears. A turnip, that's what yae are. A big, dumb, fuckin' turnip."

Tommy lunges at the Albanach. But the Albanach neatly sidesteps, getting out of the way. He falls to the floor with a loud crash. The Billy-goat gets up onto its feet. Ivy League grabs the sides of the shopping cart and pulls himself, with a great effort, up onto his knees. He must've just shot up again. I've never seen a human being look as pale as he does. His skin is tinged with a sort of blue color. My stomach nearly turns at the sight of him. Deep red blood trickles from his arm. It looks as if it's the last of it. His speech is slow and slurred like a slow tape.

"Ain't you two dumbfucks done enough fightin'?" he says, then slumps back down into his shopping cart. He covers himself with his crimson cloth. The junkie, disgusted with humanity.

Tommy gets up.

"You're too stiff, Tommy," says Finn. "You've been dead too long!"

"It was my big balls that saved your ass back then when I got killed," says Tommy. "If you hadn't been so hell-bent on gettin' that bullet outa Johnny's brain, we mighta survived, asshole."

"Hey, wait a minute, Tommy," says Johnny, hobbling on bleeding knees to center stage. "Don't get me into your fight! Anyway, Tommy, I'm glad he did that. I was a goner anyway. I was uncomfortable enough. I don't think I would've liked walkin' around with all that lead in my head."

Johnny Quinn seems really sick of the fighting. He drags his broken body into the middle of the stage and recites some more of his poetry. It's the same old poem he's been trying to finish all this time, though a different verse.

> Behind this wall wrapped around my soul
> my mother's tears are as heavy as sin
> she wonders why her son came back
> when she knew I had died already.
> I could no longer look in her eyes and smile
> I might have given all my secrets away.

But Tommy isn't having any of it, and neither is Frankie.

"Hey, Johnny, screw all that sad shit," says Frankie. "Let's sing a song. Let's sing a happy song." He runs over beside Johnny at center stage. "Let's sing *God Bless America* again!"

"Yeah," says Tommy, laughing. "Let's sing *God Bless America!*" And he begins a loud, brash rendition of the patriotic song.

Everybody joins in, even Finn. When Tommy hears Finn he stops singing and spins around once more to face him.

"Hey, you," he says. "You don't have any right to sing this song. You're a wimp remember. Anyway you're a goddamn foreigner. Foreigners ain't allowed to sing this song."

"Go fuck yoursel', Tommy. I'll sing that goddamn song any time I feel like it. I earned the right to sing that song."

Johnny interjects with another stanza from his poem.

> Behind this wall wrapped around my love
> is all I ever believed in.
> It sits there rotting in the golden sun
> among the bodies of all my heroes
> and for all these years I've wondered why
> our country had to betray us.
> No wonder there's a wall
> wrapped around my heart
> that won't let you in and won't let me out!

Johnny then slumps off into a corner and sits down heavily. Everybody else has gone quiet. Finn's trying to put on a brave face, but he's hurt after listening to Tommy. I can tell he's hurt. And he isn't so sure after all if he does have the right to sing *God Bless America*. All his old fears and insecurities come flooding back to him in an instant and he's certain that if Americans knew he'd killed Johnny they'd probably send him to Death Row. He's sick and tired of living with such a fear hanging over his head, always feeling like he's committed murder and is forever trying to hide it, acting always as if it never happened. Yeah, sure, Johnny had asked him to shoot him, had almost coerced Finn into doing it. But they were brothers after all, and as brothers they had made a pact with one another, a pact such as might never be broken. Not on a battle field anyway, no way!

Redeyes is watching Finn, watching everything intently, and his eyes blaze more fiery than ever. Gemini, the healer, can tell Finn's torn up inside.

"That's right, Tommy," says she. "He's got as much right to sing that song as any of us."

"Bullshit, Gemini," says Tommy. "He wimped out remember."

"Where have you been, Tommy?" says Gemini. "Where the hell did you go when you were killed? Must've been la-la land. I think you were wandering around the firmament wondering what the fuck hit you, and while you were wondering and wandering around out there, young Finn was killing, killing more than all of you combined, as if in doing so he'd make up for all of your spent lives. Just like he was supposed to. On the contrary, Tommy, you go fuck yourself."

"Hey, wait a minute, there, Gemini," says Romeo. "You're outa line."

"Am I?" replies Gemini.

And while everybody's getting ready for another round the sad-looking man over in the corner gets up and tries to lift his rucksack up onto his back. But the pack's too heavy. He drops it to the floor with a loud, thudding crash. Everybody turns to look at him. His shoulders are stooped wearily. He looks up at Finn.

"Come and help me, Finn," he says. "Come and help me lift this load please."

Finn recognizes the voice immediately. It's the Nazarene. He's surprised, but relieved. For some reason he feels comforted, even though his last encounter with the Nazarene hadn't ended so well. He thought back to his conversation with Stevenson on Dali's Tilting Dance floor and his dance with old Redeyes; he thought too of the kick the Nazarene had given him and the resulting drifting trip through the firmament where his search for Alba, this place they call the Albanach Theatre, had actually begun.

The beginning seems like such a long time ago. The hours seem like days. In real time it has only been hours; he is sure of that. But he's experienced so much, seen so many strange sights, met so many strange people, things, the time seems infinitely longer than it actually is. Perhaps, he thinks, I have finally gone completely stark, raving mad. Perhaps this is what madness really is. Perhaps I've finally crossed the line between sanity and madness. Perhaps that last drink I had in Paranoid Park was all I needed to give me a pickled brain. Maybe now I've got wet-brain. Maybe I'm actually sitting in a padded cell in a hospital imagining all this shit. Well, fuck it; madness ain't so bad! At least it's interestin'. He chuckles and, as he looks over at the Nazarene again, his heart goes out to him. He looks so...so terribly sad, so laden down with sadness. The poor man, thinks Finn, as he walks over to the Nazarene's corner.

"Would you help me with my pack?" the Nazarene asks. "Help me get it up onto my back."

"Aye, sure," says Finn, leaning over and grabbing the straps of the rucksack. "Goddamn, what the hell's in here?" he asks, straining to lift it.

The Nazarene manages to slip the straps over his shoulder as Finn strains to keep it high enough. The Nazarene's back straightens with the weight of the pack.

"This is all your fuck-ups," he says. "This is everything stupid, malevolent, deceitful you've ever done in your entire life. Pretty heavy, huh?"

"Yeah, I uh, I guess so," says Finn, feeling a bit confused.

"Come on," says the Nazarene. "Let's get out of here, go for a walk. I've something I want to show you."

"Where are we going?"

"Just out there, back to the Tenderloin, the jungle as you call it."

"I don't want to go back out there," says Finn. "I'm supposed to be in here!"

"You're supposed to be where you need to be and right at the moment you don't need to be here. All you're doing is fighting. Haven't you done enough of that?"

"God knows I have!"

"That's right," says the Nazarene, smiling just a little bit. "He does!"

Finn shrugs his shoulders and, as he turns to follow the Nazarene, he looks back into the theatre. Everybody's staring at him. Some of us seem happy for him, some confused. One or two of us look at him disdainfully. The Nazarene presses on without looking back, Finn follows behind looking not afraid, but apprehensive at the very least, like a schoolchild following his teacher to the principal's office.

It's a clear and beautiful day out there in the Tenderloin. Spring must have come while he was in the theatre; a great many of the cherry blossom trees lining the street have begun to blossom. Finn gasps. What a difference from the way it was before entering the theatre. The buildings are whole again too, and the streets are well-kept and clean. The garbage dumpsters are even clean; not one of them filled to overflowing as is usual in the Tenderloin. Even stranger, Finn notices, are the people walking the streets. Every single one is a Shopping Cart Soldier. All of them wear the same sun-bleached jungle fatigues as the Nazarene, and all have a rucksack strapped to their backs. They push their shopping carts with the same determination and certainty a woman might push a baby carriage. Finn casts a glance at the Nazarene, but he's walking briskly forward with the same determination as the soldiers. Finn plods quietly along beside him.

When they reach the outer limits of the Tenderloin, Finn notices more than just a few Bureaucrats darting furtively from doorway to doorway. They have AK47s slung across their shoulders. When he catches a Bureaucrat pointing up to the top of the buildings, Finn looks up too. There, dotting the skyline, on each side of the street, are more Bureaucrats. He knows they're Bureaucrats because they wear dark, pinstripe suits and have small, vacant eyes. They each wear small American flags pinned onto their lapels. They don't seem to notice Finn and the Nazarene or, if they do, they pretend not to see them, or they're just ignoring them. There's a particularly tiny Bureaucrat walking among his colleagues, calculator and notebook in hand, pencil poised above the notebook. He's making calculations with amazing speed and the dexterity with which he balances the tools of his trade is nothing short of breathtaking.

"Oh, maybe about twenty years left in that one," he says. "Ten thou' a year. That's great, lads. Keep it up! Saved two hundred thou' on that one. Kill 'em all, lads. We'll save millions this fine day. Ten years...wow, thirty years on that one...five on that one...come on, lads you're doin' great, kill 'em all...we'll save a few million today..."

Finn's wondering what the hell's going on. He hasn't seen so many AK47s since Vietnam, and he's never seen Bureaucrats looking so blatantly malevolent. But there's a pattern to their offensive behavior, and when a street-based Bureaucrat signals to a roof-based colleague his worst fear is confirmed: it's an ambush, an ambush in broad daylight, in the Tenderloin, right smack dab in the middle of San Francisco. Finn lets out a pitiful yelp. A small group of hell-bent shopping cart soldiers is walking straight into the maw of the ambush.

"Stop them, stop them!" he shouts to the Nazarene. The Nazarene shrugs his shoulders. The soldiers press on determinedly, pushing their shopping carts ahead of them. The Bureaucrats brace themselves, rifles at the ready.

"I can't stop them," says the Nazarene. "I can't interfere; it's not allowed."

Finn's bewildered, in a panic. "What d'yae mean yae can't interfere! That's your fuckin' job, ain't it? Most of those guys have been ambushed before; now you're gonnae let them be killed all over again?"

The Nazarene straightens up, pulls the rucksack off as if it were featherlight and drops it to the ground with a loud thud. His face is twisted in anger as he turns to face the Albanach.

"That's all your screw-ups," says the Nazarene. "Just like I told you. And this is your screw-up too. I can't stop this. I can't interfere. Only you can do that. Only you!" The Nazarene puts his foot on top of the bulging rucksack. "I will tell you this much, Finn," he continues. "I won't pick this up again. I'm done with it. It's bulging as you see, so what you do with it is up to you. You can keep trying to fill it as you have done, or you can empty it, one screw-up at a time; it's up to you, to you and no one else."

Finn does a dance of helplessness and exasperation in front of the Nazarene.

"For God's sake stop them; I don't know what to do. Please fuckin' stop them."

But the bullets fly, interrupting them, bouncing from wall to wall, zipping through the air like long-nosed mosquitoes on a warm summer night. They bite into the warm flesh of the Shopping Cart Soldiers and as they sink in, small erupting volcanoes of flesh throw blood and limbs and other bodybits out onto the street before them. Finn wails and screams and takes refuge in the doorway of a shop. The Nazarene crouches beside him. Finn retches. He retches once more all over the feet of the Nazarene. The Bureaucrats are having a field day. There's hardly a Shopping Cart Soldier who hasn't been chopped into a million pieces by the bitter bullets of the AK47s. Finn collapses further into the doorway of the shop and cries as hard as he ever did in all of his life.

When the grenades fall, body-bits and pieces of shopping carts rain down on the potholed streets like nightmare rain. The head of a soldier falls with a dull, heavy splat in the doorway next to Finn. He's bubbling uncontrollably, like a child. His bladder lets go a stream of piss, and he sees a picture of Soldiergirl, smiling for the last time before her head lolls to one side, the life now finally gone from her.

The smell of cordite permeates the air and a heavy cloud of smoke hangs above the ambush scene before it is dispersed in a light breeze to drift and waft high above them among the lives, the souls, of all the massacred Shopping Cart Soldiers. The Bureaucrats come down from the rooftops and out of their hiding places to congregate in front of Finn and the Nazarene. The Bureaucrats take forms out of their pockets and when they have them filled out they staple them to the telegraph poles and cherry trees lining the streets. On the forms the words *Killed In Action*, stand out for all the world to see, but no one's there to see them save Finn and the Nazarene. The Bureaucrats cover the body-bits with lightweight American flags, then disperse into the background as easily as the drifting souls of the soldiers, their day's work done.

Trembling, Finn gets up and walks over to the pile of broken bodies, dodging as best he can the rivers of blood making their way to the gutters on either side of the street. The rats'll have a fine day of feasting. He kneels before a pile of body-bits and lifts the corner of an American flag. He stares at the still-warm stuff inside. He turns to look at the Nazarene who is leaning against the shop doorway, his shoulders slumped, his head bent low.

"I'm weary, Finn," says the Nazarene. "I'm utterly and absolutely bone-weary."

"But why, Nazarene, why this. Why is the killing still going on? The war's more than twenty years over. Why is the killing still going on?"

"There's few who care, Finn. There were few back in the days of the war too; there's less who care now. Many who cared are now dead themselves. Most have forgotten. What you see here is America's everlasting shame. Come, we'll walk."

Finn picks himself up and, before joining the Nazarene, walks over by the shop doorway and stoops to pick up the heavy rucksack. He can't; it's too damn heavy. He looks to the Nazarene for help and, smiling, the Nazarene picks it up effortlessly and helps Finn put his arms through the straps. They walk back along the Tenderloin streets, leaving the scene of the carnage behind them. The streets again are neat and quiet, the blossoming cherry trees once more a delight to see. Presently, the Nazarene speaks.

"When I leave you today I won't be coming back," he says. "I've done all I can do."

"Why did those soldiers have to die like that back there?"

"Simple, Albanach. You weren't there to save them."

"What the hell are yae talkin' about. How could I have saved them?"

"By living," says the Nazarene. "That's all, just by living. Every time you put a bottle of booze to your lips, you're killing another Shopping Cart Soldier. That's why all your old buddies back at the Albanach Theatre are pissed off at you."

"Not all of them."

"Most of them are pissed off."

"How can I be responsible for so many Shopping Cart Soldiers? It's hardly my fault they're so fucked-up."

"By being responsible for yourself. I know and you know, and a great many other people know the hell you guys went through during the war. You were just kids at the time, and there was a great humankind change going on then that was absolutely opposed to war. That very same change was a universal thing that had just begun. That's why it didn't feel right for you and your pals to be in the war, that's why you had such a difficult time dealing with the mayhem, with the mayhem and carnage that Redeyes and his cronies put out into the world. It's as if you knew innately, and you did, that war sucked and that fighting in a war was pointless and obsolete. Your responsibility for the rest of your life is to avoid anything that will make you deviate from the responsibility you have for those of your fellow warriors who still live and, in turn, for the rest of humanity."

"Me!" says Finn, incredulously. "I have to do all that?"

"You have to get back out there in the trenches somehow, as you see fit, and do whatever you can to help your Shopping Cart Soldiers come back to life. You have to at least tell them there's another way out of their pain."

"But how, how can I do that? I don't even know myself!"

"I just told you. Stay away from the booze and the dope. That's what Redeyes and his cronies want—for you to stay screwed-up with booze. You're helpless then. Stay away from it and you'll have power and strength enough to help your buddies. Just think back to how well you guys fought, how hard you fought for your country and for freedom and for all the other wonderful things the generals told you you were fighting for. Well, you're not so naive now, you're wiser, and you know intuitively what's really worth fighting for. You have to get your back up, Finn. You have to get mad as hell and start fighting back for what you know is truly right. Begin by helping all the other Shopping Cart Soldiers you find. In helping them come back to life, you will be healing America. Believe me, it's in dire need of a bit of help."

The Nazarene stops in the middle of the street and looks at Finn. He takes him by the arm.

"Good luck to you, Finn. And don't be afraid; you're not alone. There's a great many others in this world of yours who are willing to help, willing to fight alongside you. Go out and reclaim the lives of your fellow warriors."

Finn is stunned. The Nazarene has spoke volumes in just a few minutes. Finn just wants to find a quiet place where he can sit and think, take it all in piece by piece.

"Go on," says the Nazarene. "There's the theatre," he says, pointing off across the street. "Remember, Finn, I won't be back, and you can continue to either fill up your rucksack, or you can empty it."

He looks quietly into Finn's eyes.

"C'mere," he says, and grabs Finn and hugs him as if he's afraid of losing him. Finn feels a terrible sense of loneliness come over him, and a few soft tears form in the corner of his eye. The Nazarene steps back and, turning, walks away. Finn watches the retreating figure for a long time. The Nazarene stops just as he's about to disappear over the horizon, turns, and waves at Finn. Then he walks over the crest of a hill and disappears forever.

◆ ◆ ◆

Stevenson's sitting just inside the door of the theatre, waiting for Finn to come back.

"It's a war zone in there," he says. "Half of them want to castrate you, the other half thinks you're a hero. Gemini's doing her best to mediate the situation, diffuse it actually."

"Well, I think I'm in better shape now for whatever's next," says Finn. "That was quite a conversation I had with the Nazarene."

"Oh?"

"Aye, indeed. He told me a few home truths."

"I hope it's enough. Redeyes is in rare form. He's getting them all riled up. It's not a pretty sight."

"I've got a few things to say to Redeyes myself," says Finn, pushing ahead of Stevenson into the confines of the theatre.

The theatre is much the same as when he left it. The streets are still cobblestoned, and the tall, damp tenement buildings still reach up to the thumbnail sky high overhead. All the other cast members are still onstage. Gemini sits atop her throne-like chair as usual. She looks distraught. Redeyes is sitting smugly on my stool. He has the same malevolent look in his eyes he had earlier on Dali's Tilting dancefloor. He's back again in the body of Soldiergirl, though he swore he'd laid her to rest. Finn stiffens. He thought he was making progress, that Redeyes and I had sorted out some of our differences, but it clearly isn't so. Redeyes looks vile and angry, perhaps even vicious.

"He said he could feel his power slipping," says Gemini. "Said he was fed-up playing games."

Soldiergirl walks over to Finn, her head tucked up under her arm. She sets it back on top of her neck. It's a precarious perch at best, and looks ready to topple at the slightest bump.

"Well," says she. "Have a nice little chat?"

"Why don't yae go back to where yae came from," says Finn bravely, though with a little less conviction than I would have liked.

"No, you listen to me; I came here to get you, to get back inside you. And that's what I'm going to do, come hell or high water."

"That's what you think," says I. "You'll have to get past me first."

"That won't be any problem," says Soldiergirl, pushing me hard against the brick wall of a building.

"Okay, that's enough," says Stevenson. "This won't get us anywhere."

"What the fuck do you know, Stevenson?" says Soldiergirl. "You're just a pussy like your countryman."

Stevenson brandishes his stick; Redeyes as Soldiergirl backs off. He's had enough experience with Stevenson's stick. He knows better than not to back off. The Shopping Cart Soldiers meantime mill around uncomfortably in the background. They're confused. They have no idea what's going on. Tommy-up-front grabs one of the shopping carts.

"Screw this," he says. "Let's get the hell outa here. Hey, Gemini, wanna go for a ride?"

"You drivin', big boy?" she asks, a wicked grin on her face.

"You betcha," says Tommy. "Come on, guys, let's get outa here. We'll go for a jaunt into the Tenderloin. Maybe we'll find some chicks, a few bottles of booze."

Finn's heart speeds up at the mention of the booze. He licks his lips, an involuntary gesture I'm sure. The Shopping Cart Soldiers ready themselves to leave. Ivy League pulls his crimson robe up around his neck and Romeo sticks his clappers into the holsters of their shopping cart. Johnny jumps into another cart, and Frankie stands by ready to do the pushing. Tommy gestures expansively.

"Your carriage awaits you, madam," he says.

Gemini steps off her throne, straightens her skirt and hops into the cart.

"You don't need other girls when I'm here," says she. "Now do you?"

"Right on, baby," says Frankie. "You're the best."

Gemini giggles, and the convoy of carts heads for the door, Tommy leading the way as usual.

"Well, I'm hittin' the road too; I'm no' in the mood to listen to you two goin' at it again," says Finn, pointing to Redeyes and me. Arkansas, meantime, has been standing all by himself, more confused than ever. He just can't figure it out.

"Maybe you should stay here," says Stevenson. "Since everything has to do with you anyway."

"Come on, Arkansas, let's get the hell outa here," says Finn. He grabs Arkansas's shopping cart. "Come on, buddy, I'll do the pushin'." There's a familiar, disturbing hunger in his eyes. Stevenson notices it too. Redeyes bursts out laughing.

"What is it they say about an old dog and new tricks?" he says.

"Fuck you, Redeyes," says Finn. "Don't yae think it's about time you came up with a better trick yourself, leave poor ol' Soldiergirl alone. She must be awful smelly by now."

"Ah, quite delicious," says Redeyes, smacking his lips.

Finn turns around and heads for the door.

"You're playing with fire!" Stevenson shouts after him.

"Ya gotta do what ya gotta do," says Redeyes, sounding like a used car salesman.

I'm troubled myself, and I really do believe that if he goes on with his drinking it might just be his last. I go after him and catch him by the door. I put my arms around him.

"Don't go," says I. "You might not make it back."

I slide my hand down the front of his trousers and rub him seductively. Two can play at the Grotesque's game. I rub him until he becomes lipsmacking-stiff. I smile and purr, and talk to him in the huskiest voice I can muster.

"Wouldn't you rather stay and make love to me, Finn? Wouldn't you like to make love to a beautiful young woman like me?"

He throws his head back and laughs so hard I feel like hiding in a corner somewhere. I didn't know he could be so cruel.

"First things first, Madman," he says, swaggering away as if he doesn't have a care in the world. "I'll do you when I come back."

I wonder if I should go after him. I decide not to. I promised myself I would never leave his side, that I would always keep the umbilical cord, whether imaginary or not, wrapped tightly around us. And for twenty-five years that's exactly what I did. Things are different now, I suppose. I must let it stretch. He is with the other Shopping Cart Soldiers after all; he must do with them what needs to be done. They'll look after him I'm sure. Stevenson, it seems, feels likewise. He beckons us to follow him. He sits at the foot of Gemini's throne, and we sit at his feet as if we were his disciples.

"I suppose we'll just have to wait now," he says.

"For what, pray tell," says Redeyes, impatiently.

"Until he gets back, of course. See if the fool's still alive!"

"Oh, he'll be back all right," says I.

"And then what?" Stevenson asks. "Then what? More bickering from you two?"

"I cringe every time I get near this one," says I, pointing to Redeyes. But for some reason I don't even believe what I'm saying myself; it doesn't ring true.

"No wonder," says Stevenson. "Come on, Redeyes. Get out of that body, leave Soldiergirl alone. You're just making things worse."

"Oh, I like to keep the lads on their toes," he says, metamorphosing quickly into his young self. "How's that?"

"How does he do that?" I ask. "Why can he do that and I can't?"

"You're too good, too innocent," says Stevenson.

"You have to feel a special need to be a chameleon," says Redeyes, laughing.

"Until you two see the wisdom in living peacefully inside him, he will always be an Empty. I wish you'd get that simple fact into your thick skulls!"

"He'd never knowingly let me back inside him," says Redeyes. "He's afraid of evil."

"Then you'll have to trick him," says Stevenson. "You'll have to be imaginative, creative. He's on his last legs, I do know that much."

"I'm not living with him!" I shout, defiantly. But there's no conviction in my declaration either. No power in it. Redeyes giggles.

"Shut up, Madman," warns Stevenson, slowly getting to his feet. He's got his hand over his chest and he coughs his horrible cough again. It's as if the excitement aggravates his illness. "I'm going to look for him," he continues when the coughing subsides. "I want to stay close to him. The Bureaucrats are all over the place these days. Seems like it's always so when a significant event is at hand. They don't want anything to upset the status quo—their apple cart. Anyway, I'll see you later," he promises, walking off towards the exit.

"I feel a tightening in my stomach," says I, "as if he's pulling the umbilical cord tighter and tighter, stretching it to the limit; I feel as if I could easily lose him, even after all these years.

"That might be the best thing that could happen," says Redeyes. "Sometimes you're like an old granny." He gets up and paces back and forth across the stage. "You know, it may seem to you that I'm too cold, a tough guy, with all my machinations, manipulations and contrivances, but I don't know how much of this I can take either. I think knowing he was gone, that our body was lost forever, would make me happy to go back to the Place of Truly Dead Souls and start from scratch. This is too much for me too."

Redeyes paces, deep in thought. He does look cute standing there with his brow all furrowed, his hand stroking his chin thoughtfully. I love his purple jacket, and his yellow buttons drive me wild. They're so irreverent, so cheeky, as Finn would say. Perhaps he's not as bad as he thinks he is after all. I don't know what to think any more. I'm just sick of being so fragmented. When I think this thought, when I think of this word fragmented, I feel a chill run through me. I think of Finn and I think of Spider. They fragmented bodies with their grenades, and I realize that it was that very fragmentation of those sentient beings, the MP's, that helped along the fragmentation of Finn's very being, his soul. Stevenson's words in the peep show come back to me. "As yae sow, Finn, as yae sow!"

"Ignore all that crap," says Redeyes, using his powerful ability to snoop on unsuspecting minds. "Like Louis here says, we must trick him! It's the only way. It's not because I'm too bad that he won't take me back; nor is it because you're too good," he says. "It's more than that. I've been thinking about it. Remember how it was when they killed the bull? He went into some kind of shock that night—as you well know! You and I were together then, Madman. I was that blast of cold, icy wind. That's when we became fragmented, divided. But it's so inexplicable too. Maybe it's just not meant to be explained."

"I know what you mean," says I. "I'm fed up trying to figure it all out myself."

I get up and pace alongside him.

"Let's get him," he says, "corner him. Once and for all—like a rat!"

"So, you corner him, that's easy enough. But then what? Ask him politely to let us back in? Demand that he let us back in?"

"Trick him!"

"Great, but how?"

He laughs. "Go back to the basics!"

"The basics?"

"Aye, Madman, the basics!"

"I don't follow you."

He begins to sing the same song Gemini was singing when I first walked into the Albanach Theatre. He waltzes across the stage and takes me into his arms, passionately. I feel his warm breath on my neck. I shiver. I've never felt anything so exciting. Shivers run up and down my back and up again, then spread across my shoulders like flickering light.

He sings: "They try to tell us we're too young, too young to really be in love...."

God, he has a beautiful voice too. I can't help myself; I run my hands up and down his back, up and down, up and down, down, down. His arse is firm, as tight as a drumskin. What a lovely boy he is right enough. My nipples grow harder and harder, more erect; my stomach quivers as if a hundred butterflies flutter there and, my God, what's happening down there between my legs? I'm tingling, vibrating, throbbing as if that part of me is separate, has become an entity all on its own, has a mind of its own, a mouth of its own, a hungry mouth of its own, salivating, wanting, needing. Kneading, kneading. He's kneading my nipples. I pull him closer to me. I feel his hardness against me. What should I do? I've never experienced this before, never been so close to another body before. What am I supposed to do now? I wonder. It's one thing to be spiritwispy and go inside Finn, but these corporeal, physical body experiences are new to me. They are an entirely different matter, an entirely different experience with their own set of laws.

"Make love to me," whispers Redeyes. "Make love to me and I will come inside you, all of me, Madman."

I look at him in disbelief. "You're mad!" says I.

"It's the only way."

"I don't understand."

"If I go inside you right at the magic moment, then that's it. That's all there is to it! We'll be as one. Accept me, that's all you have to do. If you have me inside you, then all you have to do is to somehow get inside him."

"Aye, but there's the rub," says I, only half joking.

"If you let me inside you, that's two in one. Half the battle. A twofer!" he says, laughing. "You'll be twice as strong."

"Sounds logical."

"It's the only solution."

"What's going to happen to you? You won't have a body any more."

"I don't anyway. Neither do you. These bodies we have are completely illusory. There's no substance to them. When push comes to shove, they're useless."

"Yeah, I know."

"Anyway, Madman, you know how I'm always getting a bum rap, how evil's always getting a bum rap. You'd have just as easy a time of it getting both of us inside him as you would just getting yourself back in him."

"Why should I even bother with you? It's been a free-for-all these past twenty-five years. Why should I care about you all of a sudden?"

He laughs. "Balance, baby! Pure and simple! Can't have one without the other. I guess we both know now how much we need each other—all three of us."

"I don't think Finn's convinced."

"I think he is; he just won't admit it. Anyway if we trick him he can save face. Let him think he's just going along with that old-fashioned idea of twoness. Threeness is still too much for him. He won't know the difference. If I'm already inside you, then he'll let us both in. Right at the magic moment; I'm sure of it!"

"Sounds like a done-deal, big boy," says I, in a weak but soldierly attempt to imitate Gemini when she jumped into the cart with Tommy.

"Well, shall we?" he says, nervously.

"Are you sure you want to after all?" says I. "You seem a wee bit nervous."

It occurs to me then that we're both virgins, that we've never done anything like this before, not even a kiss. We've seen it often enough, to be sure, but we've never actually done it. We've watched Finn many times, and we've been bored many times, but we've never actually felt it, the closeness of it, the skin-to-skin contact of it. Not even when we were inside him. I remember distinctly the first time he did it with Mary Quinn when they were in Hawaii, when they were virgins too. I remember how wonderful he felt, but it was still only vicariously through him that Redeyes and I knew the experience. I experienced his feelings as an observer, but I didn't feel the experience, the physicality of it. Perhaps now I will.

"Perhaps," says Redeyes, looking very solemn. "You know," he says, "I've been thinking too. When all is said and done, this is the only way it can be, you know. It just makes so much sense. But you know, Madman, when I get inside you, I can't come back out again. That's it for me. It's all up to you then."

"Yes, Redeyes, I know. I was just thinking that myself."

"You won't hurt me, will you?" he says, looking both afraid and ever so tender at the same time. I slip my hand into his.

"I wouldn't dream of it," says I. "You're too much a part of me. I can see that now."

"Then let's go somewhere and make love."

"I wonder if we'll be able to talk to each other after you're inside me?" says I, allowing him to lead me off into one of the old tenement buildings.

"I don't think it works like that, Madman. I think it'll just be as it used to be. I am you; you are me. We'll just be one, that's all."

"Did you bring any rubbers?" I ask, giggling. "Isn't that what all the girls ask the first time?"

"I wouldn't know," he says. "But I don't think we really need them."

"Well, come on then," says I, hurrying him into the nearest apartment.

◆　◆　◆

He wonders who I am, yet it's all so simple. I am a woman, a woman at last. I feel like shouting from the highest hill, "I...am...a...WOMAN!" We did it and I feel great. It was much more wonderful than I could ever have imagined. But then I wouldn't know how to describe such a thing. How does one describe lovemaking, I wonder. It would be tough enough to describe ordinary sex, even if one were used to it, but to describe what happened between Redeyes and me would be better left to the pen of a Lautreamont or to the brush of a Paul Delvaux. It is that simple; it is that great!

I feel filled up, full of Redeyes. I feel stronger than I ever have. He is inside me and, though I don't yet feel complete, I am more complete than I have been in twenty-five years. There we were, right at the magic moment, spent like dissipating thunderheads, with Redeyes lying breathless on top of me, and me trembling and shaking beneath him, both of us happy as laughter, when all at once we blend and become one. At first we are oil in water, then we are oil in oil. He blends well with me and completes his final metamorphosis. I can hear him now. He talks to me. He experiences what I experience. He is aware. He talks to me, mind to mind, thought to thought. There's a purity in our communication I haven't experienced since the moment of The Leaving. *I can see that now. I chuckle. It's funny. What will I call that moment when I get back inside Finn? The Coming? Yes,* The Coming, *what else?*

I fought with Redeyes for such a long time—just as Finn fights me. I wonder why I fought so hard, and for so long. I gave up the fight, grew tired of beating myself to death—no pun intended. When I begin to know that things are simply as they are, when I begin to accept the futility of struggling against Redeyes, struggling against that part of me known as Redeyes, I begin to know a modicum of peace at last. I wonder why it is we didn't know sooner how such a simple, ordinary act as making love could bring such peace, could feel so right, could be so right in propagating wholeness? Had I known I would have made love every day, all day.

And what of Finn MacDonald? Is he tired also of fighting me, of fighting, in reality, himself? I hope so. I think so. I know he misses us, that his life as an Empty has run its course, has reached its foregone conclusion—despair and desolation! He has other ways to go than down. I hope he goes forward; I hope he goes up. He can't stay where he is; those days are over. No more stagnation for him. He's felt me, he's seen me; he's seen Redeyes. He can't stay stuck any more. He has to move. Baby steps perhaps. But move he must. I wait. I pace. I ponder. I wonder where he is. The theatre's empty. The streets are wet. It is warm. It is dusk. At the far end of the street the gas lamp shimmers again. I pace. I pace. I hear rumblings. I hear the rumblings of many distant voices, growing closer. Beneath me I feel the tremor of marching feet, feet marching towards the Albanach Theatre, growing closer, ever closer. They're back, they're coming back! The platoon is coming back. Who's dead? Who's maimed? They're loud, rambunctious, those who are still alive. Is it the maimed who shout and scream? Or the living? Who wish they were dead. They're chanting, chanting out a hard-driving staccato chant, angrily, forcefully like a flurry of punches to the face.

Wonder what they'd be like if they lived today
wonder what they'd be like if they hadn't all died
wonder what they'd be like if you'd kept them all alive!

Stevenson enters first, looking angry and disheveled. He leans heavily on his stick, coughing and hacking helplessly. Finn follows behind, held up by Arkansas. They're roaring drunk, holding each other up, Gemini and the rest of the fellows follow behind, screaming like linties, the rapid fire of their chant zipping through the air like arrows of anger.

Ashes in the jungle stink of burning boy flesh
they gave their lives for nothin' such a mess, mess, mess
they left their asses in the jungle such a sinister sight
when they gave their little boy lives for
America...America...America the free.
Wonder what they'd be like if they lived today
wonder what they'd be like if they hadn't all died
wonder what they'd be like if you'd kept them all ALIVE!

Finn and Arkansas collapse into a corner; Stevenson sits down by my stool, exhausted. I join him, not at all willing to get caught up in the rabble-rousing before me. Everybody's drunk, it seems—even Gemini who is sitting on top of Tommy's shoulders, leading the pack like queen Boudicea, the ancient Keltic warrior-queen who held the invading Romans at bay for so long. I can feel Redeyes laughing. Tommy's laughing too.

"Well, Madman," he says, "there he is—drunk as expected."

I feel like kicking him in the balls; he's such a know-it-all, a peabrain. Finn looks up drunkenly, trying with all his might to see through the haze. He manages to get up onto his feet with a great deal of help from the wall.

"Hey, Madman," he mumbles, "let's go do it." Then he has a good laugh to himself. I look over at Tommy. He's walking around the stage like a cat ready to spring. Finn clears his head somewhat and walks into the middle of the stage.

"Hey, Johnny," he says. "Tell us a nice poem. Did yae have a good time? Just like the old days. Sittin' in the park gettin' high just like we used to. Come on, man, give us a poem. Hey, Romeo, tell him to recite a poem."

I don't know what Tommy's waiting for, but whatever it is, it has just happened. Maybe Finn simply pissed him off beyond measure; he lashes into him as if he's a lifelong enemy. He whacks the Albanach hard on the shoulder and he goes down onto his arse, his arms and legs flying in the air. He rights himself and tries to get back up, but Tommy won't let him.

"Stay there!" he says. "Stay there until I tell you to get up."

"Fuck you, meathead," says Finn. But he's in no condition to get up. Perhaps that's for the best; Tommy is furious.

"You're nothin' but a fuckin' wimp, man, a cop-out! You've been tryin' to kill yourself for years, an' when we try an' help you all you want is a goddamned poem. I'll give you a fuckin' poem! It's a good hard kick on the ass you need."

Tommy puts his foot on Finn's chest and shoves him onto his back. He circles around Finn who is now lying back, leaning on his elbows staring up at Tommy with a look of abject fear and hatred contorting his face.

"How do I get through to you?" asks Tommy, finally. "How do I make it clear that as long as you're riding that goddamned shopping cart of yours, you're negating that we ever lived, that as long as you keep pushin' it through the streets of San Francisco you're livin' the life of a loser, a complete and useless fuckin' loser? Don't you remember us like we used to be before the night of *The Leaving*? Young, healthy, fulla life. We didn't want to die. You were the only one that made it, Alba-man. And by screwin' up your own life, you're actually screwin' up the memory of us! Don't you see that. It's as if we died for nothin'. You're the only one of us left for chrissakes. You're the only one of us left who can tell other people of our goddamn NOBILITY! We were goddamn noble warriors. Sure we smoked dope an' got high like everybody else, but when push came to shove, we fought like hell. Didn't we? Goddamn it, man, didn't we?"

"Hey, lighten up, Tommy!" says Johnny.

Finn's all slumped over and there are tears in his eyes.

"Yeah, we did," he says. "We fought like tigers."

"Yeah, Tommy, cool it," says Ivy League.

"Nail him, Tommy," says Frankie, "nail the cocksucker!"

"Lighten up my ass, he's all mine," says Tommy, leaning over the Albanach, eyes ablaze. "Why is it you're tryin' to kill yourself? You don't want to grow old? Is that why you drink the way you do? You like being etherized by booze, don't you? Is that how you pretend to cope with life? Keep it up and you'll either go mad with wet-brain, or you'll just have another fuckin' seizure an' you'll be dead, bigger than shit, man. Nothin' left!"

Everybody in the room is thunderstruck, myself included. I don't think anybody knew that Tommy, the quiet man, was such an orator, such a showman. He continues to circle around Finn who is just sitting there on the floor, not daring to move. From time to time he winces and rubs his shoulder. Arkansas's lying in the corner, snoring. Ivy League, still kneeling in his shopping cart has found a saxophone. He plays. Low and slow, plaintively. The rest of the guys get into it by snapping their fingers, swaying to the sound of the sax. My foot taps of its own accord. Stevenson smiles at me and winks. Tommy, emboldened, continues. He seems to have found his forte—showmanship! He's the greatest actor the Albanach Theatre has ever seen!

"You're gonna end up just like that poor bastard over there," says Tommy, pointing to Arkansas. "You'll be lyin' there under the bushes or a goddamned bridge, an' a couple of punks'll just beat your brains in. You know that yourself. Or you'll be lyin' somewhere, drunk on your ass, and you'll freeze to death. You know that too, you *know* that's an option for you."

Finn scuttles backward, crablike, trying to disappear. He knows that everything Tommy says is true, all of it. If the drink doesn't get him, or madness, then some punk will kill him for his meager possessions or, like Tommy says, he'll die of hypothermia some winter. He's come close many times before. He remembers coming to once, covered in blood, shoes gone, wallet gone, possessions scattered all around his shopping cart. It's almost as dangerous out there on the streets as it was in the jungle, always watching his back for the predators. The predators who, like hyenas, come out only at night.

"No!" he screams. "That's not what I want!"

"Then get up!" says Tommy. "Rise above this bullshit, man. Get up, get up, get up! Unless of course you like lying in the swill an' muck. Is that where you belong, in all that swill an' muck?"

Finn cracks as Tommy stands over him, threatening him. He begins to sob.

"Ah, look! What's this? Is that a teensy weensy tear I see forming in the corner of your eye? Are you crying again, Finn? On the pity pot are you? Feeling sorry for yourself are you? Yes, yes, yes, you are, you are, you are! But you like to live in shit! You love it there, you have no responsibilities there, you can stay in your bottle and no one comes looking for you—until now, that is! It's perfect for you. Pretty soon no one will know whether you're alive or dead. No one will know you ever existed. Yes? Your epitaph will simply read, *He never existed*! You better watchit, buddy. The deeper you dig into your hole, the harder it's gonna be to get out of it. And soon enough the hole you've dug for yourself will fill up to the top with water and you'll drown, drown, drown. That'll be the end of Finn MacDonald, proud Albanach!"

When he's done, Tommy walks into center stage and takes a wide bow. He looks at each of us in turn.

"He's all yours, ladies and gentleman," he says, then walks off and sits in Gemini's throne, looking down over the stage like the Grand Inquisitor, though with a huge smile creasing his face. Then Frankie Chen with the shotoff balls takes centerstage and prepares himself for a torrent by puffing up his chest and flexing his muscles. He leans over Finn conspiratorially and speaks to him in a controlled and hushed voice.

"You're nothing, Finn," he says. "A big, bloated, bulbous blob of nothin'. All that garbage and shit you live in, that shoppin' cart life you live in, drinkin', wanderin' the streets, beggin' for pennies, all adds up to one thing—nothin'! You better get a grip, Finn, me bucko! Your mammy never taught you to live like this. Look at you! Wearin' that stupid lookin' overcoat, unshaven, filthy! Is that your disguise? Is that how you hide from reality? Let me tell you somethin', Alba man, underneath all that shit, that pile of shit you call home, is a nest of huge and bitter cockroaches, an' they're gettin' fatter an' fatter each day. They're just waitin' for you to go to sleep some night and they're gonna come crawlin' outa their holes and in seconds they're gonna be all over you, crawlin' in your ears and in your mouth and up the crack in your ass an' they're gonna start eatin' your innards, eatin' you from the inside out an' you'll be so fucked-up drunk you won't even notice it an' you'll wake up changed—the great metamorphosis! Finn the cockroach man! All the other cockroaches will eat you alive and when you wake up all that's gonna be left is nothin', nothin', nothin'! A great big, bloated, bulbous blob of nothin'! Get a grip, dumbass!"

Frankie gets down on his knees beside Finn and puts his arm around his shoulders.

"You know somethin', Finn," he says. "You make me sick! You really make me sick, an' I don't like the way you use us as fodder for your self-pity. That's the bottom line, buddy. We were in a war an' we didn't make it! God, I still remember that night when we killed the bull. Pure hell, that's what it was. The terrible fright I felt when we got ambushed. The absolute searing pain in my nuts when the bullet went through me. I could actually feel the searing pain travel up through my groin, through my stomach, and when the pain hit my heart, I could actually feel my heart exploding, like somebody blowing up a balloon too much. I saw my end, I saw my last look at life so clearly, all you guys fighting your asses off, the smoke all around us, the noise of gunfire and screams, my own included, the dripping trees, and all of us up to our asses in filthy fuckin' jungle mud, and all them goddamned snakes that come out in all that wetness. And I remember my last thought, laughable now, it was so simple, so inconsequential. I remember just thinking, with pictures of my family floating past my eyes, *Oh, no*. This is it! This is all there is to it. And you're still alive, Finn; we ain't. An' when I watch you squirming around the streets like some kinda slug I get sick to my stomach. Is that all you think of us? Is that how you remember us? By feelin' sorry for yourself? Fuck you, man! I resent you usin' the memory of me to feed your lack of fuckin' backbone!"

"Fuckin'-A, Frankie," says Romeo. "Give 'im hell, bro."

"All right, fellas," says Gemini. "That's enough!" She's up on her feet. Everybody else is too, except me and Stevenson. They pace around Finn who has been backing off towards a corner, trying to get away from them. He looks angry himself, and when he reaches the wall, he gets up onto his feet, though he's shaky still.

"You don't know what the fuck it's been like," he says. "None of you know what it's been like! I'm the only one of us that made it! Remember? Do you understand? I'm the only one of us that made it back to the fuckin' world!"

"You didn't make it back anywhere, bro," says Romeo. "You're still lyin' in the goddamn jungle pissin' your pants."

"Fuckin'-A," says Tommy. "Look at you, man. Drunk again. It's crazy! What is it you like about gettin' drunk all the time? I'm sick of lookin' at you like that! Drunk, sober, drunk, sober, drunk, sober. It's drivin' *me* mad!"

"I don't know what I'm gonnae do," says Finn. "It's no' as easy as yae think it is to quit."

"You better start thinkin' about the rest of us—an' people like him," says Frankie, pointing off to the prone figure of Arkansas. "It's too late for him—you missed helpin' him by a couple of hours. But there's a lot more like him."

"Five to seven hundred thousand at last count," says Stevenson. "So they say at least. Five to seven hundred thousand Shopping Cart Soldiers are pushing shopping carts through American streets every day. Many of them don't make it. Every year in all your little enclaves all over America half a dozen die each year. Bluidy hell,

Finn, four or five of your Veteran friends die every Winter in North Beach alone."

"Can...you...dig...it!" says Romeo, with shameless facetiousness.

"You better come out from behind the bushes and your bottles and get rid of that damned shopping cart," says Tommy. "Throw it in the San Francisco Bay; you don't need it any more."

"Force a change," says Romeo. "Take our country back, god-damnit!"

The tempo rises now as each of his old friends says his piece, as they'd been planning to do all these years. I hoped he would listen, that he could listen, that the booze hadn't completely destroyed the brain cells he would need to reclaim his life. I hoped he had enough brain cells left to make him want to live.

"Take back our country," says Romeo, "from the Bureaucrats. They don't give a rat's ass about us. That's your job, you the livin'! Ya hafta fight for us. Those assholes like to see you fucked up on booze an' dope. They like it when they know you feel as if you don't deserve to love your country."

"Right on," says Tommy. "Take back our country, even if it is fucked up. Get rid of the booze. Get rid of the lyin' Bureaucrats. That's your new job, Finn. Ya hafta fight for every vet still livin'."

"Do you know what else they say, Finn?" asks Stevenson. "They say that around one hundred and sixty thousand Vietnam Veterans have killed themselves since the war ended. That's a fact. Too much pain. Another couple of million are said to have problems with alcohol and drugs. That too is a fact. You have to help, Finn—even if it just means that you don't go down like that yourself."

"This country's yours, buddy," says Tommy. "It's ours! We fought for it, we died for it; some of us loved it so much they ran away. Sometimes I wish to hell I had. Ya hafta take it back, man. Take the mountains back, take the rivers back, take the deserts back. Shit, man, take your fuckin' dreams back. Take your goddamn life back; get rid of your nightmares. Throw away your guilt an' shame, Albanach!"

"Fuckin'-A," says Romeo.

"I need some help," says Finn. "Some soul help or somethin'.

I'm so fucked up I don't know if I'm comin' or goin', an' that's the truth!"

"That's why I'm here, Finn," says I. "I've been trying to tell you that all along."

"That's why we're all here, buddy," says Johnny. "You can help us by lettin' us go. You hafta put us in our little pigeonholes of the past. We're dead now an' you can't bring us back. Don't forget us, Finn—not that you ever could or would, but let us go! Remember us, but let us rest in peace. It was war, Finn. What happened happened. Let it go, and remember the good times. Only then can *you* rest in peace. Only then can you *live* in peace! And we can help you by tellin' you we want you to live out the resta your life the way you were supposed to, the way you woulda if the war hadn't interrupted everythin'. The truth is, we didn't come here to hurt you or be mean; we came here to help ya. Even if we have to beg, plead, or beat it into you. Ain't that right, guys?"

A chorus of fuckin'-A's rang out around the room.

"Just like the ol' days," says Frankie and everybody laughs.

"What was it you were sayin' out there in the Tenderloin, man," says Romeo. "Just before you drank that whiskey? You need to say that again."

"Yeah," says Frankie. "But get on your knees this time."

"Hey," says Gemini. "Do you have any booze left? You should make a sort of altar, and talk to it, tell it to get lost—you don't need it anymore."

"Yeah," says Frankie. "You don't have to drink it any more—it's as simple as that."

"It's true, Finn," says Johnny. "It's up to you, man. Remember back in Nam we used to call all them ol' fuckers juicers, juice freaks. Well, you've become an ol' fucked up juice freak! Ya hafta get away from that. Get fuckin' rid of that shit. Tell yourself you don't drink. It's that simple!"

"Yeah, man, that's dynamite!" says Ivy League. "Then you can tell the resta the grunts out there on the street they can do the same. Hey, man, can ya dig it! Thousands an' thousands of Shopping Cart Soldiers kickin' away their motherfuckin' shopping carts an' standin' up in the middle of the street sayin', Pardon me, but I don't drink!"

Everybody has a good laugh then. The mood is good, it is strong. Finn takes advantage of the moment. He sticks his hand deep into the pocket of his overcoat and pulls out a bottle of whiskey. When he catches sight of the booze it jolts him as it always did; a shiver runs through him. He feels a fleeting spasm of desire as if he just wants to turn the bottle up and chug from it. Tommy jumps up out of Gemini's throne and joins the rest of us down on the stage floor.

"Here, Finn," he says. "Put it up there on Gemini's throne like it's an altar. We'll make this a celebration, a sacrament. This'll be the holy sacrament of Lettin' Go. Go ahead, man, put it up there an' get rid of it."

Finn scrambles up onto the steps and sits the bottle on top of the throne. All at once the lights in the theatre dim and a golden spotlight comes up on the bottle of whiskey. I must admit it does look powerful sitting up there under the light. It looks absolutely majestic, as if it were alive, fighting for all it's worth, making itself look as attractive as it possibly can. Finn is wavering. His body trembles and shakes as he descends the stairs.

"Get down on your knees," shouts Tommy, like a preacherman. "Don't worry, brother, we'll be here to help ya!"

"Right on," chime in the other Veterans.

Finn gets down on his knees, feeling stupid I must admit but, in a quivering voice, he begins his sacramental letting go.

"Oh, sneaky bastard bottle of booze, come let me take my fill of you. Let your golden spirit course through my veins an' set my soul on fire. I love you more than words could ever hope to say. You've entranced me and enchanted me. You've courted me and wooed me. You've loved me an' possessed me. You've taken me an' captured me. You've bewildered me an' bamboozled me."

He stands and lifts his arms high up into the air. The rest of the grunts gather round him, and every time he puts a lot of stress on a word, Romeo lets out with a great whacking wallop of his clappers.

He goes on. "I am your slave and anything you ask of me I'll do for you. You have done to me what no other in this whole wide world could ever hope to do. You have shit upon me and spat upon me, you have trodden me underfoot and pissed upon me."

As he continues with his litany, the Veterans dance a war dance of sorts around him and his bottle. They are working themselves up into a frenzy even Dionysius would have been proud of.

"You have jiggled your filthy arse in front of my face. You have made me suck the tit of your hopelessness. You have trampled me with your leprous feet. You have debased me."

The frenzied dance of the Veterans grows wilder and they chant along with Finn.

"Debased me!"

"You have decayed me."

"Decayed me!"

"You have deluded me!"

"Deluded me!"

"You have defiled me!"

"Defiled me!"

"You have deducted me from the joys of life."

"Deducted me!"

"You have made me decrepit."

"Decrepit!"

"You have declared me the...MADMAN!"

"Madman!" everybody shouts just as Finn collapses to the floor.

How did this come about? What has happened to make him say so much? We're all stunned, me in particular. I run over to him and throw my arms around him. The dance of the Veterans becomes more frenzied than ever as their frenzy will somehow help Finn continue his prayer of letting go.

"Madman?" says I, hugging him more tightly. "Then you really do acknowledge me, you really, really do. You are the Madman! I am you!"

"Later, Madman," says Finn. "I ain't done yet." He scrambles to his feet and continues. The Veterans continue their frenzied dance.

"Despoiler," he says.

"Despoiler!" repeat the Veterans.

"You devious, destructive, despotic bastard!"

"BASTARD!" shout the Veterans in unison.

"Oh, dear God," Finn continues, grabbing the splendidly lit, majestic bottle of booze. "Wherever you are, as sure as this bottle of booze is in my hands, you must, dear God, help me!"

Then he sits back on his haunches, exhausted. The holy sacrament of Letting Go is over. Will he ever drink again? Who knows! But if he ever thinks again of putting a bottle of booze against his lips he'll think about this moment too. If I have my way, he won't; if Redeyes has his way, he will. Because Redeyes likes Finn most when he's overcome with the madness of the bottle. Like every other great truth, that one too is simple. I let him lie there for a while. The other vets sit around talking, reminiscing about the war. The scene is both ethereal and surrealistic at the same time. Finn's leaning on his haunches, his head bowed, his begging prayer evoking the power of his God. Gemini's up there in her throne, her head leaning in the cup of her hand, looking pensive and lonely. The other Veterans are having a good time talking about their experiences in the war. Romeo mentions The Leaving and everybody has a good laugh when he recounts the part about the bull's balls being shot off. I can't hold their laughter against them. They were kids when they died and, that being so, still don't know any better. Inside me, I hear Redeyes laughing. Finally I shake Finn back to awareness.

"Come on," says I. "It's time to go."

I walk with him into the same tenement building I'd gone to with Redeyes. I want my tryst with him to be special. I take him to the penthouse at the top of the building. I get a kick out of watching the astonishment on his face when he takes in the panoramic view of the city. Huge bay windows look out over San Francisco north, south, east and west. What's more, the interior of the penthouse is made for love. All soft colors and textures, candlelight, beautiful music playing softly. Carpets an inch thick. Two downfilled chairs sit in front of a blazing log fire. A huge, four-poster bed takes up the middle of the floor. The bed is at the dead center of this opulent room. It is draped with lace and silk. The pillows too are down-filled. They are fat like a Christmas turkey is fat. They are ready to be sat on, slept on, loved on. Next to the bed is Finn's painting of the splitapart woman he carries with him in his shopping cart, the one he does of me, over and over, without ever knowing who it is he's painting.

He's standing in an alcove by the northern window. He looks out towards the Golden Gate bridge and the mountains across the bay. Suddenly he turns and looks at me. There's a look of longing or remembrance in his eyes. When he sees his painting standing on its easel by the bed, he gives a great, heavy sigh and draws in his breath as if drawing in his last. He drops to his knees and sobs such hard, hard sobs I become alarmed. He's like a child whose heavy, heavy sobs frighten her parents into helplessness and panic. For a long time he sobs. His whole life passes through his mind. First there's the night in Alba when he meets the lone piper who warns him of the woe to come; then leaving what was still known to him as Scotland; then the war; then Mary and Finlay John Quinn, his son, and their happy years together. Finally, his years on the streets, homeless, a Shopping Cart Soldier as miserable as sin. When his sobs subside, he looks up at me.

"You know, Madman, my heart is truly broken."

And I believe him. I really do believe his heart is split in two. I can feel Redeyes inside me, panicking, urging me to comfort him. He's afraid we might lose him after all. But Finn stands, then chuckles.

"I haven't even felt a carpet in twelve years. Can you imagine! I haven't even felt a fuckin' carpet in twelve years! It's nice in here."

"Then why don't you enjoy it?" I tell him. "Make the most of it! Take a nice luxurious bath, have a shave. I believe there's a wardrobe fit for a king in there too. We'll get dressed up. I'll get rid of my robe, wear a nice dress and golden slippers. This will be our special night. The night we've both wanted all these years."

He looks at me and smiles.

"That would be fine, wouldn't it?"

Redeyes sighs with relief. I feel him strongly inside me. I have

all the abilities he once did, as well as my own. I am now a
changeling too. I'll use it if I have to, just as he did. I feel him
chuckle inside me. He thinks he's got one up on me. He thinks that
by allowing him inside me he has won a victory of sorts for himself,
a defeat for me. But I've simply become accustomed to the idea
that without both Redeyes and myself, Finn won't be complete,
won't be whole. He needs us both; it's that simple! It's up to Finn
whether he goes this way or that way. I suppose that one of the joys
of being human is to have the gift of choice. If I can get back inside
him, he'll be complete and, being complete, will have the full extent
of his gift of choice at his disposal. He'll be better able to choose
whether or not he wants to live a decent life, or remain a Shopping
Cart Soldier, tossing soulless, spiritless, across the sea like a piece
of driftwood fully at the mercy of the currents. What a shame that
would be.

I look out across the city. I hear him bathing, taking advantage
of the amenities. He's like a child playing with new toys. His new
toys are warm water and soap and the luxurious carpet under his
feet. More and more lights come on in the streets below. It seems
that as Finn becomes more whole, his broken city does too. I listen
to the water running. I think of him bathing. I think of him naked. I
think of Redeyes. He will still do his best to wreak havoc. It's his
nature, his reason for being, after all. But I'll do my best to do my
best. I can keep him in check. I am a woman after all and have
some good, strong woman talents to balance his man talents.

The water's stopped running. Finn is sitting in one of the chairs
in front of the blazing log fire. He's naked.

"What, no tuxedo, no beautiful robe," says I.

"I thought about it," he says, laughing. "But like the carpets I
haven't stood on in twelve years, I haven't been so naked in twelve
years either. It feels good."

I take my robe off and sit, naked, in the chair opposite him. I
throw caution to the wind.

"I guess this is it then," he says. "It took me a long time to get
here, Madman."

I let him talk. He is calm. The ravishes of time and his rough life have fallen from him by ten or more years. He's shaved and clean; he doesn't even have a paunch. You'd never know he's been on the streets for twelve years.

"You look fine," I tell him. "Handsome."

"And you, you're very beautiful." He laughs. "That's great," says Finn. "I have a beautiful soul.

Redeyes is laughing too. "Yes you do," I hear him reply, laughing all the more.

Finn gets up and as he's about to kneel in front of me we hear another voice, the voice of another woman.

"My name is Mui," says the voice.

Finn straightens up quickly. We look over towards the voice. It's his painting. His painting is stepping off the canvas. Finn stiffens. He looks around the room. His eyes dart furtively, this way then that. His painting stands between him and the door. There's no escape unless he goes through her, barges through her like a steamroller. His shoulders slump forward in resignation.

"You've been calling me Soldiergirl all these years," says the painting. "My name is Mui."

It's my turn to stiffen. Mui? Soldiergirl? What does she mean, Mui? She looks like me! I thought that was me in the painting.

"No, Madman," says she. "There was much confusion in the jungle that night of *The Leaving*. Souls flying everywhere. Souls mixed up. Bodies mixed up. There was much confusion that night in the jungle. My name is Mui."

She lowers her head and looks down at the separation of her body. The separation of body and soul? I wonder. She appears to be in pain, great pain, excruciating pain. The two pieces of her body come together. They melt together. The scar of the separation moves, wavelike, around her stomach like the Northern Lights rippling across the dark night sky. Then it disappears as if it's never been there at all. Mui slumps forward. She seems ready to faint. She looks up with the dreamy eyes of someone at peace with herself.

"You didn't even get that right, Finn," says she. "It was my head you lopped off. You separated me at the neck, not at the navel."

Finn darts a glance at me then back at Mui.

"That wasn't me," he says. "It was Romeo Robinson who did that. You were going to kill me and Romeo chopped your head off."

Mui smiles. "No, Finn," says she. "It was you. I was going to kill Romeo. He was on the ground, not you. You chopped my head off to save Romeo. You've been hiding it all these years. You were wrong too, Madman. It was your Finn who took my head off."

I have nothing to say. It's all too mad. This is all too mad! How could we have been so wrong? Finn slumps into his chair. He's pale.

"But I forgive you," says Mui. "What's done is done. I just want you to leave me alone now. Let me rest. Like all of your Veteran friends, I just want to rest."

She leans over and picks up my robe.

"When you get to where you need to be, Madman," says she, "you won't need this. But I will." She looks at Finn. "I forgive you, Finn. Remember that." She turns and walks towards the door. "I'm going to join the other Veterans." She opens the door and looks back. "Don't paint me any more. Leave me alone!" She closes the door behind her, quietly, and is gone. A soft light shines from the empty canvas. The canvas trembles then is still. I look at Finn; he looks at me.

"Make love to me, Finn. Take me back."

I burst into tears.

He puts his arms around me, comforts me.

"I can't take it any more either, Madman," he says.

"I have nowhere to go," says I. "I'm naked. She took my robe. Take me back, Finn. I have nowhere to go. I'm naked."

He gets up and, taking me by the hand, we walk hand-in-hand, towards the bed.

"Will it work?" he asks.

"Yes," says I.

"I want to put this part of my life behind me," he says.

"It will work," I tell him again.

We lie beside each other on top of the bed. I see the shimmer of a great many more lights coming on in the streets below, rising high above the tenement buildings.

◆ ◆ ◆

All the veterans are waiting for him when he steps out of the stairwell of the tenement building into the soft, subdued lights of the Albanach Theatre. The Veterans sit in a circle in the middle of the cobblestoned stage. Mui sits in the middle of the circle talking and laughing with the Veterans, like a young Christ talking to the elders in the temple. Stevenson sits up on Gemini's throne, smiling, taking in the scene before him, as if he were watching an exciting drama.

Inside here, inside the Albanach's body, Redeyes and I swim around in his bloodstream, all the way throughout his brain and into the far reaches of his extremities. Finn can't believe how whole he is, how complete we are, and he thanks his God profusely. He thanks Stevenson for guiding him through the Land of the Truly Alive, and he thanks all his old army pals for coming to help steer him back onto the path leading to the light.

Mui is the first to see him as he steps out of the tenement building. She goes over to him, puts her arm through his, and pulls him towards the circle of smiling Veterans. She looks good in my crimson robe, as if it were tailormade for her. The Veterans are delighted when they see Finn, when they see him looking so together, so complete, and smiling too. He's wearing dark shoes and jacket, blue jeans and a white T-shirt. He's shaved and his hair is brushed. Arkansas in particular is delighted to see him. The old pals embrace.

"Goddamn, man, it's good to see ya," says Arkansas. "Ya look great! Did ya win the goddamn lottery or somethin'?"

"No way, Arkansas, I stole this stuff from some rich sonofabitch." Arkansas laughs and slaps Finn on the back.

"Right on, buddy," he says.

"Finn, hey Finn," says Johnny, "we're gonna have a parade. You gonna come?"

"Yeah, man," says Romeo, "Stevenson said he's got a nice surprise for us."

Stevenson's still sitting up on Gemini's throne. He's having the time of his life by the looks of him. Finn looks up at him and smiles.

"We want you to lead the parade?" Finn says Tommy-up-front. "Will ya do it, will ya lead the parade."

"No way, man," says Finn, a bit embarrassed.

"You have to," says Frankie.

"That's right, Finn," says Gemini. "You have to!"

"Hey, Finn, we don't have to walk," says Ivy League. "Stevenson says we're gettin' a lift. You know, one-a them big fancy limos? It'll be fun!"

"I'll go to the parade, but I ain't goin' first," says Finn. "Remember what I was like in basic trainin'? Couldn't follow my own nose, Ivy League."

"Nah, it's up to you, Finn," says Tommy. "You have to go first. It's all on you now. You an' Arkansas get up to the topa the line'.

"Awright, awright," says Finn. "I'll do it, I'll do it! Come on, Arkansas, let's get this show on the road."

Finn looks up at Stevenson.

"You comin'?" he says.

"Wouldn't miss it for all the world," Stevenson replies, stepping down from the throne.

Before she leaves him, Mui takes Finn aside. "Remember what I told you, Finn. *I forgive you*! There's no need to go back to that place again. I forgive you, and if you can learn to forgive yourself, then you'll be able to live out the rest of your life in peace. Don't worry about us, Finn; if you let us go, we'll be fine. We'll go to the Place of Truly Dead Souls, and there we'll be able to do what we have to do. You will become a man at peace with himself. You'll be able to see the flowers again, and when the sun shines you will see it." Then she kisses him on the lips and runs off to take up her position, arm in arm, with Stevenson. Romeo turns to Finn.

"She told us everythin', bro. Thanks for savin' my life!" He laughs. "It was only a couple more hours, but it was better than nothing."

"That's right Finn," says Tommy. "Thanks for everythin'! It's funny how we got things so screwed up."

"Hey, come on you guys, we've got a parade to go to," says Gemini."

The veterans push the two old pals up to the head of the line and everybody else gets in behind them. Gemini and Tommy go first, followed by Romeo who bangs out a steady rhythm with his clappers. Frankie and Ivy League are next, supporting Johnny Quinn between them. Stevenson and Mui bring up the rear, like the Imperial Guard.

I feel comfortable in here beside Redeyes, looking out through the eyes of Finn. Redeyes and I are more content than we've ever been. How stupid we all were to remain so fragmented, but what the hell did we know—we were all so damned young after all. If nothing else, it's good to be rid of those blasted shopping carts. Finn feels better too. I can tell by the way his body feels. Comfortable and warm, with an emanating glow surrounding him.

The moment Finn and Arkansas open the doors, they are met by a sight that would melt any Albanach's heart. There sits Silverbright on top of the wooden-wheeled cart, decked out in his beautiful new saffron robe, looking every bit the seer. He holds the whisk as if it were a sceptre, as if he were king of the world. Behind the old seer stands the Albanach warrior. He too is dressed in all the finery of his ancient culture. He's playing his bagpipes fiercely, with all the pride he can muster, as if preparing to go into battle. The bull too is adorned in finery. When Finn looks at the bull and the bull looks at him, Finn is certain it is smiling. It lets out a loud bellow. The veterans pile into the back of the wagon.

"Silverbright," says Finn, "it's good to see yae again. Where've yae been; yae missed all the fun!"

"It's good to see you too, Albanach; You look good. Looks like things worked out for you."

"Aye," says Finn." "I guess I'm just one of the lucky ones."

"That's a strange lookin' limo," says Frankie with a laugh.

"All right everybody," says Silverbright. "Pile in. We're going to a parade."

"'Bout fuckin' time," says Romeo as the Veterans climb into the back of the wagon beside the Albanach warrior. When they're safely inside, the warrior plays an upbeat marching song and, with a light tap of Silverbright's whisk, the bull starts pulling the wagon through the Tenderloin.

The streets of the Tenderloin are nice again. The sun is out, pulling forth the sweet scent of the cherry blossoms. But before we've gone very far, we are suddenly met by a ragged band of Viet Cong. They're a scruffy lot, and they too still have their AK47s slung across their shoulders. They look as if they mean business.

"We're comin' too," says their leader, a tiny little man no more than five feet tall. Though he's no more than five feet, he looks as if he's got the strength of a gorilla hidden inside his wiry frame. "This is our show too you know."

The Veterans are spooked. What the hell's goin' on here? they wonder.

"This is a private party," says Finn rather lamely. "Kinda personal. Yae can't come with us."

"Fuck you, man," says the leader. "We've got too much invested in this ourselves." His comrades all nod in agreement. "Why do you think we've been following you, watching you. We need to put an end to this too, you know. We've had point men looking for you everywhere, following you—ever since you came to the Land of the Truly Alive."

"Yeah, Finn," says Johnny. "What's the big deal, man? They're Vets too. An' now we're all the same—fuckin'-A dead!"

Johnny lets out a loud, chortling laugh and all the other Veterans join in, the VC included.

"Hey, Mui," shouts their leader, "do you want to come with us?"

"Oh, no," she replies. "It's fun up here. I can see for miles and miles."

The Veterans look at one another in wonder, amazed that they're actually seeing the VC on a street in San Francisco and that they're actually talking to them.

"Fuckin'-A," Tommy shouts. "This is-fuckin'-A dynamite. The final goddamn irony. Get in there behind the wagon, fellas. This'll be the best parade in the history of parades. Okay, Silverbright, lead the way."

When the wagon passes them the VC pile in behind it, then

more and more of them come out from behind the tenement buildings and join their comrades. There are regular army soldiers among them too. Hundreds of them, thousands of them. The Veterans are astonished, then a little afraid. But as we make our way further along the streets we see more shopping carts discarded by the wayside. They're lined up neatly on the sidewalk, like boxes on a factory floor. A sign reading *25¢ deposit* is tied to each of the carts. Then one by one we're joined by an army of joyful American Veterans. There are hundreds of them too, thousands of them too. Finn and his pals lose any fear they might have had when they see the Veterans of both armies walking among each other, slapping each other on the back and shaking hands and smiling.

When I look behind me all I can see is an endless sea of Veterans stretching out all the way to the horizon. Stevenson giggles. We all have a good giggle. It's the most beautiful sight I have ever seen in my whole life.

"These are the Veterans who took their own lives," says Stevenson. "They want another chance too."

"I can dig that," says Romeo, laughing.

The buzz of the many voices behind us brings goosebumps up onto my skin. It's a magical moment. There must be thousands of us, thousands upon thousands.

"As I was saying," says Stevenson, "one hundred and sixty thousand Shopping Cart Veterans have taken their own lives since the war ended. They are all here, every last one of them."

"Goddamn," says Romeo. "Look at 'em!"

"I didn't know there was so many of us," says Frankie. "Are they all Veterans?"

"Quite so," says Stevenson.

Amidst a chorus of wows and goddamns I look back again. The army of Veterans is still streaming over the horizon, moving steadily, moving with strength, like migrating caribou who move forward on instinct alone. As we walk, the Veterans form a neat column, four abreast, as if commanded by an unseen drill instructor with coconut balls and a foghorn voice. Then, as if by some kind of magic, my thoughts become real, and I hear the drill instructor boom out a rhythm. All at once we are back in basic training, all of us I'm sure, for loud laughter in recognition erupts behind us and is carried, wavelike, towards the end of the column—if, indeed, there is an end to the column. When the laughter subsides, the Drill instructor resumes the cadence.

Oh, me name is Sammy Small, fuck you all.

Thousands upon thousands of voices repeat the chant, and as the phrase comes to an end, thousands upon thousands of feet snap down, as one, upon the concrete. The drill instructor goes on, and the Veterans continue after him.

Oh, me name is Sammy Small, fuck you all,
Oh, me name is Sammy small, fuck you all.
Oh, me name is Sammy Small, and I've only got one ball,
Oh, me name is Sammy Small, fuck you all.

The only way I know how to describe the mood, both inside Finn and in the throng all around us, is that it's blissful. Each of the Veterans is smiling ear to ear and Johnny, Frankie, Tommy, Romeo, Ivy League, Gemini and Mui are awestruck, afloat on a cloud of happiness.

As we press on through the Tenderloin, a hush falls over the marching Veterans. Way up ahead of us another group of people lines the streets. Nobody knows who they are, for we are quiet, as if wondering, as if worried. Some of the people up ahead walk into the middle of the street, blocking our way. They stare down the street towards us then disperse and join the rest of their group who line the street. As we march onward approaching them, we can see that they are dressed alike. Each wears a silver robe and, stitched upon each breast, above the heart, is a beautiful purple heart. Stevenson is jubilant.

"It's them," he says. "It's the Heroes! It's all those Veterans who died in battle during the war!"

A roar goes up behind us like the kick-off at a Super Bowl game.

We are cheering each other, hurrahing each other, and as we pass through the throng of Heroes, they stand to attention and salute us. As we pass them, the Heroes break rank and pass purple hearts out to our comrades who fell after the war. It's a sight for sore eyes. Finn is so happy he sobs. He can't help it. It's the most emotional moment he's ever experienced. There is now a throng of more than two hundred thousand Veterans marching through the cherry blossom-lined streets of the Tenderloin. The mood, exultant and jubilant, suddenly changes once more. Stevenson has his hand up and silence falls over our throng of Heroes. And they are all heroes now. Ahead of us another group of people crowds the street. There are hundreds, perhaps thousands of them, too. They crowd the street from one side to the other, from building to building. They are silent. And they are dark. There is a feel of malevolence about them. As we draw closer we can see that each has an AK47 slung across his shoulder.

"Oh, dear," says Stevenson, "it's the Bureaucrats again, it's the Empty Suits."

Sure enough there are thousands of Empty Suits blocking the street in front of us. A buzz of angry whispers comes from the Heroes as the Empty Suits point their rifles at us. We stop just a few feet from them. I wonder how many of them there really are standing arrogantly in front of us. We stand there quietly. Nobody says a word, but I can tell there isn't a one among us who is willing to move. We have faced these same rifles before. They don't make us run this time either. But this is a stand-off, an old fashioned stand-off. The Empty Suits don't seem willing to move either. They feel strong, I'm sure, and powerful. They have the rifles after all. A minute goes by, then five, then ten! All is quiet. The Empty Suits stare blankly ahead. The Heroes look at one another. Smiles break out among us. Above, a tenement window opens and a young girl leans out. She's holding a small American flag which she waves at the crowd below her. Thousands of Heroes see her and wave back.

"Daddy, daddy," she shouts, still waving at the men below. Hundreds of them wave back at her, none of them sure whose daughter she is, yet all of them hoping she is their own. Across the street, high above, an old man and his wife lean out of another window. They too wave small American flags at the throng below.

"Johnny, Johnny," they shout, "hey, Johnny," and hundreds of Johnnys look up and wave back.

Yet another window opens and a young Asian man leans out. "Frankie, hey, Frankie," he shouts, and hundreds of Frankies shout back, exuberantly, with gutloads of gusto. In our wagon, Frankie Chen's eyes are stuck on the sight above him. "Hey, man," he says, "that's my brother, that's my kid brother up there!" He scrambles to his feet, waving back, and shouts as loud as he can as tears of pure joy run down his face, "Daryl, hey Daryl, it's me, it's me!" The Empty Suits, witnessing the exuberance, the signs of recognition among the heroes, begin to fidget and squirm. More and more windows open up in the tenement buildings; more and more people lean out calling to loved ones. The Empty Suits are visibly shaken, disturbed. They try to counter the happiness they see before them by slapping bullet-laden magazines into their rifles. Click, snap. Click, snap, go the rifles, making the heroes shudder uneasily at the memory of the terrible sound. A low moan of sadness passes over the Heroes, front to back, as word of the loaded rifles is passed through the ranks of war dead. Then the tiny wee Bureaucrat with the notebook and calculator, seeing that the Empty Suits are losing ground, stands in front of them and, wishing he was Pavarotti I'm sure, tries to sing *God Bless America*, all the while urging his cohorts to join him. But the Empty suits are out of practice. They haven't sung the song since their last ball game. They cough and splutter out the words with as much conviction as a liar at a polygraph convention. When the relatives in the tenements see the pathetic efforts of the Bureaucrats, they throw whatever they can get their hands on down on the rifle-toting mob below. Pots and pans, flower pots, steam irons, and a million other heavy items come raining down on the Bureaucrats. Tommy-Up-Front, in all his glory, stands up in the wagon.

"Come on fellas, they're singin' our song. Hey, Finn, they're singin' our song. Let's show these motherfuckers how to sing our song!"

"Fuck that, man," says Frankie. "I ain't singin' that goddamn song again. Look where it got me, man! Shot off nuts an' a blown up heart."

"Yeah," says Romeo, seconding Frankie. "All it got me was a pair of clappers instead of hands. Can't even reach my pecker!"

"Come on, man," says Tommy. "That's exactly how them assholes want us to think. With hatred, just like they do! but that's what keeps us all fucked-up. Hey, listen! We fought in that goddamned war 'cause we believed! We were the believers, man. We fought like goddamn tigers for our flag and country!"

"That's for goddamn sure," shouts one of the VC, who was then joined with a chorus of *Fuckin'-A's* from the rest of his comrades. Romeo bursts out laughing, the other Veterans laugh, the VC laugh too. It's a great big joke. All of them, Americans and VC alike, fought for what they believed in; now it all seems so damned stupid.

"I'm not into all that patriotic shit any more," says Frankie.

"It ain't patriotic shit, Frankie," says Tommy. "This is about us. Them motherfuckers in the suits are tryin' to brush us under the carpet like we didn't exist, like we was dirt, man. They want to forget about us. We embarrass them, Frankie. Make 'em feel guilty!"

"That's true, Frankie," says Finn. "They still do it twenty-five years later. That's why there's so many Shopping Cart Soldiers pushin' shoppin' carts out there. Purple hearts too, Frankie, most of 'em."

"Come on, Frankie, come on, Romeo," says Tommy. "Get your back up! We've got another war to fight. Now we hafta fight for what we fought for!"

"Fuckin'-A," rang out a chorus of hundreds of thousands of Vietnamese and American war Veterans. Smiling, Romeo and Frankie join in.

And all at once, for the first time in the history of America, more than two hundred thousand voices, in unison, raise their voices to sing America's most beloved song. The happiness among the Heroes is contagious and all the relatives above them join in and there's enough tears of joy in our little wagon to float the

Queen Mary. It's as if the Heroes are finally getting the remembrance they've always wanted from the people they fought so hard to protect. The Empty Suits can see that their last stand is futile and ridiculous. Amidst the sound of rifles hitting the tarmac street, they take a long, frightened look at one another, then turn and run as fast as their office-worn legs will allow. Their retreating figures are chased by the loudest snappiest, most powerful rendition of *God Bless America* ever heard. All the Heroes are cheering along with the relatives who are now throwing rose petals down on their loved ones. Such a sight for sore eyes has never been seen before.

I'm in seventh heaven myself. I didn't think it would be so comfortable in here. But it is. And very peaceful too. I couldn't see how it would work out at first. I had my doubts. But that was then. At the same time, it's all so straightforward, so logical. Made a pragmatist out of me to be sure. Same for Redeyes; he's here too. We made it. It was easy getting back inside Finn once Redeyes came inside me. He isn't so bad you know. I just didn't understand. Not at all. I thought I was it. He is what he is. That's all. We are simply pieces of each other. I need him and he needs me; Finn needs us both so that he can be whole. The simplicity is fresh and beautiful like a flower in rain. It's good to be alive, to be where I should be. Yes, it feels good to be alive! I can feel Redeyes nod in agreement.

Tommy-up-front turns to Finn and puts his arm around him.

"Hey, man," he says. "Whenever ya need us we'll be there. Just say the word, buddy!"

"The word, Tommy?"

"And thy soul shall be healed," pipes in Ivy League, with a loud chortling laugh. He hasn't been this happy since the time before his plane went down. "And thy soul shall be healed," he repeats once more: "Ain't that a goddamned humdinger!"

Out of the mouth of babes!

"Yeah, the word," says Tommy! "The one that got us through the war."

"An' what might that be?"

Tommy, smiling, looks at Frankie and Romeo and Ivy League and Gemini and Johnny and all together they shout out The Word: "FUCKIN'-A!"

All at once thousands of Veterans throw their hands up into the air and, with a joy that can't be bought, shout out for the rest of the world to hear, "FUCKIN'-A!"

Amidst the scene of joy before him, Finn notices a Veteran wearing jungle fatigues walking away from the throng. He has long, dark hair and a dark beard, and there are red marks on his hands and feet. His shoulders are stooped as if he were sad. Before he turns the corner at the other side of the street the Veteran stops and looks back. It's the Nazarene, and there's a big, beautiful smile creasing his time-worn face. Silverbright notices the receding Veteran too. He leans over in the cart, picks up a beautiful, leatherbound book and hands it to Finn. It is *The Red Book of Seeing and Believing.*

"I almost forgot," he says. "The Nazarene told me to make sure you had this. It's the history of your people, Finn. It's yours now. Read it and be at peace."

── EPILOGUE ──

MY FATHER'S DEAD, God rest him! That's why I'm here. He died three months ago just after I got out of the hospital. I've been here ever since. They found me lying in Paranoid Park unconscious, then stuck me in the San Francisco General Hospital. I'd been lying there, in a coma, for three days! But I'm glad I'm back in Scotland again, even if I did come to bury my da. And I'm glad I didn't lose my accent. It's the only thing I had when I went to America nearly thirty years ago. My accent, and the clothes on my back. That was all! No money—nothing! Not even a pot to piss in. I still don't have a pot to piss in. I'm not complaining, mind you. That's just how it was, how it is. Again, just facts. Now that I'm back here in Scotland again I've reverted back to talking with a Glasgow accent. Kinda like I never left I suppose. It feels good to talk like this again after all those years. It's comfortable, and I don't have to repeat myself every time I talk to someone I don't know. Talking naturally might not mean much to other folk, but it sure as hell means a lot to me. It's probably not something people think much about. Aye, it is good to be home, even though I don't think I'll stay much longer. I've done what I came here to do. Bury my da, and take a good, long, hard look at myself. When I go back to America I'll go back to talking with a subdued Scots accent again just like I'm doing here. Posh that is. A posh accent. A mid-Atlantic accent, as they call it. If I didn't nobody would understand me. Hardly a soul would listen to me. Meantime, I'm going to enjoy talking with a Scots accent, the way I was born to talk, every chance I get.

My father died of a massive stroke. Everything just blew up. Bang! That was that. He left me a book. My ma gave it to me right after the funeral. It's called, *The Red Book of Seeing and Believing*, and in it is the history of my clan, the clan MacDonald. In the Gaelic, *Mac* means *son of*, so we're all the sons of Donald, the great king. The book was written in the Gaelic, and was begun three years after the '45. The 1745 that is, when Butcher Cumberland, son of the idiot King, George, delved into his filthy mind and came up with an imaginative new way to butcher the enemy. He filled his cannon with wee shards of metal and pieces of chain, and fired the lot into the midriffs of the Scottish soldiers, mowing them down like grass before the scythe. A new way of war it was, so quick, so deadly. It had never been seen on the battlefield before, that kind of brutality. Nothing like it had ever been seen before. Nothing like it has been seen since. Not, that is, until the invention of fragmentation grenades. We used them in Vietnam by the bucketful, by the truckload. A nasty piece of business to be sure. Frag grenades send out, at an angle, sprays of metal fragments that make mincemeat of anything standing in their path. A vast improvement on the great duke's inventive cannon spillings which only went forward in a straight line. When Butcher Cumberland, the duke, was done with his mowing, he and his soldiers went around the battlefield and finished off whoever was still breathing, hacking and bayoneting them till there wasn't a soul left breathing on that dark red field. No wonder indignant Scots with half a brain despise those English royalist bastards. Bunch of blueblood sonsabitches no matter how you look at it.

"He wanted yae to have it, son," says my ma, as she hands me the auld leather-bound book. I hadn't seen it since I was about eleven or twelve. "He told me that just before he died," says my ma. "That you should have it, ah mean."

Life was so bad after the '45 that the bards of the bigger clans decided to break with tradition and write down, in secret books, the histories of their respective branches. All tradition was being forced into submission or nonexistence at the time. Our Gaelic culture was being systematically destroyed. Northern Scotland became the training ground for English colonialism. The clanspeople weren't allowed to wear their clan colors or even the philibeg, the forebear of the modern kilt; we weren't allowed to speak the Gaelic; we weren't allowed to have a knife with a blade longer than three inches; we weren't even allowed to play the bagpipes since the pipes were considered to be a weapon of war. So life was bad, grim, and getting worse. In the dark years after the '45 the English and the Scottish turncoats, the backstabbers, began in earnest to clear the Scottish Highlands of the people who had lived there since the fifth century and since even before the time of Christ. Many of them were Pictish people who had mixed in with the Scottish clans over the centuries. Those hellish times were known collectively as *The Highland Clearances*, or just simply *The Clearances*. A holocaust if ever there was one. The bards knew that with the scattering of the clans, the histories had to be written down and kept secret from the rest of the world. *The Red Book of Seeing and Believing* is just such a book. And it came into my possession just after my father died. Like I said, it was written down in the Gaelic except for the most modern section which my da had written in English, but he didn't speak the Gaelic, and neither do I, more's the pity. I'll have to find somebody who does, because I'm sure that within the pages of that book is something I need to learn either about myself or my family. There's something in that book, either guidance or information, that will somehow help me get on with the rest of my life. I'm certain of it! But what it is I just don't know yet.

I do have a vague remembrance of a book while stuck in my coma. That's just part of the reason why I'm now so curious about what people remember from coma experiences. You know, how much *do* they remember? I also have a slight remembrance of a nurse who reminded me of another nurse I knew briefly in Vietnam. The nurse in Vietnam worked in triage, and the nurse at

San Francisco General worked in the emergency room. She is the first person I speak to when I come out of the coma.

We talk a lot over the next few days. She invites me to her house, offers me a place to rest while I regain my strength. I have nowhere else to go anyway. I am homeless, you see. Am I feeling sorry for myself? Nah, that's just facts. That's all. But homelessness isn't such a big deal anyway. At least that's what I'd begun to think. After all, thousands upon thousands of us Vietnam veterans live on the streets. Seems to be our lot in life, our way of life. At least for some of us. That's all the thanks we get for fighting like bastards during the war. Sonsabitches, the powers that be. Safety in numbers, it is said. I have to laugh; more like resignation in numbers. What we need to do now, us vets, is to get our backs up. Change our attitude; throw resignation out the window, and bristle with right-directed anger, bristle with righteous indignation.

The nurse told me I was talking in my coma.

When I come to, the light is blinding and warm on my face. I stiffen. I hold my arms stiffly by my sides and tense my body head to toe. I don't know what the hell's going on or where I am. I play it safe. I hear voices, both male and female, young and old, yet still I play it safe. The intense, warm light washes over me. Where can I be, I wonder. Slowly, ever so slowly, I open my eyes. I'm surrounded by half a dozen or so faces, all peering down at me. They have big, bulbous eyes, these faces, like eyes seen through a fish-eye lens. They cast quick, furtive glances at one another. They are doctors and nurses. They have clipboards in their hands, pens poised above them as if ready to strike. Stethoscopes hang around their necks like weapons. I am groggy and disoriented, confused beyond any personal experience. I remember where I've been. Pictures suddenly come back to me. Quickly. Somebody's playing the tape back. Still I play it safe. Think about it, I tell myself. Then the nurse, who looks to be just a few years older than me, sends a distinctly coy smile my way. She looks friendly, but I wonder. I trust no one. Her hair is brown, streaked with grey. A loose curl hangs over her forehead. One of the doctors, a middleaged woman, leans over me, holds back my eyelid and shines a penlight into my eye. It must be the end of her shift; her breath stinks. Keep quiet. Don't say a word. She repeats the operation with my other eye, then stands back looking at me, a self-satisfied smirk on her face.

"Do you know where you are?" she asks. Her tone is so condescending I want to slap her.

But I don't say a word. I daren't say a word. I have to figure out this strange situation first. Instead, I clench my fists, grit my teeth.

"What's your name?" asks another of the doctors.

None of your fuckin' business, I think.

The woman doctor turns and looks at her colleagues. Most of them are younger, probably students.

"He's still disoriented," says the woman doctor.

No shit, Einstein! I mumble to myself.

"Well, at least he's coming around," says one of the students.

I don't like him. I'm sure there's white stuff under his foreskin, as if he hasn't figured anything out yet, as if he doesn't yet know how to take care of himself let alone patients in a hospital.

"Anal pricks!" says I, much louder than I mean to.

The woman doctor spins around and throws her beady, fish eyes across my face.

"What was that, what did you say?" she asks.

I close my eyes. The brown-haired nurse with the errant forelock has her hand to her mouth, suppressing a laugh. The woman doctor speaks again.

"Do you know where you are?" she asks.

God help us all, but I don't move, can't move, don't say a single, solitary word, don't even breathe. Instead, I let out the loudest, brashest fart I have ever heard in my whole entire life. I don't know where it came from. It was the farthest thing from my mind. But there it was nevertheless, as if some fart goblin inside me decided just then, at that particular moment, that he needed to express himself, needed to assert himself. The boldness of it, while I stare straight at her, so startles the doctor she rocks back on her heels clutching at her breast as if gripped by a monstrous myocardial infarction. Her eyes are wide; she is visibly shaken.

The brown-haired nurse is a mess, a complete wreck. She's

laughing so hard she has to hold onto the end of a bed at the other side of the ward. My shoulders are shaking. I laugh until my eyes water. Disgusted, the doctors and nurses move away, en masse, to the next patient. I wipe my eyes and go to sleep, a self-satisfied smile creasing my angelic and peaceful face.

When I awaken, the brown-haired nurse is making her rounds again. She wipes my face with a cool, damp cloth. I smile. She smiles.

"You were out for three days, three days and three nights." says she. "Seizures, concussion, exhaustion. They didn't think you'd make it. I knew you would. You're a warrior. Just like me."

She chuckles. She takes the guard down and sits on the edge of the bed. She holds my hand. She continues.

"It was fascinating. I couldn't leave your bedside. They made me go home to rest. You wouldn't stop talking. I was there too, you know. In Vietnam. About the same time as you. It's been rough, hasn't it? I know. After listening to you, I'm sure we'll make it. We'll make it! Won't we?" The nurse pauses, thoughtful. "What are ya gonna do now?" she asks.

I shrug. "I dunno," says I.

"I've been thinking," says the nurse. "Why don't you come to my place and rest up a spell. It'll do you the world of good to rest up a spell. Get your head clear again. Then you can make a decision. Oh, don't you worry, lover boy," she continues after seeing the hungry look on my face. "There's plenty of room. You can sleep in my son's room. He's away at college you know."

I look at her, thoughtfully, then sit up. When I speak, there's an undisguised eagerness in my voice as if someone were speaking for me or pushing me to speak up.

"Mary," I blurt out, "can I call Mary? Maybe I can even talk to Finn Johnny Quinn!"

It is the strangest thing, to hear my wife's and my son's names come rolling off my tongue. I haven't seen them in more than twelve years and, lately, I haven't given them more than a passing thought, nor have I spoken their names in such a long time.

The nurse smiles. "I phoned her already," she says. "She wants you to phone her. She wants you to talk to young Finn. He wants to talk to you too. He's twenty-four now, not so young after all."

I look straight into the nurse's eyes and smile, and I can actually feel it, this smile, as if I'd never in my entire life smiled before. So strange. Then my nose begins to itch and my chin starts shaking as tears fill up my eyes. Tears of pure unadulterated happiness begin to fill up my eyes. So wonderful. Who would ever have guessed?

The nurse told me I talked a lot about the war too when I was in that other place, in my coma. That's why she took me home with her, she says. She tells me it was interesting, what I was saying, that it cut to the bone, really grabbed her, put a knot in her stomach. But she's a Vietnam veteran herself. I will call her Gemini, because I seem to remember meeting somebody called Gemini somewhere in my coma.

I don't know what happened to me in the hospital, but I do feel better than I have done in many a long year. I feel all filled up, fatter or something, as if I'd just eaten a satisfying meal. And the feeling's stayed with me too as if it were permanent, meant to be. It's a good feeling, a grand feeling! I hope it lasts, this grand, good feeling!

I feel reinvigorated when I leave the hospital. I remember walking out the door with Gemini, and pumping up my chest and flexing my muscles. Not that I have a whole lot of muscles after all those years on the streets. Twelve years it was to be exact. The muscles tend to wither away and atrophy after living like that. But no matter, I feel great! When I get to Gemini's house in the Richmond district of San Francisco I phone up my wife, or ex-wife whatever the case might be. I don't know. I'm not sure at the time how Mary might take it, you know, me calling her. Like I said, I haven't talked to her for all of those twelve years. And I haven't talked to my young Finn in all those years either. He was only eleven or twelve when Mary pissed off out of it with my son holding onto her coattails for dear life. I don't know why, but Mary is happy to hear from me.

"Hello, Mary?" says I, and there's a stunned silence at the other end of the line. Then a wee, quiet, inquisitive voice, almost timid, speaks out.

"Finn? Is that you, Finn? Are you alive? Oh, my God, you *are* alive!"

"Yeah, it's me. I'm alive, Mary. Can you believe it, I'm still alive!"

"Oh, God, Finn," says she, astonished. "This is too coincidental."

"What is Mary? What's up? Is everything okay? How's young Finn?"

"He's fine. He's better than fine. He's a great kid, Finn. But your daddy isn't doing too well. Your mom called a couple of days ago looking for you. I didn't know how to find you, get a hold of you. Your mom didn't know who else to call. He's very ill, your daddy. He had a stroke, Finn. Your mom wants you to be there, if you can make it. You should say goodbye to him, Finn. It's that bad!"

Christ, I didn't know what to think. I hadn't seen the old man in more than twenty years. After the war I stopped talking to everybody—even my mother and my father. It's sick, isn't it? But I don't have a pot to piss in, I tell Mary, and she tells me not to worry, that she'll send me the fare which she does the very next day. Seems I have a pension I've been getting from the government because of the war. I'd forgotten all about applying for it, let alone getting it. Mary has saved some of it for me. She's always been sensible that way, Mary. And the very next day I talk to young Finn as well.

"Hullo," he says in this huge, big manvoice. "Hullo, is that you, Dad?"

I nearly collapse when I hear my son's voice sounding so grown-up, so like a man, but that's when the floodgates open too, that's when I fully realize I don't even know my own boy. I've never seen tears like that in my whole goddamned life. I have to sit down on the carpet, and I cry my eyes out like a big, daft wean. I'm crying so hard I have to hang up the phone, and all those sobs are like twelve years of grief and guilt that just come tumbling right out of my body like rivers of poison. I feel even better though when it's all over and done with. I phone him back. He tells me he understands, and that he's been learning about what I've been going through in his college courses. You know, all that Post Traumatic Stress crap and all. We even have a bit of a giggle when I tell him some of my stories about the streets.

I'm looking forward to seeing him and Mary when I get back to America. I've no illusions though. Not about me and Mary anyway. Even though she never got married again. But you never know, now, do you?

The most amazing thing about this whole experience of late is that the day after talking to Mary and my boy I am back here in Glasgow. *Glesca* to the locals. I used to wonder about that particular pronunciation, because in the west coast of Scotland the language is riddled with bits of Gaelic and bits of French. We've always been good pals with the French. Anybody but those royalist bastards down the road, down south. Glesca! Then in my reading one day I discover that the Gaelic way of spelling Glasgow is Gles Chu, meaning *The Dear Green Place*. Lovely, isn't it? Gles Chu, Glasgow, Glesca! So the conclusion I have come to is that the Glesca pronunciation is very similar, phonetically, to the original Gaelic. I think it's very interesting if nothing else. Glesca! I can't help but wonder about the time when the Gaelic Highlanders were driven out of their homes down into the place with no name, and they call it, *The Dear Green Place*. My heart breaks to think of how much they must've missed their own homes after living there for hundreds and hundreds of years not bothering anyone.

I'm not trying to be facetious, but it was a trip coming back here. One day I'm in America shoving my goddamned shopping cart through the streets of San Francisco surrounded by American voices; the next I'm being shoved off an airliner by a big fat woman whose huge great tits keep jabbing me in the back, all the way down onto the tarmac covering my native soil. Her tits are so big I don't think she feels them jabbing into me. I stop off at a cafe bar in the airport, curious to hear the sound of Scottish voices after so long a time not hearing them. It's strange to hear the wee lassie's voice when she hands me a cuppa tea. "That'll be wan poun ten, mister," says she, and I nearly drop the tea, it sounds so queer in my ear. But I soon get used to it again, like riding a bike. I'm a bit worried at first, filled with fear and trepidation. Will I fit in again, will I feel like a stranger in a strange land here as well, just like I do in America? Is Glasgow still riddled with gangs? Is it worse? That's what it was like when I left. Riddled with gangs! I was always afraid to walk down the street in case some wee fucked-up hardman came running out of an alleyway past me and clouted me with a bottle, trying to make a name for himself. Nah, it can't be like that, can it? I'm tripping now, but I always was a shitebag when it comes to fighting. I hate it! I hate fighting more than anything! I still do! Perhaps now more than ever.

The first thing I do when I get into the city is to rent a wee room right in the middle of downtown Glasgow. My ma lives near there, but I don't want to sleep in the auld house; just being here all by myself after all those years is spooky enough. I don't want to meet all those new ghosts that must've gathered at the auld place. Nah, no thanks; I'll just stay in my room all by myself and let life take its course just as it's going to do anyway. And it does! That very same week. Doesn't waste any time at all.

I have just left my ma's on the evening right after my da's funeral. I have The Book in my shoulder bag which, for safety, hangs diagonally over my shoulders and across my chest. As I walk, I clutch it tightly. I am terrified that I might somehow lose it, that a bag snatcher might grab it, or that The Book will fall out of the bag or whatever. The rain is pouring down as usual, a heavy, dense rain, relentless in its efficiency to soak right through to the skin. But it doesn't really bother me, not that much; I'm too excited about reading The Book.

When I get to my room I change out of my wet clothes and into a pair of flannel pajamas I bought just for the trip. I remember growing up in Scotland, and I remember always being colder than hell at night. So I buy the flannel pajamas. I don't really need them though; there's a nice wee fire in the room. But no matter, I am comfortable. I stack the pillows up against the headboard of the bed, then jump up on top of it, book in hand, ready for a good read. I chuckle with delight, with pleasure; I can't believe how much my life's changed for the better in such a short time. Here I am in a set of nice, new, warm pajamas, I have a few bucks in the bank, and I'm sitting on top of a comfy bed in a half-decent hotel in Glasgow where I was born. A far cry from sleeping under the bushes in Paranoid Park in San Francisco, broke, drunk, and absolutely, certifiably miserable. Aye, a far cry indeed.

I open The Book, slowly and carefully, for the pages are auld, almost brittle, and the two-hundred-and-fifty-year-old ink at the beginning is fading. But that's not why I can't read it; I can't read it because, as I said before, it is written in the Gaelic. When I first take The Book from my ma I know what it is and I just skim it a wee bit before sticking it in my bag. I think I'm afraid she might take it back, not let me have it after all. The streets really do screw you up. I'll have to learn again that it's not everybody you meet who wants to kick you in the balls or into the gutter where they think you belong. It's not everybody that's out to get you. Some folk are nice and decent just because they're nice and decent. I'll have to try to remember that.

As I mentioned, the only part of The Book written in English is the part my father wrote. But his entry is brief, exceedingly brief, compared to the other entries. Not even half a page long, it reads:

> *The continuity of this book is broken. The male heir of each generation since 1745 has made an entry in this book. That tradition ends with me. My son's dead! Perhaps his son will make an entry. Better still, perhaps his son will start a new book. My son's dead! His body came back from the war, but he didn't. I don't know what happened to him over there in Vietnam, but whatever it was it killed him. He's just a wisp of his former self, an empty shell, a body without a soul. I pray for him every day.*

And that was that! There were tears in my eyes when I read my father's entry. It was hard for me to take, you know, realizing that my father had given me up for dead. Not that I blame him in the least. I understand completely. I had been missing for so long,

Shopping Cart Soldiering around the streets of San Francisco, missing in action. But it was hard to actually see how my da felt, and it written down so certainly, so concisely. He'd given up the ghost as far as I was concerned. To him I was certainly dead! He even said it twice as if he was really pissed-off at me, certain that I was dead.

I close The Book and sit it on the wee table next to the bed. I can't sleep now. But it is still early evening. I get up and look out the window. The yellow street lights shimmer off the wet road, making the street look mysterious like in a Robert Louis Stevenson novel or something. Sort of surrealistic, actually. But the rain has stopped. A few people, mostly couples, are passing by my window on the street below. I'll go for a walk myself. I'll get dressed and I'll go for a nice long walk through the wet Glasgow streets. Maybe I'll walk up the hill to Glasgow University. There are some nice views up there, looking out over the city, the dear green place.

I jump up out of the bed and into some dry clothes, sling my bag over my shoulders and step off towards the door. Just as I touch the handle though I feel something. I spin around, quickly, startled out of my churlies. What the fuck! It's like an ambush. For a split second you feel something, you just *know* something's out there though you still can't see it then, caboom! The madness begins again. I look around the room. Nothing! Then I see it, my eyes are pulled to it. The Book! I could've sworn it was The Book. "C'mere you," it seems to say. "You're not goin' anywhere without me!" I can't help it, but I seem to remember experiencing a similar feeling when I was in my coma. You know, like something beckoning me, something pulling at me from the inside out. I've always wondered what people think about when they're in a coma, or if they think of anything, or if they remember what they think about. Especially those folk who are in a coma for years. Do they have a life in their coma? I'm beginning to understand it a bit better I think, because I'm remembering certain experiences I could only have experienced in my coma. I pick up The Book and I swear I feel it pulsing as if it has a heartbeat, as if it is alive. I stuff it into my shoulder bag, and a few seconds later I'm out the door feeling

233

certain I'm embarking upon some great and mysterious adventure.

It is nice outdoors. The rain has freshened the streets and the perfume from the gardens is grassy and flowery. The overcast has broken up and the scattered bits of low, stratocumulus clouds scud past the moon. It is quite warm out too. When I first set out on my walk I head off towards the university as planned, but after a while I find that I am walking down towards the old warehouse district by the shipyards. Why? Why would I do that? I haven't been down that way since I was a child. Nah, I have no reason in the entire world to go there. But I keep on walking as if I can't help it. I don't really want to turn back. I have no reason to keep walking forward, but I have no reason to turn back either. I just keep going. I just keep walking until I am in the heart of, in the thick of the old shipyard warehouses. It's creepy! It is so quiet! I feel like I've stepped back in time. Most of the streets are still cobblestoned, and the wetness of the recent rains makes me feel, as I mentioned before, as if I'm walking through the past. It is so quiet now. The only sound I've heard in ages is a dog barking then yelping as if somebody's just given it a good hard kick right up the arse. I can't help but wonder what kind of ghouls might be out and about creeping and crawling through a night like this.

Far away, up in the distance, a lone light shines from a lamp hanging onto one of the auld buildings. I walk towards it, because I can't think of anything better to do.

I stand under the light and look at the building. It's a pub, built with the red sandstone bricks so popular with the old Glasgow builders. Green paint is peeling off a round-topped door. A huge iron knocker hangs in the middle of the door. I give it a couple of good hard raps and a few minutes later the door creaks open. Nobody's there. It's as if the door opens all by itself. I chuckle to myself; maybe it's an electronic door. I step up and walk across the threshold. It's a pub all right. And it *is* old. Sawdust covers a grey stone floor, and a weak light from the gas-lamps shimmers along the walls as if nobody wants to see too well, or even to be seen. Here and there a few customers, mostly older men, sit by themselves in the booths lining the walls. They sit there quietly, sipping at their pints of beer or knocking back short drams of whiskey. I wonder what they're waiting for. It is so quiet. Every so often a cough or the shuffling of feet interrupts the quiet. The pub smells of age. Like a crypt uninterrupted for years. A big robust barman stands behind the bar wiping glasses on the end of a filthy apron. I walk over to the bar. "Got any lemonade?" says I, looking the barman straight in the eyes. He cocks an eyebrow and looks at me queerly.

"Ah'll bring yer drink ower tae yae," he says, pointing off to the far end of the pub. I look away in the direction he's pointing. An old, old man is sitting in a booth, the collar of his overcoat pulled up over his ears as if he's freezing cold. His baldy head shines like gold leaf underneath one of the gas lamps. He beckons me with the crook of his finger. It's a bluidy good thing I'm partial to mysteries, to adventures. I walk over to the auld fella.

"Sit doon," he says, pointing to the bench across from him.

I sit down and look into deep-set, ice-blue eyes sunk way back in his head. Dark rings of fatigue hang around his eyes, but the eyes are alert nevertheless. His bottom lip nearly touches his nose. He is gumsy. There isn't a tooth in his head. He's as gumsy as the day he was born. He chuckles, and his smile I swear makes the room seem just that wee bit brighter.

"Did yae bring it?" he asks, looking straight into my own eyes.

"What? Did ah bring what?"

"The Book! Did yae bring The Book?"

I look up. The bartender is standing right by the table, as if he's just appeared there, as if he's been transported there by magic. He plops a bottle of ale down in front of me. It has a strange looking label. It is all swirls and scrolls, and in the middle of the label one word: *Fraoch*. I turn the bottle around and another label reads: *Flur na n-alba*. The auld man giggles.

"Heather ale," he says. "It's a' we drink in here. *Flur na n-Alba*. Flower of Scotland. It's also the name-a this pub yae know. *Flur na n-Alba*. We've been drinkin this ale for two thousand years. Till the sassenach, the English, banned it, that is. That's just another one-a the wrangs yae haftae right. Here ha' some."

"I don't touch the stuff any more," says I, though I don't know where that came from. I had a similar experience on the plane on my way over here to Scotland. When the flight attendant asked me if I wanted a drink I told her no, that I didn't drink. It's as if being in a coma changed me somehow. I don't know. All I do know is that I don't feel like drinking booze any more. Maybe I had enough of it on the streets, because that's all I ever did. I won't miss it.

"Ach, yae don't know what yer missin'," says the auld one, as if he just read my mind. "It's delicious!"

"That may be true," says I, "but I'll have some lemonade or even just some water if yae don't mind."

The bartender harrumphed and walked away to get me some water.

"Pleasant fellow," says I, a wee bit facetiously.

"Show me it," says the auld fella.

"Show yae what, for god's sake?"

"The book. Show me the Red Book!"

"What bluidy red book. Ah don't know what the hell yer talkin about!"

The auld man smiles. "Show me the book yer da gave yae."

"Why shoulda? Who the hell're you?"

"Iain," he says. "Iain Lom MacDonald. Ah'm your translator."

"Translator?"

"Aye, translator," he says. "Yae need a translator don't yae? Ah mean yae don't speak the Gaelic, now do yae?"

"No, ah don't."

"Well, ah do. Let me see the book, damn yae."

"Why should ah trust you?"

"Yer da did. Me an' him were good pals. Cousins actually, though distant. He told me that if a miracle ever happened, that if yae were ever tae come hame, then ah was to translate The Book for yae."

"He said that?"

"Aye, he did. In nae uncertain terms. He thought he'd lost yae forever, yae know, when yae went on yer walkabout."

"My walkabout?"

"Aye, yer walkabout. Like a bluidy aborigine. Traipsin' through yer own wee desert. Lookin for yer soul were yae?" The auld fella giggles.

I look at him, puzzled, wondering how he knows about me looking for my soul all those years. Not that I know at the time what I'm looking for, or that I have in fact lost something. When it occurs to me that looking for your soul, or feeling that you have to look for something you're sure you've lost is a common occupation, quite ordinary, I smile. It's no big deal after all that Iain Lom MacDonald, pal of my da, distant relative, would wonder if I'm looking for my soul. It is indeed an ordinary, everyday experience anyway—soul-searching, that is. It seems a natural enough thing now for me to trust this auld one with the gumsy smile. The bartender grumpily plops a glass of water down in front of me.

"Well ah'm not so sure what ah've done or where ah've been lately, but ah feel better than ah've felt in years," says I, taking a gulp of water. I watch the auld one intently. "I have it right here," says I, taking The Book from my shoulder bag and passing it to him.

"That's good, that's grand," he says. "Ah've been dying tae see it." He sticks out a bony hand and I put the book into it. I sit back then and watch him leaf through it. A big smile widens across his face as he stops and scrutinizes certain pages, or certain periods he seems perhaps to recognize.

"You're in this book, young fella," he says. "Did yae know that?" He chuckles again, pleasantly. "An' so am I..."

"How can I be in it? Must be one-a my ancestors."

"You're history," says Iain Lom. "Yae didnae even know yae were history."

"What d'yae mean I'm history?" I ask, feeling not a little bit perturbed.

"Yae'll find out soon enough," he grunts.

"Can yae translate it, can yae really do that? It's a lotta work."

"Nae bother. Take me a wee while though."

"How long?"

"Yae can either wait till ah have the whole thing done, an' that'll be a while, or yae can take it piecemeal, bit by bit."

"Bit by bit! Ah'll take it bit by bit," says I, eagerly.

"Aye, a wise decision," says Iain Lom, laughing. "Ah'd be eager too, tae see what ma ancestors were thinkin'."

Iain Lom MacDonald continues to leaf through The Book, and I continue to scrutinize him. His old overcoat with the turned up collar must be half a century old. As he reads, his jaw moves up and down in a chewing motion, his bottom lip touching the base of his nose. It's comical to watch, but the seriousness of his reading is disquieting too. Finally, after a long time, he looks up at me.

"Aye," he says, "they're a' here. Yae have a lot of work to dae here in Scotland, son. It seems yae've come back just in time!"

The way he speaks scares the daylights out of me.

"What d'yae mean?" I ask, wondering what the hell he means by "just in time."

"Away yae go hame, laddie," he says, as if dismissing a school-child. "I'll be in touch wi yae when I've enough-a the book ready for yae."

He sticks his head back into The Book then, and for some reason I know that I have indeed been dismissed and that I should do as I'm told. After squirming in my seat for a moment, I pick up my bag and get up and leave. As I walk toward the door, all the old men in the booths cast inquisitive eyes upon me. The bartender still stands at his place behind the bar wiping glasses on the end of his filthy apron.

"Did yae like yer drink?" he asks cheekily as I pass him by.

"Aye," says I. "Very much! I liked it very much. Try it yerself sometime."

I hear the barman grunt as I open the door. Outside it's pouring down rain as usual. I pull my overcoat tightly about me and, putting one foot in front of the other as if walking for the first time, begin the uncomfortable journey back to my hotel room. I am filled with wonder after meeting old Iain Lom MacDonald, and the mysteriousness of the ancient pub with its strange clientele intrigues me beyond measure. I wonder what I'll read in the translation of *The Red Book of Seeing and Believing*. What will it be that my ancestors have to say to me? I remember that books such as these are full of ancient secrets written in secrecy and kept so for centuries. What are these secrets? What strange and ancient knowledge is it that I must learn, that I must know? Goose bumps break out across my forearms and up the back of my neck. I take long, determined strides through the rain. I realize that my journey back to the hotel is only the beginning of a much longer journey for which I seem to have been chosen by something beyond the usual ken of man. I heave a deep sigh of resignation, but I smile too as I step out, one foot in front of the other, through the dark Scottish night.

A Final Word from the Author

Dear Reader,

I hope you enjoyed reading my book, and I hope it helped you find even more compassion than you already have for our homeless veterans who still push their shopping carts through our streets, through our lives, each day of the year. I hope my book will help you become an activist/advocate for homeless veterans. I realize that the following request may be a wee bit bold but, if you could, I'd like to ask you, personally, to send in a donation, however small or large, to the NATIONAL COALITION for HOMELESS VETERANS. The Executive Director of NCHV has agreed to distribute any money we do receive to various veteran's groups throughout the country, according to their need. Send in a dollar, send in a hundred; it doesn't matter! Anything you donate will help us get a Shopping Cart Soldier off the street and bring him or her back home where they belong! The mailing information is below. And thanks for all your help!

With love and peace,
John

Make your donation to National Coalition for Homeless Veterans:

Executive Director
NATIONAL COALITION for HOMELESS VETERANS
Shopping Cart Soldier Fund
333 1/2 Pennsylvania Avenue, SE
Washington DC 20003
ph: 202/546-1969
fax: 202/546-2063

JOHN MULLIGAN was born in Kirkintilloch, Scotland, in 1950, into a home with ten children. After his family emigrated to the U.S., Mulligan enlisted in the Air Force. Within weeks of turning 18 and while still a British citizen, he was on his way to combat in Vietnam. On his return to San Francisco after his tour of duty, he suffered from Post Traumatic Stress Disorder and was homeless for more than ten years. During his recovery from alcoholism, Mulligan attended a veteran's workshop run by the celebrated author Maxine Hong Kingston, who recognized his extraordinary talent and helped him edit the manuscript of *Shopping Cart Soldiers*.